Desert FANTASIES

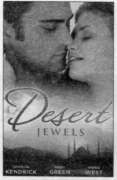

April 2014

May 2014

June 2014

July 2014

Desert
FANTASIES

TRISH MOREY
NATASHA OAKLEY
BARBARA McMAHON

MILLS & BOON

Published in Great Britain 2014
by Mills & Boon, an imprint of Harlequin (UK) Limited,
Eton House, 18-24 Paradise Road, Richmond, Surrey, TW9 1SR

DESERT FANTASIES © 2014 Harlequin Books S.A.

Duty and the Beast © 2012 Trish Morey
Cinderella and the Sheikh © 2008 Natasha Oakley
Marrying the Scarred Sheikh © 2010 Barbara McMahon

ISBN: 978 0 263 24655 1

011-0714

Harlequin (UK) Limited's policy is to use papers that are natural, renewable and recyclable products and made from wood grown in sustainable forests The logging and manufacturing processes conform to the legalenvironmental regulations of the country of origin.

Printed and bound in Spain
by Blackprint CPI, Barcelona

Duty and the Beast

TRISH MOREY

Trish Morey is an Australian who's also spent time living and working in New Zealand and England. Now she's settled with her husband and four young daughters in a special part of South Australia, surrounded by orchards and bushland, and visited by the occasional koala and kangaroo. With a lifelong love of reading, she penned her first book at the age of eleven, after which life, career and a growing family kept her busy until once again she could indulge her desire to create characters and stories—this time in romance. Having her work published is a dream come true. Visit Trish at her website: www.trishmorey.com.

CHAPTER ONE

THEY came for her in the dead of night, while the camp was silent but for the rustle of palm leaves on the cool night air and the snort of camels dreaming of desert caravans long since travelled. She was not afraid when she heard the zip of the blade through the wall of the tent. She was not even afraid when a man dressed all in black, his face covered by a mask tied behind his head and with only slits for his eyes, stepped inside, even though his height and the width of his shoulders were enough to steal her breath away and cause her pulse to trip.

Instead it was relief that flooded her veins and brought her close to tears, relief that the rescue she had prayed and hoped so desperately for had finally arrived.

'I knew you would come for me,' she whispered as she slid fully dressed out of bed to meet him, almost tripping over her slippers in her rush to get away. She swallowed back a sob, knowing what she was escaping, knowing how close she had come. But at last she would be safe. There was no need to be afraid.

But when the hand clamped hard over her mouth to silence her, and she felt herself pulled roughly against his hard, muscular body, there was no denying her sudden jag of fear.

'Do not utter another word, Princess,' the man hissed

into her ear as he dipped his head to hers. 'Or it may be your last.'

She stiffened even as she accepted the indignity, for she had been raised to accept no stranger's touch. But she had little choice now, with his arm like a steel band around her waist, the fingers of one large hand splayed from her chest to her belly and the palm of his other hand plastered hard across her mouth so that she could all but taste his heated flesh.

Unnecessarily close.

Unnecessarily possessive.

Every breath she took contained his scent, a blend of horseflesh and leather, of shifting sands and desert air, all laced with a warm, musky scent that wormed its way into all the places he touched her and beyond. Those places burned with heat until unnecessarily possessive became unnecessarily intimate, and some innate sense of survival pounded out a message in her heartbeat, warning her that perhaps she was not as safe as she had supposed.

Something inside her rebelled. Foolish man! He might be here to rescue her but hadn't she been ready and waiting? Did he imagine she had prayed for rescue only to scream or run and risk her chances of escape?

She was sick of being manhandled and treated like a prize, first by Mustafa's goons and now by her own father's. She was a princess of Jemeya, after all. How dared this man handle her like some common sack of melons he might have picked up at the market?

He shifted and she squirmed, hoping to take advantage of his sudden stillness while his focus seemed elsewhere, but there was no escape. The iron band simply pulled her tighter against the hard wall of his body, his fingers tightening on her flesh, punching the air from her lungs. She gasped, her lips parting, and felt one long finger intrude between her lips.

Shock turned to panic as she tasted his flesh in her mouth.

She felt invaded. She felt violated with the intimacy of the act.

So she did the only possible thing she could. She bit down.

Hard.

He jumped and spat out a curse under his breath, but, while he shifted his fingers away from the danger of her teeth, he did not let her go. 'Be still!' he hissed, holding her tighter, even closer to his rigid form, so that she was convinced he must be made of rock. Warm, solid rock but with a drum beating at its core. Once more she was reminded that this man was not just some nameless rescuer, not just a warrior sent by her father, but a man of flesh and blood, a beating heart and a hot hand that touched her in places no man's hand had a right to be. A hand that stirred a strange pooling heat deep in her belly...

She was glad she had bitten him. She hoped it hurt like hell. She would gladly tell him that too, if only he would take his damned hand off her mouth.

And then she heard it—a short grunt from outside the tent—and she froze as the curtains twitched open.

Ahmed, she realised as the unconscious guard was flopped to the carpet by a second bandit clad similarly in black. Ahmed, who had leered hungrily at her every time he had brought in her meals, laughing at her when she had insisted on being returned to her father, telling her with unrestrained glee exactly what Mustafa planned on doing with his intended bride the moment they were married.

The bandit's eyes barely lingered on her before he nodded to the man at her back. 'Clear for now, but go quickly. There are more.'

'And Kadar?'

'Preparing one of his "surprises".'

All at once she was moving, propelled by her nameless rescuer towards the slash in the tent wall, her slippered feet barely grazing the carpeted floor. He hesitated there just a fraction, testing the air, listening intently, before he set her down, finally loosening his grip but not nearly enough to excise the blistering memory of his large hand spreading wide over her belly.

'Can you run as hard as you bite?' he asked quietly, his voice husky and low as he wrapped his large hand around hers, scanning the area one last time before he looked down at her.

The glinting light in his eyes made her angrier than ever. Now he was laughing at her? She threw him an icy look designed to extinguish any trace of amusement. 'I bite harder.'

Even in the dark she thought she sensed the scarf over his mouth twitch before a cry rang out across the camp behind them.

'Let's hope you're wrong,' he muttered darkly, tugging her roughly into a run beside him, his hand squeezing hers with a grip of steel, the second man guarding their rear as together they scaled the low dune, shouts of panic and accusation now building behind them.

Adrenaline fuelled her lungs and legs—adrenaline and the tantalising thought that as soon as they were safe she was going to set her father's arrogant mercenary right about how to treat a princess.

From the camp behind came an order to stop, followed by the crack of rifle fire and a whistle as the bullet zinged somewhere over their heads, and she soon forgot about being angry with her rescuer. They would not shoot her, she reasoned. They would not dare harm a princess of Jemeya and risk sparking an international incident. But it was dark and her captors were panicking and she had no intention of testing her theory.

Neither had she any intention of complying with the command to stop, even if the man by her side had any hint of letting her go. No way would she let herself be recaptured, not when Mustafa's ugly threats still made her shudder with revulsion. Marry a slug like Mustafa? No way. This was the twenty-first century. She wasn't going to be forced into marrying anybody.

So she clung harder to her rescuer's hand and forced her feet to move faster across the sand, her satin slippers cracking through the dune's fragile crust until, heavy and dragging with sand, her foot slipped from one and she hesitated momentarily when he jerked her forwards.

'Leave it,' he snapped, urging her on as another order to stop and another shot rang out, and she let the other slipper be taken by the dune too, finding it easier to keep up with him barefoot as they forged across the sand. Her lungs and muscles burned by the time they had scaled the dune and plunged over the other side, her mouth as dry as the ground beneath her bare feet. As much as she wanted to flee, as much as she had to keep going or Mustafa's men would surely hunt her down, she knew she could not keep going like this for long.

Over the sound of her own ragged breath she heard it—a whistle piercing the sky, and then another, until the night sky became a screaming promise that ended with a series of explosions bursting colour and light into the dark night. The cries from behind them became more frantic and panicked and all around was the acrid smell of gunpowder.

'What did you do to them?' she demanded, feeling suddenly sickened as the air above the camp glowed now with the flicker of flame from burning tents. Escape was one thing, but leaving a trail of bloodied and injured—maybe even worse—was another.

He shrugged as if it didn't matter, and she wanted to pull her hand free and strike him for being so callous.

'You did want to be rescued, Princess?' Then he turned, and in the glow from the fires she could make out the dark shape of someone waiting for them, could hear the low nicker of the horses he held. Four horses, one for each of them, she noted, momentarily regretting the loss of her shoes until she realised all she would be gaining. She didn't care if her feet froze in the chill night air or rubbed raw on the stirrups. It was a small price to pay for some welcome space from this man. How she could do with some space from him.

'Surely,' she said, as they strode towards the waiting horses, 'you didn't have to go that far?'

'You don't think you're worth it?' Once again she got the distinct impression he was laughing at her. She looked away in sheer frustration, trying to focus on the positives. Her father had sent rescuers. Soon she would see him again. And soon she would be in her own home, where people took her seriously, and where men didn't come with glinting eyes, hidden smiles and hands that set off electric shocks under her skin.

She could hardly wait.

She was already reaching for the reins of the closest horse when his hand stopped her wrist. 'No, Princess.'

'No? Then which one's mine?'

'You ride with me.'

'But there are four...'

'And there are five of us.'

'But...' And then she saw them, two more men in black running low across the dunes towards them when she had been expecting only one.

'Kadar,' he said, slapping one of the men on the back as they neared, making her wonder how he could tell which one was which when they looked indistinguishable to her. 'I'm afraid the princess didn't think much of your fireworks.'

Fireworks? she thought as the man called Kadar feigned disappointment, her temper rising. They were only *fireworks*?

'Apologies, Princess,' the one called Kadar said with a bow. 'Next time I promise to do better.'

'They served their purpose, Kadar. Now let's go before they remember what they were doing before the heavens exploded.'

She looked longingly at the horse she had chosen, now bearing the man who'd been waiting for them in the dunes. A man who, like the others, was tall and broad and powerfully built.

Warriors, she guessed as they swung themselves with ease onto their mounts. Mercenaries hired by her father to rescue her. Maybe he had spent his money wisely, maybe they were good at what they did, but still, she couldn't wait to see the back of them.

Especially the one who took liberties with his hands and with his tongue.

'Are you ready, Princess?' he asked, and before she had time to snap a response she found herself lifted bodily by the waist onto the back of the last remaining horse, her impossible rescuer launching himself behind and tucking her in close between him and the reins, before wrapping a cloak around them both until she was bundled up as if she was in a cocoon.

'Do you mind?' she said, squirming to put some distance between them.

'Not at all,' he said, tugging the cloak tighter and her closer with it, setting the horse into motion across the sand. 'We have a long way to go. You will find it easier if you relax.'

Not a chance.

'You could have told me,' she said, sitting as stiffly as she could in front of him, pretending that there was a chasm between them instead of a mere few thin layers of fabric. She tried to ignore the arm at her back cradling her and wished away the heat that flared in every place where their bodies rocked together with the motion of the horse.

'Could have told you what?'

'That they were only fireworks.'

'Would you have believed me?'

'You let me think it was much worse.'

'You think too much.'

'You don't know the first thing about me.'

'I know you talk too much.' He hauled her even closer to him. 'Relax.'

She yawned. 'And you're arrogant and bossy.'

'Go to sleep.'

But she didn't want to go to sleep. If she went to sleep, she would slump against him, closer to that hard wall of his chest, closer to that beating heart. And princesses did not fall asleep on the chests of strangers mounted on horseback. Especially not strangers like this man: arrogant. Assuming. Autocratic.

Besides, she had stayed awake most of the last night. It would not hurt her to stay awake a little longer. She looked up at him as they rode, at the strong line of his jaw under the mask, at the purposeful look in his dark eyes. Then, because she realised she was staring, she looked upwards to where it seemed as if all the stars in the universe had come out to play in a velvet sky.

She picked out the brightest stars, familiar stars that she had seen from her suite's balcony at home in the palace.

'Is it far to Jemeya?'

'Too far to travel tonight.'

'But my father, he will know I am safe?'

'He will know.'

'Good.' She yawned again, suddenly bone weary. The night air was cold around her face and she snuggled her face deeper under the cover of the cloak, imagining herself back in her own bed at the palace. That was warm too, a refuge when the winds spun around and carried the chill from the mainland's cold desert nights.

The horse galloped on, rocking her with every stride, but she knew there was no risk of falling, not with this man's arms surrounding her, the cloak wound tightly around them both, anchoring her to his body. She breathed in the warm air against his body, deliciously warm. His scent was so different from her father's familiar blend of aftershave and pipe tobacco, which shouldn't smell good but still did; this man smelled different and yet not unpleasantly so. This man seemed to carry the essence of the desert, warm and evocative, combining sunshine and sand, leather and horseflesh, and some indefinable extra ingredient, some musky quality all his own.

She breathed deeply, savouring it, tucking it away in her memory. Soon enough she would be back in her own bed, with familiar scents and sounds, but for now it was no hardship to stay low under the cloak, to drink in the warmth and his scent and let it seep bone deep.

After all, she was safe now. Why shouldn't she relax just a little? Surely it wouldn't hurt to nap just for a moment or two?

She let her eyelids drift closed as she yawned again, and this time she left them closed as she nestled against the hard, warm torso of her rescuer, breathing deeply of his scent, relishing the motion as the horse rocked them together. It wasn't so bad—a nap would refresh her, and soon she would be home with her father again. Nobody would know she had fallen asleep in the arms of a stranger.

And nobody would ever know how much she enjoyed it.

Zoltan Al Farouk bin Shamal knew the precise moment the princess had fallen asleep. She had been fighting it for some time, battling to remain as rigid and stiff in his arms as a plank of wood.

He almost laughed at the thought. She was no plank of wood. He had suspected as much from the first moment he had pulled her into his arms and spread his fingers wide over her belly. A chance manoeuvre and a lucky one, as it happened, designed to drag her close and shut her up before she could raise the alarm, but with the added bonus of discovering first-hand that this princess came with benefits: a softly rounded belly between the jut of hipbones, the delicious curve of waist to hip and the all-important compunction to want to explore further, just to name a few. It had been no hardship to hold her close and feel her flesh tremble with awareness under his hand, even while she attempted to act as if she was unaffected.

Unaffected, at least, until she had given into her baser instincts and jammed her teeth down on his finger.

This time he allowed himself to laugh, a low rumble that he let the passing air carry away. No, there was nothing wooden about her at all.

Especially now.

The rhythm of the horse had seduced her into relaxing, and bit by bit he had felt her resistance waver, her bones soften, until sleep had claimed her and she had unconsciously allowed her body to melt against his.

She felt surprisingly good there, tucked warm and close against his body, relaxed and loose-limbed, all feminine curves and every one of them an invitation to sin.

Exactly like her scandal-ridden sister, from what he had heard. Was this one as free and easy with her favours? It would not surprise him if she were—she had the sultry good looks of the royal women of Jemeya, the eyes that were enough to make a man hard, the lush mouth that promised the response would not be wasted. At her age, she must have had lovers. But at least, unlike her sister, this one had had the sense not to breed.

It would be no hardship making love with this woman. His groin tightened at the prospect. In less than forty-eight hours she would be his. He could wait that long. Maybe duty and this unwanted marriage would have some benefits after all.

Maybe.

As he looked down in the bundle of his arms, one thing he was sure of—spoilt princess or not, she was far too good for the likes of Mustafa.

Around him his friends fanned out, sand flying from the horses' hooves as they sped across the dunes. Better than good friends, they were the brothers he had never had, the brothers he had instead chosen. They would stay for the wedding and the coronation, they had promised, and then they would each go their separate ways again—Kadar back to Istanbul, Bahir to the roulette tables of Monte Carlo and Rashid to wherever in the world he could make the most money in the shortest time.

He would miss them when they were gone, and this time he would not be free to join them whenever the opportunity arose. For he was no longer the head of a global executive-jet fleet with the ability to take off to wherever he wanted if he had the time. Now everything he had built up might have been for nothing. Now he was stuck here in Al-Jirad to do his duty.

The woman in his arms stirred, muttering something as she shifted, angling herself further into him, one hand sliding down his stomach and perilously close to his groin.

He growled into the night air as he felt himself harden, growled when her hand slipped even lower. If she could do this to him when she was asleep, how much more would she be capable of when she was awake?

He could not wait to find out.

CHAPTER TWO

AISHA woke and sat up in bed, confused and still half-dreaming of mysterious desert men with broad shoulders and glinting eyes, of solid, muscled chests and strong arms with which to cradle her.

No. Not men. Just one man who had taken possession of her dreams as if he had a God-given right to.

Ridiculous. Thank God it was the morning after and she would never have to see him again.

She felt a sudden, bewildering pang of regret that she hadn't had the chance to thank him.

Baffling, really. The man had been arrogant beyond belief, he'd laughed at her every chance he'd had, and her father would have no doubt paid him handsomely for rescuing her—and she was actually sorry she hadn't had the chance to thank him?

What mattered now was that she was safe! Relief that they had got away turned to exhilaration running through her veins. She had been rescued from her kidnappers and the sick promise of a marriage to that pig, Mustafa. She let herself collapse back into the pillows with a sigh.

She was free.

She looked around the dimly lit room, searching for clues. Where was she? A palace or a plush hotel, given the dimensions of the room and the opulence of the furnishings. A palace with a bed almost as comfortable as her own at home, a bed she couldn't wait to reacquaint herself with tonight.

She was still wearing her robe, she realised as she slipped from the bed. Whoever had brought her here hadn't bothered to change her, merely put her to bed in the robe she had been wearing when she was rescued.

The man who had cradled her in his arms on his horse?

She stopped, halfway to the window, turned and looked back at the big, wide bed. Had he been here, in this room, leaning over to lay her softly on the bed, cautious not to wake her? Had he gently pulled the soft quilt up to cover her and keep her warm?

She shivered, remembering the warmth of his breath against her cheek when he had held her in the tent, remembering the solid thump of the heartbeat in his chest.

And then she remembered the way he had laughed at her, and she wondered why she was wasting so much time thinking about him when there were far more important things to consider.

Like going home.

She padded to the window, curious for a glimpse outside if only to give her a clue as to where she was. Maybe her father was already here, anxiously waiting for her to wake up so he could greet her.

She curled her toes into a luxurious silk rug as she pushed aside a curtain. She squinted into the bright sunlit day—later than morning, she estimated from the height and power of the sun. How long had she slept?

Blinking, she shielded her eyes with her hand and peered out again, letting her eyes adjust. Below her was a large courtyard garden, filled with orange trees and flowering shrubs, pools of water running between and a fountain in the centre, its splashing water sparkling like diamonds. Around the square ran a cloistered walkway beyond which the palace spread, grand and magnificent, topped with towers and gold domes that shone brightly in the sun. The scene was utterly beautiful.

Except for the black flags that flapped from every flagpole. She shivered in spite of the heat of the day, a sense of foreboding turning her blood cold.

Why were they all black? What had happened?

There was a knock on the door and she turned as a young woman bearing a tray entered, her eye drawn to the window. 'Oh, you're awake, Princess.' She bowed, put the tray down on a table and poured a cup of hot, aromatic liquid. 'You've slept almost the whole day. I've brought tea, some yoghurt and fruit in case you were hungry.'

'Where am I? And why are there black flags flying on the flagpoles?'

The girl looked as if she didn't know how to answer as she held out the cup of steaming beverage. Aisha caught the sweet scent of honey, spices, nutmeg and cinnamon on the steam. 'I will let them know you are awake.'

'Them?' She took a hopeful step closer as she took the cup. 'Is my father here?'

The girl's eyes slid away to a door. 'You have slept a very long time. You will find your clothes in the dressing room. Would you like me to select something for you while you bathe?'

She shook her head and put the cup aside. 'No. I want you to answer my question.'

The girl blinked. 'You are in Al-Jirad, of course.'

Al-Jirad? Then not far from Jemeya. No more than

thirty minutes by helicopter from the coast, an hour from the inland. 'And my father? Is he here, or is he waiting for me at home?'

'Someone will come for you shortly.' The girl bowed, looking uncomfortable and already withdrawing, heading for the door.

'Wait!'

She paused, looking warily over her shoulder. 'Yes?'

'I don't even know your name.'

She nodded meekly and uncertainly, her hands clasped in front of her. 'It is Rani, Princess.'

Aisha smiled, trying to put the girl at ease. She had so many questions and the girl must know something. 'Thank you for the tea, Rani. And, if I might just ask…?'

'Yes?'

'The man who brought me here… I mean the *men* who brought me here. Are they still somewhere in the palace, do you know?'

The girl looked longingly in the direction of the door.

'I wanted to thank them for rescuing me.'

The girl's eyes were large and wide, her small hands knotted tightly together in front of her. 'Someone will come for you, Princess. That is all I can say.' And with a bow she practically fled, her slippered feet almost soundless on the floor, the door snicking quietly closed behind her.

Aisha sighed in frustration as she sipped more of the sweet tea, relieved to know where she was, but still left wondering and worrying about the black flags. Maybe the King's aged mother had finally succumbed to the illness that had plagued her these past few years. The last she had heard, the old queen had not been responding to treatment. The Al-Jiradans would justifiably be sad at her passing, she mused. Queen Petra had been universally loved and adored.

But, beyond that, the knowledge she was in Al-Jirad was welcome. Relations between Al-Jirad and Jemeya— one little more than a patch of bare desert at the end of a sandy peninsular, the other a dot of an island a short distance off-shore—were close and went back centuries. Strategically positioned either side of the only navigable waterway into the desert interior, a deep trench that gave access to shipping, the two had forged a strong bond over the years, their geography assigning them the role of gatekeepers to the inland access route.

And Al-Jirad's King Hamra was one of her father's closest friends and allies. This must be one of the several palaces he had dotted across the kingdom.

She bathed quickly, anxious to find out more, and all the time wondering why she'd bothered to ask the girl about her rescuers. Would she really want to see him again, even if he was still in the palace, knowing how he had affected her? Did she really want to thank him?

Because how could she face him and not remember how intimately he had held her? How could she stop herself from blushing when she remembered how good— and, at the same time, how disturbing—it had felt?

No. She dried herself and slipped into a gown hanging in the bathroom. It was better they remained strangers. It was just as well he had never taken off his mask and she had never seen his face. It was far better she had no idea who he was.

She paused by the tray and nibbled on a fat, juicy date while she poured herself more tea, savouring the sweet, spicy brew, feeling more human after her shower and confident that soon she would be on her way home.

Then she pulled open the dressing-room doors to find something to wear.

And felt the sizzle all the way down her spine to her toes.

The relief she'd been feeling at being rescued, the relief at finally being safe, started unravelling from the warm ball of contentment in her gut and twisted, tangled and knotted into something far more ominous.

Because the wardrobe she'd been expecting to hold one or two items was full.

Of her own clothes.

Her own gowns and robes met her gaze, her own shoes, slippers and purses. She gazed around the walls of the room, at the shelves and the mirrored recesses where her jewellery box sat in pride of place. Even Honey—the tiny teddy bear she'd had as a child, its ears shiny and bare after years of stroking them with her thumb as she fell asleep—sat jauntily winking at her with his one remaining eye from on top of a chest of drawers. She picked up the worn, well-loved toy and held it to her breast, wishing for the comfort it had always lent as a child before dropping to a sofa, confusion scrambling her brain.

'What does it mean, Honey?' she whispered quietly to her toy, just as she had done as a child when she could not understand what was going on in the grown-up world around her. Just as she had done when her father had told her that her mother was never coming home from the hospital where she had gone to have a baby. 'Why?'

Part of her wanted to run like that child had run, find the girl called Rani and ask her, demand to know this instant, what was happening, what it was she wasn't telling her. But she was an adult now, and a princess, and could hardly go running around a palace in a dressing gown.

No, that way was not her way, no matter how confused she felt, no matter how much she needed answers to her questions. Besides, there had to be a logical explanation for why all her things had been shipped to a palace somewhere in Al-Jirad. There had to be.

So she would not make a spectacle of herself. She would choose something from her own clothes, get dressed, and only then, when she looked like the princess she was, would she go looking for answers.

And she intended to find them!

A man calling himself Hamzah came for her one interminable hour later. The Sheikh's vizier, he had told her, bowing deeply, and when she had started to question him he had promised that the Sheikh would answer all her questions. So she duly followed the wiry old man along the shaded cloister she had seen from her window, her impatience building by the minute.

The sun was lower now, turning the golden stone of the palace to a burnished red, though it was still almost too hot for the white linen trouser suit she had selected from her wardrobe.

She didn't care. She had chosen smart travelling clothes over one of her cooler silk abayas for a reason: she wanted it to be clear that she intended travelling home to Jemeya the first chance she got, today if it was at all possible. They could pack up and send her clothes after her.

The merest hint of a breeze, cooled by the fountains and the garden, tickled the patch of bare skin behind her neck, making her thankful she'd knotted her hair behind her head. Cool serenity she had been aiming for in her look, which was what she most needed. Along with confidence. Which she had for the most part, she felt, until she thought about the mystery of the clothes so neatly filling the dressing room and the absence of any kind of answers to her questions.

The strangeness of it all once again sent skitters down her spine. No matter how much she had tried to find a logical reason, to try to explain what possible reason they had sent her entire wardrobe here, it made no sense at all.

She shivered despite the warmth of the day, the relief she'd felt at escaping Mustafa's desert camp rapidly dissipating in the wake of all of her unanswered questions.

And in the shadow of a growing suspicion.

Something was wrong.

The vizier led her deeper into the palace, through a maze of corridors; between walls lined with beautiful mosaics set with gemstones, the colours leaping out at her; past rich wall-hangings and tapestries of animals frolicking on the banks of rivers. And water, water was always a theme—in the murals, mosaics and in the tiny fountains, trickling from stone jars in every corner over rocks, making music with water.

It was beautiful.

No doubt designed to be quite restful.

If you weren't already seething with impatience, turning every watery tinkle, every babbling and burbling rivulet, into the sound of someone scraping their nails down a blackboard.

By the time they came to a set of carved doors that rose imposing and ominous before them, she was ready to scrape her nails down anything.

Strange; she wasn't normally a violent person or prone to biting or scratching.

'Can you run as hard as you bite?'

She remembered the laughter in his words and she wished she'd bitten down harder. Then Hamzah beckoned her to follow, and she promised to put that man out of her mind once and for all. He was gone, probably busy blowing his reward at the nearest casino or fleshpot.

Mercenaries would be like that, she figured. In it for the money. The thrill of the hunt. The quick buck.

They entered a library, the floor and columns of the massive room decked in marble, smooth and cool, the occasional chairs and tables gilt and inlaid with precious stones, the walls lined with books and manuscripts. And there, in one far corner of the room, sat a man behind a computer, his hair shining blue-black under the lights.

He looked up as they approached, his eyes narrowing as he sat back in his chair. A secretary, she assumed with a sigh, wondering how long it would be and how many more layers of bureaucracy she would encounter until finally she found this mysterious sheikh and maybe even someone who could answer her questions.

'Princess Aisha.'

She stepped forward, her patience having reached its limit. 'Can you answer my questions? Or can you at least point me in the direction of someone who can? Because, as much as I am grateful for your hospitality, I need to know why I am not already on my way home to Jemeya but instead find the wardrobe in my room stuffed full of my clothes.'

The older man reared back as if he'd been physically struck. 'Excellency, I am sorry.'

Her eyes snapped around to the vizier. *Excellency?*

'Thank you, Hamzah. I'll handle this now.' And something in his voice made her turn back to the man in the chair, even while the older man withdrew. Almost in slow motion, it seemed, he pushed back his chair and rose to his full height.

Tall, she registered. Broad-shouldered.

And there was something about that voice…

Her mouth went dry.

It could not be him! She must be going mad if she imagined this man to be her rescuer. That man was a mercenary, sent by her father to rescue her. And this man was some kind of…*royalty*?

'Why did he call you Excellency? Surely that term is reserved for King Hamra, the ruler of Al-Jirad?'

She swallowed as he rounded the desk, long-limbed and lean, before propping himself against it, crossing his arms over his broad chest as he coolly surveyed her with dark, unreadable eyes. His hard face was constructed of too many harsh angles and too many dark places to be considered conventionally handsome. And, with the dark blue-black shadow of his beard, he looked—dangerous.

'So, who are you?' she asked, raising her chin in defiance, willing her voice not to crack. 'Why is it so impossible to get answers to my questions?'

'You are impatient, Princess. I was not warned of that particular trait. But then, I suppose you have been through an ordeal and we can excuse it this once. Did you sleep well?'

She was impatient but he could excuse it *just this once*. Who the hell did he think he was? What was it about Al-Jirad and the men here that brought out the worst in them? 'And I am expected to answer your questions while you choose not to answer mine?'

He smiled then, and for a moment he almost looked human. Almost. Before his face reverted to dark, shadowed planes and grim eyes. 'Touché.' He gave just the merest inclination of his head. 'I am Sheikh Zoltan Al Farouk bin Shamal, but of course you may call me Zoltan.'

'And I am Princess Aisha of the royal Peshwah family of Jemeya, and you may address me as Princess Aisha.'

This time he laughed, a rich, deep sound that sounded far too good to come from someone like him, a man she wanted to dislike everything about.

'Where is my father?' she demanded, cutting his laughter short. 'Why is he not here to greet me? I was promised he would know I was safe, but instead I find myself still here in Al-Jirad, instead of already being on my way home to Jemeya.'

He spread his arms out wide. 'You have an issue with your suite? Have we not made you comfortable here? Is there anything you lack?'

'I was assured my father would know I was safe.'

'And he knows, Princess Aisha. As he has known since you were plucked from that desert encampment last night. I spoke to him again once you were safe within this palace's walls. He is overjoyed beyond measure. He wanted me to tell you that.'

She blew out a breath she hadn't realised she'd been holding. At least something made sense. They were the exact words she would expect her father to use. 'So he's still in Jemeya, then, waiting for me to return home.' It still didn't explain why he would send her entire wardrobe—surely her lady in waiting could have selected a few likely outfits for her to choose from? But maybe he panicked.

'No. He is not in Jemeya, but right here in Al-Jirad,

at the Blue Palace, attending to some business. He will be here tomorrow.'

She blinked. The Blue Palace was the ceremonial palace of Al-Jirad, and the seat of the kingdom. Her father must have business with the King. But then she remembered the black flags flying atop the palace roof. Of course he would be here in Al-Jirad at such a time. 'Did something happen to Queen Petra? There are black flags flying.'

His brow furrowed, his eyes narrowing, drawing her eye to the strong black lashes framing his dark eyes. 'Yes, as it happens. It did.'

'Oh,' she said, 'that's so sad. So I'm not leaving just yet.'

He smiled again. 'No, Princess, you are not.'

'Then I will just have to wait for him here.'

He smiled and crossed his ankles, drawing her eye to the long, lean line of his legs encased in what looked like the finest fabric, superbly tailored. Superbly fitted everywhere. 'I get the impression you are not used to waiting, Princess.'

She realised she was staring, and where, and snapped her eyes back to his face. She caught a glimmer of laughter in the crease of his eyes and the curve of his lips. Laughter, and something entirely more menacing, and she got the impression he thought he was toying with her, like a cat with a mouse, prodding it one way and then the other, wanting it to run so he could pounce...

Well, she was no mouse and she would not run. And, sheikh or no sheikh, she didn't like his tone, nor his words that told her he was busy adding to her list of character faults. As if it mattered to her what he thought of her. She stiffened her spine.

'Maybe it's because I seem to have done nothing else

lately. I spent many hours out in the desert, waiting for escape. But I can wait one more night.'

He nodded, his smile growing wider. 'Excellent. I am sure you will find your time here most entertaining.'

She sensed she was being dismissed, and she realised that she was doing most of the 'entertaining', for he seemed more than amused. But she also realised that, no matter how much the man irritated her, she could not go without at least thanking him for offering her a safe haven. 'Then thank you, Sheikh Zoltan, for your hospitality. I apologise if I seemed impatient earlier but naturally I became frustrated when nobody seemed willing or able to answer my questions.'

'Perfectly understandable, Princess. You have been through a testing time.'

She nodded and gave a matter-of-fact smile, relieved she hadn't plunged their two countries into some kind of diplomatic crisis. After all, she was being offered protection here in a neighbouring country. Sanctuary. She should not abuse that courtesy. 'Then I will not waste any more of your time, Sheikh Zoltan. I will wait in my suite until my father arrives.'

He took her hand and she felt a sizzle of recognition, of having held a hand like this one before, a hand that belonged to a man who ran with long, powerful strides…

Impossible!

'Tell me one thing,' she said, disturbed enough to remember another niggling question that had not been answered. 'Why did my father send all of my belongings here when I will be in Al-Jirad such a short time? Surely he must have realised I could have made do with a suitcase-full at the most? Why do you think he did that?'

He shrugged, her hand still wrapped securely in his.
'Maybe he thought you would need them afterwards.'

'Afterwards? After what?'

'After we are married, of course.'

CHAPTER THREE

SHE wrenched her hand away. 'You must be mad!' The entire world must be going crazy! First Mustafa and now this man claiming she must marry him! 'I'm not marrying anyone,' she said, wanting to laugh so insanely at the very idea that maybe *she* was the one who was mad. 'Not Mustafa. And certainly not you.'

'I am sorry to break the news this way, Princess. I had intended to invite you to dine with me tonight, and convince you of the merits of the scheme while I seduced you with the best food, wine and entertainment that Al-Jirad can offer.'

'It does not matter how you planned the delivery. Your message would still be insane and my answer would still be the same. I am not marrying you! And now I intend to return to my suite and await the arrival of my father. I'm sorry that someone went to the trouble of unpacking all my belongings when they will only have to repack it all for the journey home tomorrow. Good night.'

She wheeled around, already taking a step towards the door that looked a million miles away right now, when her wrist was seized in an iron clasp.

'Not so fast, Princess.'

She looked down to where his hand curled around

her slender wrist, his skin a dark golden-olive, making
her own honey-coloured skin pale to almost white. Or
was that just because all her blood had drained away
and turned her ghostlike?

She lifted her gaze to his dark, glinting eyes. 'Nobody
touches a princess of Jemeya without consent.'

'Surely the betrothed…'

She pulled her wrist from his grip. 'I have no betrothed!'

'That's not what your father thinks.'

'Then you *are* indeed crazy. My father would never
give his permission for a marriage I did not want.'

'Maybe your father has no choice.'

'And maybe you're dreaming. For when he arrives
tomorrow he will surely set you straight. He did not
send his men to rescue me from the hands of one mad
despot to simply hand me over to another.'

'You are so sure they were your father's men?'

His words blindsided her. What kind of question was
that? Of course her father had sent her rescuers. 'They
came for me,' she asserted, hating this man right now
for making her question her own father's actions, for
making her doubt that he would do anything and everything in his power to get her back. 'As I knew they
would from the first moment I was kidnapped. I knew
my father would send someone to rescue me and I was
right. And they told me that my father would be told I
was safe. So who else would have sent them?'

'And if I told you that it was my men who rescued
you from that desert camp and from a future bearing
Mustafa's fat and plentiful sons?'

She threw her hands up in the air. 'I've heard enough
of this. I'm leaving.' She turned away and started walking. She was going to walk out of here and through that

door, and this time, when she did, she would forget all about being a princess and looking like a princess and acting like a princess—she would run as fast and hard as she could back to her suite and lock the door behind her. And she did not care who might see her, or what they might think of her, and she would not come out until her father had arrived and ensured her safe passage back to Jemeya.

This time there was no iron manacle around her wrist, no move to stop her. And for a moment she even thought she might make it. Until she heard him utter the fateful words behind her.

'And if I said I came for you with your father's blessing?'

Her feet shuddered to a halt on the marble-tiled floor, fear clamping down so hard on her muscles that it was impossible to move. She was suddenly aware of the pounding of her blood, her heart racing like that tiny mouse's must have, knowing the cat was behind it, ready to pounce if she moved so much as a tiny whisker.

I came for you?

Did he mean what he had said? Had he been there after all last night? Had he been one of the men in the rescuer's party? Or had he been the one to slice his way into her tent, to plaster her to his body too tightly and set off a low, burning heat deep in her belly, to cradle her in his arms as his stallion galloped across the dunes?

For that man had been tall and broad, supremely fit and sure of himself and unbearably arrogant with it. Yet her rescuer had been a mercenary, dressed all in black, his face completely covered but for his dark, glinting eyes.

No, it couldn't be him. She would not allow it.

She spun around. 'You are bluffing! You admit speak-

ing to my father this morning. He told you about the
rescue and now you try to make me feel so indebted to
you, so happy to have escaped the clutches of Mustafa,
that I will agree to this—' she searched frantically for
a word that might convey just how crazy this marriage
idea was '—insanity!'

Not a chance.

'But by all means,' she continued, 'do share this little
fantasy of yours with my father when he arrives tomorrow. I'm sure he'll be most entertained.'

Zoltan pushed himself from the edge of the desk,
then strode towards her with long, purposeful strides
that ate up the distance between them until he stood before her, tall and impossibly autocratic, his eyes fixed
with a steely determination, his jaw set like concrete.
'If you want to talk fantasy, Princess, let me share one
with you right now. Would you be similarly entertained
if I told you that I cannot wait to see what that mouth
of yours can do when you are in the throes of passion
rather than in the grip of fear?'

Shock thunderbolted down her spine, ricocheted out
to her extremities and made her clenching and unclench-
ing hand itch to slap one darkly shadowed cheek. 'How
dare you speak to me like that?'

'How dare I?' He reached out a hand, put the pad of
his thumb to her lip. 'But you're the one who put the
idea into my head, Princess—you and those sharp, white
teeth of yours.'

She gasped, took a step back. 'You!'

And then he smiled and, seemingly casually, crossed
his arms over his chest. She saw it then, on the index
finger of his right hand: the imprint of her teeth etched
deep and angry-looking on his skin.

He watched her eyes widen. He saw the realisation dawn and bloom. He smelt her fear.

And it felt strangely good.

'Yes, Princess. Me. Wearing your brand, it would appear—some quaint Jemeyan custom, I assume, to mark one's intended?'

She looked back up at him, her features tight and determined. 'It doesn't matter who you are or whether you were there last night. It doesn't matter if you were in the party that rescued me from that desert camp. I owe you nothing but my thanks, and you have that. But there is still no way I will marry you. And there is no way on this earth that you can make me.'

'You can fight this all you like, Princess, but there is no other way.'

'And if I still say no?'

He smiled. 'In that case, if you feel that strongly, maybe there is one other way after all.'

'Yes?'

'I can take you back to that desert encampment, leave you there and let Mustafa have his way with you. Your choice, Princess.'

She looked as if she was going to explode, face red with heat, her hands clenched at her side and her eyes so alight they were all but throwing flames. 'When my father finishes his business with the King and comes for me tomorrow, he will tell you the same as I do. There will be no marriage!'

All of a sudden he was tired of the game, of baiting her for her reactions, of toying with this spoilt princess, even though she had provided the only entertainment value in a world suddenly turned upon its head. The need to rescue her had brought him and his three friends together again for the first time in five years, and plucking her from beneath the nose of his hated half-brother had presented a moment of such sublime satisfaction that he would revel in the victory for years to come.

Except now he was faced with a precocious, precious princess who thought she had actually some say in what was happening. Why had he ever let her think that? Why had he tolerated her demands, deflected her questions and allowed her that privilege when she had never had it?

He knew damned well why—because he was still so angry about being put in this invidious position himself. Because he couldn't see why he should be the only one to suffer and sacrifice, the only one mightily frustrated at the choiceless situation he found himself thrust into. So why the hell shouldn't he extract some measure of glee from seeing her tossed right out of her precious, princessly comfort-zone?

And what right had she to feel so mightily aggrieved when marriage was the only thing required of her? Whereas his marriage to her was only one tiresome necessity in a long list of requirements his vizier had put before him in order to enable him to take the throne of Al-Jirad. And who had the time for any of this? The ability to speak fluent Jiradi as well as Arabic; the need to be able to quote from the sacred book of Jiradi which he must learn by heart before the coronation; having to honour the alliance between commitment to replenish the blood stock of Al-Jirad with a princess of noble birth from their sister state of Jemeya.

No. Suddenly he was tired of it all.

He sighed as she looked up at him, eyes defiant and openly hostile. He was sick of this whole damn situation before it had even properly begun.

'King Hamra is dead.'

She blinked. Once. Again. And then it seemed her entire face turned into a question mark, eyes wide, mouth open in shock. Then she shook her head. 'No.' Her hands flew to her mouth. 'You said it was Queen Petra. No!'

He watched those hands. He remembered them. Slim, he recalled. Long-fingered. Hands that had come perilously close to grazing the fabric covering his swelling organ last night. Hands that would soon have that privilege and that right, a right he hoped they would soon exercise.

Then he noticed her eyes and found them already filling with tears, threatening to spill over. He simultaneously wondered at her ability to distract him and cursed it when he knew the news he had to deliver was only going to make her feel worse. 'But how?' she cried. 'When?'

'The morning before you were kidnapped. King Hamra was on his way to Egypt for a holiday—he and the Queen in one helicopter with his close advisers, his mother and sons, their wives and families in the other. For some reason the two helicopters ventured too close to each other. Nobody knows why. But it seems that their blades touched and both helicopters plummeted to the ground.'

He gave her a moment to let the news sink in before he added, 'There were no survivors.'

Her face was almost devoid of colour, her dark eyes and lashes suddenly starkly standing out on a skin so deathly pale that he worried she might actually collapse.

He took hold of her shoulders before she might fall and steered her to the nearest chair where she sagged, limp and boneless.

'But surely not all of them? Not Akram and Renata?

Not Kaleem and Akra? And, please, no, surely not the children? They were so young, just babies…'

He could offer her nothing, so he said nothing, just gave the slightest shake of his head.

'Nobody told me!' she cried when she realised the truth and the extent of the disaster. 'I knew nothing. All the time I was in that desert camp they told me nothing. Oh yes, they laughed and smirked and made crude jokes about what Mustafa intended to do with me, but nobody told me that the King and his family had been killed. Nobody told me…'

She looked up at him, the shock, hurt and misery right there in her eyes to see, and for a moment he almost felt sorry for her and sorry for the upset all this damned mess would cause her. But, hell, why should he feel sorry for her, when his life had been similarly turned upside down, his future curtailed by the rules laid down by those of centuries past? The fact was that they were both the victims in this situation.

'Is this why all this is happening? Because it is somehow connected to that tragedy?'

Why did she have to look so damned vulnerable? He wanted to be angry with her, the spoilt princess who was having to do what her nation needed instead of what she wanted for a change. The last thing on earth he wanted was to feel empathy for her. To feel sorry. Especially when he was being subjected to the same external forces. He sucked in air. 'Al-Jirad needs a king.'

She looked up at him through glassy eyes, her long black lashes heavy with tears. 'That man—the vizier— he called you Excellency. Are you to be that king?'

'I am one possibility. King Hamra was my uncle. My father had two sons to two different wives. One was Mustafa. The other was me.' He paused. 'And, of course, whichever one of us it is to be is decided by the pact.'

She nodded, her eyes hardening with the realisation of what this came down to, the grief still there, but framed in anger now. 'So that's what this is all about, then, this game of Hunt the Princess. Whoever marries the princess first wins the crown of Al-Jirad.'

'It is what the pact requires. Where the crown of Al-Jirad is compromised, the alliance will be renewed by the marriage between the royal families of our two countries. Because of your older sister's situation...'

'You mean, because she has two children to two different fathers and she never actually bothered marrying either of them, she's no longer eligible for the position? But surely she has a proven track-record. If it's heirs you need—and when has any monarchy not been all about heirs?—Marina has proven child-bearing capabilities, where sadly I do not.'

'Your sister is, to put it mildly, over-qualified for the position. The fact you have not yet bred is still in your favour.'

Have not yet bred. She itched to hit something. Anything. Maybe him. Except princesses were not supposed to do such things, were not expected to give in to such base instincts. But still, the claim that this agreement was somehow in her favour rubbed, and rubbed raw.

'How can it be in my favour when it forces me into this situation?'

'It is duty, Princess. It is not personal.'

Not personal? Maybe that was why she hated it so much. Because it wasn't personal. And she had dreamed—oh, how she had dreamed—that being so far down the line to the crown, and a woman into the deal, would ensure she would never be subjected to the strictures of the first or even the second-born sons. She had watched her brothers with their tutors, seen how little rope they had been given. And she had watched her sister, who had been given too much too quickly while all the attention was on her brothers and their futures. She had been foolish enough to think she could somehow escape the madness of it all unscathed and lead a near-normal life. She had stupidly hoped she might even marry for love.

Zoltan watched her as she sat there, trying to absorb the enormity of the situation that confronted her. But it was hardly the end of the world, as she made it out to be. He would be the one on the throne, a position he'd never been prepared for, whereas she would go from princess to queen, a job she'd been primed for her entire life. What was so difficult about that?

They could still have a decent enough marriage if they both wanted. She was beautiful, this princess, long-limbed and lithe, with skin like satin. It would be no hardship at all to bed her to procure the heirs Al-Jirad required. And she had a fire burning beneath that cool, princessly exterior, a fire he was curious to discover more about, a fire he was keen to stoke for himself.

Why shouldn't it work, at least in the bedroom? And, if it didn't, then there were ways and means around that. An heir and a spare and they both would have done their duty; they could both look at different options. So just because they had to marry didn't make it a death sentence.

Then she shook her head, rising to her feet and brushing at the creases in her trousers, and he got the impression she would just as simply brush away the obligations laid upon her by the pact between their two countries.

And just as fruitlessly.

'So marrying you is to be my fate, then, decided by some crusty piece of paper that is hundreds of years old?'

'The pact sets out what must happen in the event of a situation such as this.'

'And of course we all must do what the pact says we must do.'

'It is the foundation stone of both our countries' constitutions—you know that. Are you so averse to doing your duty as a princess of one of those two countries?'

'Yes! Of course I am, if it means my fate is to marry either you or Mustafa! Of course I object.'

'Then maybe it is just as well you do not have a choice in the matter.'

'I refuse to believe that. What if I simply refuse to marry either of you? What if I have other plans for my life that don't include being married to some despot who thinks he can lay claim to a woman merely because of an accident of her birth?'

'That *accident of birth*, as you put it, gives you much wealth and many privileges, Princess. But it also comes with responsibilities. Your sister chose to shrug them off. Being the only other member of the royal Jemeyan family who can satisfy the terms of the pact, you do not have that option.'

'You can't make me marry you. I can still say no and I *do* say no.'

'Like I said, that is not an option available to you.'

She shrieked, a brittle sound of frustration and exasperation, her hands curled into tight, tense fists at her side. He yawned and looked at his watch. Any moment now he expected she would stamp her feet, maybe even throw herself to the floor and pound the tiles with her curled-up fists like a spoilt child. Not that it would do her any good.

'Look,' she started, the spark in her eye telling him she'd hit on some new plan of attack. Her hands unwound and she took a deep breath. She even smiled, if you could call it that. At least, it was the closest thing to a smile he'd seen her give to date. 'This is all so unnecessary. The pact is centuries old and we've all moved on a long way since then. There must be some misunderstanding.'

'You think?'

'I know.' She held out her hands as if she was preaching. Maybe she thought she was, because she was suddenly fired up with her building argument, her eyes bright, her features alive. He was struck again with how beautiful she was, how fine her features, how lush her mouth. His groin stirred. No, it would be no hardship bedding her. No hardship at all.

'My father loves me. He would never make me marry a man I didn't love, not for anything.'

'Not for anything?' He arched an eyebrow. 'Not even for the continuing alliance between our two countries?'

'So, maybe…' she said, with sparks in her eyes, really getting into it, 'maybe it's time we drew up a new agreement. Times have changed. The world has moved on. We could lead our respective countries into a new future, with a new and better alliance, something more applicable to the modern era that covers communication and the Internet and today's world instead of one that doesn't exist any more.'

He crossed his arms, nodded, fought to keep the smile from his own face as he pretended to give it serious thought. 'A new agreement? I can see how that would appeal.'

She failed or chose to ignore the sarcasm dripping from his words. 'Besides, of course, there is my work in Jemeya. My father would not expect me to walk away from my duties there.'

'Ah, yes, your *work*. Of course, someone like you would consider sitting down with a bunch of homeless kids and reading them fairy stories to be work. Very valuable work, no doubt. Makes for a few good photo opportunities, I dare say.'

Her eyes glinted, the smile wiped clean from her face. 'I teach them our language! I teach them how to read and write!'

'And nobody else in Jemeya can do that? Face facts, Princess.' He kicked himself away from the column. 'You are needed by Jemeya as much as a finger needs a wart.'

'How dare you?'

'I dare because someone needs to tell you. Jemeya does not need you, and the sooner you face facts the better. You have two older brothers, one of whom will inherit the throne, the other a spare if he cannot. So what good are you to Jemeya? Don't you see? You are surplus to requirements. You're a redundant princess. So you might as well be of some use to your country by marrying me.'

Her eyes were still glinting but now it was with ice-cold hatred.

'I have told you—I will not marry you and my father will not make me. Why would anyone in their right mind want to marry you? You led me to believe I had been rescued from one mad man when all along you were planning captivity of the same kind with another.

'Maybe it's time you faced facts yourself—you're arrogant beyond belief, you're a bully and you're so anxious to be Al-Jirad's next king that you would stop at nothing to get on that throne. I won't marry you now and I wouldn't marry you if you were the last man left on earth!'

Blood pounded in his temples, pounding out a drumbeat of fury, sounding out a call to war. What must he have done wrong in some former life that he would be lumbered with this selfish little princess for a wife? What gods had he somewhere and at some time insulted that they would visit upon him this poisoned shrew? For if he had a choice right now, if he didn't know Mustafa would otherwise get the crown, he would take her back and dump her back in that desert camp and be finished with her.

'Do you actually believe that I want to be king? Do you actually think that even if I wanted a wife I would want to marry someone who does not know when she is being offered the better end of the deal? Do you really think I want to marry such a spoilt, selfish little shrew?'

'Bastard!' He heard the crack, felt the sting of her hand hard across his cheek, and the blood in his pounding veins turned molten.

He seized her wrist as it flashed by, wrenching her to him. 'You'll pay for that!' She tried to pull her arm free and when he did not let go she pounded his chest with her free hand, twisting her shoulders from side to side.

'Let me go.'

Like hell.

He grabbed her other wrist, and she shrieked and tugged so hard against his restraint until she shook the hair loose behind her head and sent it tumbling down in disarray. 'Let me *go*!'

'Why?' he ground out between clenched teeth. 'So you can slap me again?'

But she twisted one arm right around, her wrist some-how slipped free and she raised it to lash at him again. He caught it this time before she could strike and pulled her in close to his body, trapping her arm under his and bringing her face within inches of his own. She was breathing hard, as if she'd just sprinted a mile, her chest rising and falling fast and furiously against his, her eyes spitting fire at him, her lips parted, gasping for air and showing those neat, sharp teeth, whose bite he could still feel on his hand.

He looked at her mouth and wondered how she would taste—something spicy and sweet with a chili bite. He looked at those wide, lush lips, parted like an invitation, looked at the teeth again and decided it might even be worth the risk.

And then he shifted his gaze and realised she was watching him watching her, her eyes wide, her pupils so dilated they were turning her eyes black.

'I hate you!' she spat, twisting her body against his, friction turning to heat, heat turning to desire.

Desire combusting to need.

'I know,' he said, breathing just as hard and fast. 'I hate you too.' Before his mouth crashed down hard on hers.

And even as she turned rigid beneath him, even though shock stilled her muscles, he felt the warmth of her blossoming heat beneath his kiss, tasted the honey and spice he knew he'd find there, tasted the chili heat—

and there, in the midst of the honey, cinnamon and chili, he tasted the promise of a woman beneath the princess.

And he wanted more.

CHAPTER FOUR

SHOCK punched the air from her lungs, sent all thoughts scattering from her mind. But God, she could still feel!

He seemed to be everywhere, the strong wall of his chest pressed hard against her, the steel bands of his arms surrounding her, the rough of his whiskered cheek against her skin and the press of his lips against her own.

Even the very air that intermingled between them, their heated breath, seemed full of his essence, his taste.

And for a moment that recognition blindsided her because it was so powerful. She did recognise his scent and the very feel of him, and she knew it was truly him—the man who had cradled her tightly in his arms, whose chest she had turned into to breathe more of him in while his horse had carried her away from the desert camp and away from that slug, Mustafa, who thought he could just take her at will...

Revulsion blossomed inside her, welling up like a mushroom cloud, giving her frozen limbs strength and purpose and her blank mind the will to act.

She thrust her chin up, twisted her face away, seeking escape from his relentless kiss. 'No,' she cried. *'No!'*

But he did not stop. He gave her no space, no release. He showed no mercy. Instead she felt herself lifted from her feet and swung around until she felt the hard marble of a column at her back. She felt herself sandwiched between it and him, pinning her to his long, lean body while his seeking mouth found hers again and she was full of him and the taste of him. Coaxing. Demanding. Persuading.

So persuasive.

Her body stirred. Her body responded, and she hated herself for it, even as she angled her head to give his mouth and his hot tongue better access to her mouth.

Then his hand slid down her arm, brushed one aching nipple on a straining breast, and suddenly it was Mustafa's greasy fingers she saw in her mind's eye, it was the smack of *his* lips as he walked towards her...

Oh God.

And that image was enough to give her the strength she needed. 'No!' she cried, twisting hard against the steel-hard shackles of his strong limbs. 'Get away from me!' And somehow she managed to unleash one wild hand and lashed out with it to push him away, her nails finding purchase on flesh as she dragged them down.

She heard his curse and suddenly she found herself thrust away, panting and reeling and having to search for the bones in her legs in order to stay upright while he stood there looking like a thundercloud, dark, grim and threatening, rubbing his scored cheek. She waited, gasping for air, shocked by what she had done, appalled that she, a princess of the royal house of Jemeya, had performed such a base act. Yet she was not sorry she had done it. Not one bit.

But she was afraid.

The reality of her position was never starker, never more terrifying. For she was alone in this palace, with no allies, no-one to protect her. He was big, powerful and angry, and she had struck him and drawn blood.

The way his chest heaved, the way his pulse pounded angrily at his temples and his eyes looked wild and vengeful, she knew he would not let her get away with that.

Just when she feared he would act, that he might actually raise his hand to strike her, he surprised her by smiling, a long, lazy crocodile smile. 'What quaint customs you Jemeyans have. What does this second brand signify, I wonder? Eternal fidelity? Ever-lasting love? Or a promise of many years of wild, passionate nights in my bed?'

'You flatter yourself! You know exactly why I hit you. How else was I supposed to make you stop acting like a barbarian?'

'Maybe it was not clear you wanted to stop.' And, maybe because he saw the disbelief etched so clearly on her features, he added for good measure, 'Your body told me you did not want to stop.'

'Then you weren't listening!'

He lifted his hand, exposing the three angry red lines marring his cheek, his eyes widening at the blood smeared on his hand. 'You will be sorry for this.'

She almost laughed out loud. His threat meant nothing to her. 'No. I don't think so. What I'm actually sorry about is for assuming I was being rescued last night rather than being kidnapped into some other nightmare. I'm sorry for having to listen to this ridiculous scheme of yours and argue its insanity, and I'm really sorry you do not seem to have any concept of how mad you are. But I am not sorry for hitting you. You asked for that!'

His lip curled. 'I should take you back to Mustafa's camp and leave you there.'

Fear crawled up her spine, even though she knew that there was no chance of it, even though she knew that he would never do such a thing—not when he wanted the throne for himself. Yet still she remembered the old crone's probing fingers, the humiliating inspection, and she remembered what Mustafa had promised to do to her the moment they were married and he was safe...

'My half-brother deserves a woman like you,' Zoltan continued. 'He deserves someone who can give him grief and make his life hell.'

But the poison of his insults washed off her, only serving to fuel the fire in her veins. She tossed her hair back, refusing to be cowed by his kind. 'If you think you're so different from him you are kidding yourself mightily.'

His face turned as red as a pomegranate, the tendons in his neck standing out in thick, tight cords, his pulse dancing in his throat. 'I am *nothing* like him!'

'Then you don't know him at all. You are both contemptible! Unfit to rule a line, let alone an entire kingdom. Al-Jirad is better off without the both of you.'

'Then who will be king?'

'I don't care. Someone else can sort that out. But I tell you this much, just as I'll tell my father when he comes: I am not marrying either of you.'

'You do that, Princess. You tell your father. You tell yourself. You tell whoever you like. Maybe if you say it often enough, you might even believe it.

'But you would be wasting your breath. For in less than twenty-four hours we will be married, whether you like it or not.'

'Over my dead body!'

His eyes glinted dangerously, the three scratches down his cheek standing out bold and angry. 'If that's what it takes.'

If the vizier hadn't chosen that exact moment to arrive, she would have hit him again—harder this time.

Princesses didn't hit, she knew. Princesses were serene, kept their cool and never lashed out—so she had been taught by endless tutors. But she had grown up with older brothers. They might have been princes, but they'd certainly not treated her and her sister like princesses. Oh yes, she was more than capable of dealing with bullies.

'Hamzah,' he said to the bowing vizier. 'What is it?'

The vizier took one look at Zoltan's cheek before glancing over at Aisha with disdain, taking in her unkempt hair, her reddened cheeks, clearly disapproving of what he saw. Then he blinked as if she didn't matter and turned back to Sheikh Zoltan.

'Sheikh King Ashar has called from the Blue Palace. He asks if he can speak to the princess.'

At last! Zoltan looked at her and now it was her turn to smile, because finally this was her moment. The sooner she spoke to her father, the sooner a halt could be put to these crazy wedding plans. Finally she had a chance to talk to someone who would listen to her, someone who cared about her, rather than trying to reason with a man who was like a brick wall and gave not a toss for what she wanted. 'Where can I take the call?'

When the vizier bowed and gestured towards the big desk in the corner, it was all she could do not to run over and snatch up the receiver simply to hear her father's voice again, just to let him know that, while she might be safe from one despot, it was only to be landed in the lap of another. He could not know the full details of what was planned. He must have been deceived. He must have no idea what this man was really planning.

But she wouldn't let herself run across the floor to

the phone. She could do serene when she wanted to, she could do regal. She was just finding it *harder* when this man was around, the urge to act rather than think decidedly more tempting.

'We will leave you in privacy, Princess,' Zoltan said behind her, about to withdraw after Hamzah. On a wicked whim she turned and held up one hand, one-hundred-per-cent confident in what her father would say.

'No. You wait. I'm sure you will be interested in what my father has to say.'

For as much as she hated him, as much as he threw her off-balance, she wanted him here to witness this, she wanted no more misunderstandings between them. Finally she could talk to her father, someone reasonable, someone who made sense and cared about her as a person, not just as some chattel to be exchanged in a business deal. And afterwards she would hand the phone over so her father could tell Zoltan the same thing because he would surely not believe her. She picked up the receiver, still smiling. God, after what she'd been through, she was really going to enjoy this. 'Papa, it's so good to talk to you!'

She listened and laughed as he expressed his delight, thanks and apologies for not being there to meet her. She assured him that she was unharmed, that neither Mustafa nor his men had hurt her, not physically, and that she couldn't wait to go home.

She threw a smile across to Zoltan, imagining his teeth gnashing together, relishing that thought. Thinking that the last thing he would have wanted was for her father to call, someone who would surely take her side in all of this.

Until there was a pause on the end of the line she could no longer ignore.

'Papa?'

The words she heard chilled her blood and made her dizzy with shock and disbelief. 'But, Papa, I do not understand.' And this time he said the words slower, so there could be no mistake, so she could not misunderstand.

'Aisha, you are not going home. Why has no-one told you yet? *You must marry Zoltan.*'

She made the mistake of looking up, caught the suddenly smug look on Zoltan's face, as if he had caught the gist of her conversation and knew it was not in her favour. Then again, he had probably read her reaction on her face. She spun around, turning her back on him, hating his air of casual boredom, hating the sudden curve she'd witnessed on his lips.

Hating everything about him.

'But, Papa...' she pleaded into the receiver, curving her free hand around the mouthpiece, shielding the panic in her voice and cursing her impulse to let Zoltan stay in the room while she took the call. But she was not done yet. 'I don't *want* to marry him!'

He wanted to choke. Did she for one moment actually imagine that he actually wanted to marry her? Laughable. But it wasn't laughable. It was painful, really, having to listen to one half of a conversation when that half was clearly going so wrong.

There were plenty more 'but, Papa's, a fair sprinkling of 'but why?'s and a lot of time where she said nothing but listened to what her father was telling her before she tried to get a word in. He had to admit the one that almost plucked at his heart strings was the 'Please, Papa, please!'

Said in her Poor Little Princess voice, it was quite touching, really. If you cared.

Even if you did, what could anyone do? Hadn't he explored every option himself?

But then the final cruncher—the 'Yes, Papa,' in a voice that sounded like a child's who had just been rebuked and told to be good—before she turned back to the desk and put the receiver down.

It was awkward witnessing someone else's humiliation, especially after they'd insisted you stayed and had acted as if it was going to be some kind of victory for them.

Awkward and yet, at the same time, supremely satisfying.

She didn't look up at him, but she didn't have to for him to realise she'd been crying. Her long lashes were clumped into thick black spikes, moisture glazed her eyes and he had to wonder why she insisted on making it so difficult for herself.

He'd learned early in life that some things were worth fighting for and some things were a lost cause from day one. 'Choose your battles,' his uncle, the King, had told him when he was just a young boy and still steaming after his father had, as usual, accepted Mustafa's side in a dispute. 'Don't waste your time on the things you can't change. Save your energy for the battles that count.'

He hadn't really understood the message back then; it had all just seemed so unfair that his father had never taken his word, no matter the truth of the matter. But bit by bit he'd learned that nothing would ever change and that arguing only made things worse.

Gradually he'd learned to accept the inevitable and save his energies for the battles he could win.

Someone should have told this woman the same thing.

Didn't she see there was no changing this? She was stuck. As stuck as he was in this centuries-old time warp. There was no getting out of it. There was no escape.

'So you managed to sort it all out?' he asked when she had stood there, her hands on the replaced receiver, for way too long.

She drew in a long breath then, blinked, straightened and made the tiniest concession she could to her tears by flicking them from the corners of her eye while making out as though she was pushing the weight of her long, dark hair back behind her ears.

'My father will be here tomorrow, as you said.' Her voice was low and flat, as if all the stuffing had been knocked out of it, all the life.

He waited longer still, struck by how much this admission of defeat cost her in her too-stiff spine and forced control, almost—if he had to admit it—admiring her. Maybe she wasn't as fragile as he had supposed or she would have been wailing on the end of the phone, dissolved into shrieks and fits of tears by now. Facing him after the instruction to stay, only for it to mean he had witnessed her humiliation, would be no easy task. Not for anyone, let alone some brittle, spoilt princess.

She blinked then as she looked up at him. 'My father—Sheikh Ashar—says I have no choice. Apparently neither of us do. It seems it is more complicated than a mere alliance. He says our countries are inexorably linked and that if this marriage doesn't happen both of our families forfeit their right to their respective thrones. So, if I say no, it will not only be Al-Jirad without a king.'

He waited. He had known this to be the truth, but she would never have believed him if he had told her. It was better coming from her father.

'So then, it is settled. There is no escaping this marriage, for either of us.'

She blinked up at him, her eyes as empty as her voice. 'Not unless I wish my father to lose the crown and my brothers to lose their birthright.'

She drew in breath and seemed to grow taller then, her chin raised, her eyes resigned but still, he noted, with a glimmer of defiance, even if still glassy. 'I would not do that to my family, of course.'

'Of course.'

'In which case, it seems there is no choice. Apparently I am stuck with this marriage.' Her chin grew higher then, her eyes grew colder, with an icy surface you could skate over. 'And so, it would seem, stuck with you.'

He watched her leave, her head held high, her posture impossibly straight and regal.

Haughtiness becomes you, he thought as she swept from the room, back to her princessly best, if you didn't count the riotous freefall of her hair tumbling down her back, hair that had felt like a silk curtain in his hands. He remembered the feel of her in his arms, the heat from her mouth, the softness and suppleness of her body against his, and he growled low and deep in his throat.

For all her protests, for all her pretence, there was a live woman under that haughty exterior, hot and wanting, and he would take great pleasure in peeling that harsh shell away piece by inevitable piece.

'What happened to you?' There was laughter in Rashid's words as he led the other two friends into the library and caught sight of Zoltan's cheek.

'Let me guess,' Bahir said with a knowing grin. 'The princess happened to him.'

Kadar perched himself on the edge of the desk where Zoltan sat and studied the three lines down his friend's cheek. 'No wonder she wasn't impressed by my fireworks. Looks like she's packing her own.'

Zoltan leaned back in his chair, pinching the bridge of his nose with his fingers, his head full of ancient verse after hours of study. No surprise that his friends would find this intensely amusing. They would no doubt find it doubly so if they knew exactly what he had been doing right before she had raked her claws down his cheek.

'I'm glad you all find this so entertaining. What are you doing here anyway? I thought you were falconing today.'

'We thought you might be lonely,' Rashid said, picking up a paperweight from the table and tossing it from one hand to the other. 'Didn't realise you were otherwise occupied.'

'Don't drop that,' Zoltan warned, thankful for the opportunity to change the subject. 'It's Murano glass, three-hundred years old. A present from the then-king to his sheikha. Worth a fortune, apparently.'

Bahir stopped tossing the paperweight for a moment, peering into the colours of its mysterious depths. 'Oh well,' he said, tossing it in Rashid's direction. 'Easy come, easy go.'

Kadar spun around the heavy tome sitting in front of Zoltan and peered down. 'What's this?'

'The Sacred Book of Al-Jirad. I have to know it by the coronation.'

'What? All of it?'

'The entire thing, chapter and verse. Ready to be

quoted from at the appropriate moment, to spout the wisdom of the ages.'

Rashid whistled. 'Then, brother, you really do need rescuing.'

Kadar slammed the book shut before Zoltan could stop him. 'Come on, then,' he said, jumping to his feet.

'I don't have time,' he growled. 'I'll see you at dinner.'

'What, you're too busy to spend a few minutes with your best friends when we've all come so far to help you? Nice one.'

'Lame,' Rashid agreed, tossing the paperweight casually in one hand. 'Besides, you have to exercise some time. We're heading for the pool.' And he threw the paperweight at Zoltan so fast he almost fumbled the catch and dropped it to the marble floor.

'Reflexes a bit slow today?' he teased, looking at his cheek. Zoltan knew he wasn't talking about the paperweight. 'I reckon I might actually beat you over twenty laps today. What do you say?'

Zoltan was already on his feet. 'Not a chance.'

Aisha could not believe it had come to this. She lay on the big, soft bed, her pillows drenched with tears. But now, hours after she had returned from that fateful meeting in the library, her tears were spent, her eyes sore and scratchy, and she was left with just the aching chasm in her gut where hope had once resided.

There was no hope now. There was nothing but a yawning pit of despair from which she could see no way out.

For tomorrow she was required to marry Zoltan, an arrogant, selfish, impossible man who clearly thought her no more than a spoilt princess and who had made it plain he considered she was getting the better end of the deal in having to marry a barbarian like him, and that there was not a thing she could do to avoid it. To renege on the deal would result in bringing down the royal families of two countries and smashing apart the alliance that had kept their countries strong for centuries.

And, for all the power that knowledge should bestow upon her—that she was the king-maker of two countries—she had never felt more powerless in her life.

She had never felt more alone.

She rolled over on the bed, caught a glimpse in the corner of her eye of the magnificent golden wedding-robe sitting ready and waiting on a mannequin in the corner of her room and squeezed her eyes shut again.

Such a beautiful gown. Such a work of art. *Such a waste.* A gown like that deserved to be worn to a fairy-tale wedding, whereas she was to be married to a monster. Expected to bear his sons, destined to be some kind of brood mare. Doomed to never find the love for which she had once hoped.

Such foolish dreams and hopes.

After all, she was a princess. She swiped at her cheeks. What right had she had to wish for any kind of normal life, even if her two brothers had the future crown of Jemeya well and truly covered?

Yet still, other princes and princesses around the world seemed to marry for love these days. Why shouldn't she have dared hope for the same?

She shook her head. It was pointless feeling sorry for herself. She forced herself to move, found herself a wash cloth in the bathroom to run cold water over and held it to her swollen, salt-crusted eyes. She could mope for

ever and it would not change things. Nothing she could
do, it seemed, could change things.

She returned to her room, passing by the open balcony doors when the curtains shifted on a slight breeze
as she still held the cool, soothing flannel to her cheeks.
Rani must have opened them, she guessed, before she
had left her to her despair, for she was sure the doors
had not been open before.

Poor Rani. She had been so excited to show her
the gown when she'd returned from her meeting with
Zoltan, so delighted to tell her what was planned for her
preparations the next day—the fragrant oil-baths, the
henna and the hairdresser. Aisha had taken such strides
to hold herself together until then, all the way from the
library through the convoluted passageways and along
the cloistered walk to her suite. It had been so much
effort to hold herself together that, in spite of all of the
young girl's enthusiasm—or maybe, in part, because of
it—she had taken one look at the dress, collapsed onto
the bed in tears and told the girl to go away.

The breeze from the open doors beckoned her, carrying with it the late-afternoon perfume of the garden
below, the heady scent of jasmine and the sweet lure of
orange blossom. It drew her to the window, to where
the soft inner drapes danced and played upon the gentle
breeze. She stood there for a moment before venturing
out onto the balcony of her suite. The sun was dipping
lower now, the evening rays turning the stone and roof
of the palace gold, even in the places it was not. The
garden was bathed in half-light, the sound of the splashing fountain and birdcalls coming from its green depths
like an antidote to stress.

It all looked so restful and beautiful, so perfect, even

when she knew things were far from perfect, that she could not resist the lure of the perfumed garden.

A set of stairs led down from the balcony. She looked back into her suite and realised someone had already taken away the jacket she had torn off and discarded en route to her bed, but it didn't matter, because she probably wouldn't need it anyway. It was deliciously warm and without the sting of the sun's rays. It wasn't as though she was planning on running into anyone.

She wasn't in the mood for running into anyone. A lifetime of training had told her that she must be presentable at all times, in all situations, prepared for every contingency; given a lifetime of doing exactly that, only to find that your life could take a bizarre turn and force you into marriage with someone just because some crusty old piece of paper said you must, what then did it matter how she looked? She finger-combed her hair back from her face and smoothed her creased trousers with her hands. That would do. Once, she might have cared, but today, after all that had happened, she felt a strange sense of detachment from her former life.

It didn't matter any more.

If she could be married to someone she hated because the ancient alliance between their two countries dictated it, then nothing mattered any more—not how you looked, how you acted or certainly not what you dreamed and wanted from your life. Only that you were a princess. Only that you came from the right breeding stock. And Zoltan hated her anyway. It wasn't as though he cared how she looked.

Zoltan was stuck with her, just as she was stuck with him, and somehow that thought was vaguely comforting as she descended the stairs into the garden. After all, why should she be the only one inconvenienced by this arrangement? Why should she be the only one to suffer?

Her legs brushed past lavender bushes intruding onto the path as she walked, releasing their scent onto the air. She breathed deeply, taking it in, wishing herself the soothing balm it promised.

The garden was deserted, as she had hoped it would be, silent but for the rustle of leaves on the breeze, the play of water and the call of birds. She drifted aimlessly along its paths, breathing in the scented air, delighting in the discovery of the ever-changing view and the skillful placement of a bubbling bird-bath or a flowering frangipani to surprise and delight. She stopped by one such frangipani tree laden with richly scented flowers, picked a cluster of bright white-and-yellow flowers to her face and drank in their sweet perfume.

Her mother's favourite flower, so her father had told her when she had leafed through her parents' wedding photos. She could see her parents' wedding photos now, and her mother's bouquet, all tight white rosebuds amidst the happy brightness of frangipani flowers as she drank in that sweet scent.

She wondered what her mother would tell her now. Would she be as cold and clinical as her father, who had told her today that there was no point thinking or dreaming or wishing for things to be different, because she was what she was and that was how it was to be? Or would she be more understanding, at least empathetic of her situation?

And not for the first time she wondered about her own parents' marriage, wishing she knew more of the circumstances of how they had met. But her mother had died way too early for her to be interested in any of that, and now it was all so long ago.

She arrived at an opening in a wall, keyhole-shaped, potted palms on either side. A path to another garden? she wondered. But as she looked through it she could see it was not one but a series of archways through which she caught a glimpse of greenery and whispering palms that beckoned to her.

She looked back, trying to get her bearings so she would not get lost, saw what must be her balcony above the tangle of vegetation and realised she was in the far corner of the square, the other side of the palace to where the library lay.

Further from Zoltan, she figured, so maybe it wouldn't hurt to venture a little further, especially not if this was to be her new home.

She encountered only one other person, a maid, who blinked up at her, bowed and soundlessly and quickly moved on.

She passed by a bird-bath with a bubbling fountain where birds splashed happily, oblivious to her passing, and the breeze whispered through the palms, the promise of the archways luring her on. She loved them all. Every one of them was decorated slightly differently, one whose walls were covered with blue-and-white mosaic, another inlaid with mother-of-pearl, the last with a pair of peacocks with bright and colourful plumage, every one of them a work of art.

It was as she passed beneath that last richly decorated arch and wondered what she would find beyond that she heard it, a voice, a shout, and then splashing and laughter. *Men's laughter*, coming from some kind of pool. She swallowed as she swung around, pressing her back hard against the cool, tiled wall, grateful she had heard their voices before stumbling unknowingly into their midst. She should not be here. She had come too far.

And then she heard his voice amongst the others, Zoltan's, and the bitter taste of bile rose in her throat as she remembered how supremely difficult it had been to walk from that library with her back straight and her head held high when all she had felt like doing was collapsing in a heap in despair—how it had taken every shred of her self-control to force herself to wait until she had walked through the door of her suite before she could let her tears go. She could not bear to see him again with those memories so vivid in her mind.

His voice rang out again, issuing some kind of challenge. There were calls and laughter, and the challenge seemed to be accepted by another. The unfairness of it all grated on her raw nerves, rubbed salt into her still-fresh wounds. Clearly Zoltan was not agonising too much over the stress of a forced marriage, for all his protests about not wanting to take a wife. Clearly he was not suffering unduly, if he could take time out to frolic in a pool with his friends without a care in the world. And clearly he had not felt the need to cry his heart out on his bed at the unfairness of it all. The truth of it struck home again. She was nothing in this world but a pawn in a game where she didn't even merit a move.

There came a splash then, the sound of thrashing water and cheers, and curiosity got the better of her. Who were these men with Zoltan? Could they be the ones who had accompanied him to the desert encampment last night? Maybe she could take one look. It wasn't as though the pool was private; there was no gate and she was simply out walking.

Making sure she stayed in the shadows under the

archway, she peered out past the garden surrounding the pool. There were two men there, neither of them Zoltan, standing cheering at the far end of a broad sapphire pool, partly shaded by twin lines of palms. Though it was nowhere near shady enough to hide the scars that marred one man's back, the skin twisted and brutal-looking, and she wondered what could have caused such a mess as the water of the pool was torn apart by churning arms, going stroke for stroke as two more men devoured the length of the pool.

Until they reached the end and the water erupted as someone emerged, using powerful arms to springboard out a mere head before his rival.

'I win,' the first said, offering his hand to the second.

Zoltan, she realised, disappointed as her eyes drank in the sight of him dripping wet. How typical that he should win the race. How unfortunate. She would have loved to see him lose. She would love to see something or someone wipe that smug look of superiority off his face and the sheer arrogance that infused every part of his body, every glistening muscle, every hard-packed limb.

Of course he would not have an ounce of fat on him, she thought with added resentment, he would not allow such a thing. She had seen enough. And she almost managed to turn away until he flexed his shoulders as her eyes caught the play of muscles under broad shoulders and tracked down the vee of his torso, to where his hips were encased in black lycra above the start of those long, powerful legs.

She sniffed, refusing to be impressed. So maybe she had been wrong before. Maybe he was not *exactly* like Mustafa, at least not in this one respect, she thought as she remembered the fat man scratching the bulging of his gut through his robe with long, almost feminine fingernails ending fingers adorned with gaudy rings. She shuddered, knowing how close she had come to that repulsive fate.

Still, it made no difference to her how many muscles Zoltan had, and she did not care that his skin glistened a golden-olive in the light. Not when in essence he was exactly the same as his half-brother. Not when there were still so very many reasons to hate him with every fibre of her being.

And she was sure, with time, she would find more.

'I gave you a head start,' his vanquished rival claimed as she watched furtively from the shadows. 'Let's make it best out of three.' Zoltan laughed and slapped his friend on the back, turning his face to the sky to shake the water from his dark hair. She had to blink and look again to make sure it was him.

Zoltan actually laughed? Was this the same man as the monster she had met today in the library? Was this the dark barbarian who had snarled and growled and so smugly informed her that she had no choice? For when he smiled, when he laughed so openly, his face was transformed. Not handsome, exactly. He would never be handsome. His face was too dark, his features too strong, like the strongest, bitterest cup of coffee imaginable. But with laughter lighting his dark features he almost looked human.

Almost—*good*.

Electricity sizzled down her spine and her mouth turned ashen. Tomorrow—*tomorrow*—this man would be her husband. This hated man would lie next to her in bed, wearing even less than he was wearing now. And expecting her...

She shivered, feeling a growing apprehension that the unknown would soon become known.

She clutched the flowers in her hands to her face, burying herself in their fragrant scent.

This was not how she had imagined it would be.

'Princess Aisha?'

CHAPTER FIVE

THE flowers fell from her hand as she turned, the vizier behind her bowing respectfully. 'One of the maids saw you walking. Is there something in particular you were looking for, Princess?' He glanced across at the pool, and she followed his gaze to where all four men were now gathered at the near end, laughing together, all four of them bronzed and built, with strong masculine features, all of them impressive in their own way. Once again she wondered whether they might be the same men who had helped pluck her from Mustafa last night. Her gaze returned to the enigma that was Zoltan. There was something about him that set him apart and that caused her pulse to trip. 'You are a long way from your suite.'

She turned to see him watching her. 'I was enchanted by the garden,' she said, her cheeks blazing with embarrassment at being caught peering covertly from the shadows and now openly staring. 'I did not know where the path would lead me. I was about to head back.'

He nodded. 'Rani has brought your meal. Perhaps you would permit me to show you back to your suite?' he said, and she knew it wasn't a question. She also knew she wasn't about to refuse.

'Of course,' she said, wanting to be as far away from

the mystery that was Zoltan—the laughing barbarian with the gleaming skin, the man who would be her husband tomorrow—as she could get.

'Princess!'

Too late.

She felt his call in a searing sizzle of heat down her spine, guilt-stricken that she had been discovered, a voyeur in the shadows, and not only by the vizier but now by Zoltan himself.

She wondered how much humiliation it was humanly possible to suffer in one day, for right now, the supply seemed endless. And this time she had no-one to blame but her own wretched curiosity.

Would he be angry with her for spying on him? Or would he laugh at her, the way he did, with unsubtle jibes, mocking words and that unmistakable upturn of his lips?

Either way, she hated him all the more for it. And she hated her own stupid lack of judgement for not leaving the moment she had realised he was here. Hated that he made her feel so off-balance and uncertain. Hated that he so badly affected her judgement.

She dragged in the scented air as she turned, praying for strength, steeling herself for the confrontation.

But nothing could have prepared her for the full impact of that near-naked body approaching. Her mouth went dry, her heart rate doubled and kept right on going, and her eyes didn't know where to look. He was so big, his glistening golden-olive skin beaded with moisture, his chest sprinkled with black hair circling dark nipples before arrowing south, over a taut, hard-packed torso...

She dared not look too far south. Instead she focused on the white towel he had picked up and which he now used to pat his face dry as droplets continued to rain from the slicked-back tendrils of his hair. But the snowy whiteness of the towel only served to highlight the rich glow of his skin, to contrast against the darkness of his features, and would have been of much more help to her right now if he lashed it firmly around his waist.

'You should have brought your swimsuit if you wanted a swim,' he said, dismissing the vizier with a brief nod over her shoulder, before taking in the cool shell-top and her bare arms.

She realised he was not angry, as she had feared he might be, but was laughing at her again. Right now she would have preferred the anger.

'Unless of course,' he added, his dark eyes raking over her heated face, 'you prefer swimming *au naturel*?'

'No!' Her prissy-sounding outburst escaped before she could stop it, just as she could no more prevent her cheeks flushing with embarrassment. The thought of being any more exposed to his scrutiny than she already was made her skin tingle and goose bump. But the thought of being naked in the same pool with him triggered an entirely new and more potent kind of reaction. She could already imagine the feel of the water cool against her tight nipples, the pull of the water tugging at her curls as it slipped between her aching, heated thighs...

She squeezed her legs together, wishing to God she'd bothered to find her jacket so that he might not witness any more of her body's reaction to his presence, crossing her arms over her breasts so that they could not betray her. 'I was just going for a walk,' she said, her nails pressing into her arms, harder and deeper, while she wished fervently that he would use that damned towel and cover himself, if only so she was not so tempted to look *there*. 'To clear my head.'

'A good plan,' he conceded, dashing her hopes when he balled the towel in one fist and flung it to one side. *Yet another reason to hate him*, she told herself, for any reasonable man would surely cover himself up in front of a lady—*a princess*. But this was clearly no reasonable man. He was a barbarian who had treated her, and continued to treat her, appallingly. Definitely a barbarian, arrogant, self-assured and clearly used to parading near-naked around women. So what if he managed to look almost human when he smiled and when he laughed? He did not smile for her, he did not laugh with her.

This man laughed at her.

And she hated him for it.

She might have told him that too, but just then he reached down before her and picked up the flowers she had dropped and long forgotten. 'It is a good time to walk in the garden. All the evening flowers send out their perfume to sweeten our sleep and make us forget the heat of the day and let us dream of cooler seasons.' Then he held the floral sprigs to his nose, breathing in their heady scent, closing his eyes for a second, giving her the chance to study him more closely—his sooty lashes and brows, the strong blade of his nose and the three long, red marks left so unashamedly by her own raking nails. 'Beautiful,' he said, surprising her again. And then he looked across. 'Did you drop them?'

When she nodded, because her throat was suddenly too tight to speak, he gently tugged one of the flowers and slipped it into the tumble of her hair behind her ear, presenting her with the rest of the scented bouquet.

'I should go,' she said, taking them and already backing away, disturbed beyond measure by even just the brush of his fingers in her hair, the touch of his fingers against hers. She was unsettled by his proximity and how it put all of her senses on high alert. Confused by a man who suddenly seemed once more like her rescuer of last night, the man whose warm body she had huddled against, rather than the barbarian who had attacked her today and so mercilessly dismantled her defences.

How could a man she hated on such a fundamental level stir such feelings within her?

For this was the same man, she battled to remind herself, the same ruthless man who had only rescued her so he could be king. But of course he could afford to look more relaxed now. He had no need to argue with her because he had got what he had wanted. He knew that she had been forced into compliance with this marriage, that she knew she had no choice. He knew she wasn't going anywhere and that he had won.

He didn't want a wife.

He just wanted to be king. She just happened to be the one who could make it possible. She was merely the means to an end.

Oh yes, there was good reason why he could laugh and smile with his friends now and afford to be more civil to her, and that knowledge only served to fuel the burning hatred she felt for him. Because he assumed she was a done deal. He assumed that, once her father had told her straight, she would do what she was required to do without any more complaint and become his compliant bride.

Like hell.

And that thought gave her strength.

It gave her back the power to be herself. 'You are busy and I am interrupting,' she said. But when she looked over to the pool and scanned its surrounds for the proof to support her argument, she found it empty, the sapphire surface of the water unbroken, his friends nowhere to be seen. She frowned. How had they left and she not even noticed? For now she was alone here with him, with him wearing nothing more than a stretch of black lycra. She looked down at the flowers in her hand and swallowed, trying hard to focus on them and not let her gaze wander from the detail of their cleverly sculpted petals, the delicate curve, the subtle shading of colours. Anything that might stop her gaze or her focus from wandering further afield where she might catch a glimpse of his powerful legs or that bulging band of black lycra hinting at what lay below. 'I really have to go.'

'So you said.' He smiled, enjoying the start-again stop-again nature of her icy armour. For a moment she'd seemed to be regaining some composure, some of that haughtiness he'd witnessed in the library, but now once again she seemed unsure of herself, almost confused, like an actor having trouble staying in character.

How long had she been standing in the shadows watching? What had she been thinking that turned her cheeks such a deliciously guilty shade of red?

Whatever it was, she didn't look haughty now, like she had when she had marched so erect and cold from the library. She looked shy and vulnerable, a woman again, rather than an ice princess. A woman who didn't seem to know where to look.

'Is something wrong, Princess? You seem—agitated.'

She looked up at him then, her once kohl-rimmed eyes now a smudgy grey and overflowing with exasperation. 'You could cover yourself! I'm not used to talking to a near-naked man.'

'Only watching them, apparently,' he said, while secretly pleased to hear it. He didn't want to think of her with other men. She would have had them. God, she was nearly twenty-four—of course she would have had them. But at least, unlike her sister, she had chosen to be discreet about them.

'I didn't know you were here!'

'And when you did, you left immediately.' He was already reaching for the towel he'd flung down earlier. In one smooth movement he had it wrapped low around his hips and knotted it tight. He held his hands out by his sides. 'Is that better?'

'A little,' she said, though still her eyes skated away every chance they got. 'Thank you. And now I must go.'

'Stay a moment longer,' he said, enjoying his prickly princess too much to let her go just yet. She was a strange one, this one, moving through a range of emotions and reactions too fast for him to keep up with or to understand, frustrating him to hell because he didn't know what he was dealing with on the one hand, intriguing him on the other. 'There are some friends of mine you should meet. Or meet again, without their masks this time.' Then he glanced over his shoulder, wanting to call them over so that he could introduce them, surprised when he found they had disappeared without his noticing. More surprised that they were not already queued up to congratulate the woman who had left her mark on him not just once but twice in the space of twenty-four hours.

Maybe they had realised that this was his battle and his alone and it was better to leave him to it. Not that they wouldn't relish the opportunity to rub it in every chance they got.

But there would be time to introduce her to them tomorrow at the wedding and maybe by then the marks on his face and hand would have faded and they might have forgotten.

And maybe camels might grow wings and fly.

More likely they were just hoping that by tomorrow she might have added to his list of injuries.

'Your friends have gone,' she said. 'And so must I.'

On an impulse he didn't quite understand himself, but knowing his friends would understand a rapid change of plans, he almost asked her to dine with him.

Almost, except he stopped himself at the last moment. For the dinner he had planned with his friends would take no time at all, and then he would be back to his books and his study, which was where he needed to be if he was ever going to be prepared for the requirements of his new role.

Whereas dinner with this woman? Who knew where that would lead, given the startling turn events had taken today? He didn't even know how it had happened. But he did remember the feel of her in his arms, the way she'd turned so suddenly from a rigid column of shock to lush feminine need with just one heated, molten kiss. Would he be tempted to linger if he dined with her tonight, tempted to make her truly his before she became his bride? It made no difference to him.

But then he remembered the cold slash of her claws down his cheek.

He did not need another reminder of how much she objected to this marriage, certainly not before the wedding. And they would be married soon enough. She would be his tomorrow night in every sense of the word, and he could wait that long. He didn't need another battle at this stage, not when he had already won the war.

'Then good night, Princess,' he said with a bow. 'Sleep well. And when next we meet, it will be at our marriage.'

And he let her go. He watched her turn and walk

purposefully away from him, watched the sway of her hips as she moved through the arched walkway to where Hamzah joined her to guide her back to her suite along the archway walk.

He turned away before she disappeared, cursing duty and all that came with it—the duty that forced him into this situation, the duty that insisted he marry this particular woman at this particular time, the duty that meant he would spend his night trying to memorize a crusty old book rather than burying himself in the body of a woman who looked and walked like a goddess. A woman who apparently hated the thought of doing her duty even more than he did.

Or maybe she just needed a bit more time to get used to the idea. That would make sense. He'd had three days since being informed of the disaster and what its implications were—that he should prepare himself for the fact he could be the one to inherit the throne. She'd had little more than that number in hours. And, even though her father had told her there was no other course of action, of course she would still be in denial, wanting to wish away her fate.

So maybe it was a good thing he had not asked her to dine with him. Because now she would have this night by herself, this one last night to enjoy her freedom.

And tomorrow, and for all the nights that would follow, her duty would be clear. Her duty would be with him.

In his bed.

CHAPTER SIX

'IT IS time, Princess.'

Startled, Aisha looked up from the cushioned seat where it seemed a hundred willing hands had been busy making the final adjustments to her veil and make-up until only a moment ago, whereas now she felt only the cold fingers of dread clawing at her insides. Surely it could not be time for the ceremony already? The day had passed in a blur of preparations, starting with a warm, oil-scented bath and moving on a seemingly never-ending conveyor-belt of sensual indulgences: a massage that had promised to soothe the tightness between her shoulders and yet had proved ultimately futile, before a facial, manicure and pedicure and the delicate, tickling touch of the henna artist creating golden swirling patterns on the backs of her hands and feet, a gesture of her acceptance of the Al-Jiradi ways.

It had all taken hours, yet surely it could not already be time? But the hands of the mantel clock offered no respite. Rani was right. The ceremony would begin in less than ten minutes.

She squeezed her eyes shut, feeling physically ill despite having barely eaten a thing all day.

'Do not be nervous, Princess,' reassured Rani. 'You look beautiful.' Clearly she mistook her reaction for normal pre-wedding jitters. But how could this be normal wedding nerves when most brides actually chose to get married? Or at least had a say in who they married? No, there was nothing normal about this marriage. Even if the mirror that Rani suddenly produced and held in front of her made her gasp.

She blinked, and looked again. Was that woman in the mirror, that woman adorned in golden robes, with her dark hair twisted with ropes of pearls and curled behind her head, really her? Her eyes looked enormous, rimmed with kohl and shimmering with glitter, her lips plumped and gloss-slicked ruby red. She looked every bit a real bride.

The enormity of what she was being forced into was like a lead weight on her chest. Married to a stranger. A despot.

A barbarian who cared nothing for her, but only what she could do for him.

What a waste it had been, feeling relief at escaping from Mustafa's slimy-fingered clutches, for here she was, being forced to marry yet another arrogant captor.

One of the other women tinkered with the fall of her veil, while Rani searched her face for any flaws. 'You look perfect, Princess. Sheikh Zoltan will not be able to resist his new wife.'

Oh hell! She jammed her lips shut. It was either that or bolt for the bathroom, with metres of golden embroidered silks fluttering in her wake, to throw up the few sips of sweet tea she had managed to swallow.

She clamped her eyes shut and concentrated, swallowing down on the urge, concentrating on her breathing. She would not let that happen. She was a princess of Jemeya, after all. She would not shame her father or her country in such a fashion.

Instead she willed her body to calm until she was back in control again, smiled the best she could at the waiting group of women all glowing with satisfaction with the results of their handiwork, and said with only a hint of irony, 'Then we must not keep Sheikh Zoltan waiting.'

It was to be a brief affair—just a small gathering, she had been advised—in deference to the recent demise of the royal family, which was the reason why it was being held here at this palace rather than the Blue Palace. The actual coronation would be held there in a few more days after the traditional mourning period, but his wedding now would cement Zoltan as the next king.

The ceremony itself was painfully brief. Her stomach still in knots, she was led slowly to a gilded ballroom where both her father and Zoltan stood waiting for her at the front of a small gathering of guests and officials, already seated at low tables for the feasting to follow. She searched the faces looking at her but failed to find her sister amongst them and felt a bubble of disappointment that she hadn't bothered or been able to attend. But that was her sister and it was half of why she loved her so much. Instead of following convention and trying to do the right thing, Marina made her own rules and lived by them, and she didn't blame anyone else when they went wrong.

Maybe her sister had been right all along.

The attendees fell silent and rose as one as she arrived, and to the sound of music, the beat of drums, the stringed oud and the haunting ney reed pipe, she moved across the room and forward to her fate. Her father nodded and beamed at her approvingly, partly, she knew, the smile of a man who had not seen his daughter for a few days, but also the smile of a man who would keep his crown. And she could not find fault with him for that. He had been born to be king. He knew nothing else. Jemeya knew no other way.

Besides, he was her father and she loved him, and so she did her best to warm her frozen face and smile back, not sure whether she had succeeded.

The other man stood a good head taller, and she almost missed her step when she saw the evidence of her nails still clear on his cheek. She lifted her gaze higher, saw his dark, assessing eyes on her, and felt an instantaneous rush of heat blossom in her bones and suffuse her flesh with what she saw there.

Oh, there was still the resentment, hard-edged and critical and matching the unrelenting set of his jaw. There was still the smug satisfaction at achieving what he had set out to do in order to become king. But it was the savage heat she saw burning inside those eyes that started fires under her own skin. A savage desire.

For her.

Her gaze dropped to the floor as she took those final, fateful steps. She could not breathe. Could barely think. Was only half-aware as the music ceased except for the drumming, only to realise it was her own heartbeat she was hearing. And then someone—the vizier?—uttered something and took her hennaed right hand and placed it in her father's palm. After barely a handful more words, her wrist was lifted and passed to Zoltan's waiting hand and, as easily as that, it was done. She was married.

Somewhere outside a cannon boomed, while inside the music resumed, brighter now and faster, signalling the end of the formalities and the start of the wedding celebrations and the feasting to come, but the music washed over her; her father's congratulations washed over her.

She was married.

They were led to their seats. She went as if in a daze, and all the time Zoltan kept hold of her hand, his warm fingers wound tightly around hers, almost as if he feared she would run if he let go. Foolish man. He should know there was nowhere for her to run now.

There was no escape.

She was married.

But she would not look at him, afraid that if she did she might once again witness that burning need and feel that potent reaction in her own body.

His thumb stroked her hand and she squeezed her eyes shut, trying to stop the warmth from his touch coursing up her arm. Why did he do that?

She did not want to feel this way. She hated him. She must not feel that way. And yet still her flesh tingled and burned, her breasts felt plumped and heavy and her thighs bore an unfamiliar ache...

It was not fair. And while she grappled with the reactions of a traitorous body, she was barely aware of the staff descending from every direction, filling glasses and delivering steaming platters until the table was sagging under the weight of food that she knew must smell wonderful and taste delicious. But she smelt nothing, could bring herself to taste nothing.

'Perhaps you might smile,' Zoltan leaned close to say.

Through the fog of her senses, she heard the bite in his voice, the rebuke, and it woke her from her stupor. This was Zoltan next to her, the barbarian sheikh. If she had witnessed need in his eyes, it was the need to possess her to take the crown of Al-Jirad. That was what she had witnessed in those greedy eyes. Nothing more.

She pulled her hand from his and used it to reach for her water so he could not take it back and stir her senses with the gentle stroke of his thumb again. 'Perhaps I do not find reason to smile.'

'This is our wedding day.'

She glared at him then, allowed her eyes to convey all the resentment and hatred she had for him and for being forced into this position. 'Precisely!' she hissed. 'So it is not like there is anything to smile about.'

A muscle in his jaw popped. His eyes were as cold and flat as a slab of marble, and she knew at that moment he hated her, and she was glad. There would be no more hand stroking if she could help it.

She sipped her water, celebrating her good fortune, but her success and his fury were short-lived, his features softening at the edges as he scooped up a ripe peach from a tray of fruit. 'Oh, I don't know,' he said, running his fingers over the velvet skin of the peach almost as if he was caressing it, holding it to his face to breathe in its fresh, sweet scent. 'There's always the anticipation of one's wedding night to bring a smile to one's face, wouldn't you say?'

And he bit deeply into the flesh of the peach, juice running down his chin, his eyes fixed on hers. Challenging. *Mocking.*

'You're disgusting!' she said, already rising to leave, unable to stand being alongside him a moment longer.

'And you,' he said, grabbing hold of her wrist, the corners of his lips turning up, 'are my sheikha. Do not forget that.'

'What hope is there of that?'

'None at all, if I have anything to do with it. Now sit down and smile. You are attracting attention.'

She looked around and saw heads turned her way,

the faces half openly curious, the other half frowning, except for the three men who sat at a table nearby who looked to be almost enjoying the show, the same men who had been with Zoltan last evening at the pool.

'Who are those men?' she asked, sitting down to quell curiosity and deflect attention from herself rather than because she wanted to, determined not to accede to his demand quietly. It worked. People soon returned to the feast and to the conversation.

'Which men?'

'The three you were with last night,' she said, rubbing her wrist where he had held her, damning a touch which seemed to leave a burning memory seared on her flesh. 'The ones sitting over there looking like the falcons that caught the hare.'

He knew who she was referring to before he followed her gaze to see his three friends sat talking amongst themselves, openly amused by the proceedings. 'They are friends of mine.'

'Are they the ones who were with you the night you came to Mustafa's camp?'

He looked back at her, amused by her choice of words. 'You mean the night we rescued you?' The glare he earned back in response was worth it. 'Yes, they are the ones. On the left is Bahir, in the centre, Rashid, and the one on the right is Kadar.'

Her eyes narrowed. 'He is the one with the scar on his back?'

'That is him.'

He waited for her to ask for details, like most women he knew would, but instead she just nodded, surprising him by asking, 'And you are the only one married?'

'As of today.'

'Why?'

'What do you mean, "why"?'

Alongside him she shrugged and took a sip from her glass of water, taking her own sweet time to answer. 'Oh, I don't know. I see three men who are clearly of marriageable age and who all look fairly decent with their clothes off. Your friends are all—what is that expression they use in women's magazines?—ripped?'

Her words trailed off, leaving him to deal with the uncomfortable knowledge that she thought his friends looked good with their clothes off, his gut squeezing tight in response. He didn't like that. He didn't want her looking at them. He looked over to where the trio sat, knowing that if they only knew they would never let him live it down.

'And of course,' she continued, 'you all seem quite friendly.'

'What's that supposed to mean?' he said, already suspecting where this was going.

For the first time she chose to look directly at him, rather than choosing to avert her eyes. She arched one eyebrow high, her eyes brimming with feigned innocence. 'Naturally, I was wondering, maybe you're all gay or something? Not that that's a problem, per se, you understand. But it would explain why none of you have wives or women.'

He could not believe what he was hearing. If they had been anywhere else... If they had been anywhere but sitting in the midst of a crowded room where they were the centre of attention, he would have rucked up her golden skirts and shown her just how far from gay he was right here and now.

But he did not have to resort to such means, not given

their eventful, albeit brief, history. She could not have forgotten already. 'I seem to recall a certain incident in the library yesterday. I seem to recall you being there. Do you really have cause to wonder if I am gay?'

She shrugged again and picked a grape from a bunch, the first item of food he'd seen her take. 'So maybe you swing both ways,' she said, her eyes outlined and as bold as that sharp tongue of hers. 'How am I supposed to know? After all, you were the one who said you never wanted a wife. And you are only marrying me so you can get the throne of Al-Jirad. What do you expect me to make of that?'

He growled, looking around at their guests, happy, loud and deep in the celebrations, and wondered if anyone would actually notice if he did drag her off to some sheltered alcove and put her concerns about his sexuality to bed this very minute. The thought made him stir, and not for the first time today. The moment she had walked into the ballroom, shrouded from head to toe in her golden wrapping, looking more like a goddess than any woman he had ever seen, he had lusted to peel each and every one of those robes and veils from her until she stood naked before him.

'Let me assure you,' he said, aware of three pairs of eyes studying them intently, judging their interaction, instead of watching the dancers like everyone else, no doubt hoping for more sparks to further entertain them. 'You need have no concerns on that score.

'And one more thing,' he added almost as an afterthought, when he noticed she was now making an entire course of grape number two. 'If I might suggest something?'

'What?'

'In the interests of allaying any and all concerns you have about my sexuality, you would be wise to eat something much more substantial. You're going to be needing your strength tonight.'

The grape went down the wrong way, the dancers finished, and it was only that the applause drowned out the sound of her coughing that hardly anyone realised she was choking.

Bastard!

Her father topped up her water but she was already on her feet, one of her attendants coming to help her manage her robes. 'Where are you going?' Zoltan demanded to know, rising to his feet beside her.

'The bathroom. Is that permitted, Your Arrogance?'

He let her go this time and she swept from the room, on the outside a cloud of sparkling gold, on the inside a raging black thundercloud.

She bypassed the bathroom, needing to stride the long corridors, needing to pound the flagstones in an effort to pound the man out of her psyche, until finally she stopped by an open window looking over yet another shady garden. She breathed deeply of the fragrant air, praying it lend her strength. She needed space. Space from that barbarian she was now wedded to. Space from the knowledge that tonight he would expect to make her his wife in every sense of the word.

And she was so very afraid.

She should never have goaded him. She should have known he would find a way to strike back at her, that her tiny victory would be only short-lived.

She looked up to see the vapour trail of a jet neatly bisecting the endless blue of the sky with a thin white line, the tiny plane no more than a diamond sparkling in the sun. She wished with all her heart that she were on that plane right now, flying as far, far away from Al-Jirad, Zoltan and her birthright as she could possibly get.

But she was not, because she was a princess, and duty ordained that she do this thing, that she marry a man she didn't love.

Duty.

Such a little word. Such a huge impost. And tonight Zoltan would expect her to do her duty again and let him bed her.

She shuddered at the thought, suddenly assailed by myriad images and sensations cascading over her: the feel of his strong arms around her in the library, his hot mouth seeking hers, plundering hers, the sight of his body, fresh from his swim, the slide of droplets down his satin-skinned chest...

She breathed in the perfumed air and watched the tiny speck of a plane disappear into the distance as she thought of her shattered dreams and hopes. No hope of marrying a man she loved. No escape from a forced marriage. Not now.

But that did not mean she was completely powerless.

'Princess,' Rani said beside her, 'the Sheikh will be worried.'

She nodded as an idea formed and took shape in her mind, but knowing what Rani said to be true. Any moment Zoltan was sure to send out the storm troopers to find her and drag her back.

So there was no escape. She was stuck in this marriage with him. But Zoltan was a fool if he thought that meant he would have it all his own way and that she would deliver herself up to him on a platter.

She would not waste herself that way.

She had not saved herself all these years to be taken by a barbarian.

'What are you doing here?'

She stilled at the desk where she was sitting, pausing mid-sentence in the letter she was writing longhand to her sister to tell her about the wedding. In all likelihood it would never be sent, the details too baring, too revealing, but it was cathartic, writing it all down, putting her thoughts and shattered dreams into words.

But partly it had been something to pass the time, something to placate her mounting nerves, to do while waiting for the inevitable knock on the door.

She'd known that eventually he'd finish his drinks with his friends or whatever it was that he'd excused himself to do and that had kept him so long after the ceremony, wonder where she was and come looking for her. She should have known that he wouldn't wait for her to open the door to barge in, all aggrieved and affronted masculine pride.

She rose to face him, willing away the heat in her cheeks. Against Rani's shocked protests, she'd unwound herself from the metres and metres of golden fabric, pulled down her hair and scrubbed her face clean, dressing instead in a simple white nightdress, with a white robe lashed at her waist. Now only the henna tattoos adorning the backs of her hands and feet remained, but even they would fade in time and at least she no longer felt like some kind of prize to be fought and waged war over and dressed up like some kind of triumph. She felt like herself. Not even a princess any more, but a woman.

A woman with a mind of her own. A woman who

knew about duty, but who also had her own hopes and dreams for the future.

That woman faced up to him now.

'Why wouldn't I be here?' She swallowed and tugged on the ends of her robe's ties, taking both mental and physical reinforcement from the action. 'After all, this is *my* suite, Sheikh Zoltan.' She put the emphasis squarely on the 'my'.

'And this is our wedding night!'

Packed with memories she would cherish for ever. What a laugh. She shrugged, realising she hadn't been the only one to divest of her wedding garb. He'd changed too out of that crisp, white wedding robe and into a pair of perfectly tailored trousers and a smooth fine-knit shirt that clung to his chest like a lover's caress. But no, she would rather not think of his lovers right now, or how many he must have had, or what their hands might do with a chest like that to explore. Not that she was jealous, exactly. It was just that she did not care to know the details.

She lifted her gaze to his face, plastering a disingenuous expression on her own. 'Your point being?'

'You are supposed to be in my chamber. Didn't they tell you I was expecting to find you in my suite?'

She sniffed, looking down at the desk and fingering the hand-written pages, thinking about all the things she'd talked about, all her hopes and her disappointments, exposing herself and her pointless dreams. No, she probably wouldn't end up sending it, come to think of it. Her seize-the-moment sister would probably only laugh and say that no man was worth waiting for, especially the one you didn't even know existed. She looked back up at Zoltan, waiting like a mountain before her. 'I do believe someone mentioned something like that, yes.'

'Then why did I have to come looking for you here?'

'Because there seemed no point in going to your room.'

He raked one hand through his hair. 'What the hell are you talking about? Why not, when you knew I had been expecting to find you there?'

'Simply because I thought it might give you the wrong idea,' she said, pausing to enjoy the mess of confusion on his features and the questions flashing across his eyes before deciding to put him out of his misery. 'Given the fact I have no intention of sleeping with you.'

CHAPTER SEVEN

THE mountain before her turned volcanic, the face glowing hot with the magma so close below the surface, eyes wild. She braced herself for the eruption, knowing she was courting disaster and yet feeling a strange sense of elation that she'd succeeded in throwing him so completely off-balance. But the expected eruption did not eventuate. Zoltan somehow managed to hold himself together, his rage rolling off him in searing waves of heat. 'Is this some kind of joke?'

'Rest assured, Sheikh Zoltan,' she said, aiming for meekness. 'I would never joke about such a thing. I am deadly serious.'

'But you are my *wife*!' he roared, rigid with fury. 'Let me remind you of that fact, in case today's ceremony had somehow slipped your mind.'

This time she could not help but laugh. 'Do you seriously think for a moment I could forget, when I was handed over to you like little more than a stick of furniture?'

'Oh,' he said, pacing out the width of the Persian rug that took up one half of the room before turning to devour the distance back in long, purposeful strides, his thumb stroking his chin as if he were deep in contemplation of some highly complex problem. 'I see your problem. You think it should have been all about you, the poor little princess forced to do her duty for once in her life? Do you think we should have got down on hands and bended knees and thanked you for so generously sacrificing yourself on the altar of martyrdom? For so generously agreeing to do what was your duty?'

She closed her eyes as she took a despairing breath, ignoring his barbs and insults except to use them to fuel her resolve. If she had a problem, it was standing not ten feet from her. 'No, I don't think that at all. For, while I'm not overly fond of finding myself a pawn in someone else's game—a game, it seems, where I find myself a loser from the very beginning—I actually don't think I'm the one with the problem here.

'You needed a wife—a princess, no less—in order to be king and today you got one. So now you can be crowned King of Al-Jirad. You have my heartiest congratulations.' She looked towards the door. 'And now, if you wouldn't mind leaving, Sheikh Zoltan, I will finish my correspondence.'

He stood, slowly shaking his head. 'You are kidding yourself if you think that, Princess. You think this ends here? You know Al-Jirad needs an heir. Two at least before your work is anywhere near done.'

She angled her chin higher. 'I acknowledge that my services are also required as some kind of brood mare. I do not particularly like it, but I accept that it is so.'

His eyes gleamed in the light. 'Then what are you doing here and not already in my suite?'

'Simple,' she said, crossing her arms over her chest, refusing to be cowed. 'I don't know you. I won't sleep with a man I don't know, whoever he is, whether or not he believes he has some kind of legal entitlement to my breeding services.'

He came closer then, so close she could feel the air shift and curl between them, carrying his scent to her on a heated wave. It was all she could do to stand her ground and not turn and run, and only half from fear of his anger. The other half was from fear that, in spite of her anger and her hatred for him, she might yet be drawn towards an evocative scent that brought back memories of lying wrapped in his arms, close to his heated body.

She swallowed as he came close. But surely he would not try anything here, in her suite? Surely he was not that ruthless that he could come here to take what she had denied him elsewhere?

'You don't know me, Princess?' He scooped the back of one finger down her cheek, an electric, evocative gesture that sent ripples of sensation radiating out under her skin. 'Not at all?'

'No,' she said, hating it when he slid his hand around the curve of her throat. 'I know practically nothing about you.' She willed herself to be strong, to remember his cruelty and the fact he was using her, even as her skin tingled, her traitorous body yearning to sway into his touch. 'And to tell you the truth, I'm not particularly fond of the bits I have seen.'

'Strange,' he mused. 'When I had been sure there was a definite connection between us.' He angled his head. 'Did you not feel it then, when we kissed?'

'I felt nothing but revulsion!'

'Then I am mistaken. It must have been your sensual twin sister in my arms in that library. That woman was warm and willing and had a fire raging inside her that I longed to quench.'

She spun away, discomfited by his words. Shamed by the parts that hit too close to home. 'You are very much mistaken!'

He stood there where she had left him like a dark thundercloud. 'It is you who is mistaken, Princess, thinking you have a choice about this, barricading yourself away in your room like some kind of virginal nun seeking sanctuary when you should already be on your back working to provide Al-Jirad with the heirs it requires.'

Her blood simmered and spat, turned molten in her veins and seared its way under her skin. It was all she could do to swallow back on the bitter bile that ached to infuse her words. 'How tempting you make it sound, Sheikh Zoltan. You paint a picture in which any woman would be mad not to want a starring role—on her back, ready to be serviced by the barbarian sheikh!'

She turned away, unable to look at him a moment longer, unable to banish the unwelcome pictures in her mind's eye—and the unwelcome rush of heat that had accompanied them—needing air and space and everything she knew she would never find in this marriage where she was stuck with him for ever.

A hand clamped down on her shoulder and wrenched her around. 'What did you call me?'

She looked purposefully down at his hand on her arm, and then up to him. 'Only what you are. A barbarian.'

He smiled then, if you could call it that, baring his teeth like a wild animal before it lunges for the kill, his eyes alert and anticipating her every move. Her simmering blood spun faster and more frantic in her veins.

'I seem to recall you calling me a barbarian once before, Princess,' he said, tugging her closer, sliding his free hand down her arm, and then so slowly up again. 'Maybe you are right. Maybe I am only a barbarian— the princess's personal barbarian. Do you like the sound of that? Would that excite you? Does it heat your blood like it did yesterday in the library?' He looked past her shoulder to the massive, wide bed that lay so broad and inviting across the room, and when he looked back at her his eyes gleamed with purpose. 'Is that why you stayed here in your room?' He looked down at the simple robe she was wearing, flicking the collar under his thumb, and she could tell he was working out how easy it would be to discard. 'Is that why you changed out of your wedding gown, so that when I came and got angry, as you knew I must, it would be no challenge to tear off your robe and gown and bare you to my gaze?'

'You kid yourself,' she whispered, her breath coming rapid and shallow. She hated what he was doing to her body, hated herself for imagining the scene he portrayed and for wondering what it would be like to be taken by one so powerful. And she felt confused and conflicted—she hated him, and he was being a monster, yet still heat mounted inside her, still the excitement of his touch and his words tugged and awoke some deeply buried carnal self.

'Do I?' He touched the pad of his thumb to her parted lips, and she trembled and saw his answering smile when she did. 'For, given that I am a barbarian, I could take you now and save myself the trouble of carrying you all the way to my suite.'

His predatory smile widened. He stepped in closer, let go his grip on her arm and used both his hands to scoop behind her neck and into her scalp, under the weight of her thick black hair. 'Would you like that, Princess?'

She swallowed, having to put up her hands against his hard chest to stop herself from falling into him. 'You wouldn't dare.' But she wouldn't bet on it.

'And maybe it would be better this way,' he countered, lifting her chin, angling his head. 'For some say familiarity breeds contempt. Maybe we should consummate this marriage now, right now, lest in time you decide you hate me.'

His face drew closer and she remembered all the reasons why it shouldn't, remembered how she felt, remembered the promise that she'd made to herself. 'I already hate you.'

His nostrils flared, his eyes flared, then immediately descended into utter blackness. She knew she was playing with fire. 'In which case, sweet princess, what is the point of waiting? Let's finish this now.'

'No!' She pushed against his chest with every bit of strength she could muster, twisting away from him, almost stumbling in her hurry to get away. 'Get out! I do not want this! I do not want you!'

'You are fooling yourself, Princess,' he said, his chest heaving as his eyes burned like coals. 'Once again your body betrays you. Why shouldn't we finish what we started?'

'I'll tell you why,' she said. 'Because if you do not leave now, if you do not go, then it will be on your own head. And you need never seek my respect or love or even the tiniest shred of civility, because I will hate you as much as it is physically possible to hate anyone if you take what is not freely given!'

There were sparks spitting fire in her eyes, there was a bright slash of colour across her cheeks, and right now he burned for her—burned for this woman who was now his wife and yet not completely. He burned bright and hot, his blood heated and heavy in his groin, and it took every bit of the restraint civilisation had wrought over the aeons upon the male mind that he did not throw her bodily to the floor and take her now.

'Then I warn you, Princess. Do not take too long to decide to give what you must, because when it all comes down to it, for the sake of Al-Jirad, I will gladly risk your hatred!'

He left her then and his blood turned to steam, his fury a living thing, tangling in his gut, fuelling his feet into long, purposeful strides. He should never have given her time to prepare. He should have accompanied her to his suite, got their necessary coupling over and done with before returning to his studies. Instead he had got lost in the endless pages and had given her too much time, it seemed. Time to think and plan and plot how she could evade her duty.

But it would not last.

In three days he would be crowned King of Al-Jirad, and like it or not, the princess must by then be his wife in all senses of the word. He had studied the pact in detail long enough to know that, searching for any way out, for any concessions.

He headed back to the library, back to his endless books and study. There was no point wasting time thinking about a spoilt princess and her pathetic, 'I will not sleep with anyone I do not know' now.

She would know him soon enough.

Her resistance would not last.

He could not afford to let it.

He'd already churned his way through twenty laps when he noticed Bahir at the end of the pool, and he cursed his decision not to return to his studies.

'You're up early,' his friend said, sitting himself down

on the edge of the pool as Zoltan finished the lap and checked his watch. 'Barely six a.m. Honeymoon already over?'

Zoltan glared at him as he made a rapid change of plans. The ten extra laps could wait. He put his hands on the side of the pool and powered himself out, intending to grab his towel and just keep right on walking. He wasn't in the mood to talk to anyone this morning, let alone one of these clowns. They knew far too much about him as it was.

'Uh oh,' Bahir said behind him. 'Maybe the honeymoon hasn't even begun.'

'I didn't say anything,' Zoltan protested as he bent down to scoop up his towel.

'Brother, you didn't need to. It's written all over your body language. What happened? How could the princess manage to turn down the legendary Zoltan charm? Although admittedly all that brooding intensity must be tiresome to endure.'

He glared at his so-called friend. 'There's nothing to tell.'

Bahir grinned. 'So long as it's not because she plays for the other team.' He whistled. 'That would be one cruel waste.'

The urge to laugh battled with the urge to growl. He didn't want anyone speculating about his wife's sexuality. Besides, if Bahir only knew which team she'd openly speculated they all played for he wouldn't think it nearly as funny himself. He sighed. Clearly Bahir would not stop until he knew. 'She says it's because she doesn't know me.'

'What?'

He shrugged. 'She says she won't sleep with any

man she doesn't know. Apparently—' he ground out the words between his teeth '—that includes her husband.'

'But she has to. I thought you said so.'

'I did. According to the terms of the pact she has no choice.'

'Did you tell her that?'

He thought back to their argument and how bitter and twisted it had become at the end. 'Under the circumstances, I really don't think it would have helped if I had.'

'But she has to eventually, right? She has to give you heirs and she knows that?'

'True.'

'So don't tell anyone in the meantime,' Bahir said, shrugging. 'I won't tell if you won't, kind of thing.'

He shook his head. 'That won't work. I have to swear on the book of Al-Jirad that we are married in every sense of the word. '

'So lie.'

He shook his head. 'That is hardly an honourable way to start my reign.' He'd spent hours last night trying to work a way around the requirement—had lingered some time over that very option—until finally concluding that lying would not work even if he could bring himself to act so dishonourably. Besides, she would know the truth and she could hold that over him the entire time. It would not work if she could bring down the kingdom at any moment she chose.

His friend nodded. 'True. Still, I can see her point of view.'

'What's that supposed to mean?'

'Well, it has all been kind of sudden.'

'It's been sudden for everyone. And it's not as if she has a choice.'

'So maybe that's what this is all about. She wants to feel like it is her choice.'

Zoltan looked up. 'What are you talking about? Why should that matter?'

'She's a woman.' He shrugged. 'They think differently. Especially Jemeyan princesses.'

Zoltan looked at him. 'So what did happen between you and her sister?'

It was Bahir's turn to look uncomfortable. 'It's history. It doesn't matter. What you have to worry about is how your princess feels right now. She's a princess in a desert kingdom who has probably been hanging out all these years for her prince to turn up. She wants to be romanced. Instead she gets lumbered with you and told she has to make babies.' He shrugged. 'Frankly, who could blame her? Nothing personal, but who wouldn't be a tad disappointed?'

'Thank you so much for that erudite summation of the situation.'

Bahir was back to his grinning best. 'My pleasure. So, what are you going to do?'

He snorted. 'I don't have time to do anything. I've got too much to do before the coronation as it is.'

'Well, you'd better do something, or by the sounds of it there won't be a coronation and Mustafa would be within his rights to come steal that pretty bride right out from under your nose—and next time he won't leave you a window open to rescue her.'

'I've been wondering about that,' Zoltan said. 'What was Mustafa waiting for? If he'd slept with her that would have been the end of it.'

'Maybe,' Bahir mused, 'he was waiting to be married?'

Zoltan shook his head. That didn't sound like the

Mustafa he knew. 'More likely he was so sure that nobody could find them that he thought there was no rush; he could take his time torturing her by telling her in exquisite detail exactly what he had planned for her.'

'Then it's lucky we found her in time.'

Was it? Zoltan wondered as he padded back into the palace. She sure as hell didn't think so. He was still thinking about the words Bahir had used.

'She wants to feel like it is her choice.'

'She wants to be romanced.'

How could he do that? What was the point of even trying? Here in the palace it was like being in a fishbowl, full of maids and footmen and the ever-present Hamzah, uncannily always to hand when he was needed and plenty of times when he was not. How was he supposed to romance her and somehow study the necessary texts to complete the formalities he was required to before he could be crowned King?

It was impossible.

And then he remembered it—a holiday his family had taken when he was just a child, a shared holiday with his uncle, the then-King, and his family. In a spot not far from the Blue Palace, a jewel of a location on a promontory reaching a sandy finger out into the sapphire-blue sea. They had slept in tents listening to the waves on the shore at night, woken to the early-morning calls of gulls, fished, swum and ridden horses along the long, sandy beach.

Maybe he could take her there, where she could unwind and relax and forget about duty and obligation for a while and maybe, just maybe, tolerate him long enough that they could consummate this marriage.

He could only hope.

* * *

'Where are we going again?' Aisha asked as the four-wheel drive tore up the desert highway. Outside the car was golden sands and shimmering heat, while inside was smooth leather and air-conditioned luxury. And the scent of him beside her was mixing with the leather, evocative, damnably alluring and much too likeable—much too annoying. She was almost tempted to open her window and risk the heat if it meant she wouldn't have to endure it.

'A place called Belshazzah on the coast,' Zoltan said without shifting his gaze from the road. The tracks of her nails, thankfully, were fading on his cheek. He stared at the road ahead, dodging patches of sand where the dunes crept over the road on their inexorable travels. A man in control, she thought, looking at him behind the wheel. A man used to taking charge, she guessed, unable to let someone else drive for him, so that the necessary bodyguards were forced to squeeze into the supply vehicles that trailed behind them. He looked good, his dark hands on the wheel, the folded-back sleeves of his white shirt contrasting with his corded forearms and that damned scent everywhere...

'How far is it?'

'Not far from the Blue Palace. No more than two hours away.'

Aisha buzzed down her window a few inches and sniffed.

'Are you cold?' he said, immediately moving to adjust the temperature.

'Not really,' she said, gazing out behind her dark glasses at a horizon bubbling under the desert sun. *Not at all.* When he'd turned up at her door this morning and asked if she'd like to accompany him to the beach encampment, she'd remembered the things he'd said to

her last night and how close he'd come to forcing himself upon her and she'd almost told him where he could
shove his beach encampment.

But something had stopped her. Whether it was the
look in his eyes, that this unexpected invitation was
costing him something, or whether it was just because
for the first time he was actually asking if she would
accompany him rather than telling her and riding roughshod over her opinions and views as was his usual tac-
tic—whatever it was—she'd said yes.

'And remind me again why we're going there?'

He shrugged. 'The palace is too big, filled with too
many people, too many advisers. I thought you might
appreciate somewhere a little quieter.' He turned to her
then. 'So we could get to know each other a little more.'

Even from behind his sunglasses she could feel the
sizzle his eyes sent her all the way down to her toes.

'You mean so you can finally get what you expected
you would get last night?'

He didn't look at her, but she caught his smile behind
the wheel. 'Do you really think I need go to so much
trouble when the palace is full of dark corners and secret places? Not exactly the kind of places you want to
hang around and hold a meaningful conversation, but
perfectly adequate for other, more carnal pleasures.'

Her window hummed even lower. She did not want to
hear about dark places and carnal pleasures. Not when
it made her body buzz with an electricity that felt uncannily like anticipation.

Impossible.

'It's not going to happen, you know,' she said, as
much for her benefit as his.

'What?'

'I'm not going to sleep with you.'

'So you said.'

'I hate you.'

'You said that too. You made that more than plain last night.'

'Good. So long as we understand each other.'

'Oh,' he said, taking his eyes off the road to throw her a lazy smile, 'we may not know each other, but I think we understand each other perfectly.'

Dissatisfied with the way that conversation had ended, she fell silent for a while, looking out at the desert dunes, disappearing into the distance in all directions. She shuddered when she remembered another desert camp. 'How do you know Mustafa's not out here somewhere, waiting for you to make a mistake so he can steal me away and take the crown before you? Aren't you worried about him?'

'Are you scared, Princess? Are you worried now you should have consummated this marriage last night when you had the chance?'

She crossed her arms over her chest and turned her gaze pointedly out the window again. 'Definitely not.'

'Then you are braver than I thought. But you have nothing to fear. My sources say he's moved out of Al-Jirad for now.'

'So he knows he's beaten and given up?'

'Possibly.'

'And he won't be at the coronation?'

His jaw clenched, his hands tightening on the wheel. 'He wouldn't dare show his face.'

She hoped he was right. If she never saw the ugly slug again, it would be too soon. She looked around, wondering at the words he had spoken, about the punch his words had held. She wondered why he was so certain, and she guessed it was not all to do with her kidnapping.

'What did he do to you?'

There was a pause before he spoke. 'Why do you ask that?'

'You clearly hate him very much. He must have done something to deserve it.'

He snorted in response to that. 'You could say that. I grew up with him. I got to see how his twisted mind works first-hand.'

'Tell me.'

'Are you sure you want to hear this, Princess?'

'Is it so bad?'

'It is not pretty. He is not a nice person.'

She swallowed. 'I'm a big girl. I can handle it, surely.'

He nodded. 'As you say.' He looked back at the road for a moment before he began. 'There was a blind man in the village where we grew up, a man called Saleem,' he started. 'He was old and frail and everyone in the village looked out for him, brought him meals or firewood. He had a dog, a mutt he'd found somewhere that was his eyes. We used to pass Saleem's house on our way to school where Saleem was usually sitting outside, greeting everyone who passed. Mustafa never said anything, he just baited the dog every chance he got, teasing it, sometimes kicking it. One day he went too far and it bit him. I was with him that day, and I swear it was nothing more than a scratch, but Mustafa swore he would get even. Even when the old man told him that it was his fault—that even though he was blind he was not stupid. He knew Mustafa had been taunting his dog mercilessly all along.

'One day not long after, the dog went missing. The whole village looked for it. Until someone found it—or, rather, what was left of it.'

She held her breath. 'What happened to it?'

'The dog had been tortured to within an inch of its life before something more horrible happened—something that said the killer had a grudge against not only the dog, but against its owner.'

'What do you mean?'

'The dog had been blinded. So, even if it had somehow managed to survive the torture, it would have been useless to Saleem.'

She shuddered, feeling sick. 'How could anyone do such a thing to an animal, a valued pet?'

'That one could.'

'You believe it was Mustafa?'

'I know it was him. I overheard him boasting to a schoolfriend in graphic detail about what he had done. He had always been a bully. He was proud of what he had done to a helpless animal.'

'Did you tell anyone?'

Her question brought the full pain and the injustice of the past crashing back. He remembered the fury of his father when he had told him what he had heard; fury directed not at Mustafa but at him for daring to speak ill of his favoured child. He remembered the savage beating he had endured for daring to speak the truth.

'I told someone. For all the good it did me.'

Choose your battles.

His uncle had been so right. There had been no point picking that one. He had never been going to win where Mustafa was concerned. Not back then.

She waited for more but he went quiet then, staring fixedly at the road ahead, so she turned to look out her own window, staring at the passing dunes, wondering what kind of person did something like that for kicks and wondering about all the things Zoltan wasn't telling her.

He was an enigma, this man she was married to, and, as much as she hated him for who and what he was and what he had forced her into, maybe she should be grateful she had been saved the alternative. Because she would have been Mustafa's wife if this man had not come for her. She shuddered.

'Princess?'

She looked around, blinking. 'Yes?'

'Are you all right? You missed my question.'

'Oh.' She sat up straight and lifted the heavy weight of the ponytail behind her head to cool her neck. 'I'm sorry. What did you ask?'

He looked at her for a moment, as if he wasn't sure whether to believe her or not, before looking back at the interminably long, straight road ahead. 'Seeing as we were talking about Mustafa,' he started.

'Yes?'

'There is something I don't understand. Something you told me when we rescued you.'

'Some rescue,' she said, but her words sounded increasingly hollow in the wake of Zoltan's revelations about his half-brother's cruel nature. Maybe he had saved her from a fate worse than death after all. 'What about it?' she said before she could explore that revelation any further.

'How did you convince Mustafa not to take you right then and there, while he had you in the camp? Why was he prepared to wait until the wedding? Because if Mustafa had laid claim to you that first night he held you captive, if he had had witnesses to the act, then no rescue could have prevented you from being his queen and him the new king.'

She swallowed back on a surge of memory-fed bile,

not wanting to think back to those poisoned hours. 'He told me he did not care to wait, you are right.'

'So why did he? That does not sound like the Mustafa I know.'

She blinked against the sun now dipping low enough to intrude through her window and sat up straighter to avoid it, even if that meant she had to lean closer to him in the process, and closer to that damned evocative scent.

'Simple, really. I told him that he would be cursed if he took me before our wedding night.'

'You told him that and he believed you?'

'Apparently so.'

'But there must have been more reason than that. Why would he believe that he would be cursed?'

Beside him she swallowed. She didn't want to have to admit to him the truth, although she rationalised he would find that truth out some time. And maybe he might at least understand her reluctance to jump into bed and spread her legs for him as if the act itself meant nothing.

'Because I told him that, according to the Jemeyan tenets, if he took me before our wedding night the gods would curse him with a soft and shrivelled penis for evermore.'

'Because you are a princess?'

'Because I am a virgin.'

'And he believed you?' He laughed then as if it was the biggest joke in the world, and she wasn't tempted in the least to rake her nails down his laughing face again—this time she wanted to strangle him.

Instead she turned away, pretending to stare out of the window and at the sea, fat tears squeezing from her eyes, but only half from the humiliating memories of being poked and parted and prodded by the wiry fingers of some old crone who smelt like camel dung.

The other half was because it never occurred to Zoltan to believe her. It never occurred to him that she might be telling the truth, that she might actually be a virgin. And the rank injustice of it all was almost too much to bear. She angled her body away from him to mask the dampness that suddenly welled in her eyes.

To think she had saved herself all this time only to be bound to someone like him instead. The one thing she had always thought hers to give; the one thing she had thought hers to control, and when all was said and done she had no control at all. No choice. It was not to be given as a gift, but a due.

What a waste.

'It would seem your half-brother is superstitious,' she managed to say through her wretchedness to cover the truth.

And from behind the wheel, Zoltan's words sounded as though he was still smiling. 'Yes. He always was a fool.'

CHAPTER EIGHT

She could smell the salt on the air long before she could see the sea. They had left the highway some time ago. The track across the desert sands was slower going, until they topped one last dune and suddenly a dry desert world turned into paradise.

From their vantage point, she could see the rocky peninsula jutting into the crystal-clear sapphire waters, and where before she had seen no signs of vegetation beyond small, scrubby salt-bushes clinging to the sand for their meagre existence for miles, now the shores and rocks were dotted with palms, the rocky outcrops covered with lush, green vegetation.

'It's beautiful,' she said as they descended, heading for the long, white strip of sandy beach. 'But how?'

'A natural spring feeds this area. If you like, I will take you and show you where the water runs clean and pure from the earth. If I try hard enough, I'm sure I'll remember the way.'

The offer was so surprising, not only because he was asking her again, but because he had revealed a part of himself with his words—that he had been here before, and clearly a long time ago.

'I would like that,' she said, wondering what he would have been like as a child. Overbearing, like he was now?

Although that wasn't strictly true, she was forced to admit. He wasn't overbearing *all* the time.

Which was a shame, really, because he was much easier to hate when he was. And she didn't want to find reason not to hate him, because then she might be tempted to wonder...

But no. She shook her head, shaking out the thought. She didn't wonder. She didn't care. She didn't want to know what it would be like to be made love to by a man like this one, who clearly was no virgin himself, who had no doubt had many lovers and who probably knew all about women and what they might enjoy...

'Is something wrong, Princess?'

She looked up at him, startled. 'No. Why do you ask?'

'Because you made some kind of sound, kind of like a whimper. I wondered if there was something wrong.'

'No.' She turned away, her cheeks burning up. 'I'm fine, just sick of sitting down. Are we nearly there?'

Thankfully they were. A cluster of tents had been erected below a stand of palm trees in preparation for their arrival, one set apart from the rest.

'Is that one mine?' she asked, half-suspecting, half-dreading the answer.

'That one is ours, Princess,' he said, pulling open her door and offering her his hand to climb from the car. 'It would not do to let everyone know the true state of our marriage.'

'But I told you...'

He found it hard not to grind his teeth together. So she had—how many times already? Did she think he wanted to be reminded how much she did not want to lie with him? 'I am sure you will be more than satisfied with the sleeping arrangements.'

She looked down at his hand, as if assessing whether he was telling the truth. 'Fine,' she said, finally accepting his offer of assistance. 'But, if not, then I will not be held accountable for the bruise on your ego.'

'I'm sure my ego can take it, Princess. It is the damage you do to the monarchy that is my more immediate concern, and indeed the damage you could do to your own father's. So perhaps you might keep that in mind.'

Her face closed, as if she'd pulled all the shutters down to retreat into herself.

So be it.

She might be used to having things all her way when she was at home leading her sheltered spoilt-princess life, but she was here now, she was his wife, and she would start doing her duty and acting like his wife before they left and before the coronation. Nothing was surer.

Still, for what it was worth, he let her lead the way into their tent to inspect the sleeping arrangements, to check out the large sofa that could double for a bed if needed, and the large bed he was hoping would be the only sleeping arrangement required.

Besides, following her was hardly a hardship. Not when he had the chance to check out the rhythmic sway of her hips under the coral-coloured abaya she wore today.

As he followed her he could not work out whether he liked her dressed more like this—in a cool cotton robe that only hinted at the shape beneath, but did so seductively and unexpectedly when a helpful on-shore breeze ventured along and pushed the fabric against her shape—or in trousers, like she'd worn that first day at the palace, that fitted her shape and accentuated her curves.

Then again, he hadn't yet seen her without her

clothes. And, while he'd felt the firmness of her flesh under his hands, and felt the delicious curve of her belly and roundness of her bottom hard against him, there was still that delicious pleasure to come.

Now, there was something to think about...

She turned, her hand on the tent flap, just about to enter. 'Did you say something?'

'No,' he said, struggling to adjust to the conscious world. 'Why do you ask?'

'Because I thought you said something. Though, now I think of it, it sounded more like a groan. Are you sure you're all right?'

But before he could find the words to answer, she had angled her head to the notes being carried intermittently on the breeze. 'What's that?'

Never had he been more grateful for a change of topic as he strained his ears to listen. The knowledge that she had made him so oblivious to his own reactions was a cold wake-up call. He could not afford to let such lapses happen, not if he was to be King.

And suddenly the notes made sense on the breeze and reminded him of something he'd been told. 'There is a camp of wandering tribes people nearby. A few families, nothing more. They will shortly move on, as they do.'

'They are safe, then, these tribes people?'

And he realised that even to ask that question showed she wasn't as unconcerned at the thought of being recaptured by Mustafa as she wanted him to think.

'They would not be here if they were not. But they have been advised of our coming and they value their privacy too. So rest assured, Princess, they will keep their distance and they will not harm you.'

* * *

She'd only been here an hour and already she loved it. Being on the coast meant on-shore breezes that took the sting from the heat of the day and made being on sand a pleasure, rather than torture—at least if you had taken off your sandals to paddle your feet in the shallows.

And she hadn't minded a bit when Zoltan had had to excuse himself to take care of 'business', whatever that meant. Because it gave her the chance to truly relax. Despite all the beauty of this place, the endless sapphire waters, the calming sway of palm trees and the eternal, soothing whoosh of tide, there was no relaxing with that man about.

But still, she was glad she had come. Already, without the overwhelming weight of the palace and the duty it carried, she felt lighter of spirit. She knew there was no way of evading that duty for long. She knew she could not forever evade the chore that life had thrown her way.

But for now the long beach had beckoned her, drawing her to the point at the end of the peninsula, and she was thinking it was time to return when she heard it, the cry of a child in distress.

It came on the breeze, and disappeared just as quickly, and for a moment she thought she'd imagined it or misread the cry of a sea bird, and already she'd turned for the walk back when she heard it again. Her feet stilled in the shallows. A child was definitely crying nearby and there was no hint of any soothing reply to tell her anyone had heard or was taking any notice.

She swivelled in the shallows, picked up the hem of her abaya in one hand and ran down the beach towards the headland as fast as she could.

It was only when she rounded the rocky outcrop at the end she found the child sitting in the sand and wailing. She looked around and saw no-one, only this young girl squealing and clutching at her foot. Her bleeding foot.

'Hello,' she said tentatively as the girl looked up at her with dark, suspicious eyes, her sobs momentarily stopping on a hiccup. 'What's wrong?'

The young girl sniffed and looked down at her foot, saw the blood and wailed again.

Aisha kneeled down beside her. 'Let me look,' she said. She took her foot gently in her hands and saw a gash seeping blood, a broken shell nearby, dagger sharp, that she must have trod on with her bare feet.

'Ow! It hurts!' the young girl cried, and Aisha put a hand behind her head, stroking her hair to soothe her.

'I'm sorry, but I'm going to have to wrap this up and it might hurt a little bit.' She looked around, wishing for someone—anyone—to appear. Surely someone must realise their child was missing and take charge so she didn't have to? Because she had nothing with her that might help, and the swaying palm trees offered no assistance, no rescue.

'Where is your mother?' she asked, once again scanning the palms for any hint of the girl's family as she ripped the hem of her abaya, tearing a long strip from the bottom and yanking it off at the seam. She folded the fabric until it formed a bandage she could wrap around the child's foot.

'Katif was crying. And Mama ran back to the camp and told me to follow.' And then she shrieked and Aisha felt guilty for tying the bandage so tight, even when she knew the girl was upset about not being able to follow her mother and her mother not coming back.

'Your mother knows you are okay,' she soothed, sensing it was what the child needed to hear. 'Your mother is busy with Katif right now, but she knew I would look out for you and she could check on you later.'

The girl blinked up at her. 'You know my mother?'

There was no way she could lie. 'No, but I know she is good to be taking care of Katif, and I know someone will be here soon for you.'

And even as she spoke there was a panicked cry as a woman emerged running from the trees. 'Cala! Cala!'

'Mama!'

'Oh, Cala,' she said, relief evident in her voice as she fell to the sand and squeezed her child tightly in her arms. 'I am so sorry, I did not see you fall behind.' And then she noticed the improvised bandage on her daughter's foot. 'But what happened?'

'I cut my foot on a shell. This lady found me.'

For the first time the woman took notice of Aisha. 'The wound will need cleaning before it can be properly dressed,' Aisha offered. 'There was not much I could do here.'

The mother nodded, her tear-streaked face caked with sand. 'Thank you for taking care of her. Katif was screaming again; he's sick and I don't know what's wrong with him but I had to get him back to camp and I thought Cala was right behind me.' She gulped in air as she rocked her child in her arms. 'I was so afraid when I realised she was missing. I was so worried.'

Aisha stroked her arm. 'It's all right. Cala is fine.' She looked over her shoulder, thinking that she should be getting back. 'I must go. Will you be all right getting back to camp?'

'Of course,' the mother said, letting go of her child for a moment to take Aisha's hand and press her forehead to it, noticing the torn hem of her robe. 'Oh, but you have ruined your abaya.'

'It is nothing, really. I have many more.'

And the woman really looked at her this time, her eyes widening in shock, tears once again welling from their dark depths. 'Blessings to you,' she said, prostrating herself on the sand before her as her wide-eyed daughter looked on, contentedly sucking on two fingers of her hand. 'Bless you.'

'What are you doing?' she asked Zoltan when she returned. All the way back she had felt the sun warm her skin. All the way back she had felt the warmth of the woman's blessings in her heart.

Now she found Zoltan sitting at a desk under the shade of a palm tree, a massive tome before him.

He barely looked up from his study. 'It was too hot inside the tent.'

'No, I mean, what are you reading?'

He looked up then, suddenly scowling when he saw her torn robe. 'What happened to your abaya?'

She looked down. 'Oh, there was a child on the beach. She'd cut her foot.'

He leaned back in his chair, his frown deepening. 'And so you tore your robe?'

She shrugged. 'There was nothing else to use.' And then she remembered. 'Is there a doctor somewhere close?'

This time he stood. 'Are you hurt, Princess?'

'No, not for me. There is a child—a baby, I think. It sounds like he should be seen by a doctor. The mother is worried...' He was looking at her strangely. 'What's wrong?'

He shook his head. 'Nothing. And yes, Ahab—one of the chefs—has some medical expertise. I will ask him to visit the camp, to see if there is anything he can do.'

She nodded, majorly relieved. 'Thank you. It is probably worth him checking the cut on the girl's foot too, in case there is still some shell lodged inside.' She looked down at her torn robe. 'I should get changed.'

He watched her turn, wondering about a spoilt princess who would tear her own abaya to make a bandage for a child she didn't know. A stranger.

And he didn't want her to go. He slammed the book shut. He'd had enough of crusty old prose for one day. Besides, he was supposed to be getting to know her.

'Princess, seeing you're getting changed...?'

'Yes?'

'Now that the sun is past its worst, I was thinking of taking a swim to cool down. Would you care to join me?'

He saw a slideshow of emotions flash over her eyes: uncertainty, fear, even a glimmer of panic, but then she gave a longing look out at the ocean, where the water sparkled and beckoned and promised cool, clear relief under the dipping sun.

He recognised the moment she decided before she'd said the words, in the decisive little pout of her lips.

'Yes,' she said, with a nod. 'Why not?'

It's only a swim, she told herself as Zoltan went to instruct Ahab and she changed into her swimsuit. *In bright daylight and in clear sight of the beach.*

It wasn't as though he could actually try anything.

But that didn't stop her skin from tingling as she pulled on her tangerine-coloured one-piece, didn't stop the tiny hairs on the back of her neck from lifting or stop her remembering how good he had looked wearing nothing but a black band of lycra.

Only a swim.

She belted a robe around herself and tugged it tight

before pinning her hair up. If she got into the water before he returned to get changed himself, it wasn't as though he would even see her.

The beach was deserted. She dropped her towel and sunglasses on one of the recliners that had been put there expressly for their use, and, with a final look over her shoulder to check that Zoltan was nowhere to be seen, she slipped off her robe and padded to the sea.

It was warm in the shallows, so no shock to the system, the temperature dropping as the water deepened, cool currents swirling around her knees and sliding inexorably higher with each incoming wave. She waded deeper into the crystal-clear sea, her hands trailing through the water by her sides until her thighs tingled with the delicious contrast of cool and heat and she dived under an incoming wave to truncate the exquisite torture.

She was a goddess. There was no other way to describe her that could possibly do her justice. And he thanked whatever gods were watching over him that had brought him to this part of the beach at this particular moment in time. He'd witnessed her furtive glance over her shoulder and watched her wade into the sea, all long, honey-gold limbs and sweeping curves, the sweetly seductive roll of her hips like a siren's call.

He growled low in his throat.

He had never been one to resist the call of a siren. Even one who at the same time appeared so timid and shy. Why was she so nervous around him? Because she knew what was in store for her?

No. Because she knew what she did to him and she wished it wasn't so.

Because she felt it herself.

He watched her strike out in the water, swimming expertly along the shore, long, effortless-looking strokes, measured and effective, the kick of her feet propelling her along.

Dressed in that colour she looked like a luscious piece of fruit.

A piece of fruit he could not wait to sample.

And as his groin ached and tightened he thought that maybe this swim wasn't going to provide quite the cooling-off he'd had in mind.

The water was delicious, the repetitive rhythm of her strokes soothing in its own way, and a swim was turning out to be a very good idea. Until something grabbed hold of her ankle and pulled tight.

She screamed and tugged and whatever it was let go. She came up spluttering, coughing sea water, and pushed a tangle of hair out of her eyes.

'You!' she said between coughs when she found Zoltan standing there grinning at her. 'It's not funny. You scared the hell out of me.'

'Did you think you'd caught a shark, Princess?'

'A shark would be preferable,' she spat back and dived under the water to swim away. He was alongside her when she came up for air. 'It's a big ocean, you know. Go find your own bit to play in.'

'Your strap is twisted,' he said, ignoring her frustration and building on it by putting a hand to her shoulder, slipping his fingers underneath the strap and gently turning it up the right way. She gasped as his fingers brushed her skin, turning it to goose bumps and her nipples to hard peaks as he left his hand there longer than he needed. 'That colour suits you, Princess. You look good enough to eat.'

Nothing could stop the heat from flooding her face or the heavy, aching need pooling between her thighs. He was so big before her, so powerful, his shoulders broad, his chest dripping wet, and it was all she could do not to reach out a hand and feel if his skin felt as good as it looked.

She yanked her eyes away, looked to the shore. 'I should go back.'

'Already?'

'I had a head start. And I need to wash my hair.'

He smiled one of those wide, lazy smiles that made his face look boyish, even a little bit handsome. 'So you did. But of course you must go, Princess. Such a pressing need must be urgently addressed.'

She knew he was laughing at her but she almost didn't mind. Worse still, she almost found herself wishing he would make her stay. *Which made no sense at all.*

CHAPTER NINE

HER hair was almost dry when he found her brushing it in a chair under the palms. The air was filled with the scent of lamb on the spit and at first she assumed it must be time to eat.

'You have a visitor, Princess,' he said. 'Or several of them, to be more precise.'

'Me?' She put her brush down and followed him.

They stood in a small group, looking uncertain and talking quietly amongst themselves—a woman holding a baby, a man alongside and a little girl holding a small package in her hands.

The girl from the beach.

When the woman saw her she broke into a wide smile, tears once again welling in her eyes, but it was the man who stepped forward. 'I am so sorry,' he said with a bow. 'I told Marisha this was a bad time, but she insisted we come and thank you both. But you see, the helicopter comes soon after dawn tomorrow morning.'

She looked across at Zoltan to see if he understood and the mother came forward. 'Princess, Katif needs a small operation—his coughing has torn his muscles and they need to stitch it up so he will not cry any more. They are coming to take us to the hospital and I will not have a chance to thank you again.'

She reached down and urged the young girl forward with a pat to her head. 'Now, Cala.'

The little girl blinked up at her, and suddenly seemed to remember the package. She stepped tentatively forward, limping a little on her tender foot, a bandage strapped around it under her satin slipper. 'This is for you.'

Aisha smiled down at her. 'You didn't have to bring me a present.'

'We wanted to, Princess,' the mother said. 'To replace the abaya you ruined to bandage Cala's foot.'

Aisha knelt down and touched a hand to Cala's head. 'How is your foot now, Cala? Is it still hurting?'

'It hurts, but the doctor-man fixed it.'

And she smiled her thanks up at Zoltan, who was watching her, a strange expression on his face.

'It will feel better soon, I promise,' she said, accepting the parcel and pulling the end of the bow till the ribbon fluttered open. She pulled back the wrapping and gasped.

'It is all hand-stitched, Princess,' the woman offered proudly as Aisha lifted the delicate garment spun from golden thread and gossamer-thin.

'It's beautiful,' she said, fingering the detailed embroidery around the neckline. 'It must have taken months.'

The woman beamed with pride. 'My family has always been known for our needlework. It was the least your generosity deserved.'

Aisha gathered the little girl in her arms and hugged her. 'Thank you, Cala.' Then she rose and hugged her mother too, careful of the now-sleeping baby in her arms. 'Thank you. I shall wear it with honour and remember you always.'

She looked across at Zoltan and wondered if she should ask him first, but then decided it didn't matter.

'You will stay and eat with us, won't you?'

The adults looked unsure, clearly not expecting the invitation, not knowing if she was serious. 'We did not mean to intrude.'

'You are not intruding,' she assured them, hoping Zoltan thought the same.

'Please, Mama,' Cala said, tugging on her mother's robe. 'Please can we stay?'

'Of course,' Zoltan said in that commanding voice he had, as if there was never any question. 'You must stay.'

They sat on cushions around a campfire, supping on spiced lamb with yoghurt and mint, with rice and okra, washing it down with honeyed tea under a blanket of stars. Afterwards, with the fragrant scent of the sisha pipe drifting from the cook's camp, Cala's father produced his ney reed pipe from somewhere in his robes and played more of that haunting music she had heard wafting over the headland when they had first arrived.

Cala edged closer and closer to the princess as the music wove magic in the night sky until she wormed her way under her arm and onto her lap. 'Cala,' her mother berated.

'She's fine,' Aisha assured her.

The girl looked up at her with big, dark eyes. 'Are you really a princess?'

Aisha smiled. 'Yes, it's true.'

'Where's your crown?'

She laughed. 'I don't wear a crown every day.'

'Oh.' The girl sounded disappointed. 'Is Princess your name?'

'No. Princess is my job, like calling someone "doctor" or "professor". Of course I have a real name. My name is Aisha.'

Aisha.

Moon goddess.

Strange. He had never thought about her having a name. He had always thought of her simply as 'princess', but how appropriate she would have a name like that. Little wonder she looked like a goddess.

And here she was, his precious little spoilt princess, cuddling a child and looking every bit as much a mother as the child's own mother did.

This woman would bear his children.

She would sit like that in a few years from now and it would be his children clambering over her. It would be the product of his seed she would cuddle and nurture.

And the vision was so powerful, so compelling, that something indescribable swelled inside him and he wished for it to be true.

Aisha. Sitting there with near-strangers, giving of herself to people who possessed little more than the clothes on their back and who had gifted her probably their most treasured possession. Giving herself to *his* people.

Maybe she was not such a spoilt princess after all.

And the thought was so foreign when it came that he almost rejected it out of hand. Almost. But the proof was right there in front of him. Maybe there was more to her after all.

'Thank you,' she said after the family had gone and they walked companionably along the shoreline under a sliver of crescent moon. It had seemed the most obvious thing in the world to do. The night was balmy and inviting, and he knew that she was not yet ready to fall into his bed, but he was in no hurry to return to his study of the centuries-old texts.

'What are you thanking me for?'

'Lots of things,' she said. 'For sending Ahab to look at their children, for one. For arranging the necessary transport to hospital for the operation Katif needs, if not the operation itself. And for not minding that the family shared our meal.'

'Be careful, Princess,' he warned, holding up one hand. 'Or one might almost forget that you hate me.'

She blinked, though whether she was trying to gauge how serious he was, or whether she had been struck with the same revelation, he could not be sure. 'So you have some redeeming features. I wouldn't go reading too much into it.' But he noticed her words lacked the conviction and fire of her earlier diatribes. He especially noticed that she didn't insist that she did hate him. He liked that she didn't feel the compunction to tell him. He sighed into the night breeze. It had been right to get out of the palace where everything was so formal and rigid, where every move was governed by protocol.

In the palace there was always someone watching, even if it was only someone on hand and waiting to find out if there was anything one needed. For all its space, in the palace it was impossible to move without being seen. He curled his fingers around hers as they walked: in the palace it would have been impossible to do *this* without his three friends betting amongst themselves whether it meant that he would score tonight.

'You were good with that child,' he said, noticing— *liking*—that she didn't pull her hand away. 'I suspect you found a fan.'

'Cala is very likeable.'

'You were equally good with her family, making

them feel special. If you can be like that with everyone, you will make a great sheikha. You will be a queen who will be well-loved.'

She stopped and pulled her hand free, rubbing her hands on her arms so he could not reclaim it. 'If I'd imagined this walk was going to provide you with yet another opportunity to remind me of the nature of this marriage, and of my upcoming *duty* in your bed, I never would have agreed to come along.'

He cursed his clumsy efforts to praise her. 'I am sorry, Princess. I did not mean...'

She blinked up at him, her aggravation temporarily overwhelmed by surprise. He was sorry? He was actually sorry and he was telling her so? Was this Zoltan the barbarian sheikh before her?

But then, he wasn't all barbarian, she had to concede. Otherwise why would he have sent anyone to look at a sick child? Why would he have approved his uplift in a helicopter, no less, and the required operation if he was a monster?

'No, I'm sorry,' she said, holding up her hands as she shook her head. 'There was no need for me to respond that way. I overreacted.' *Because I'm the one who can't stop thinking about doing my duty...*

The night was softly romantic, it was late, soon it would be time for bed and she was here on this beach with a man who came charged with electricity.

'What did you do before?' she asked, changing the subject before he too realised why she was so jumpy, resuming her walk along the beach under the stars. 'Before all this happened. Were you always in Al-Jirad? I attended a few functions at the Blue Palace, but I don't remember seeing you at any of them.'

'No, you wouldn't have,' he said, falling into step

beside her as the low waves swooshed in, their foam bright even in the low moonlight. 'I left when it was clear there was no place for me here.'

'Because of Mustafa?'

'Partly. My father always took his side. I was twelve when my mother died and there seemed no reason to stay. Mustafa and I hated each other and everyone knew it. For the peace of the family, my father sent me to boarding school in England.'

She looked up at his troubled profile and wondered what it must have been like to be cast adrift from your family because you didn't fit in, when you were possibly the only sane member in it.

She slipped her hand back in his and resumed walking along the shore, hoping he wouldn't make too much of it. She was merely offering her understanding, that was all. 'Is that where you met your three friends?'

'That was later. We met at university.'

'And you clicked right away?'

'No. We hated each other on sight.'

She looked at him and frowned. He shrugged. 'Nothing breeds hatred faster than someone else telling you who should be friends.'

'I don't think I understand.'

'It's a long story. Basically we'd all come from different places and somehow all ended up in the university rowing club, all of us loners up till then and intending to row alone, as we had always done to keep fit. Until someone decided to stick us in a crew together, expecting we "foreigners" should all get along. For a joke they called our four the *Sheikh Caique*.' He paused a while, reflecting, and then said, 'They did not laugh long.'

'And over time you did become good friends with them.'

He shrugged and looked out to sea, and she wondered what parts of the story he was not telling her. 'That was not automatic, but yes. And I could not wish for better brothers.'

They walked in silence for a while, the whoosh of the waves and the call of birds settling down to sleep in the swaying palm trees the music of the night.

And then he surprised her by stopping and catching her other hand in his. 'I owe you an apology,' he started.

'No, I explained—'

He let go of one hand and put a finger to her lips. 'I need to say this, Princess, and I am not good at apologies, so you must not stop me.'

She nodded, her lips brushing the pad of his finger, and she drank in the intoxicating scent of him. It was all she could do not to reach out her tongue so she might once again taste his flesh.

'I was wrong about you, Princess. I know I messed up trying to tell you before, but you are not who I thought you were. I underestimated you. I assumed you were lightweight and frothy, spoilt and two-dimensional. I assumed that because you called what you did with children your "work", that it must be no kind of work. But after seeing you forge a bond with that little girl today, the way you knelt down and listened to her and treated her like an equal, I realised this is a gift you have.

'And I apologise unreservedly for my misjudgement, because I was wrong on every single count. I had no concept of the person you really are.'

She waited for reality to return—for this moment to pass, this dream sequence to pass, for the real Zoltan to return—but instead she saw only this Zoltan waiting for her answer.

'You're wrong, you know.'

'About you?'

'About being no good at apologies. That was one of the best I think I've ever heard.'

It was true. His confession had reached out to her, warming her in places she would never have suspected him reaching. His previous assessment of her was no surprise. She had known he had resented her from the start, assuming she was some shallow party-girl princess who cared nothing for duty. But what was a surprise was the way his words touched her. And, even though he had not realised yet in how many ways he had misjudged her, his words touched her in places deep inside, places she thought immune to the likes of anything Zoltan could say or do.

He smiled. 'I am so sorry, Aisha,' he said and she blinked up open-mouthed at him.

'You called me by my name. You have never called me that before.'

He nodded, his eyes contrite. 'And it is to my eternal shame that I did not do so from the very beginning. You deserved to be called by your name rather than your title. A name that spoke of the goddess you were surely named for, the goddess who must be so jealous right now of your perfection that she is hiding away up there behind the blinds.'

And, even though he'd gone too far, she could not help but smile. 'You should not suggest such things of the gods,' she said, still battling to find balance in a world suddenly shifted off its axis. 'Lest they grow jealous and seek their revenge against the mortal.'

'A goddess could be jealous of you,' he said, curling his hand around her neck. 'Except that you are bound in marriage to me, and no goddess could possibly ever envy you that. They would figure you are already pay-ing the price for your beauty.'

She swallowed, wondering where the other Zoltan was hiding, the one who would come out at any moment breathing hell-fire and damnation and demanding that she do her duty by him, if not willingly, at least for the good of their respective countries.

Yet she didn't want that other Zoltan to appear, be-cause this Zoltan made her feel so good—not only be-cause he awakened all her senses, but because he spoke to her needs and desires and touched her in dark, secret places she had never known existed.

'Do you have an evil twin?' she asked on impulse, remembering another conversation where he had im-plied the same of her, because she needed something—anything—to lighten the tone of this conversation and defuse the intensity she felt building inside.

His lips turned up. 'Not that I know of.'

She smiled as she shook her head and looked up into his dark eyes, wondering if it would be some kind of sin if she wanted to enjoy this other Zoltan just a little while longer. 'I'm not entirely convinced.' She allowed her smile to widen. 'Because this twin I wouldn't mind getting to know a little better. If I thought he was going to stick around a while, that is.'

He dragged in a breath, his dark eyes looking per-plexed, even a little tortured. 'I'm not sure that's pos-sible,' he said, his gaze fixed on her mouth. 'Because right now I want to kiss you. And I'm not sure I should. I'm not sure which twin you might end up with.'

'Maybe,' she said a little breathlessly, watching his mouth draw nearer, 'there's only one way to find out. Maybe we just have to risk it.'

Something flared and caught fire in his eyes. 'I think you might be right.'

He dipped his head, curled one hand around her neck and drew her slowly closer, pausing mere millimetres away, forcing their breath to curl and mingle between them, a prelude to the dance to come.

Then even that scant separation was gone as he pressed his lips to hers.

One touch of her lips and he remembered—sweet and spice; honey, cinnamon and chili; sweet and spice with heat. But there was so much more besides.

For this night she tasted of moonlight and promises, of soft desert nights and whispered secrets. She tasted of woman.

All woman.

He groaned against her mouth, let his arms surround her, drawing her into his embrace. She came willingly, accepting his invitation, until her breasts were hard up against his chest, her slim body curving into his, supple and lithe, while he supped of her lush mouth. And when he felt her hands on his back, felt her nails raking his skin through his shirt, he wanted to lift his head and roar with victory, for the goddess would be his tonight.

Except there was no way he was leaving this kiss.

She was drowning. One touch of his lips and the air had evaporated in her lungs and it was sensation that now swamped her, sensation that rolled over her, wave after delicious wave. His lips on hers, his taste in her mouth, his arms around her and her body knowing just one thing.

Need.

It bloomed under the surprisingly gentle caress of his lips. It took root and spread a tangle of branches to every other place he touched. It built on itself, growing, becoming more powerful and insistent.

He held her face in his hands and kissed her eyes, her nose, her chin before returning to her waiting lips, seducing her with his hot mouth while her hands drank in his tight flesh.

And in the midst of it all she wondered, how could this be the same man who had kissed her in the library? The same man who had so cruelly punished her with his kiss and had demanded her presence in his suite so he could impregnate her with his seed?

Yet it must be the same man, for she recognised him by his taste and his essence and the far-reaching impact he had upon her body.

But in between the layers of passion and the on-slaught of sensation, in between the breathless pleasure, a niggling kernel of doubt crept in: how could he be so different now and yet still be the same person?

'Aisha,' he said, breathing as heavily as she, resting his forehead on hers, his nose against hers. She almost forgot to care that he seemed different, because he was so warm now, so wonderful, and the way he said her name made her tremble with desire. This man, who was now her husband. That thought made her shudder anew.

'You are a goddess,' he said, his big hand scooping over her shoulder and down, inexorably down, to cup one achingly heavy breast. Breath jagged in her throat, her senses momentarily shorting before he brushed the pad of his thumb against her nipple and she gasped as her entire circuitry lit up with exquisite pleasure that made her inner thighs hum.

She mewled with pleasure. 'I think,' she uttered, breathless with desire, 'maybe you must be the evil twin after all.'

And he growled out a laugh that worked its way into her bones and stroked her from the inside out. 'Make love to me, Aisha,' he said, before his lips found hers again. 'Be my goddess tonight.'

Tonight?

Already?

But before she could protest and say it was too soon, he sucked her back into his kiss with his hot mouth and his dangerous tongue and drew her close against him, shocking her when she felt his rigid heat hard against her, frightening her with the realisation that she must take that part of him inside her body. And, even though her logical mind told her that men and women the world over made love this way and had done for centuries, the unknown was equally as persuasive. Surely not all men were so large? How was she—the untested—supposed to accommodate him? There was no way he could not know she was a virgin. There was no way it would not hurt.

Yet something about that rigid column pressing against her belly, something wild and wanton that was written on the pulsing insistence of her own body, made her yearn to try.

'Please,' she cried between frantic breaths, not knowing let alone understanding what she was asking for as he dipped his head to her breast and suckled her nipple in his hot, hot mouth, sending spears of sensation shooting down to where her blood pulsed loud and urgent between her thighs.

'Aisha,' he said, his breathing as wild as hers as he reclaimed her mouth, her lips already tender from the rub of his whiskered cheeks. She wondered why she was hesitating and not already in his bed.

It wasn't as if she had a choice. She was already married to this man. She was expected to bear his children and provide the country with heirs, and the officials would already be counting the days.

Why should she wait when the night was so perfect and her own need so insistent?

Why wait, when she already hungered to discover more?

His mouth wove magic on her throat, his hands turned her flesh molten and made her shudder with delight, and through it all she sensed the greater pleasures that were yet to be discovered, yet to come.

And still a crack opened in the midst of her longing, a flaw in the building intensity of feeling, a space in which to give rein to her doubts and fears.

For this was not how she had planned her first time to be.

Even though her breasts were heavy with want, and her body pressed itself closer to this man of its own wicked accord, this was not how she had imagined giving away her most private, guarded possession.

She had wanted to give it up with love, not merely in the heated flames of lust.

She had wanted to give it to a man she loved because she wanted to. Because she had made that choice.

And through that widening crack came the mantra, the words she'd rehearsed and practised and that had seemed so important to cling to.

'I won't sleep with you,' she breathed. Yet she faltered over the words even as she spoke them out loud, struggling to comprehend what they meant and why they had suddenly seemed so very necessary to say, why they now seemed so strangely hollow.

'But that is good news,' he said, his mouth at her throat, his hands scooping down the curve of her back to press her even closer to him, 'because I don't want you asleep. When I make love to you, I want you very much awake. I want to see the lights in your eyes spark and shatter when you come.'

She gasped, her heart thudding like a drum in her chest at the pictures so vividly thrown up into her mind's eye. And once again she felt herself drowning under the waves of desire, lust and all things sensual. Unable to breathe or think or make sense of where she was.

Able only to feel.

And the fear welled up inside that soon she would have no choice; that maybe it was already too late.

'I'm afraid,' she admitted. 'It's too soon.'

'You want me,' he said, his mouth once again on hers, coaxing her into complicity, convincing her that this was the best way. The only way. 'It's not too soon to know that.'

He might be right, but still she wavered, because she had seen her sister give in to passion and take what she wanted of a man, had seen her left with his child and nothing else.

She did not want that for herself. She did not want a fleeting affair that might rapidly turn from lust to resentment or worse. She did not want a marriage that could turn so quickly empty, and from where she could not simply walk away.

She wanted the real deal. She didn't know how that was possible now, but that didn't stop her from wanting it. She had held on to that dream for too long to give up on it completely.

'It's not that easy,' she whispered against his stubbled jaw. 'I can't just—'

'Of course you can,' he soothed, his hot mouth stealing her words and making magic to convince her it would be the easiest thing in the world. 'I am a man, you are a woman and we want each other. What else matters?'

His hand scooped down her back, squeezing her behind, his fingers so perilously close to her heated core. She knew she must tell him or she would be on her back before he found out. She did not want him to find out that way. She could not bear it.

'Then maybe there is one more thing you should know,' she said, looking uncertainly up at him, feeling herself colour even as she spoke the words, 'because I have never done this before.'

The side of his mouth turned up, and the eyes that had so recently been molten with heat turned flat and hard. 'If you're still trying to get out of this, Princess, you should know I am not as gullible as my half-brother.'

CHAPTER TEN

HE SAW her flinch and caught the hurt in her eyes before she shoved herself away from him. He let her go, watched her putting distance between them as disbelief bloomed and grew large in his gut. A virgin? There was no way it could be true. 'You can't be serious. You're how old? And your sister…'

She spun around. 'Oh, of course! Because I'm twenty-four, and because my sister has two illegitimate children, then I must have slept with any number of men and somehow got lucky and escaped the same fate? How many men did you think, Zoltan? A dozen? One hundred? How many men did you think had broken down the gates and paved the way for your irresistible advances?'

'Princess,' he said. '*Aisha*, I never thought—'

'Of course you did. You didn't believe me before when I told you why Mustafa had not touched me. You thought it was some kind of joke. Well, the joke's well and truly on you. And if I had my way, even though we are married already, the gods would surely curse you as I now do.' Then she turned and strode away down the beach.

He watched her go, adding his own curses and feeling the effect of hers already. What a fool! He'd had her

in the palm of his hand, supple and willing, so close to
exploding she was like unstable dynamite. If only he'd
reacted to her confession by telling her he'd be gentle
with her, or that he thought her all the more precious for
it—as he would have, if he'd thought for a moment she
was speaking the truth—then she would have been his.

And that *should* have been his reaction, given what
she had told him earlier. But back then he'd heard her
story and had seen in it only the chance to laugh at
Mustafa's stupidity. Because that was what he'd wanted
to see.

He hadn't considered her in any part of it.

But then, he had never considered her.

He'd only seen what he had to do to satisfy the terms
of an arrangement he'd had no part in making. He'd only
wanted to grind his half-brother down to the nothing
that he was in the process.

He was a fool, on so many counts. He'd been the stupid one.

As for Aisha? She was indeed a goddess.

A virgin goddess.

He watched her walk towards the camp as long as
he could along the dark stretch of beach, watched until
her flapping abaya was swallowed up by the night. Only
then did he look up at the silvery moon and stars and
feel the weight of his obligations sit heavily on his shoulders, feel the watchful eyes of the gods looking down
on him, no doubt laughing at this sad and pitiful mortal who threw away destiny when it was handed to him
on a platter.

And what to do? For she must be his wife in all senses
of the word in time for the coronation if he was to become king, and there was one more night for that to
happen.

That should be his most pressing imperative. But right now he wondered, for right now he was faced with choices he'd never seen coming.

He could have the kingdom and a wife he lusted after but who might hate him for ever if he took her before she was ready. Or he could have a wife who wanted him but who might take her own sweet time falling into his bed, in which case the kingdom might well in the meantime fall into the hands of a man he hated more than anyone.

And, when his duty to his country had been his prime motivating force until now, why was that suddenly such a difficult choice?

He slept badly that night. But how could he not when he'd lain awake not ten feet away from her all night? He'd heard her toss and turn through the night, he'd heard her muffled, despairing sighs and pillow punches when it was clear sleep was evading her too despite the gentling sounds of the sea on the shore. He'd registered the exact moment her breath had steadied and calmed and then he'd listened to the sounds of her sleeping. And all the time he thought about the waste of night hours and what they could have been doing if only he hadn't been such a damned fool.

When he rose early, he tried not to dwell too much on how good she looked asleep with her hair rippling over the pillow, or how easy it would be to climb into bed with her and finish this thing now. Except that she would truly hate him then, and somehow he didn't want her to hate him any more. If she could like him, even just a little, it would make this whole thing so much easier.

But he took one look at the table under his palms waiting for him to resume his studies and baulked. He had a problem to contend with and there was no space in his head for study. Besides, there was still way too much tension in his body to sit there quietly and take anything in, tension he needed to work off to give himself the headspace to think. He looked out at the ocean, inviting and calm, but swimming would involve going back to the tent to change. Besides, the thought of swimming made him think about her, looking lush and edible in that citrus-coloured swimsuit, and he needed to untangle his thoughts if he was to work out what he was to do, not scramble them completely.

And she was more than capable of scrambling his mind.

Already he was half-tempted by the thought of giving her as much time as she needed to fall into his bed. But that would mean leaving the door open for Mustafa, and how could he do that to Al-Jirad? How could he so callously evade his duty?

But, for a prize like her, it would be almost worth giving up the throne.

He shook his head, though he knew it would take more than that to clear it. He heard the nicker of horses and swung his head around.

Perfect.

Zoltan was nowhere to be seen when she rose, her head feeling as if someone was pounding inside her skull trying to break their way out. She could not remember a worse night. But then, she had not had much experience of sharing a tent with a man who simultaneously drove her wild with passion one minute, and so foaming with fury the next. And somewhere in the midst of those extremes she felt a strange hurt, a sadness, that things had gone so very wrong. But she would not dwell on how cheated she felt that they had not made love last night, or how her body had refused to relax, remaining so achingly high-strung half the night. She would not dwell on that at all.

Rani bringing her tea was just the distraction she needed. If she was going to worry, it might as well be about something important, and someone must have heard from Marina by now. 'Is there any news of my sister this morning?' she asked as the steam from the fragrant, spiced liquid curled in the air.

'No news, mistress.'

For the first time, Aisha felt a prickly discomfort about her sister's failure to arrive. Sure, Marina might be headstrong and wayward, and abhor anything to do with the constraints of convention, but why would she not attend her sister's marriage, and now the coronation? Surely she would attend for her sister's sake, at least?

'The master is riding, Princess,' Rani continued, breaking into her thoughts. 'Would you like a horse prepared for you?'

Aisha almost said no. Almost. But then she thought about riding along the beach, the wind in her hair, the closest she would ever get to being free again, and the idea held such appeal that she agreed. Maybe it might even blow away this growing concern in her gut that Marina hadn't shown up. Maybe it might make her see that her sister was just making a statement that she disapproved of this marriage and its terms and she was staying away as a protest. *Maybe.*

'Which way did Sheikh Zoltan go?' she asked when her horse was brought to her a few minutes later. When the groom pointed one way down the beach, she pointed her mount the other way.

* * *

It had been worth visiting the rest of the tribes people, Zoltan thought as he neared the point, taking a circular route back to the camp. Talking with them had made his path clearer and shown him what was needed. Al-Jirad had progressed in many areas under the rule of King Hamra, but there were still advances to be made in education and healthcare delivery, especially for these wandering people.

It was clear he should thank Aisha for breaking the ice and putting him in contact with them. He would not have thought to visit them otherwise.

It was also clear that he could not entrust the future of anyone, let alone his people, to the likes of Mustafa. That man did not want the throne of Al-Jirad for any reason other than his own personal aggrandisement. He cared nothing for the people.

Strange, he mused as his mount nimbly negotiated the rocky shoreline, how quickly he had come to think of the people of Al-Jirad as his people. He had taken on this role begrudgingly out of a sense of duty, and because the alternative was too ugly a prospect to entertain. He had taken it on all the while resenting the changed direction it meant for his life, and the loss of a business he had created from the ground up, the biggest and best executive-jet leasing business in the world. He had been only months away from achieving that goal when he had taken the call and realised he could not do both. Where was his resentment now? Where was his anger? Instead he felt a kind of pride that he was able to follow in his beloved uncle's footsteps. He would honour King Hamra's memory by being a good king.

The coronation must proceed.

Which meant he could not wait for Aisha to make up her mind. They would have to consummate the marriage before the coronation, which meant he would have to go back to the camp and explain, once again, that she had no choice. But after the mess he had made last night, he just hoped he could word it in a way she would understand. She *had* to understand.

It was duty, pure and simple, after all.

Except, thinking about it, his groin already tightening, maybe this part was not so much duty...

He saw her as he rounded the point, probably one hundred metres down the beach. He stopped for a moment to watch her gallop along the shore, her long hair flying behind her, the hem of her abaya flapping in the wind, the rest of it plastered against her body as spray from the horse's hooves scattered like jewels around her, and he realised the word 'goddess' came nowhere close to describing her.

Then she saw him, and he lifted one hand in greeting, but she pulled her horse up and turned before galloping in the other direction.

So she was still angry with him about last night, he thought as he set off in pursuit. Not entirely unexpected, but nevertheless not a good start when she was probably only going to get angrier with what he had to tell her.

His stallion powered down the shore. She was a good horsewoman and she had a decent head start, but her horse was nowhere near as big or as powerful as his and steadily his stallion narrowed the lead until they were galloping side by side across the sand.

She glanced across at him and dug her heels into her mount's flank. It responded with a spurt of speed but it was no trouble for his powerful horse to catch her. 'We need to talk,' he shouted into the air between them.

'I have nothing to talk to you about.'

'It's important.'

'Go to hell!'

'Listen to me.'

'I hate you!'

And she wheeled her horse around and took off the other way. He pulled his mount to a halt, its mouth foaming, nostrils snorting as he watched her go.

'You want a race, Princess,' he muttered into the air as he geed the horse into pursuit. 'You've got one.'

He was gaining on her again. She knew he would, she knew she couldn't escape him for ever, but he wasn't even supposed to have come this way. And she didn't want to talk. She didn't want to have to listen to him. She didn't even want to see him. How dared he look so good on a horse, with his white shirt flapping against his burnished skin, looking like some kind of bandit? How dared he?

She glanced over her shoulder, saw him just behind and urged her mount faster.

Barbarian!

All night he had lain there as if she didn't exist, as if he didn't care that she was hurt and upset and angry. All that time he had made not one attempt to try to make up for what he had done. Not even one. He had let her lie there waiting for him to do—something—and he had done precisely nothing. He had let her lie there aching and burning and he had made not one move to comfort her.

Bastard!

'Aisha,' he called, alongside her once again. 'Stop!'

He reached across, snatched the reins out of her hands and pulled the two horses to a halt.

She shrieked and smacked at his hand and realised it was useless, so she slid off the saddle, swiping at the tears streaming down her face. She splashed through the shallows, her abaya wet and slapping against her legs, tiny fish panicking and darting every which way before her frantic splashing feet.

She did not even know why she was crying, only that now the tears had started she didn't know how to turn them off.

'Aisha!'

She felt his big hands clamp down on her shoulders, she felt the brake of his body and his raw, unsuppressed heat, and she sobbed, hating him all the more for reducing her to this. 'Leave me alone!'

But he did not leave her alone. He turned her in his hands and she closed her eyes so she could not see his face. There was nothing but silence stretching taut and thin between them. And just when she could not stand it any more, just when she was sure he must be enjoying this moment so very, very much, he crushed her to his chest. 'Oh, Aisha, what have I done? What have I done?'

If he hadn't been holding her, she would have collapsed in tears in the shallows.

Instead she sobbed hard against the wall of his chest.

'Aisha,' he said, one hand stroking her head, the other behind her, holding her to him, 'I do not deserve you. I am afraid I will never deserve you.' He cradled her head in his hand and she felt the press of his mouth on the top of her head; felt the crush of her breasts against his chest; felt the stirrings of unrequited need build again, as if they had been lying in wait for just such an opportunity, ready to resume their pulsing insistence.

'Can you ever, ever forgive me for the way I have treated you?'

She sniffed. His shirt was sodden against her face. 'I don't want to forgive you,' she whispered against his skin, afraid to pull her face away. Afraid to look at him. 'I want to hate you.'

There was another achingly long pause and this time she was sure the thin wire connecting them would snap before he answered. 'I don't want to be hated.'

'I can't,' she said, releasing another flood of tears. 'I want to. I've tried, but I can't. And I hate you for it.'

He laughed then, no more than a rumble in his chest, and she wanted to hit him for being able to find humour where there was none—until he said, 'You do not know what a relief that is. I don't think I have ever heard more wondrous words in my life.' He lifted her chin between his fingers and she resisted at first, hating that he was seeing her like this, tear-streaked and swollen-eyed. But his persuasive fingers had their way, and she blinked up at him, saw his dark eyes upon her, the dark features of his face so—tortured.

'I could never live with myself if you hated me, Aisha, even though I know I deserve it, even though I have made such a mess of this. Can you ever, even in some tiny way, forgive me?'

The tears welled anew. She sniffed. He leant down and kissed first one eye, and then the other. 'I do not enjoy knowing that I make you cry.'

She pressed her lips together, her skin tingling where his lips had pressed. He leant down and kissed the end of her nose. And, in spite of herself, she jagged up her chin so her nose butted up harder against his lips, wanting the contact, needing more.

His hands grew suddenly warmer around her, scooping down lower and less soothing, more *appreciative*; the air around them was suddenly super-charged and electric and his dark eyes spoke of more than torture.

For in their dark depths she saw heat and desire and the promise of pleasure like she'd never known before.

'Aisha...'

And she knew before his head dipped that he intended to kiss her. She knew it and did not a thing to prevent it. Because it was what she wanted, this kiss with this man in this time.

His arms tightened around her as he drew her close. *'Aisha,'* he whispered in the second before their lips connected.

It was like coming home. It was like every time she'd been away from home and returned to the palace in Jemeya and felt its welcome warmth and familiarity wrap around her. It was just like that. Only one thousand times better.

For his kiss didn't just deliver familiarity. It offered a new dimension. It promised pleasures unbound.

And as she feasted on his hot mouth, and fed from the magic dance of his lips and tongue, all she knew was that she wanted all of those pleasures and she wanted them now. She could all but taste them.

She groaned into his mouth, her hands clutching at his shirt, fisting in the fine cotton as his hands cupped her behind and pulled her close, pulled her hard against the long, hot heat of him. And this time, she knew, she would not be left waiting and wondering. This time she would discover the pleasures she had waited for all these years.

It would not be so bad, she told herself; she would not be giving up on her dream, merely recognising life had changed the parameters. It did not mean it could not still work eventually. And meanwhile...

Meanwhile she could not breathe. Someone had sucked the oxygen out of existence and all that was keeping her going was the heated sweep of his hands on her body, the molten lure of his mouth and the rigid promise of his erection. Those things fed into her own need and stoked the fire beneath her until she was red-hot and rabid with desire. Until she knew kissing was not enough.

'Please,' she begged. 'Please!'

He lifted his hot tongue from her throat. 'What do you want, my princess?'

And her hunger and desire coalesced into one indisputable fact. 'I want you, Zoltan. I want to feel you inside me.'

CHAPTER ELEVEN

SHE felt him lift his head from hers and look up to the sky. She heard his roar. She felt his triumph in hers. Because she knew she was right.

He carried her back to the camp as he had done that first night, in front of her on his stallion, but this time she was not wrapped in a cloak and bound to him. This time she clung to him herself, looking up at all the harsh angles and dark shadows of his face, wondering how she had never thought them beautiful before.

For he was. Darkly, supremely beautiful.

When they arrived back at the camp, he slid out of the saddle and reached up for her, taking her in his arms as if she were weightless and looking at her as if she were the only woman in the world.

She liked that look as he swung her down. At that moment she wanted to be the only woman in the world for him for ever. But this moment and how it made her feel would do, even if there was no other. Because surely it couldn't get better than this?

He carried her into the tent and pulled the flap closed, signalling they were not to be disturbed. She swallowed at that. Everyone outside would know what they were doing inside, yet instead of stultifying her somehow that only managed to heighten her excitement.

Then Zoltan was there in front of her again and there was no room to care about anyone else because there was only the two of them. He slid one hand behind her neck. 'You are so beautiful,' he said, and even though she knew he was being generous, that her kohl must be smudged and her eyes swollen from tears, the knowledge he could see past that fed into her very soul.

As did the assurance they were already married. He didn't have to impress her now. He didn't have to pretend. She was already his wife in name and he could take his time making her so in fact.

She was so grateful he hadn't pushed her. Maybe she might have taken longer to get to this stage if they hadn't already been married, but for now there was no reason to delay. This was the man she was wedded to. This was the man she was bound to.

And when she looked up at him, tall and broad and wanting her, it felt not such a bad place to be.

'Are you still scared?' he asked as he gathered her into his arms. She nodded, afraid to speak lest he hear the quake in her voice, before he said, 'Then I will do my best to make it as pleasurable as possible. I owe you that, at least.'

His hot mouth went to work on her to smooth her concerns away as he laid her reverently on the bed. He made no move to undress her, and she wanted to cry with relief, for she wasn't yet ready to bare everything to him. It felt so good, anyway. He made it feel so good.

He made *her* feel so good.

She liked the way he kissed, giving her all he had to give. Their mouths meshed, his tongue inviting hers into the dance. She liked the way his hands skimmed her body, curving over a hip or cupping a breast, making her gasp when his thumb flicked over a sensitive nipple.

She liked the way his body felt under her hands. Firm. Strong. Sculpted.

Except she was too hot and he was wearing too many clothes. Way too many clothes. She pulled his shirt from his trousers so she could slide her hands up the bare skin of his back, relishing the feel of skin against skin, only it was not nearly enough to satisfy her.

And all the while the need inside her built, the heat inside her escalated. She felt as if she was losing herself, drowning under a wave of sensations, but wanting more, driven to find more.

He gave her more.

His mouth dipped to her breast, his hot tongue laving at her nipple, and she gasped as heat met need in a rush that sent sensation spearing through her, a direct line from breast to her heated core.

She was way too hot, and if his hand hadn't already been at her knee, smoothing her abaya up from her legs, she would have ripped it off herself. His hand scooped higher, deliciously higher, as his mouth wove magic at her breast and she wound her fingers through his hair hoping that he would pause, *there*, where her need was so great.

But he did not pause. She whimpered a little as he moved on and drew her gown higher over her belly. He lifted his mouth now, so that he could slip her gown higher, his fingers trailing sparks under her skin, or so it seemed. She unwound her arms and he eased the gown over her head and rocked back on his knees, looking down at her in just her underwear, drinking her in from her toes to her eyes, looking at her in a way that banished her fears that he might find fault with her now when she was so close, that put a fire under her blood. 'You are beautiful, Princess,' he said as he unbuttoned his shirt. 'You are perfection.'

His voice was so thick and tight that it was like gravel against her senses. His dark eyes were almost black, and brimming with need.

She knew little of love-making apart from what she had read in books, but she knew that it must be taking too long because this need inside her burned so hot!

'I want you,' she said, wanting him to know that in case he was taking his time because he thought she might yet change her mind. He growled deep in his throat, tore the shirt from his shoulders and undid the buckle of his belt. She watched, transfixed, as his busy, clever hands worked the trousers undone, watched hungrily as he slid them over his hips and kicked them aside.

She gazed at his masculine beauty, at the perfection of his form, at the bulge in his underwear, before he joined her once again on the bed, scooping her back into his arms.

Skin brushed by the cooling air was now brushed with the smooth of his hand and with his heated lips. He kissed her lips, nose and eyes, he trailed kisses down her throat, took her hand and kissed his way up her arm, her wrist, the inside of her elbow and down the other.

He didn't so much kiss her as worship her body, and when he dispensed with her bra she let it go with no protest. Why would she protest when her breasts wanted his mouth on them with no barrier between them?

His tongue took a wicked trail across her belly and it was almost too much, her body never more alive, never more on fire. And then his hand cupped her mound and her spine arched into the bed. 'Please,' she begged.

'What do you want, Princess?'

'I want you,' she gasped. 'Inside me.'

Laughter rumbled from him and into her as his mouth found her thigh and he proceeded to kiss his way down one leg.

Why was he taking so damned long? Her hands fisted in the covers as she was driven wild with desire, wild with need. She needed him inside her, and he was raining kisses on her instep.

'Someone is impatient,' he said as she kicked at him, urging him on.

'Haven't I waited long enough?' she came back with, her chest heaving, pulling her leg away.

'But if you have waited this long, surely a few more minutes won't matter?'

'I might die before then,' she replied and threw her head back into the pillows as he kissed his way up her inner thigh. 'Oh God.'

'Do you like that?'

'Mmm,' she managed. He must have been listening because she felt his fingers trace the waistline of her lace panties, felt them sneak under and scoop them down, felt his hands gentle her legs apart.

Oh God.

Every cell in her body tensed and clamped shut. This was it!

It was, and yet it wasn't, for in one shocked moment she realised his head was still between her thighs. 'You can't,' she said, then he parted her and she felt the sweep of his tongue against her inner lips and she almost cried out with the utter pleasure of it—did cry out when she felt his tongue circle that tiny, concentrated nub of nerve endings.

Already she was lost. She was panting now, lost in a new world with no idea how to find her way out and with no wish to find her way out any time soon. Not until she found this magical place he was taking her.

She hated him for making her wait, for delivering such exquisite torture, hated him and loved him for making her feel so very much.

Just when she thought she could not take any more, she felt his fingers upon her, circling her very core, working in train with his busy lips and tongue. One finger pressed inside her and her muscles clamped down at the invasion. But it was hardly unwanted. A swish of his tongue and she sighed and relaxed, only to feel another push into her alongside it.

Suddenly it was too much. There was too much to enjoy. Too much pleasure. She felt that pleasure spiral upwards, felt her whole being reduced to sensation, and then with a final flick of his clever tongue and press of his fingers inside her she was sent catapulting into the sky.

He held her while she rocked back to earth. He pressed kisses to her belly and breasts and lips where she tasted herself on his mouth.

'But you...' she managed, feeling as limp as a rag doll.

'Think you're amazing.'

And some part of her that still registered compliments glowed. She had done nothing and he could still say that? She sensed him rise up, heard the swish of fabric over skin and opened her eyes to see him between her legs, his hand guiding his erection towards her. So large. So alive and wondrous.

'You're so beautiful,' she whispered in awed reverence. 'Do you think...?'

'Oh,' he said, leaning down to suck her into his kiss, 'I know.'

She tasted his mouth on hers then, felt it tug her into his world, convincing her with the persuasive play of his tongue and losing her until with a start she realised he was there, butting and straining against her entrance. Even when she panicked, his hand was there below her to lift her and ease the angle.

But he was there, *right there*, and she would have panicked but he was also right there with her, taking her higher again with his kiss. Suddenly a pressure became a presence and, with a flash of pain that went as quickly as it had come, he was inside her.

She stilled then, stunned by what had happened, feeling his fullness deep within her body. He was inside her and, now the moment of pain had gone, she felt only that amazing sensation. But was that it? Was this how it was supposed to be?

He kissed her eyes. 'Are you all right?' She blinked up at him, seeing his concern in the tiny creases around his eyes, and she knew she loved him, just a little, even then. He shifted his elbows, a movement that shifted his body subtly so very far below and she gasped at the unexpected friction.

'I'm good,' she said. 'You *feel* so good.'

He growled at that and raised his hips, and she felt the sliding loss of him even as muscles she'd never realised she possessed battled to hang on.

He thrust back into her, this time with greater force. Why had she never done this? she wondered as her head was driven back into the pillows. Why had she waited when the pleasure was so exquisite, so addictive?

Then he withdrew and thrust into her again and she knew why—because she had wanted to save herself for the one who was special, the one who could make her feel this good. Zoltan made her feel this good.

Zoltan was the one.

She had saved herself for the very best.

And with every thrust of his hips she knew that to be true; with every thrust of his hips she knew she would never find a higher place.

But she found it now, when the slide of him inside her turned incendiary, and she combusted in a shattering explosion that featured the sun, moon and stars.

It could have ended there, but she heard his roar, felt his shuddering climax, and it drove her still further through the galaxies until he launched her again into nothingness and the sky gave way to the glow of a tiny kernel of knowledge.

She loved him.

Something had shifted the sands beneath his feet. Something had shifted the foundations of his very world while he wasn't looking.

Something?

Or *someone*?

For, while Zoltan's body pulsed with the post-release hum as he lay back against the pillows, his breathing slowly steadying, his mind grappled with the impossible. She was perfect in every way. How could she be? Yet she had responded instinctively to his every move, naturally and sometimes even wantonly, despite being uneducated and unrehearsed, and her unskilled reactions had stoked the fire raging inside him, higher and higher, until he had even felt himself consumed.

When had that ever happened before?

How could she, a virgin before this night, do such a thing? He had expected to pleasure her, to make this coupling as easy as possible. Never had he expected that he would find paradise himself.

He turned to her, touched the fingers of one hand to the line of her cheek, wanting to put into words how he felt but unsure how to go about it, surprised when he felt moisture there. He sat up. 'Did I hurt you?'

She shook her head, blinking away the tears. 'I had no idea. I didn't know it could be that good.'

'Usually it's not,' he said, sliding one arm beneath her. Then, because some part of him realised that honesty could be couched in better terms, he went on. 'It's never been that good for me. Never before.' She looked up at him, her dark eyes wide and a tiny frown between her brows, as if wondering whether to believe him or not. Suddenly she shuddered in his arms and her eyes and lips squeezed shut, a woman battling to keep control.

'Aisha,' he said, smoothing her brow with his free hand as tears insisted on squeezing past her closed lids, 'I did hurt you. I'm sorry. I was trying to be gentle.'

She shook her head, tried to turn away, but he gathered her closer into the circle of his arms. 'No. I was thinking about Mustafa and what he said he'd do to me. Zoltan, if you had not come I would still be there. If you had not saved me, it would be him in my bed. It would be him...' She shook her head. 'Oh God, it would be him in my bed.'

He tried to gentle her with his hands as his own heart grew weightier in his chest. 'He cannot hurt you now.'

'He would have.' She sniffed back on the threat of more tears. 'He had an old woman examine me,' she said, her voice thready and thin. 'He wouldn't believe me until she had poked and prodded and confirmed what I had told him. Only then he believed. Only then he left me alone.'

Her voice cracked on the last word and this time she

dissolved into tears. He pulled her in, cradled her head against his chest and let her cry, her tears ripping at his soul.

He did not deserve her thanks. She had been right all along—he was a barbarian. He—who knew Mustafa better than anyone—had paid no heed to what she must have suffered at his half-brother's hands. He had seen her rescue as a way of evening the score between them. And once she had been in his hands he had asked her nothing. He had demanded everything.

Worst of all, he had not believed her.

He was no better than his half-brother and that knowledge tore at his gut. He dropped his head to hers, pressed his lips to her hair. 'I am so sorry, Aisha, that I did not believe you. I was so wrong.'

He lifted her tear-streaked face to his, kissed her damp eyes and the tip of her nose. 'Can you ever forgive me for the way I have treated you?'

She blinked up at him, her soft lips parted, looking so lost and vulnerable, so very kissable, that he felt the kick all the way down in his groin. She gave a tentative smile, touched a slim hand to his chest and down his side, her fingers curling deliciously into the flesh of his buttock. 'Maybe,' she said hesitantly, taking his hand, putting it to her breast, her eyelids fluttering closed as his hand cupped her breast, his thumb stroking her nipple.

'Anything,' he said as she set both her hands on him, exploring, tracing every detail, setting his skin alight, turning his voice to gravel. 'Name it.'

'Make me forget him. Make love to me again. I mean, when it is possible.'

He growled low in his throat and, still holding onto her, flipped onto his back so she straddled him, his eyes drinking in the sight of her rising up from him, his hands drinking in her satin-smooth skin.

'Oh,' she said, her eyes widening as she realised he was already primed beneath her, 'I thought it would be too soon.'

'No,' he said as he encouraged her hips higher so he could position himself, loving the way she so naturally assisted with the movement of her lush body to find her centre. 'With you, Aisha,' he said, as he drew her down his long length, 'anything is possible.'

CHAPTER TWELVE

FOR the first time in days she felt that things were finally going right and falling into place. They had woken in the tent to the sound of waves breaking on the shore. They had made slow, lazy love as the sun had risen over the horizon. They had held hands while travelling across the sands to the Blue Palace.

And now, sitting in the front row of the Blue Palace's magnificent twelfth-century arched reception hall, grandly fitted out for the coronation of Al-Jirad's new king, she felt not only happiness but immense pride as well.

For in front of her stood Zoltan, now only minutes from being crowned King of Al-Jirad. The building was full of assembled guests from countries near and far, and her father sat alongside, beaming widely, no doubt at the knowledge he would be keeping his crown and that the Jemeyan legacy and the pact between their two countries would live on.

As for Aisha? She was so full of the new wonders of love-making that she could not begin to describe how she felt: glowing. Buzzing. Electric, with a heightened awareness of all things of the flesh. For Zoltan had awakened in her the pleasures of the flesh in a way she had never dreamed possible. She smiled to herself, thinking of the latest way he'd pleasured her—asking her to don the gossamer-thin robe she'd been gifted, pleasuring her with his clever tongue and seeking lips before taking her again. Was there no end to his talents?

Not so far, apparently.

He had told her that with her all things were possible. Could it be true? Could they find love out of the madness of a forced marriage neither of them had wanted? Might Zoltan grow to love her as she so wished to be loved?

Last night he had made it seem possible.

Only one thing could temper her joy this day and it was that there was still no word from Marina. She tried to tell herself not to be surprised—it was Marina, after all, and she had never been one for protocol and obligations, especially when it involved anything remotely connected to duty. But still, after all that had happened, Aisha had so very much wanted to have the chance to talk to her sister again.

Around her the formalities dragged on longer than she expected, and she zoned out, listening with only half an ear. It was not entirely intentional, but there was only so much pomp and ceremony one could take in when one had other, much more carnal pleasures on their mind, and right now she had the memories of last night's activities to savour as well as the upcoming night's activities to anticipate.

And there was really no need to listen. It was all just a formality, after all. And it was all so long…

Until she heard the name of her island home mentioned, and the pact. She blinked into awareness and she realised why the ceremony was taking so long, because an extra segment had been added to the ceremony due to the unusual circumstances of the ascension, a series of declarations Zoltan was required to respond to.

'And do you solemnly swear,' the Grand Vizier said, 'on the covenants of the Sacred Book of Al-Jirad that you have married a Jemeyan princess?'

She glanced from her father to Zoltan, not knowing she would be mentioned as part of this, and suddenly wishing she'd paid more attention, for neither of them looked surprised or perplexed.

'I declare it to be true,' Zoltan said.

'And do you also solemnly swear, on the covenants of the Sacred Book of Al-Jirad, that you have impregnated with your seed the Jemeyan princess you have married so that Al-Jirad and Jemeya might both prosper into the future just as your family will prosper?'

'I declare it to be true.'

'Then you have fulfilled the covenants of the Sacred Book of Al-Jirad and I declare…'

But Aisha heard nothing more. For her blood had turned to ice and the thunder of it in her ears drowned out the proceedings while her mind focused on the words *you have impregnated with your seed the Jemeyan princess*…

He had been *required* to impregnate her before the ceremony take place, as part of his requirements to become king?

The blood in her veins grew even colder. Was that what their trip away to Belshazzah had really been about, even while he had told her it was merely to get to know each other better?

For he must have known he would need to sleep with her before the coronation. The vizier would have told him.

He must have known.

Yet he hadn't told her. He'd let her think that it didn't matter how long it took, so long as they were married and gave the impression of sleeping together.

He'd let her think that she could take her time to get to know him.

He'd let her think she had a choice.

But he had known!

All the time he had known. She thought back to their time at Belshazzah, and to the skilfull way he had given her space and then reeled her in again, like a fisherman playing a fish. Giving it line, letting it think it was free, only to reel it back before letting it run again. He'd done the same with her, letting her think she had space, letting her walk alone, letting her make choices. But she'd been on a line all along and he'd known that all he had to do was reel her in and *impregnate* her.

She shuddered at the very sound of the word. It sounded so cold, formal and clinical. It sounded a million miles from what she thought they had been doing that day.

And all the time he had let her believe that it had meant something.

What had he told her? *It's never been that good for me.* She had wondered then whether he was telling her the truth, wanting in her heart to believe it but so scared to.

He had wanted her to believe it too. So she would become the biddable, complicit wife he needed.

And she had wanted so much to believe him. When would she learn?

She felt sickened, physically ill, and when she gasped in air to quell the sudden unwanted surge of her stomach her father frowned across at her and she did her best to send a reassuring smile back in his direction. It would not be the done thing for a Jemeyan princess to throw up at her own husband's coronation.

Somehow she made it through to the end of the ceremony, avoiding eye-contact as she placed her arm on his, stiff and formal, as the royal party departed.

Somehow her legs managed to carry her all the way from the ceremony to the balcony of the palace.

Somehow she even managed to smile stiffly at the crowd gathered in the square spread out below to celebrate their first sight of the new King and Queen of Al-Jirad.

Their cheers didn't come close to touching her. The only word she heard over and over in her mind was *impregnate*.

'You seem tense, Aisha.'

'Do I?'

She had suffered through the interminable state reception, putting up with inane small-talk and diplomatic and ultimately meaningless mutterings with as much grace as she could muster. But now, as she removed one of the heavy chandelier earrings from her lobe, she could enjoy a brief respite in their suite as they changed before a formal dinner.

Or she could have enjoyed it, that was, if Zoltan hadn't also been there. She pulled the other earring loose and dropped it to the dressing table in a clatter, just wanting the heavy weight gone from her ear, and wishing that the heavy weight on her heart could be so easily discarded.

Across the room Zoltan stopped tugging at his tie. 'It appears the stress of becoming queen is getting to you.'

'Tell me about it.'

'So maybe you need to relax.'

'And what did you have in mind?' she said, the taste of bile bitter in her throat. 'Perhaps a little *impregnation* to calm me down and turn me back into your oh-so-biddable wife?'

He blinked. Slowly. His jaw set. 'Is that what you're upset about, the wording of the ceremony?' He shrugged. 'It's ancient. It is required by the texts.'

'As, it seems, was the need to *impregnate* me before the coronation.'

'Aisha,' he said, coming closer, putting his hands to her shoulders, 'don't be like this.'

'Don't touch me!' she said, brushing his hands away. 'You knew, didn't you? You knew before we went to Belshazzah that you had to get me to sleep with you.'

'Princess,' he said, holding out one hand to her. 'Aisha, what is the point of this? It is already done. Did you not enjoy it?'

Her chest heaving with indignation at his inference that everything must be all right if the sex was any good, she demanded, 'What would have happened if you had not impregnated me before the coronation? If your answer to that question in the ceremony had been no?'

His jaw ground together, his eyes glinted. 'I would not have been crowned king.'

'And you knew that all the time we were at Belshazzah.'

'I knew.'

'And not once did you bother to tell me.'

'I tried. I was going to—'

'I don't believe you!'

'It's the truth! I was going to—'

'No! You told me you were taking me there so we might get to know each other, because the palace was too big, too public. You never once told me it was so you could secure the throne by ensuring I slept with you in time for the coronation. Don't you remember what you told me in the car on the way, that you didn't need to go to so much trouble to get into my pants because you could so easily find a dark corner in the palace to perform the task?'

'"Getting into your pants" are your words. They were never mine.'

'Don't get semantic, because playing with words won't work in this case. It doesn't matter which words you use. Because when it all comes down to it that's what you needed, that's what you wanted, wasn't it? Getting into my pants—impregnating me with your seed—only that would ensure you the throne.'

'I never lied to you,' he said, 'just because I didn't tell you the intimate details of the pact.'

She scoffed, indignant at the way he could worm his way around the truth. 'Not openly, perhaps. You didn't tell me what you knew. Instead you let me think that sleeping with you was my choice, that I had some say. While all the time you knew the clock was already ticking.

'Your lie was a lie all the same. It was one of omission.'

'Princess. Aisha, listen.'

'No! I am through with listening to you. Do you have any idea how betrayed I feel right now? How shattered that you could not entrust me with the details of my own future?' She put her shaking head in her hands before she raised her head and flung her arms wide. 'No. I am done with it, just as I am done with you and anything to do with you.'

'What are you saying?'

'I'm saying I have had enough of this farce of a marriage. I want out of it.'

'You can't just walk away from this marriage. You are bound to me just as I am bound to you.'

'Why shouldn't I walk away? You're king now. You don't need me any more. Don't try to tell me that the Sacred Book of Al-Jirad, the font of all knowledge and power, would prevent a queen who has been lied to and manipulated from escaping the chains of her captives? I am sure the wisdom of the ages would be on her side. And, if not, I am sure the weight of modern justice would support her.'

'Even though you have not yet finished your duty? You have yet to deliver the necessary heirs expected of this union.'

She tossed her head. 'Who knows, maybe there is a little bastard prince already implanted in my womb.'

'We are married. He would not be a bastard.'

'You don't think so?' From somewhere she managed to dredge up a smile. 'Though maybe you're right. Maybe he won't take after you. In any event, I am not staying here in this place a moment longer. I am going home to Jemeya.'

'You forget something, Princess—you need to supply two heirs.'

She raised her chin. 'So send me your sperm, Zoltan, and I will gladly save you any more pretence and any more of your lies and I will happily *impregnate* myself!'

He'd always known she was shallow. Zoltan crashed through the air as he strode down the passageway towards his suite, sick of a night spent making excuses, tired of explaining the new queen was unfortunately 'indisposed'.

She wasn't indisposed. What he'd really wanted to tell people was that she was a spoilt little princess who wanted everything all her own way—expected it—as if it was her God-given right. Well, he'd never wanted this marriage in the first place himself. He was better off without her. He would cope just fine. He tugged at the button at his collar, needing more oxygen than the suddenly tight collar allowed.

But—damn—maybe not Al-Jirad.

He would have to talk to Hamzah, find out how the queen's sudden absence would change things, to see if there was a workable way around her absence. There was nothing he could recall in the Sacred Book of Al-Jirad, but Hamzah would know the legalities of it all. Although her father would no doubt talk her around eventually; he was as hard-nosed about doing one's duty as anyone when it all came down to it. He had promised Zoltan tonight when they had exchanged a quiet word earlier on that he would soon talk sense into his precious daughter's head.

Wall hangings fluttered as he passed like a dark storm cloud, creating turbulence in the formerly serene air.

And the thing that made him angrier than ever, the thing that made him steam and fume, was that for just one day, just a few short hours, he had actually believed that this marriage might work.

He'd actually believed they had something that could take this marriage beyond the realms of duty and into something entirely more pleasurable.

Fool!

He'd been blinded by sex, pure and simple. So blown away by the delights of her sweet, responsive body, he'd forgotten what he was dealing with: a skin-deep princess who wanted the entire fairy-tale, from the once-upon-a-time to the happy-ever-after. When was she going to realise this was real life, not the pages from some child's picture book?

He paused as he came to the door of her suite, wondering if she'd already had her belongings removed and shipped. Nothing would surprise him.

He pushed open the door. It was silent inside and eerily dark with the closed curtains, only the light from the still-open door spilling in. There was no trace of her. He crossed the floor to her dressing room and tugged open the door. Nothing. She'd had them pack every single thing and wasted no time about it. They had taken every trace, until one might think she had never been here at all.

He ground his teeth together as he contemplated her mood when she had given the instructions to collect her belongings. Clearly she did not consider her return to Jemeya to be in any way temporary. Clearly she had no wish to be here. Maybe he should cut his losses and let her go. He would be well rid of her. He would have to ask Hamzah if that was an option that could be tolerated.

He was on his way out when his passing caused something to flutter, like loose papers riffling in the breeze, and he turned towards where the sound had come from. He pulled open a curtain, let light flood in and found them straight away. There were some loose papers on a desk tucked haphazardly under a blotter. He frowned, remembering a letter she'd been writing the night they'd been married when he'd come looking for her; remembering the way her fingers had shifted the pages as she'd looked down at them. The rushed packers had not done such a thorough job after all.

He pulled them out, intending to fling them in the nearest bin, when her neat handwriting caught his eye. Of course she would have neat handwriting and not some scrawl, he thought, finding yet another reason to resent her. She had probably been tutored in perfect script from an early age.

He didn't intend to read any of it, but he caught the words 'foolish' and 'naive' and he thought she must be talking about him, compiling a list of his faults.

That would be right. She had sat here on her wedding night and made a list of his failings—and to her sister, no less. No wonder it was such a long letter.

So what did his little princess really think of him? This should be amusing.

But as he read it wasn't amusement he felt. It was not him she was calling a fool. It was herself, for wishing she could choose a marriage partner, for ever thinking that she might one day marry a man for love, a good man who would love her for who she really was.

A ball formed in his gut, hard and heavy. He knew he shouldn't read on, but he could not stop. And he felt sick, knowing he was not that man she had wished for, and knowing that she saw herself as flawed when life and circumstances had conspired against her, when he knew it wasn't life she should be blaming. For he was the one at fault, he was the man who had shattered her dreams.

And he still wasn't sure why he cared.

When had duty got tangled with desire? Maybe about the time he had realised she was who she had said she was—an innocent.

Or maybe about the time duty had tangled with need. *Aisha.*

All she had wanted was a man to love her the way

she should be loved. Those words had meant nothing to him before. Her hopes and wishes had been like so much water poured on sand, for they had been thrown together, strangers, and what did it matter what either of them wanted when neither of them had a choice?

But he knew her now, better than before, and seeing her thoughts written down so clearly, knowing how she'd been hurting all that time...

The ball in Zoltan's gut grew heavier, and heavier still as he saw her call herself naive for saving herself for some mythical and ultimately non-existent male, and as she apologised to her sister for all the times she'd thought Marina had tossed her virginity away lightly, because at least she'd chosen who she'd gifted it to. For it had been hers to give, and she'd been the one to make that decision, and now Aisha applauded her, even envied her, for she would never experience that privilege.

But beyond that she was sorry, she wrote, that she had ever considered herself something special for the choice she had made. A choice that had clearly backfired spectacularly.

The ball in Zoltan's gut grew spikes that tore at his vital organs.

She thought she wasn't special? She was the most special of them all.

A woman so perfect and pure that he had felt honoured that he had been the one to receive her precious gift.

Yet clearly that wasn't how she had felt. And, even though she had come willingly to him that night, ultimately she had had no choice. No wonder she felt so cheated and betrayed now. No wonder she had not hung around long enough for him to explain.

She had lost her most guarded possession to a barbarian who had apparently taken it out of duty and purely to satisfy the dusty requirement of some ancient covenants.

And now she was gone and all he was left with was that memory. It killed him to realise that he had never told her what that day had meant to him, had never put into words how wondrous that experience had been. He cursed himself that he had assumed she must have known how he felt. For surely she must have known?

Why the hell hadn't he told her?

Why hadn't he thought to warn her of the ancient declarations in the coronation ceremony before she could imagine how he felt about what they had done, that he had been merely impregnating her?

And he remembered her frosty demeanour, her shutdown expression. He had wounded her so deeply. It destroyed him to think he had hurt her and that she might still be hurting.

He replaced the pages on the desk. He should not have read as much as he had; in truth he should not have read anything, but he was not sorry that he had. For now he knew what he must do. He must go to Jemeya and seek Aisha out. He must explain; he had to tell her what he felt for her, he must seek her forgiveness. For he had to get her back.

He had to.

Still, he wasn't sure why.

Only that he had to.

And from the mists of time he remembered those words his uncle, the King, had told him, the only positive lesson from his youth that had stuck. 'Choose your battles, and choose them wisely.'

He would go to her today. Tell her that he was sorry. Ask her if she could trust him enough to give him one more chance. Because this battle was worth fighting. This battle was one he could not afford to lose.

He could not let Aisha go. He could not bear the thought of her not being here with him.

Behind him the door was pushed open. 'Excellency,' the vizier uttered with relief, 'I have been looking for you everywhere. You must come quickly, there is news.'

For a heartbeat he hoped that Aisha had changed her mind and returned of her own accord.

'What is it?' he said.

'It's Mustafa,' the vizier said. 'He has taken Princess Marina hostage.'

Zoltan's blood ran cold.

As much as he hated his half-brother, his first thoughts went to his wife.

Aisha.

How would she feel when she learned the news? How terrified she would be, knowing what kind of man was holding her beloved sister.

Aisha had already suffered enough at the hands of his half-brother. She had suffered more at his own clumsy and ham-fisted efforts to possess her. He could not bear her to suffer more.

He would not allow it.

CHAPTER THIRTEEN

AISHA was sick with fear, sick with worry. Mustafa had Marina, had taken her hostage on her way to the coronation. Even though her father swore that she would be rescued and brought safely back to Jemeya to be reunited with her family, and despite the relief of learning that her two children were safe at home with their nanny, Aisha wondered when this nightmare would ever end.

The only positive thing that Aisha could see was that at least worrying about her sister took her mind off thinking about Zoltan.

Most of the time.

She picked up her childhood bear, from where it winked at her on its shelf, and hugged it, wandering to the window of her bedroom, the treasured bedroom she had yearned so desperately to return to. She looked out over the cliffs of her island home to the shoreline of Al-Jirad in the distance. For there lay another palace that stood encircled by sandy deserts ruled by a king she had once imagined she had felt something for.

Two days now she had been back in Jemeya, and she could not deny the truth any more, for each passing day piled a heavier weight on Aisha's heart than the one that had gone before. The fact Zoltan hadn't tried to stop her from leaving, the fact he had let her return to Jemeya in the first place—didn't that say something about how little he actually valued her as his wife? Didn't the fact he hadn't come after her speak for itself? Surely she had been right to leave when she had, no matter what her father had tried to tell her?

Two days. A world ago, it seemed now. And her time with Zoltan could almost be some kind of dream. Imaginary. Unimportant.

Except then she remembered the touch of heated hands and the brush of a whiskered cheek against her breast, the thrust of him deep inside her, and she knew that so long as the memories remained in her mind there was no way she could ever easily forget him.

Damn him.

Damn herself!

For now she was here, back in her own room where she had always maintained she wanted to be, and after the places he had taken her it seemed a hollow victory indeed.

A spoilt princess?

Maybe Zoltan had been right all along. For, yes, she still felt betrayed and manipulated, but when things hadn't gone her way she'd as good as stamped her feet and run away.

Fool.

She looked down at the bear in her arms. Maybe it was time she grew up. Maybe instead of sitting here locked away in her room, waiting for Zoltan to make a move, she should be the one to make an effort, to reach out with an olive branch. After all, they were married and bound together. They had slept together—made love together. And no matter what she had spat out in her anger to Zoltan, there was no way she did not want to feel his body between her thighs again.

Maybe, if that was to happen, it was time for her to reach out to him, and if he didn't want her back, well, she wasn't an inexperienced virgin with dreams of falling in love with the man of her dreams any more. She was a woman. She would cope with whatever happened.

But first she owed it to herself to try.

There was a commotion outside her room, raised voices and someone shouting her name, and then the door was flung open and her father burst through, the smile on his face a mile wide, and next to him, her beaming sister.

'Marina!' she cried, and flung herself into her open arms.

It was a noisy reunion, filled with laughter and tears of joy, and it was only when her father went off to order a feast that Aisha had the chance to draw Marina aside to talk. They curled their feet beneath them on a sofa overlooking the sea and held hands as they had done ever since they were children.

'I was so afraid,' Aisha confessed. 'Did he hurt you? Mustafa, I mean. He must have been so angry that he had lost me.'

Her sister patted her hand and for a moment her eyes grew serious, the muscles in her face tight. 'He was angry. And bitter. He delighted in telling me in how many ways he would have me.' Her eyebrows raised. 'And in great detail.'

Aisha shuddered, remembering her own ordeal, and her sister put a hand to her arm, squeezing it.

'But don't worry. I now know why he had to spell it out. Because, my dear sister, it seems the man is impotent.'

'So why did he say those things? Why did he take you?'

She shrugged. 'I think he knew there was nothing he could do to challenge the ascension but he still wanted to frustrate things. I'm sure he was hoping the coronation would be delayed. As it was, apparently the news didn't make it to the palace in time.'

She patted the back of Aisha's hand where the remnants of the henna tattoos were still just visible. 'Which reminds me, you are a queen now, and a married woman! Congratulations. Zoltan is such a wonderful man. You must be so happy.'

She shook her head. 'No. Please don't,' she said, pressing her lips together, tears once more springing to her eyes, but this time not from joy.

'Why? What's wrong?'

'It's off. I left him. I don't know if he'll want me back.'

'What?'

She shrugged. 'I left him.'

'How could you do that? Didn't he rescue you from Mustafa?'

Aisha could sit no longer. She jumped up and walked slowly to the window to where the sandy coastline of Al-Jirad appeared as a thick white line in the distance, all the while trying to make sense of all her actions, trying to remember why leaving him was so necessary. 'That was only so he could become king. Everything he's done, it was to become king. That's all he wanted. He didn't really want a wife. He told me that. And he didn't want me.' She spun around, clutching her hands together. 'And, before you say anything, it's been two days now since I left his palace and he hasn't bothered to so much as contact me. So, you see, he doesn't care.

'I will contact him, though,' she said, before scraping her bottom lip with her teeth. 'I've decided to try to make it work, if he wants to try.'

Her sister's eyes opened wide. 'You have no idea, do you? Nobody told you.'

'Told me what?'

'That Zoltan couldn't call you because he was too busy rescuing me.'

'What?'

'It's true. How do you think I got away if not for Zoltan and his friends?' She looked up at the ceiling and blew out a breath. 'Bahir included, as it turns out. Seeing him again was a blast from the past, I can tell you.'

'You know Bahir?' she said, distracted.

It was her sister's turn to shrug, as a strange bleakness filled her eyes. 'It was a long time ago. I'm not sure he wants to remember it either.' She blinked and smiled. 'But that's not the point right now.' She uncurled her long legs from underneath her and padded to where her sister stood. Aisha was still shocked from the revelation that Zoltan had been busy rescuing her sister all the time she'd been thinking he had written her off; still trying to work out why he had done that when there was no risk to his reign. He hated Mustafa, it was true, but why would he risk everything to rescue her sister? Unless...

A tiny and no doubt futile glimmer of hope sparked into life. Unless he had done it somehow for her. But no; he didn't want her.

'The thing is, dear sister,' Marina said, taking her hands in hers, 'what are you going to do now?'

'I don't know,' she said, her heart racing, trying to assimilate and understand everything her sister had told her about Zoltan, everything that made no sense, except that it was Zoltan, and in a way it did. Who else had a grudge against Mustafa and felt he had to prove himself at every turn? Who else would delight in humiliating him further? 'I was going to get in touch anyway.'

'Well, maybe you'll get your chance in a few minutes.'

Realisation skittered down her spine in a tingling rush. 'He's here?'

'He said he wanted to freshen up before he saw you. He said he smells of horse.'

'I like the way he smells,' she mused out loud.

Her sister smiled. 'Maybe you could start by telling him that.'

'My father told me I'd find you here.'

They were in the library, all four of them, freshly showered and looking dangerously dark and sexy. And one of them looked darker and sexier than all the others as he perched on the edge of a desk. He watched her, with those impenetrable dark eyes, his jaw clamped shut, his expression closed.

One by one the other men peeled away, Bahir slapping him on the back, Kadar on the shoulder. Rashid uttered a quick, 'Later,' and with a bow of their heads in her direction they were gone.

He stood and bowed his own head. 'Princess,' he said. 'Queen.'

She looked up at him, at this man she had once had and lost, at the dark planes and sharp angles of his face, and wondered how she could ever have thought he wasn't the most handsome man on the planet. How had she missed such an obvious fact? She wished she could have flung herself into his arms, as she had done with Marina. But if he rejected her, if he pushed her away, she would die.

'I came to thank you. For rescuing Marina.'

'Your sister is well?'

She nodded. 'Very well, and very grateful. We all are.' She searched for something else to say, something to broach the veritable abyss that seemed to stretch between them. And then, because she needed to know if the tiny spark in her heart would be fanned into life or would quickly be extinguished, she went on. 'Why did you do it and not leave it to someone else? Why did you risk yourself on such a rescue now that you are king?'

He dragged in a breath. 'I should never have left Mustafa free to continue to make trouble, after what he had attempted with you. He is the worst kind of opportunist. He saw an opportunity when King Hamra's entire family was wiped out and he kidnapped you to try to steal the crown.'

She frowned. 'You don't think he—?' She stopped. It was too ugly a thought to entertain, too horrible, even for someone like him.

'Do I think he was behind the crash from the start?' He shook his head. 'No. I wondered that once too, but no. Mustafa is a bully, he always has been. But even he would not be capable of murdering so many of his own family. The early reports from the crash investigators seem to support that it was a tragic accident. So, like I said, he saw the opportunity to seize the throne and he took it by kidnapping you.

'And then when that went wrong he saw the chance to frustrate the coronation by taking your sister hostage. I promise he won't try anything again, not where he is now, but how could I do nothing when I felt responsible for what had happened, for letting him go after what he had done to you?'

'Oh.' She looked at the floor as the tiny spark of hope

fizzled out. 'I see.' He felt responsible. But he would. When would she ever learn? When would she stop her silly dreams and hopes getting in the way of reality? 'Well, thank you.'

'And, of course, there was the consideration that Marina is your sister.'

She warily lifted her head. 'Because she is now sister-in-law to the King?'

'More than that. I knew you would be upset. I know how much your sister means to you.'

She blinked up at him, touched beyond words, the beginnings of a tentative smile forming on her lips, the spike of tears behind her eyes. 'I'm sorry,' she said, and then wondered why she'd said that when she'd been intending to thank him again. And then she realised it didn't matter if he rejected her apology out of hand and never wanted to see her again—she owed him this apology. 'I'm so sorry for causing you so much trouble.'

'It was Mustafa—'

'No—for being such a spoilt princess. I'm sorry for leaving you the way I did. My father tried to talk sense into me but I wouldn't listen. I thought you didn't care that I'd gone, but all that time you were out there finding my sister.'

She squeezed her eyes shut and put her hands over her face, feeling the dampness on her cheeks from the tears that would be contained no longer. 'I'm such a fool.'

She felt his arms close around her, felt herself pulled against his chest, and the sheer joy of it brought forth a fresh burst of tears.

'Aisha,' he said, stroking her hair, pressing his lips to it.

She lifted her tear-streaked face, blinking away the

moisture in her eyes, and he swept the hair from her face with his fingers. 'You're not still angry with me?' she asked.

He shook his head, the corners of his mouth turned up the slightest fraction. 'It's me who should be asking that. I have treated you appallingly. I was so angry and so resentful with being forced into this position, that I took it out on you. And I understand why you were so hurt the night of the coronation. I'd betrayed your trust once again. And I was going to follow you and tell you that you were right that same night, even though I knew you wouldn't believe me, and tell you that I cared for you.

'And then came the news that Marina had been taken. Hamzah was against me going. But I thought, *I hoped*, that if I could help reunite you with your sister you might understand, just a little, how much you mean to me.'

Her heart swelled in her chest. 'I still can't believe you did that, that you risked everything.'

'But none of it matters, does it?' he said. 'If you can't have what you truly want.'

'What do you truly want?'

He looked down at her with his dark, potent eyes. 'I want you. I want all of you. I want you to be my queen. I want your body. I want your soul. I want you for ever.'

She gasped as he pressed his lips to her forehead before pulling back and she hungered for more of his kiss. 'And I know I fall short of the kind of man you wanted to marry. I know this has all happened the wrong way around and that you have every right to hate me for ever. So I am offering you a choice.'

'What choice?'

He dipped his mouth, kissed the tip of her nose, and

she drank in his air and the very essence of him while her lips searched in vain for his.

'You can walk away from our marriage and all that it entails, or you can stay and settle for my flaws and imperfections and, ultimately, my love.'

Her swelling heart sang. 'What did you say?'

'I said I'm giving you a choice.'

'No, not that bit. The other bit.'

'About walking away?'

'No!'

He smiled and kissed her eyes, first one and then the other, but when she angled her face higher, to give him access to her hungry mouth, he withdrew. 'The other choice is my love. You see, I have nothing to offer you, Aisha, that you cannot find in a million other more worthy men, nothing but the one thing only I can give you—my love, if you will accept it.'

'You never told me. I never knew.'

'I didn't know it myself. Not really, not until you walked away and left my heart in pieces on the floor. I love you, Aisha. And I know I am so unworthy. I know I am the last person who deserves it. But will you come back and be my wife? Will you let me love you? Will you find it in your heart to love me one day, even just a little?'

'Oh, Zoltan, yes—a thousand times yes. I love you so much. And now...'

'Now?'

'Now will you kiss me at last?'

He laughed, a low, delicious rumble that vibrated through her all the way to her bones. 'Only a kiss, Aisha, my queen?'

'Don't tell me—you are giving me another choice already?'

His hands scooped down her back to cup her behind, bringing her into even closer contact with the evidence of his desire. 'Only if you want it.'

She smiled up at him, her blood fizzing in anticipation, dizzy with love. 'Oh, I want it, Zoltan. I want it all.'

As his head dipped and his lips brushed against hers with that first delicious contact, she heard him say, 'Then you shall have it.'

And she knew, in her heart, mind and soul, that she already did.

* * * * *

Cinderella and the Sheikh

NATASHA OAKLEY

Natasha Oakley told everyone at her primary school that she wanted to be an author when she grew up. Her plan was to stay at home and have her mum bring her coffee at regular intervals—a drink she didn't like then. The coffee addiction became reality and the love of storytelling stayed with her. A professional actress, Natasha began writing when her fifth child started to sleep through the night. Born in London, she now lives in Bedfordshire with her husband and young family. When not writing, or needed for 'crowd control', she loves to escape to antiques fairs and auctions. Find out more about Natasha and her books on her website www.natashaoakley.com.

For my Dad

CHAPTER ONE

'SHOULD I know him?' Polly Anderson pulled the A4 photograph across the table so she could see it more clearly. She squinted down at it, trying to bring it into focus.

Her friend smiled. 'Forget your contact lenses this morning?'

'I didn't forget them.' Polly accepted the black coffee Minty handed her and took a quick sip of the scalding liquid. 'It was a late night and my eyes feel like they're filled with grit if you really want to know.'

'And you're too vain to wear your glasses, of course.'

Polly grimaced. More that she'd put them down somewhere and had absolutely no idea where. She set the blue and white mug down on the table. 'I'm sure I've not met him. He's not exactly in the usual run of sheikhs that do business with Anthony, you know.'

'Not fat or old.'

'Something like that.'

Minty laughed her husky laugh and slid a second photograph along the table. 'You should see him without the headscarf. Then we just get tall, dark and deliciously dangerous.'

'Nice,' Polly said, looking down at the image of an

aggressively handsome man. Actually *very* nice. Her sight wasn't so short she couldn't see that. It was all about the eyes, she decided. *Mostly about the eyes.* Unexpectedly blue in a face that was unmistakably Arab.

Exotic and familiar at the same time. And incredibly sexy. Those eyes seemed to promise feelings and sensations she'd no experience of. Or very little.

She smiled. Maybe there was more of her scandalous great-great-grandmother in her than she'd supposed. Now *that* was an interesting thought—and probably one her mother would prefer her not to dwell on. 'So, who is he?' she asked, looking up.

'Officially, His Highness Prince Rashid bin Khalid bin Abdullah Al Baha. But for Western consumption he's generally known as Sheikh Rashid Al Baha. Much simpler. Twenty-nine. Six feet two and a half inches. Single. Keen horseman. Rich beyond your wildest dreams.' Minty leant forward. 'Pretty damn sexy all round.'

Polly laughed. 'Not that you're interested or anything.'

'Actually I'm not. He's a bad idea as anything other than eye candy. He's Crown Prince Khalid's second son. The one he had with his English wife—'

'Oh, okay…I've heard of him,' Polly interrupted. 'He's Amrah's playboy sheikh, right?'

Minty nodded. 'That's him. Plays hard and fast. Only thing he really exhibits any sort of commitment to is his horses. I don't understand all that, but he's something big in the horse world. Breeds them or something. Which is why I thought you might have met him through that slimy stepbrother of yours. But if not it doesn't really matter. We'll manage.'

Polly picked up the more traditional of the two pictures and held it out in front of her. Long flowing white robes and his dark hair concealed beneath a white headdress.

Minty was right. Prince Rashid bin thingy was really very sexy. If he'd been to Shelton she'd have remembered.

She closed one eyelid to focus more clearly. 'A couple of sheikhs did come over from Amrah but they were both much older. And I doubt they were royalty because Anthony would have been much more impressed. I can probably get their names for you if you need them.'

Minty shook her head and bent over to open the file resting against the leg of her chair. 'I don't. But while we're at it, have a look at his elder brother,' she said, passing across another glossy A4 picture. 'His Highness Prince Hanif bin Khalid bin Abdullah Al Baha. Again he tends to contract all that to Sheikh Hanif Al Baha. And who can blame him?'

Polly picked up the photograph.

'Now their daddy's so ill Hanif's probably the one we should be talking to,' Minty said slowly, her eyes focused on her notes. 'They've both got the "bin Khalid bin Abdullah Al Baha". Exactly the same. Not very imaginative, is it? The only difference is the Hanif-Rashid bit.'

There was more difference between the brothers than that. Sheikh Hanif looked like a 'safe pair of hands'. At least, he did as far as you could ever judge anything from a single photo when you weren't wearing your glasses.

Polly closed one eyelid and brought the blurry image into sharp focus again. He had a solid sort of responsibility. Maybe a hint of sadness in his dark eyes? Certainly steeliness.

But Rashid was something else. There was a restlessness about him. A man who exuded an edginess. Danger. As Minty said, a *bad* idea. Unquestionably. Why *were* bad boys always so attractive?

'Neither of them have been to Shelton. I'm sure.

They're both a good twenty years younger than the men I met.'

Minty flicked through the pages of her notebook. 'I can't get my head round these names at all. The dad is Crown Prince Khalid bin Abdullah bin Abdul-Aalee Al Baha. *Jeez.*'

'"Bin" means "son of",' Polly said, putting the photographs down and picking up her coffee. She wrapped her fingers round the comforting warmth and blew across the top of the mug. 'Think of it like a family tree. And Baha is King Abdullah's family name so that pinpoints them as being close to the centre of things.'

'That makes it all as clear as mud.' Minty rubbed at her forehead. 'Not that it matters. I think as long as you cover your shoulders and don't wear miniskirts while in Amrah we'll be just fine even if we don't get all that sorted.'

'Right.' Polly stretched out long legs encased in the finest ten-denier stockings. 'I can manage that. Seems a bit of a pity to hide my best feature, though, don't you think?'

'Better than getting arrested for immorality in a public place.'

'Do they do that?'

'I've absolutely no idea. Let's not risk it.' Then as she caught the edge of Polly's startled gaze, 'Don't let it worry you. I've got a team working on the practical side of things. Nothing horrible will happen to you, I promise.'

Polly nodded, only partially reassured.

'And Matthew Wriggley, the tame historian we found, is painstakingly putting together some wonderful detail on your Elizabeth Lewis. Really exciting. You'll love it.' She gathered the photographs together and put them inside her slip file. 'It was all going great until Crown

Prince Khalid fell ill and the permission to begin filming was mired in red tape.'

Polly said nothing. She took another sip of her coffee and waited. She'd known Minty for something like nine years and she knew there was more to come.

'So now I need you to cultivate Sheikh Rashid, get his support and encourage him to fast-track it all or we'll miss the best of the weather. Convince him we don't have any kind of subversive agenda.'

Two frown lines appeared in the centre of Polly's forehead. 'I thought you said we needed to negotiate with the elder brother now Crown Prince Khalid is ill.'

'I knew you weren't paying attention to me. Sheikh Hanif is the brother we *should* be talking to since he's generally thought to be his father's right-hand man, but he's completely un-get-able-at.'

'That's not a word.'

'You know what I mean,' Minty said, ripping the top off a sachet of artificial sweetener and dropping the contents in her coffee. 'He's doing the bedside vigil thing. Which leaves us with Sheikh Rashid—'

'Ah.'

'—who isn't, and who *fortunately* has a well-documented soft spot for English blondes.'

'How fortuitous,' Polly said dryly.

'Isn't it? Even better is that he's going to be at your place for the big charity bash this weekend. I've no idea why he isn't also sitting at his father's bedside but that's not important—'

Polly shook her head. That couldn't be right. 'His name isn't on the guest list,' she said with the quiet certainty of someone who'd been through it twice last week.

'He is. He's in the Duke of Aylesbury's party. Part of the "plus six".'

'How the *heck* do you know that when I don't?'

'One very boring dinner party sat next to an inebriated old Etonian and hey presto. It's all in the flirting.' Minty picked up her spoon and stirred her coffee. 'Apparently big brother Hanif was at Eton with the Duke of Aylesbury and they're close friends. Presumably that friendship has extended to little brother, too, I don't know. Whatever the reason, he'll be at Shelton on Saturday.'

Polly sat back in her chair and gazed in frank admiration.

'So, if you do your "charming lady of the castle" thing and get his support that should speed everything up beautifully. We've had all the appropriate forms in now for about four months—'

'Do my what?'

Minty looked up and laughed. 'You know what I mean. Foreigners love that stuff. Take him to see the Rembrandt or something. Talk about your mother the dowager duchess. Toss your hair a bit. Don't mention you're more the Cinderella of the outfit. He'll love it.' Distracted, she glanced over her shoulder, then back at Polly. 'What *is* that noise?'

'*Aargh!* That's my phone. Sorry.' Polly made a dive for her handbag. 'I should have switched it off.' The handle caught on her chair arm and by the time she'd opened her bag the ringing had stopped.

'Important?'

Polly glanced down at the number. 'Probably not. It's Anthony.' She turned it off and returned the phone to the depths of her bag. 'I'll call him later.'

'Good plan! Let him sort out the latest crisis. It's about *bloody* time he did something.'

Polly allowed herself a tiny smile. Loyalty to her late stepfather meant she always stopped short of joining in criticism of Anthony.

'How long is it now since Richard died?' Minty asked suddenly.

'Three years. Almost. It'll be three years in May.' Was it really that long? Polly replaced her bag back on the floor and picked up her coffee once again. In another four months her mother would have been widowed longer than she'd been married. Unbelievable. So much had happened.

'Plenty of time for him to have got used to the idea of running the show—'

If only. Anthony still showed absolutely no inclination to do anything of the sort.

'And if his well-bred wife thought of something other than horses that'd help.'

'They'll have to manage while I'm away filming—'

'*If* we get our permit.'

'*If*,' Polly agreed mildly.

'Well, try to sound like you mind one way or the other!'

'I do.' Her smiled twisted. *Sort of.* It was just…leaving Shelton was going to be difficult, particularly since she knew it wasn't in safe hands. Every time she tried to imagine herself packing her case and walking away from it…she couldn't.

Instead she'd think about how much there was to do. The Burns Night Supper, for example, or the Valentine's Ball, or the craft fair held at the castle each Easter weekend…

All bringing in desperately needed revenue if the conservation programme was to continue. The trouble was she *cared*. Somehow, and she didn't really understand how, it had got into her bones. Shelton Castle had become her raison d'être.

And, the truth was, it wasn't hers to love. It was Anthony's. *His* birthright. *His* privilege to nurture and succour the castle for future generations. And if she didn't manage to detach herself she would eventually be left with nothing.

Minty watched her with narrowed eyes. 'We agreed. It's time you left Shelton.'

They had agreed that.

'And way past time you did a job for which you're being properly paid.'

Also true. Her head agreed. It was her heart that was more difficult to control.

'You've got no savings, no pension, no career structure—'

'I know.' *And she did.* It wasn't something that kept her awake at night, but she did know she'd allowed herself to drift for too long.

And she knew Amrah could be the answer. The first real attempt she'd made to cut the umbilical cord that tied her to the castle.

'Well, then, be nice to Sheikh Rashid and I'll have you on a plane within twenty-four hours of getting the paperwork through.'

'Be nice to Sheikh Rashid.' That was easier said than done. There was no getting near the man. Polly moved back to conceal herself behind an extravagant white floral display of alstromeria, lisianthus and roses so she could watch him more easily. Or, more accurately, so she could watch him without anyone noticing that was what she was doing.

Sheikh Rashid sat facing out across the ballroom. As he'd done all evening. His long legs stretched out in front of him, a look of faint boredom on his face. Silent. Arrogant. And rude, if she was honest.

From the very first moment he'd arrived he'd been

permanently surrounded by women who looked as if they'd stepped out of a Bond movie, but they could have been invisible for all the attention he paid them. Perhaps he was so used to it he didn't notice they were there?

But it was rude all the same. And, speaking as someone who'd often been all but invisible, she didn't like it.

Of course, they should have moved away rather than continue to try to attract his attention. That would have been classier, but they didn't. *Of course they didn't.* They hovered about, smiling and laughing. Hoping he might notice them.

All of which made Minty's cunning plan just that little bit more difficult to bring to fulfilment and left Polly stuck behind a large floral arrangement completely uncertain what to do next.

Polly bit her lip. Minty would have powered her way across the ballroom and flicked aside all competition like flies off a trifle, but she wasn't Minty.

And he wasn't the kind of man she'd ever be comfortable approaching. Contact lenses in, she was able to confirm her initial assessment of His Highness Prince Rashid bin Khalid bin Abdullah Al Baha as sex on legs. Or would be, if you liked that kind of thing. Which she didn't.

He was all too much. Too tall. Too handsome. Too... powerful. He looked like the kind of man who could crack a nut with his bare hands and wouldn't hesitate to do the same to people if he had to. And, from all she'd read, he came from a long line of men who'd had to. Centuries of tribal disputes, years of colonial occupation and violent coups had shaped Amrah into the country it was. They'd shaped the men who ruled it, too.

It was strange to think her great-great-grandmother had been an active participant in all that history. Or a small slice of it at least.

'Something wrong?'

Polly turned to look down at her mother. 'No. Why?'

'You're frowning. I wondered if the ice sculpture was melting or the fireworks had got damp,' she said, bringing her wheelchair into line. 'It's not often I see you frowning.'

'Nothing like that. As far as I know.' Polly smiled and set her glass of untouched champagne down on the window sill behind her. 'But I ought to stop standing about and check.'

'Polly—'

She stopped.

'I just wanted to say you've done a beautiful job tonight. Again.' Her mother reached out and lightly touched her hand. 'I know Anthony doesn't appreciate the work that goes into something like this, but I do.'

'I know.' Polly spontaneously bent down and placed a kiss on her mother's cheek. 'Have you got everything you need? Can I get you a drink?'

The dowager duchess laughed. 'I'm fine. Any more champagne and I'll be arrested for being drunk in charge of a wheelchair. You do what you need to do, darling.'

'Get someone to come and find me if you want to go to bed,' she said, taking in her mother's tired face. 'There's no need for you—'

'Stop fussing. I'll be fine.' Then, her attention snagged, 'Who's that man? I don't recognise him.'

Polly followed the direction of her mother's eyes.

'With the Duke of Aylesbury? Front table, beneath the Mad Duchess oil painting?'

'That's—' She stopped as Rashid's eyes met hers. The sensation was akin to how she imagined it would feel if you stuck a wet finger into an electrical socket. He was quite, quite still…and, *heaven help her,* he was definitely watching her.

What was more he'd probably seen her watching him. Polly straightened her spine and summoned up her 'perfect hostess' smile, resisting the temptation to check that her hair was still firmly pinned in its chignon. Then, abruptly, he leant forward and spoke to the Duke of Aylesbury sitting immediately to his left.

She forced her chin that little bit higher as Sheikh Rashid's blue eyes locked with hers once more. It had to be pure imagination that made her stomach clench in…

God only knew what. The word that had sprung into her mind had been *fear*. Except that didn't make any sense.

'He looks so angry.'

'That's His Highness Prince Rashid bin Khalid bin Abdullah Al Baha.' His formal title came easily from her lips, absolutely no trace of the uneasiness she felt appearing in her voice. She dragged her eyes away. 'Why do you think he's angry?'

'I just did,' her mother said slowly, and then smiled. 'For a moment. He has a very uncompromising face.'

That was one way of putting it. It seemed to Polly he had an uncompromising everything.

Her mother released the brake on her wheelchair, apparently having lost interest. 'I hope Anthony isn't intending to do business with him. I don't think that would be a good idea at all.'

On that slightly obscure observation the dowager duchess moved away, her gloved hands moving lightly on the wheels of her chair. Polly watched her for the shortest of moments and then, deliberately not looking back at the Amrahi prince, walked towards the Long Gallery.

Or tried to. Every step she felt as though his eyes were boring into her back. All of a sudden it became difficult to walk in a straight line. She felt conscious of how her arms swung in relation to her legs. Wondered what would be the best thing to do with her hands. She hadn't felt so self-conscious since she'd left puberty.

Polly slipped out into the Long Gallery and pulled the door shut behind her with a satisfying click. She rubbed a hand over the goose bumps on her forearm. What was the matter with her? Surely if she'd learnt one thing in the last six years it was not to let these people get to her. They could look down their long patrician noses any which way they wanted. It didn't touch her. Couldn't, if she didn't let it.

But...

Still the words she needed to put a frame around what she was feeling eluded her. There was *something*. Something she couldn't quite catch at.

Call it feminine intuition, but she was certain the mind behind those blue eyes wasn't thinking about anything as pleasant as her state-school education and her mother's temerity to marry 'out of her class'.

Polly frowned. The way he'd looked at her had felt personal. He'd looked at her as though she were...

Damn it! What *was* the word?

He'd looked at her as if she were the...*enemy*. That was it. As though it were only the finest of veneers layered over his anger.

Polly shook her head. She was being ridiculous. The dark hair, olive skin, blue-eyed combination had really done something peculiar to her common sense. She didn't know him. Didn't even know very much about him and he'd have to know even less about her.

At best she'd be a name on their application for permission to film in Amrah. Maybe he just wasn't keen on a film crew coming to his country? But that hardly made sense because he could say 'no' and Minty would have to move on to another project. It was hardly something he needed to lose any sleep over.

But she might. Polly walked the length of the Long Gallery and through into the library with the wonderful smell of leather, polish and really old books. If Sheikh Rashid *did* veto the project, what would she do then? It was past time she left this place and it wasn't as though she had alternatives leaping out at her.

'Everything all right, Miss Polly?'

Polly spun round and smiled up at her stepbrother's elderly butler who'd come through the Summer Sitting Room. 'Fine. I'm just on my way to check everything's ready for the fireworks.'

'You'll find the two gentlemen from "Creative Show" in the staff room,' the butler said, the merest flicker in his eyes communicating how annoying he'd found them.

Polly smiled and gathered up the folds of her peacock-blue dress. 'We're nearly done. And the rain seems to be holding off all right so I think we'll revert to midnight. Let's get this over as soon as possible and send these people home.'

'Very good, Miss Polly.'

Miss Polly. She liked that. Henry Phillips had managed to find the perfect solution as to what to call someone who was almost one of the family but not quite.

No, not quite. She would always be the housekeeper's daughter even if her mother had married the fourteenth duke. And Henry Phillips would always remember he'd taken her into the kitchens and made her hot milk and sugar during her father's wake. It was a bond between them that would never be broken even if she was *almost* 'a member of the family'.

'Henry...?' She stopped him as a new thought occurred to her. 'What do you know about Sheikh Rashid Al Baha? He's not been to Shelton before tonight, has he?'

'No,' the butler answered with one of his rare smiles, 'but I fancy he's the money who bought Golden Mile all the same.'

'By himself?'

'Indeed.'

'He must be worth billions!'

'A little more than that,' the butler said with another thin smile. 'I doubt it was pocket change, but nothing that need worry him, I gather.'

'So why didn't he come here?' she asked with a frown.

'I imagine all the negotiations were carried out through his agent. His Grace and the anonymous buyer of Golden Mile both wished the transaction to be private.'

'Oh.'

'Why do you ask?'

'No reason.' *Almost no reason.* It had suddenly occurred to her that the look in Rashid Al Baha's cold blue eyes might have had something to do with Anthony after all. Her stepbrother made enemies easier than anyone she knew.

'And they met tonight?'

Henry nodded.

'What happened? Did they argue?'

'That would be very unusual for someone from his culture, I believe. They spoke and it was extremely cordial. But—' the elderly man searched for the correct word '—it was...shall we say, cold.'

Why? An Amrahi prince with the reputation and disposable income of this one would normally have Anthony exerting himself to charm. And even she had to own he was good at that when he saw a reason to be.

But 'cold' was exactly the word to describe the way Rashid Al Baha had looked at her earlier. Cold, angry and speculative.

CHAPTER TWO

RASHID watched the Hon Emily Coolidge finger the large diamond nestled against her rather bony chest and felt a familiar wave of boredom wash over him. This was his mother's country, the country in which he'd received much of his education, but he felt very little affinity with it. Or with the people who lived in it.

It felt empty. Soulless. Emily had to know he'd never choose her, or anyone like her, as the mother of his children. It made her behaviour inexplicable.

The brunette's finger moved again across the cool plains of the diamond droplet. There'd been a time, not so long ago, when that unspoken offer would have been appealing. In fact, he wouldn't have stopped to think about it. He'd merely have lost himself in mindless pleasure, content that Western women seemed to view these things differently.

'Will you be in London next week?'

Rashid twisted the champagne glass between thumb and forefinger, concentrating on the play of light on the liquid in his glass. He really hadn't thought much about who the mother of his children would be. It was always something for the future. Something far distant.

But now things were changing. He felt a mortality that had never touched him before. There had to be something inbuilt that made a man long to pass on his genes. To feel that he would go on...

Was that it? Was that what this gnawing dissatisfaction with his life was about? A wanting to set his place in history? To find meaning?

'I'm returning to town after this evening.' Again the brunette moved her hand suggestively across her low décolletage. 'Wouldn't it be fabulous if we could spend some time together before you fly back to Amrah?'

'No.' And then he cursed himself for what had been a staggering lack of good manners. His shoulders moved in an apologetic shrug. 'My father...'

Rashid let the sentence hang unfinished. The doctors, he knew, would do everything they could, but neither he, nor any man, could hope to foresee what the next few months would bring.

Emily leant forward and touched his hand, outwardly concerned.

Rashid studied her face. She didn't care. There was no genuine emotion in her painted eyes.

And he couldn't be bothered.

The truth of that slid into his brain like a dagger through silk. He wanted to shake these people off, move away, find space to breathe. And yet he had the responsibility of a guest towards his host's friends. A responsibility he was shirking.

It was a relief when a loud crack ripped across the general murmur of conversation. He looked out towards the formal gardens stretching down to the ornamental lake and at the white firework cascading down like some overblown pompom.

'Oh, my God, how lovely.' Emily unwound her overly

long body and stood, hand raised to shield her eyes as though that would somehow make it easier to see what was happening out in the landscaped gardens. 'Fireworks! Oh, Rashid, how beautiful.' She turned her long neck so she could look directly at him.

Another sharp crack, followed by a hiss and sizzle, and he caught sight of a particularly spectacular cascade of golden shards.

'I love fireworks!'

Vaguely, very vaguely, he was aware of the movement around the table. Chairs scraped back and then Nick's hand touching his arm. 'Coming to see?'

Rashid shook his head. He looked up and met his friend's understanding blue eyes. Nick knew why he was here and would be tolerant if his behaviour wasn't quite as it should be.

Rashid's head jerked upwards as he felt the spurt of anger flicker deep inside him. Under any other circumstances he wouldn't be here. Given half a choice he'd be back in Amrah, ready to spend precious time with his father if he was sent for. And he'd have been watching his brother's back, holding off the factions that were all too eager to turn recent events to their advantage.

His friend smiled and deftly manoeuvred the rest of the party outside. Rashid pulled a weary hand across his face and then let his eyes wander along the panelled walls. So different from home, but no less beautiful. Shelton Castle was a place of wealth. A little shabby, but in the English style of conserving all that was old regardless of fashion.

He'd come hoping to understand—and he didn't. The fifteenth Duke of Missenden was feckless and without honour. He fully deserved the destiny he had created for himself, Rashid thought, and if he'd scared him by coming here, so much the better.

Rashid was distracted by a flash of peacock-blue dipping in and out of the black-dinner-suited men clustered by the doors to the terrace. He sat back in his chair and watched Miss Pollyanna Anderson weave her way through the tightly packed throng watching the fireworks.

She was his one uncertainty. Where *did* she fit into all this? Last night he'd finally accepted Nick's statement that the dowager duchess and her daughter were not accepted by the late duke's children and therefore unlikely to be complicit in anything underhand.

But Pollyanna was too confident. She'd worked the room tonight with the assurance of someone who knew she belonged.

It had been Pollyanna who'd orchestrated the staff so they were largely inconspicuous. Pollyanna who'd managed the minor fracas earlier. He couldn't see her as someone passive. She appeared strong and capable.

So, given all that, was he prepared to accept Pollyanna Anderson's sudden desire to come to Amrah was a mere coincidence? His strong mouth twisted. And if it were not a coincidence, what he wanted to know was what she hoped to gain. And by what means did she intend to gain it?

His eyes narrowed. Did she hope to coerce him into silence by distorting what she saw in his country? Or was she some kind of a honey trap? Set to embarrass him and discredit his evidence?

That didn't feel right. She moved gracefully enough, but she didn't walk in a way that suggested she expected to be looked at. Her dress was a stunning colour, which brought out the deep blue of her eyes, but he doubted it had been made by any of the designers the women he'd spent time with would have deemed worthy of notice.

She *was* attractive, he conceded, but in a very English

way. Wide blue eyes, pale alabaster skin and hair the
colour of desert sand. But no femme fatale. And, baring
the fact he was certain she'd known exactly who he was
and where he was to be found at any given time this
evening, she'd not tried to approach him.

She'd been too busy working, controlling the events of
the evening with a skill born of practice. He watched her
as she paused, looking back towards the fireworks with a
slight smile. Then she raised a hand to rub her neck and
turned away. Her movements were rapid and she walked
with obvious purpose across the highly polished floor
towards a narrow door in the back wall.

It was the small furtive glance she made back across
the now almost empty ballroom that had Rashid on his
feet. Curiosity had always been his besetting sin and this
was beyond temptation.

Rashid sidestepped the table and followed her across the
ballroom. The door she'd walked through opened easily
and he slid quietly into what appeared to be an intimate but
ornately furnished sitting room. Gilt mirrors hung on the
opposite wall and the furniture looked as if it belonged in
a museum rather than a family home. All with a faded air
of grandeur befitting one of England's foremost stately
homes.

It took less than a second to locate Ms Anderson. She
was sitting at right angles to the fireplace on one of a pair
of brocade sofas, as yet completely unaware he'd come
in. Via her reflection he watched her slip off her shoes and
reach down to rub at her toes.

The rhythmic movement of her fingers over stock-
inged feet was unexpectedly sensual and his eyes were
riveted. Even more to the tantalising glimpse of her full
breasts as the front of her dress gaped.

Rashid forced himself to look away and his eyes

snagged on the back of her neck, with the two soft tendrils of honey-gold hair that had escaped the tight twist she'd favoured. It was the kind of neck made to be kissed. Long. Soft.

Maybe he'd underestimated her success as a potential honey trap? Pollyanna possessed a natural sensuality.

'Ms Anderson, my name is Rashid Al Baha.'

Her head snapped round to look at him and her mouth formed an almost perfect 'o'. 'Wh—?'

'I apologise,' Rashid said, moving farther into the room, 'for disturbing you.'

She hurriedly returned her feet to the torturous-looking heels she'd been wearing and stood up, letting the soft folds of her dress mass around her ankles. 'No. That is, I…' One agitated hand twisted the loose curls back into her chignon. 'I'm sorry, did you need something?'

Rashid stopped a few feet away from her. 'I'm no great lover of fireworks.'

'Oh.'

Again that almost perfect oval. His eyes flicked across her flushed face and over a body that he knew Western convention would deem too curvaceous. She was not a conventional beauty, perhaps, but he felt a vague sense of disappointment that she was not a consolation prize.

Centuries ago he might have taken this woman in recompense for her stepbrother's sins. Maybe there'd been wisdom in that. It was just possible that a few weeks in the arms of Miss Pollyanna Anderson might go some way to dissipating his anger.

He watched the tremulous quiver of her full lips and felt a renewed rush of sexual awareness. Rashid clenched his teeth and forced himself to look at the famed Rembrandt hanging over the ornate fireplace.

'I thought this might be a good opportunity to talk,' he said, looking back at her, determined to regain control.

'Talk? I…' Her hand smoothed out the front of her dress, drawing attention to her curves.

'Or are you not aware your request to film in my country has been passed to me?'

'W-we did think it might have been.' And then she smiled.

She had an amazing smile. Rashid felt the full impact, particularly when it was combined with the feel of her hand in his. 'It's really kind of you, Your Highness.'

'Rashid, please.'

The beating pulse at the base of her neck was the only indication he had that she wasn't entirely comfortable. She had such pale skin. So white.

'Rashid,' she repeated obediently. 'And I'm Polly.'

It took him a moment to catch up. A moment he spent remembering that he needed to let go of her hand.

'Minty suggested I try to speak to you about it tonight, but I doubt I'd have had the courage.'

'Minty?'

'Araminta Woodville-Brown. She's the producer.' Polly hesitated. 'Hasn't she been in contact with you? I thought…'

Had she? Faced with a pair of clear blue eyes looking up at him he wasn't sure that he remembered.

'I thought that must be why you wanted to talk to me.'

'I've merely seen the paperwork,' he said in a voice that sounded overly formal. He couldn't seem to help it.

'Oh. Well…' she moistened her lips with the tip of her tongue '…Minty thinks…that is, she believes it would make a good programme and I…'

She broke off again and took a deep breath. Then she smiled. Her blue eyes glinting with sudden laughter. 'I'm making a real hash of this, aren't I? I'm so sorry.'

If she'd been hoping to deliver a polished presentation in support of the application sitting on his desk she certainly was, but at this precise moment he was more inclined to approve it than he would have believed possible.

She took another deep breath and Rashid found himself watching the rise and fall of her breasts. The fact they were now demurely covered made it more erotic than anything the Hon Emily Coolidge had managed in a dress practically slashed to her navel.

'Perhaps I could get you something to drink and we could start again?'

'I need nothing.'

'D-do you mind if I pour myself some water?'

'Not at all.'

Polly walked over to the mahogany bow sideboard and lifted a glass from the top of the water jug, chinking the two together. The noise was loud in the quiet of the room. Behind her, Rashid stood perfectly still. He was like some great big black spider. Motionless, and poised to strike.

Did spiders strike? Not that it really mattered. Rashid Al Baha looked as if *he* might strike. And, honestly, the reality of him was unnerving enough without adding the curse of her imagination. Tomorrow morning, the *minute* she opened her eyes, she was going to ring Minty and tell her the next time she had a good idea for smoothing out a bureaucratic hiccup she was to do it herself.

'I—I always keep some water in here in case I need it,' she said, trying to regulate her voice. Her hand shook slightly as she poured and a splodge landed partly on the tray and partly on the wood.

Everything slowed to half speed as the water spread out on the highly polished surface. 'Oh, God, please no!' she said, swiping at it with her hand. 'Oh, help!'

This was like a waking nightmare and it couldn't be happening to her. It couldn't. What was it about her karma that sent everything around her into free fall? Her fingers made no impact on the puddle of water and she turned round, looking for something that would be more effective.

'Here.' Rashid stepped forward, holding out a clean, starched white handkerchief.

She grabbed it and started to mop up the water, then carefully wiped the underside of the glass. 'Thanks. I'm not usually that clumsy.' And then, 'Actually, I am. I'm jinxed,' she said, handing back his handkerchief. 'But, look, no permanent damage. I live to destroy another day.'

She looked up and caught the waft of something tangy on his skin. A clean masculine smell. And she could see the dark shadow on his chin.

Powerful. That was the only word to describe Rashid Al Baha. It was apt for everything about him. Hard, masculine features, a honed physique that confirmed everything she'd read about his predilection for dangerous sports and a steady blue gaze that was startling against the black of his hair.

'Th-that sideboard came to Shelton in seventeen ninety-two.' Polly could feel the heat burning in her cheeks. 'It would be dreadful if I was the first person in all that time to put a mark on it.'

Rashid smiled. He'd smiled before, politely, but this was something different. For the first time it reached his eyes. Maybe he was human, after all? Wouldn't that be a surprise?

'I'm sorry. Please take a seat.' She pulled at the chain around her neck. 'I should have said that before. I'm afraid I'm a little nervous.'

That devastating smiled widened. 'There is no need to be.'

'You clearly don't know Minty. I'm no good at this type of thing.' Polly took her water with her and sat back down in the corner of the sofa. 'She'd do this so much better than I can.'

Rashid chose the sofa opposite. His eyes were still firmly resting on her face. It was unsettling. And that was putting it mildly.

'Take it to him.' Minty's final words to her were echoing in her head. She was fairly sure her friend hadn't factored in spilling water over a valuable antique, tripping over her words and generally not being able to think of anything anyway. Her mind was a complete blank.

And all the while those blue eyes watched her. Polly looked away and gently chewed at her bottom lip.

'I would be interested to know how you come to be involved?' he prompted, as though he knew she was never going to be able to get started alone.

He had an amazing voice, too. His accent wasn't so dissimilar to the ones she heard every day, but the way he put his words together, the stress he placed on the syllables was certainly different. Unmistakably foreign despite his English-public-school education.

'I suppose it's because it was my idea. In a way. Although I didn't expect it would happen.' She raised her eyes back up to his face. 'Minty's the film-maker. She wants to make an hour-and-a-half programme which could be broken up into three half-hour slots. Something like that.'

His feet moved and Polly found herself looking down at his highly polished Italian shoes. She was sure they were Italian. Expensive and very beautiful. Everything about him screamed an understated wealth. The kind of wealth that could buy a racehorse like Golden Mile as an individual rather than as part of a consortium. Even in her stepbrother's world that was unusual.

And here she was, sitting in the North Sitting Room with her heart in her mouth and her future, it would seem, resting on her ability to convince this man it was a good idea.

'With you presenting?'

'Yes, that's the idea.'

Rashid inclined his head. He was like a panther. The thought slid into her head. That was a far better analogy than a spider. He was all contained power, unpredictable and dangerous.

'I know we'd be the first film crew allowed into Amrah—'

'The second.'

'Second?'

'When my grandfather became King he was eager to open our country to the West. Fourteen years ago he allowed a programme to be made and the result was deeply offensive to both my family and our people.'

Talk about wanting the ground to open up beneath you. 'I didn't know that.'

Any other man and she'd have asked what had been offensive about it, but she didn't feel she could. There was an impenetrable barrier around Rashid Al Baha.

Polly moistened her lips and tried to find the words that would convince him that their intention was not to offend. Not in any way.

'Our programme would focus on Elizabeth Lewis's journey across Amrah in the late eighteen eighties. We'd like to retrace her steps, see some of the things she describes.'

'Such as?'

'The desert. Fortresses.' This was so difficult. She was

floundering and she knew it. She hadn't thought much about what she would see as the decision wasn't hers. 'Camel-riding. Maybe even camel-*racing*. I believe she did that at one point.'

Rashid sat back on the sofa. 'An important part of Amrah's culture, but not one that is generally looked on favourably in the West.'

'But the king has forbidden child jockeys by law. It— it was that,' she struggled on, 'which people found difficult to accept. Over here, I mean.'

Was she imagining a hint of a smile in those cold blue eyes? He really was the most unfathomable man. But, if his reputation with women had any basis in reality, he must be able to use that smile to good effect sometimes.

What would that feel like? If Rashid Al Baha looked at her with desire? With wanting? She felt a slightly hysterical bubble of laughter start in the pit of her stomach and spiral upwards. If His Highness Prince Rashid bin Khalid bin Abdullah Al Baha turned his notorious playboy charm on her she'd run in the opposite direction. He was an absolutely terrifying man.

'I see. It is helpful to have it explained.' The smile in his eyes became more definite.

Polly just hoped she'd wake up in a few minutes and realise this whole conversation had never happened.

Of course he didn't need her to tell him what the international community thought about child jockeys. He was a highly educated man. A leader of men. He'd probably even been instrumental in implementing the ban.

She could feel the heat rise in her face and a dry, nervous tickle irritate the back of her throat. Just wait 'til she got Minty on the phone tomorrow. If it turned out she had known about the 'offensive' programme made earlier Polly was going to personally shoot her.

'What I meant to say was that we wouldn't be saying anything…contentious. It's more a human-interest type of thing. A personal journey.'

'Personal?'

'Yes. Well, yes. That's the plan.'

'But not yours?'

She shrugged. 'Only in as much as Elizabeth Lewis is my great-great-grandmother.'

'Your great-great-grandmother?'

'On my father's side.'

A frown snapped across his forehead. 'That wasn't in the paperwork.'

'I suppose because it's not really relevant, is it?'

For a moment Rashid said nothing. 'Her legacy is still remembered in Amrah.'

Polly risked a smile. 'I still don't know very much about her, but I gather she was…ahead of her time.'

This time she was left in no doubt that his eyes were smiling, but his voice was still dry. 'An unusual woman.'

Did he consider that a good or a bad thing?

'That's it, really. Minty and I made a short programme on Shelton Castle about two years ago—'

'I've seen it.'

'You have?' she asked, her eyes nervously flicking up. 'Anyway, it was fun—and quite successful in ratings terms so Minty found it easy to get the funding for this one. And, well, th-that really is it…' She tailed off lamely. 'She's put it all together and I know she'll be more than happy to talk it over with you. I'm just there to provide a personal connection to the subject.'

And because Minty was quite determined her friend would find a life for herself away from Shelton. There was no need to mention that. It made her sound incredibly wet.

Besides, Minty might change her mind when she heard

how this conversation had gone. If Rashid had even the slightest inclination to open his country to a film crew again he'd want to be sure the resulting programme would be well executed and she hadn't done much to instil him with confidence.

Rashid stood up in one fluid movement. It was that panther thing again. He was all restrained power and energy, his mind finding an outlet in movement, and yet she would never describe him as agitated. In fact, you couldn't really imagine anything much throwing this man off his balance.

All of a sudden she didn't care one way or the other. She'd done her best and that was all anyone could do. If this didn't come off something would. Life was like that. It couldn't go on for ever without a bend in the road.

Polly finished off the last of her water and stood up, cradling the glass in two hands. 'W-what do you think? Can we come?'

His blue eyes flashed across at her. 'There would need to be conditions.'

'Of course. Not that I'd have anything to do with any of that. But Minty was wonderful when she made the programme on Shelton. Everyone involved was really considerate of the castle and there was nothing intrusive or unpleasant about the experience.'

Much to her annoyance Polly could hear a tremor in her voice. She wanted to sound confident and yet, somehow, in front of this man it wasn't possible.

'She's your friend.' He brushed her comment aside as though it wasn't worth nothing. It was the spur she needed.

'The programme on Shelton was one of five Minty made about different English stately homes. No one complained. She's a talented and very successful documentary film maker.' Polly raised her chin. 'So, what do you think?' she asked, forcing herself to meet his eyes. There was nothing to see. Not by so much as a flicker did he give away what he was thinking.

'Why now?'

She'd been braced for an outright rejection and his question surprised her. 'Now? You want to know why now?' she echoed, and then gathered herself together. 'Because of the weather. If we want to film in the desert—'

Rashid cut her off. 'I will think about it,' he said, turning away and striding across the room.

Polly stood, slightly stunned as the door shut behind him. She drew in a shaky breath. Heaven help her. That had been scary. But…he *had* left her with a little bit of hope— and, even ten minutes ago, that was more than she'd expected.

CHAPTER THREE

POLLY adjusted her long dark head-covering, trying to pull it farther over her blond hair. 'How do I stop this thing slipping off?'

Pete, standing closest to her, gave the front a gentle tug. 'Maybe a hair clip? I don't know. Do your best. It's not required of Westerners to cover their heads unless they're entering a holy place.'

Yes, she knew. But Minty's thirty-two-page ring-bound instruction booklet had also said a simple covering was sensible in the heat and generally considered respectful.

'Just relax about everything. So, where is this interpreter guy? Ali something, isn't it?' he said with a look over his shoulder at the cameraman.

Ali Al-Sabt. She knew that, too. She'd gone through Minty's 'bible' and highlighted anything that might be important in fluorescent yellow. She practically knew it verbatim, but there was no point saying anything.

'He should be holding up a card. Easy enough to spot,' Baz said, scanning the crowded concourse.

'You'd have thought.'

Polly let the conversation wash over her. The five men Minty had assembled were all veteran travellers. They'd worked together before, knew each other well and clearly considered her dead weight in their team. It didn't matter. She was here. And it was absolutely incredible.

There were people everywhere. The guidebook had said that Amrahis regarded travel as an event and that whole families tended to see their loved ones off and meet those coming home. It was all a world away from her quiet and controlled departure from Heathrow, but she loved it. The noise, the bustle, the general excitement of the place.

'There! John's over there.'

A hand waved high above the crowd and Polly allowed Pete to steer her towards it, struggling to keep the wheels of her case straight.

A smiling man in a traditional white *dishdasha* nodded as they approached. *'As-salaam alaykum.'*

Polly murmured, *'Wa alaykum as-salaam.'* Which she seriously hoped meant 'Peace to you' or something like. Leastways that had been what her *Phrases for the Business Traveller to Amrah* had said, though her pronunciation was bound to be hit and miss despite the accompanying CD.

'This is Ali Al-Sabt—'

Behind them there was a loud shout and then a general hum of excitement. Polly's eyes went to the glass-protected VIP walkway, high above. At first she noticed the speed at which a group of men on it were walking, their sense of purpose—and then recognition hit her.

She felt as though her stomach had plummeted a couple of hundred feet. Even in the traditional robes of his country Rashid Al Baha was unmistakable. *Powerful.*

For the tiniest fraction of a second she fancied his footsteps slowed and his eyes met hers. She felt as though everything around her had frozen in a blur of colour.

There was only him…and her. Everyone else was as still as if they'd been paused by a TV remote. He looked directly at her. She was sure he did.

For a moment.

And then the world around her restarted, the noise of the concourse louder than before.

'That's Sheikh Rashid Al Baha. He must be returning from the summit in Balkrash.'

Polly wasn't sure which member of the team said that. She watched as Rashid disappeared from sight, still feeling a little shell shocked. She wasn't alone either. Judging from the reaction of the people around her, the Crown Prince's second son enjoyed a film-star status in his own country. There were fingers pointing all around. An excited chattering, which punctured the general hubbub of airport noise.

'What was the summit about?' she asked, bending to adjust the label on her bag.

'Perhaps best if we don't ask those kind of questions,' Steve, the one American of the team, said quietly. 'Let's keep ourselves out of the politics. Contravene that one and I guess we'll be on the first plane out of here.'

Polly agreed and stood quietly by while they waited for Graham to join them with all their equipment.

Seeing Rashid had brought back all the feelings she'd experienced when she'd met him at Shelton. He unsettled her. *Worried* her. It wasn't as though she felt he was attracted to her. Not that. It was that he…was watching her.

Watching her, looking for something that would mean he could make a decision about her. And because she knew he wasn't a man to have as your enemy it…*bothered* her. At least, she thought that was what she thought.

'Ready to go, Polly?' Baz said, coming behind her.

She nodded and let herself be steered towards the exit.

Once outside the intense heat hit her like a wall, driving everything else from her mind. She'd come expecting the temperatures to be high, but this was searing. Direct sunlight made her grateful for the scarf she had fashioned into a hijab covering her head. Less about modesty, perhaps, and everything about practicality.

'Please to come this way,' Ali said, indicating a line of waiting cars. Sleek, expensive and so black you might imagine they'd been dipped in oil. And more incredibly they were surrounded by uniformed guards. *Guards with guns.*

'Please. This way.'

Polly looked over her shoulder in time to see Pete duck down into the third car. Graham was anxiously watching their expensive equipment safely stowed away, and John, Baz and Steve had already vanished.

'Miss Anderson,' Ali said, indicating the second car. As she moved towards it the door was held open. Disorientated, she meekly did what was wanted, only hesitating when she realised there was a man already inside. A man she recognised.

'You?' she said foolishly.

Rashid Al Baha's blue eyes met hers. 'As you see.'

'I—I wasn't expecting to see... I mean...' *Oh, hell!* Polly pulled at the scarf covering her blond hair in what she recognised was a nervous gesture. 'Were you supposed to be meeting us? I'm sure we weren't told—'

His eyes seemed to dance. 'This is a spontaneous gesture of hospitality. There is no way I could have arranged my timetable today to coincide with yours.'

'Oh.' And then, rather belatedly, 'Thank you.'

'*Afwan.*'

You're welcome, she mentally translated, foolishly pleased the hours she'd spent poring over her phrase book were paying dividends. 'Are you sure we're allowed to be travelling together?'

Rashid settled himself more comfortably in his seat, resting his head back on the rest. 'You have an inaccurate view of my country.'

'I merely wondered whether it was appropriate with you being a member of the royal family.'

'Ah.' He turned his head so that he could look at her. 'I think you'll find that, as a member of the royal family, I'm permitted to do as I choose.'

Polly wasn't sure what to answer. Her explanation hadn't been true either, because she *had* wondered whether it was usual for a woman to travel alone in a private car with an Amrahi man who wasn't a family member. And it seemed Rashid was totally aware of that. His blue eyes were still glinting. Teasing.

Well, if he didn't care, why should she? This wasn't her country. She deliberately concentrated on fastening her seat belt. With the door shut and the tinted windows closed the atmosphere was pleasantly cool. Polly sighed and settled back into the softest leather seat she'd ever sat in. Soft as butter. She let her fingers rest on the suppleness of it and tried not to think how close Rashid Al Baha was to her. Or how much he unnerved her.

And he *really* did unnerve her. On every level there was. This close she could feel him breathe, strong and even. It seemed to pulse through her. As did her awareness of his taut body, thighs slightly apart and feet firmly planted against the sway of the car.

'You've just returned from a summit, I gather,' she said in an effort to break the silence.

'Yes.'

'D-did it go well?' Steve's words of caution came flooding into her mind. Politics was a no-go area. Part of the stipulations Rashid had made was that they didn't film anything that could be construed as military or politically sensitive. 'I don't mean to pry, obviously.'

He said nothing, merely watched her beneath hooded eyes.

'I still can't believe I'm really here.' Polly nervously pleated one end of her scarf. 'One minute I'm discussing whether we need to take the chandelier in the Great Hall down for cleaning and the next I'm here.'

Not the greatest conversational gambit she'd ever tried, but it was the best she could do. Every sense she had was throbbing with awareness. Every hair on her body standing to attention. She couldn't remember reacting to a man like this…ever. But then she'd never met a man quite like him.

Polly turned to look out of the tinted car window. Partly because she needed to have something other than Rashid Al Baha to focus on, and partly because she was captivated by what she was glimpsing.

The guidebooks she'd devoured hadn't really prepared her. She'd come expecting desert and wide blue skies and was confronted by modern glass, steel constructions and six-lane motorways.

'Amrah is a place of great contrasts,' Rashid said, as though he'd been able to read her thoughts.

'I had no idea Samaah would be like this. How old a city is it?'

He shifted in his seat, drawing her attention back to him as much by that as his voice. 'Centuries old, but its current incarnation is only forty. It has become a financial centre and brought a great deal of wealth to the country.'

She'd known that. Only that wasn't part of Elizabeth Lewis's story and she'd not focused her attention on what that would mean. 'Amrah doesn't have oil, does it?'

'Some, but the reserves are fast running out.'

Polly turned again to look out of the window. She watched as the buildings sped past, unwilling to miss anything.

If they'd arrived by sea, she knew from guidebooks she'd have been met with fortified ramparts dating back centuries. A testament to its troubled history. But this…was all so newly constructed.

'Are you disappointed?'

'Stunned.'

'We have the camels and the Bedouin tents, too.' His voice was laced with humour.

Polly turned her head to look at him and smiled. Her first since getting into the car. She settled back into her seat. 'Do you spend much time in the desert?'

'Like most of my countrymen I return at least once a year to reconnect myself with my heritage. A tradition, if you will. Something you English seem to understand.'

He said it as if she were a different species. 'You're half English.'

'My mother is English, but I am entirely Arab.'

How did he manage to turn his voice to flint? Polly adjusted her scarf, tucking one end carefully over her shoulder.

'I'm flattered you have so obviously researched me,' he continued, his voice slicing through the silence.

Polly glanced up at his calmly arrogant face. Did he honestly think that? That she'd consciously sat down and 'Googled' him?

She *had*. But she'd infinitely prefer it if he didn't think it. 'Merely read the magazines in the hairdresser's,' she corrected. 'You're often featured. Being royalty.'

'Then I should be the one asking the questions, perhaps.'

'There's nothing particularly interesting about me—'
She broke off as she caught sight of the Majan
International Hotel. 'Isn't that where we're staying?'

'There's been a change.'

Polly looked at him sharply. 'What kind of change?'

'I have decided to offer you the hospitality of my home
while you are in Samaah. You and your colleagues,' he
added as blandly as though he hadn't seen her quick
glance through the back window to make sure they were
still being followed.

She wasn't particularly reassured. Why was he doing
this? He might have given them permission to film here,
but even Minty hadn't imagined he'd wanted them here.

'Is that a spontaneous decision?'

'Not at all. How else could I have arranged for cars to
be here to meet you?'

Quite. And Polly had the definite feeling very little in
Rashid's life was left to chance.

'My sister is waiting to receive you. I was to have
joined you later.'

His sister?

'Is it far from the airport?'

'No.'

Through the window to her left Polly could see they
were still flanked by motorcycle outriders. It deflected her
interest. 'Are they necessary?'

'It is wise.'

'Because we might be attacked?'

'Because I might be,' he returned coolly.

Rashid watched the blond Englishwoman process that.
He could sense her uncertainty, see the questions she
wanted to ask but felt she couldn't. For now that suited
him perfectly well.

He stretched. 'It is a minimal threat but a significant

one, particularly while there is uncertainty about Amrah's political future.'

'I've read about that.' Her blue eyes met his. 'I was sorry to hear your father's ill again.'

Just that. No spurious sympathy in her face. He'd spent much of last week receiving condolences from men he knew would be pleased to hear his father had died and one of his more conservative uncles named as successor. Words meant nothing, but her quiet statement felt genuine.

It was that dichotomy again. The difference between what he knew and what he felt. She *seemed* genuine—but there was no one as plausible as someone who was making it her business to appear so.

'His doctors have been able to buy him a few months, but I think he will shortly be in paradise.'

'I'm so sorry.'

'I think your sympathy should be reserved for the people he is to leave behind.'

Pollyanna clutched at her scarf as it threatened to slide off her head. 'That's what I meant. It's incredibly hard to lose a parent.' Then, 'Are you sure this is the right time to have visitors like us? We would be perfectly comfortable at the hotel. And we only mean to stay in Samaah for a couple of nights.'

'I'm aware.'

'Wouldn't you rather be with your family?'

'If I'm needed I will be called.'

He watched her hesitate and then bite back whatever observation she had been tempted to make. That was just as well. He'd given more away in that single sentence than he'd intended.

Her perfume, light but exotic, swirled around him like a wisp of smoke. It seemed to drug his mind, pull truths from his lips he'd prefer left unsaid. And the truth was she was probably right. This wasn't the best time to have visitors in his home.

And certainly not this one.

Despite the dossier he'd read on Miss Pollyanna Anderson he remained uncertain of her motives in coming here. And, until he was, he'd every intention of controlling everything about her visit.

'Your family is well?'

Her blue eyes widened slightly. 'My mother's well enough.'

'And your brothers?'

'I don't have any brothers.'

It was very convincing. Yet she presumably chose to live in the home of her mother's stepson, a man he knew for a liar and a cheat, because she wanted to.

'I should have said stepbrothers,' he corrected smoothly. 'Your mother's late husband had three sons, I believe?'

'Yes. Anthony, the current Duke, is well, but I haven't seen Benedict or Simon for months. They rarely come to the castle.'

Did he believe that? All three brothers were directors of Beaufort Stud Farm with a financial stake in its success. It was inconceivable one brother should act alone in what was a family business.

Polly twisted her gold chain bracelet with long, slender fingers. *She was nervous.* He had to be wary of her, yet when he looked at her he found himself wanting to reach out and place a kiss on the inside of her wrist.

He wanted more than that if the tightening of his body was anything to go by.

Another time, another place. Rashid let the silence stretch between them. His brother had asked him to act as his right arm and Hanif couldn't afford negative publicity in the West. Not now. Not when his grandfather was looking to him to keep Amrah's financial markets steady and praying for an easy handover of power.

For now there was no choice but to keep this film crew close. Time enough to decide how much freedom he could allow them. Plenty of time to reach a conclusion about Pollyanna Anderson.

The cavalcade approached the outer gates of his home. He felt Pollyanna stiffen beside him and she turned to look at him with wide eyes.

'Welcome to my home,' he murmured.

'I-it's so beautiful.'

'*Shukran.*'

The gates opened seamlessly and the cavalcade moved forward, coming to a gentle stop. Polly unfastened her seat belt and adjusted her scarf once again, wrapping it tightly round her hair and letting both ends fall down her back. Even through the heavily tinted windows the magnificence of the place they'd been brought to was immediately obvious.

And it was old. How old she couldn't possibly judge, as the architectural style was completely unknown to her. Her door was opened and Polly accepted the wordless invitation to get out of the car. She stood, speechless, looking up at the white marble columns and the huge carved wooden doors, as intimidating as they'd surely been designed to be.

So incredibly beautiful. Breathtaking, really.

'Not bad, is it?' Pete remarked, coming up to stand beside her. 'I'm sorry you had to travel with Sheikh Rashid alone. You were there one minute and not the next. I'm not sure how that happened.'

Didn't he? Polly was in very little doubt. She watched

as Rashid paused to speak to one of his staff. She had no doubt he'd orchestrated everything that had happened. Nothing at all was left to chance.

Which meant he'd intended to ride with her alone. Intended to talk to her.

'Better be a bit careful about that. He's got a reputation. Probably because he's not allowed to play at home, if you know what I mean.'

Polly's eyes involuntarily wandered over to where Rashid was.

'But those rules might not extend to you since you're English. I can't believe this,' Pete said, looking about the palace with professional interest. 'It's incredible. I wonder if we can wangle filming here.'

Rashid walked towards them, an Amrahi prince to the ends of his fingers, Polly thought. And, for the first time in her hearing, he spoke in Arabic she didn't understand.

'Come. We will have refreshments.' The interpreter was almost beside himself with excitement. He was hovering about and practically rubbing his hands together in glee.

John moved closer to where she was standing and spoke quietly, 'This is a quite amazing honour. Try to follow my lead if you can. Hospitality is very important in this part of the world. There will probably be some kind of coffee-drinking ritual.'

Polly nodded and moved to follow. John stopped her. 'It's possible you might not be included. You might be taken to have refreshments with the women. I don't know. Just go with the flow. No point in upsetting him.'

She wasn't at all happy with that. The idea of being taken off, goodness only knew where, to make conversation with women who might or might not understand her language wasn't appealing. Particularly when she knew

Rashid was perfectly able to bend things to his will if he wanted to.

Still, she'd fight that battle if she had to. Polly adjusted her scarf once more, conscious of the heat burning through the dark fabric.

Rashid came to stand within six feet of her. 'I wish to introduce you to my sister, who is acting as my hostess and who will be able to help you with anything at all while you are staying in my home.'

'Thank you.' She looked past him to where a very beautiful woman was standing.

'My sister, Her Highness Princess Bahiyaa bint Khalid bint Abdullah Al Baha. Bahiyaa, this is Miss Pollyanna Anderson.'

The other woman moved forward to shake her hand. Polly automatically extended her own.

'You are very welcome, Miss Anderson.'

'Polly, please.'

'And I am Bahiyaa.'

Older than Rashid? Younger? She couldn't tell.

'You must be tired from your flight.'

Polly wasn't sure about that. The only thing she knew with certainty was that beside Bahiyaa she was impossibly creased. Minty's guide to all things Amrahi hadn't led her to expect anything like the exquisite gold embroidery on Bahiyaa's tunic, or the carefully co-ordinated scarf she wore over her head. The sunlight caught the gold bangles at her wrist and the overwhelming impression was one of shimmering beauty.

Erring on the side of caution, she, on the other hand, had picked a long-sleeved too-thick cotton top and paired it with an ankle-length linen skirt, both in olive-green. In the glamour stakes she was coming a very poor second.

'Shall we move in out of the heat?'

It seemed to be expected that the men would go first. Somehow with Bahiyaa beside her that didn't seem rude. It was simply different from the way things were done in England. And, anyway, she'd never quite understood why it was polite to encourage a woman into a room first. She always hated being thrust into a room of people she didn't know.

They walked across a central courtyard and through another pair of intricately carved wooden doors. The ceiling of the room beyond soared and Polly's eye was immediately captivated by the geometric decoration that seemed to cover every available surface.

Another pair of doors, another room beyond. And then they came to a room that was exquisitely beautiful for an entirely different reason. Glass doors had been opened out onto a garden. Polly couldn't see much of it but the scent of flowers wafting in was heady. *Roses.* Was that possible? Surely in these kinds of temperatures they must be incredibly difficult to grow?

A low table was central to the room and around it there were long couches in rich port-coloured silk. Polly watched carefully as Bahiyaa sank gracefully down and copied her, carefully tucking her skirt around her legs.

'As soon as you have had some refreshments I will take you to your room,' Bahiyaa said with a warm smile. 'By then your luggage will have been unpacked.'

Would it? Oh, heck! Polly had this terrible mental picture of the contents of her suitcase. She'd thought she'd imagined every possible scenario, but staying in an Amrahi palace hadn't been one of them. Having staff unpack for her was another.

Opposite, John was lounging comfortably on his couch, deep in conversation with his host. Minty had said she'd wanted him particularly because he'd worked so often in

Arab countries. He did make it look easy, but all the other team members seemed to be taking this whole experience in their stride. The Amrahi interpreter was smiling as though his life would never reach a greater height than this moment.

Polly tried to think of it in terms she would understand. This must be like being invited to Royal Lodge, the Duke of York's home. And, yet, it wasn't quite the same because the Al Baha family wielded real power rather than mere influence.

Today, only a few hours ago, Rashid had been at a summit with other Arab leaders. When she stopped to think about it, how *incredible* was that? She understood how important it was they kept themselves out of Amrahi politics, but how could you not be curious to know what had been discussed? A summit was something that would be reported worldwide. The decisions made there would impact on a whole region.

And *this* man was a part of that.

'Playboy sheikh' maybe, but on his home turf he was something else entirely. Every eye in the room seemed to be resting on him. It was his personality that was the dominant force.

'This is your first visit to Amrah?' Bahiyaa asked.

'My first visit anywhere, unless you count a long weekend in Paris with some university friends.'

'Then we must make absolutely sure your stay is delightful.' She paused while staff quietly came in with small plates of fresh dates, recognisable but only just. They were plump and almost jewel-like. Another couple brought plates of what looked like deep-fried balls together with bowls of a syrupy-looking sauce.

She'd read about the importance of coffee in this part of the world in her travel guides, but she'd expected her first experience of it would be in one of Samaah's modern coffee houses.

And she'd not expected to be tasting it under Rashid's watchful eye. He was aware of everything. A little out of her sight line, but she was certain he was listening to her conversation with his sister while he conducted a different one.

Polly had never felt so out of depth in her entire life. Not even when her mother had first announced her engagement to Richard and her bedroom had moved from the staff quarters to the family wing. That had been strange. But *this* was completely and utterly alien. There were no familiar points of reference at all.

She cast a surreptitious glance in his direction. Rashid's mother might have been English, the largest part of his education undertaken in her country, but it was hard to believe Rashid had had any Western influences in his life at all.

A man walked forward holding a silver tray on which was a type of coffee-pot and eight small china cups. He stopped by Rashid, who murmured something in Arabic before pouring coffee into one of the cups. Then he sipped. Placing the empty cup back on the tray, he poured a second cup and passed it to her.

She knew enough about this ritual to know it was considered the height of bad manners to refuse. Careful not to touch his fingers, she took hold of the handle-less cup with her right hand, as instructed in Minty's 'bible', and looked down into a thick translucent yellow drink.

It looked…foul, if she was perfectly honest, and it smelt incredibly strong. Polly looked at Bahiyaa for guidance as to whether she was expected to drink now or wait.

'This must be your first taste of *gahwa*. It is so much a

part of our culture that I often forget how strange it is to Western visitors. I think you'll find it quite similar to espresso.'

That wasn't especially comforting, since she'd never managed to acquire a taste for espresso.

'Try.'

Polly sipped. It was strong, with a mixture of flavours she found very strange. Her palate wasn't sufficiently developed for her to separate them out.

Bahiyaa reached out one heavily hennaed hand for a date and Polly copied her. The contrast between the bitter-tasting coffee and the sweet, succulent date was heavenly.

She looked up and caught Rashid watching her, his blue eyes openly focused on her. Her stomach clenched in recognition. Somehow, and she honestly didn't understand how, this man attracted her. Not just that. He *mesmerised* her.

Charisma. Power. *Danger.* He took her world and he changed it. He made her feel as though everything she'd ever known was now open to question. Every fundamental belief about how men and women reacted to each other now needed to be rethought.

Rashid's piercing blue eyes burned through her. The heavy scent of roses, the bitter taste of coffee in her mouth, the feel of heat surrounding her all combined. Polly watched, fixed like a rabbit in headlights, as Rashid drank his coffee.

She noticed the movement of his throat as he swallowed. Noticed the way his hand held the cup. Strong, beautiful hands. The kind of hands you would want to caress your body. And then her eyes travelled up to his lips. The kind of lips you would *want* to kiss you.

This was fantasy. She didn't know him. Knew very little about him, even. He wasn't, and couldn't ever be, part of her world, but what she was feeling was as old as time itself. She knew it, even though it frightened her.

She wanted him. And that wanting had nothing to do with liking or a desire to nurture. It owed nothing to shared values and goals. All the things she thought were important. This was about passion. Desire. An instinctive knowledge that sex with this man would be amazing.

Polly raised a hand up to her forehead. Blood was pulsing in her temples and she felt as if an iron band were tightening around her chest. She couldn't breathe in the heat. There was only an overwhelming need to lie down. To sleep. To…

'Polly.'

She heard Bahiyaa's voice as though it were some way away. And then there was nothing.

Rashid was on his feet.

'She's fainted.' Bahiyaa looked up, Polly's wrist held in her hand. 'It must have been the heat.'

He stood back as water was brought in a large iced jug and placed on the central table.

'Polly? Can you hear me?'

There was no sign of life other than the gentle rise and fall of her breasts. Her blond hair was splayed out across the ruby fabric of the couch. She looked pale and vulnerable. Beautiful. Rashid clenched his hands into fists by his side. His sister was certainly right in thinking that Polly had fainted, but he was less certain the cause was the heat.

Whatever it was that had passed between them was mutual. He'd seen the open desire in her eyes, read her thoughts as clearly as if she'd spoken them aloud. He'd seen the surprise in them, too, and knew she wasn't used to reacting to a man the way she did to him.

He watched her eyelids flutter and the soft parting of

her lips. 'Gentlemen, might I suggest I show you the rose garden while Ms Anderson recovers?' he said, his voice clipped. 'My sister will stay with her.'

The words were sensible, but Rashid stayed looking down at Polly.

'I will come and tell you how she is later,' his sister promised, brushing a gentle hand across Polly's forehead.

He wanted to push her aside. If there were no one in this room it would be his hand touching her face... And he *wanted* that with an intensity that amazed him.

'Rashid.'

Still he hesitated.

'Rashid,' Bahiyaa prompted again, 'you have guests.'

It had been no part of his plan to find Polly Anderson sexually desirable. And, yet, in that moment when he'd looked at her bravely drinking her first cup of *gahwa* he'd felt something shift.

He swore silently. No, before that. He'd felt it back in Shelton Castle. It was why Polly was in Amrah now when the sensible course of action would have been to refuse their application to film.

They were here because *she* fascinated him. Against all logic.

And his sister knew that. Her dark eyes looked up at him, a soft smile on her lips. She *knew*.

Rashid forced his hands to relax by his sides. It was the lure of the forbidden and he *would* master it. He had no place in his life for a woman like Pollyanna Anderson—even if she were not related by marriage to a man he fully intended to ruin.

'I'm sure my sister will manage better alone.' Abruptly he turned and moved towards the garden.

CHAPTER FOUR

POLLY awoke in a comfortable bed, cool cotton covering her, and it took a moment for her to realise where she was. Not at Shelton. Not any more. She was in *Rashid's* home. *Rashid Al Baha's palatial home.*

Her eyes took in the strange room. Presumably she'd been carried here because she sure as heck couldn't remember walking. *Carried.*

Polly raised a hand to shield her eyes, as though that would block out the image of that. Who had carried her? One of her colleagues? *Rashid?*

The last thing she actually remembered was the world slipping away and the overwhelming feeling of sickness that had accompanied it.

'There is nothing to worry about,' a female voice spoke softly. 'You fainted in the heat.'

Polly took her hand away and looked across the shadowy room to where Princess Bahiyaa was sitting reading by soft lamplight. Rashid's sister set the book down on the small hexagonal table and stood up.

'The heat and humidity here in Samaah is very different from anything in England. I should have arranged for refreshments to be served in an air-conditioned part of the palace,' she said, pouring out a glass of water from the jug set out beside the bed. 'I'm so sorry.'

Polly raised herself up on her elbow and pulled the pillow up behind her, only then noticing she was still in her clothes. Time to be grateful for small mercies. 'Carried' was humiliating enough, 'undressed' would have been terminally mortifying.

She brushed her hair off her face. 'I've never fainted before. I'm really embarrassed.'

'There is no need. The fault is mine.'

It wasn't. Polly knew it wasn't, but then it hadn't been her fault either. Nor had it been Rashid's, but his blue eyes were the last thing she remembered.

'*Shukran,*' she said, accepting the glass Bahiyaa gave her.

'Do you speak Arabic?'

'Only a few words and I'm not sure how useful they'll be.' She took a sip of water. '"*Ma-atakallam arabi*" might be, I suppose, but there's not a lot of point in saying "I don't know much Arabic" in anything other than English.'

Bahiyaa laughed. 'It is lovely that you have tried. May I?' she asked, indicating the side of the bed.

Polly nodded.

'While you were sleeping I arranged for some of my clothes to be brought for you. I saw that much of what you have will be uncomfortably warm even at this time of the year.'

Princess Bahiyaa had seen the contents of her suitcase. Oh...*hell*! Polly's toes squirmed at the thought of how she'd packed her case: socks balled down the sides and underwear she really should have binned months ago tucked inside her interpretation of 'modest and conservative' clothing. 'I couldn't, I—'

'It is no matter. Please.' Bahiyaa smiled. 'And it is my

pleasure. And maybe you would like a refreshing shower,' she said, pointing at a door in the far corner, 'before having a little to eat? You will feel much better, I think.'

Polly glanced down at her wristwatch. She made a quick mental calculation. Five o'clock UK time would mean it was a little past nine in Amrah. Too late to be asking her hosts to organise food...

But...the prospect of food was too tempting to put up a really convincing fight. And a shower would be wonderful.

'I will organise it now and be back shortly.'

Polly waited until Bahiyaa quietly shut the door before setting her glass down on the side table and gingerly pushing back the light covering that had been placed over her. The floor beneath her feet was tiled and cool. The room was impossibly beautiful, with dark wood furniture that was so burnished it seemed to shimmer.

Carved wooden screens were at the windows and bright jewel-coloured fabrics were draped over *the* most enormous bed. Polly bit back a smile. There'd be room for a sheikh and his entire harem in a bed that size. It was incredible and, if she set her English reserve to one side for a moment, wasn't it just the most exciting thing to stay in an Amrahi palace rather than some impersonal hotel?

Her great-great-grandmother would certainly have thought so. Elizabeth would probably have had no hesitation in borrowing Princess Bahiyaa's clothes either, Polly thought, fingering the silk of the pale pink tunic laid out across the foot of the bed. For just this little while wouldn't it be wonderful to set aside all of her inhibitions? To live boldly?

Polly let the tunic drop back on the bed and padded over to where Bahiyaa had said she'd find a shower. She stopped on the threshold, stunned by the acres of black marble and a highly decadent sunken bath.

Aware Rashid's sister could return at any moment, Polly opted for a shower, and in the quickest time possible, before scurrying back to the bedroom. Bahiyaa's clothes were waiting for her. Tempting her. The silver threads in the fabric glinting in the lamplight. She felt as if she'd got the devil himself sitting on her shoulder whispering, 'Just do it.'

Polly picked up the silk…trousers and stepped into them. She supposed that was what they were called. They were loose fitting with a drawstring waist and came in tight around the ankles. And were incredibly comfortable. Already she could feel that the fierce heat of Amrah's sun would be more bearable without a tight waistband.

And the tunic felt like gossamer. She'd never worn a fabric so light, or decorated with such exquisite embroidery. Minty's instruction to dress 'conservatively' and 'modestly' had suddenly taken on a whole new meaning. This outfit was far sexier than anything she'd worn before.

It was the colours, the geometric patterns in the embroidery and the way the silk caressed her skin. It was…*glamour* with a capital 'G'.

Taking the path of least conflict at Shelton meant she had precious little experience of that. The knack of survival had been to blend into the background as much as possible and no one wearing something like this could ever hope to do that.

She felt beautiful in it. She felt as if she really had wandered into an Arabian adventure. She felt like someone else and that was exciting.

There was a soft tap at the door.

'May I come in?' Bahiyaa called.

'Yes.' Polly moved to open the door. 'Yes, of course.'

'That pink is a wonderful colour for you,' Bahiyaa said, coming into the room. 'I thought it would be. It makes your pale skin bloom.'

If any woman had said that to her in England Polly would have found it strange, but coming from Bahiyaa it was charming. She smiled. 'You're very kind to lend—'

'It is a gift,' the other woman stopped her. 'Please.' She turned and picked up a loose wraplike cloak in the same shade of dusky pink. 'There is a little more before you are ready. This we call a *thub* and you wear it over the *dishdasha*.'

'The tunic's called a *dishdasha*? I thought that was for men?'

'Similar, but a little more fitted,' Bahiyaa said with a laugh. 'Women here are not so very different from those in your country. And men are the same the world over. These,' Bahiyaa said, pointing at the loose-fitting trousers, 'we call *sirwal*.'

'*Sirwal*,' Polly repeated obediently.

'And finally,' Bahiyaa continued, reaching behind her for a long length of fine pink silk, slightly darker than either the *sirwal* or the *dishdasha* but picking out some of the embroidery in the over jacket, 'you have a *lihaf*.'

'*Lihaf* not *hijab*?'

Bahiyaa smiled and gently arranged the *lihaf* in place. 'Arabia is made up of many countries and there are many tribes within each of those. Each tribe has its own traditions, its own way of dressing and distinctive dialect.'

'I didn't mean—'

'You are looking beautiful. All we need now is sandals. I thought that since we are a similar size you might be able to manage with a pair of mine? I am a European size thirty-nine.'

Polly was beginning to feel so overwhelmed by the whole situation she'd have put on anything—and it was magical to be given the chance to wear something so romantic and feminine. She slipped her feet into

Bahiyaa's high gold sandals, a size too big but perfectly manageable.

'Perfect.' Bahiyaa stepped back to admire the effect. 'Now come.'

Polly found it hard to pull herself away from the mirror. She looked completely different. Transformed. Bahiyaa laughed as though she knew exactly what Polly was thinking. 'I never understand why some Amrahi women adopt Western dress. Our traditional clothes are…deceptively seductive, don't you think?'

Sexy, Polly amended silently. Layers of finest silk that skimmed the body were *very* sexy.

'They're gorgeous.'

'Come. I thought you would enjoy eating in the cool of the gardens.'

Reluctantly Polly let Bahiyaa lead her away from the mirror. She'd never been one for admiring herself, but she couldn't quite believe she could look so different. Even more amazingly she *felt* different.

Bahiyaa led her through a maze of narrow corridors. Polly's eyes snagged on the intricately carved archways and a fleeting glimpse of a small courtyard filled with lemon trees in pots. Then they were back in the room in which she'd fainted.

'The rose garden is one of my favourite places,' she said, leading her outside. 'Rashid's, too.'

Polly could understand why. If anything the scent of roses was stronger now than in the heat of the day. And there were other unfamiliar smells. Jasmine, maybe?

'It is a romantic place, I think.'

Like something out of an old Hollywood version of *Arabian Nights*, a real mix of East and West. Polly followed, acutely conscious of how the heels of her borrowed sandals tapped on the mosaic-tiled floor and charmed by the creamy candles placed in large ornate holders.

Bahiyaa walked on in a jangle of gold bangles. 'These gardens were here in the time of your great-great-grand-mother.'

Were they? Really? Polly looked around with new eyes. Was she looking at something Elizabeth would have seen?

'You must ask Rashid to tell you something of their history.'

'Yes, I…' *will*. That was what she'd meant to have said, but the single word dried in her throat as Rashid came out of the shadows to meet them.

Unlike her, he was no longer in traditional Amrahi clothes. He wore jeans and a light cotton shirt open at the neck, his dark hair uncovered…

'He is something of an authority.'

Sexier even than she'd thought him at Shelton. More intimidating than he'd ever been before.

'Bahiyaa.' He spoke his sister's name on a breath.

Polly glanced back over her shoulder as the suspicion Bahiyaa had orchestrated this 'accidental' meeting took hold and that her brother was not happy about it.

'I have brought your guest to see you, Rashid, now Polly is feeling so much better. Please,' his sister in-structed, gesturing towards a sumptuous pile of cushions on a raised dais, 'sit with Rashid for a while. He will love to tell you about these gardens while I organise for your food to be brought out here.'

Then, with a mischievous smile at her brother, she was gone.

Rashid's eyelids quickly came down to cover his ex-pression, but Polly was sure he didn't want her here. She was intruding. What was more she felt a little as though she'd been caught dressing up.

When she was in her own clothes, in her own country, Rashid made her feel uncomfortable enough. Here it was almost unbearable. And, face to face with Rashid again, it didn't take any thought to understand why she'd fainted. Around him she found it difficult to remember to breathe. He was scarily beautiful in an aggressive, masculine way.

And not at all likely to be interested in her. Best she remember that. A man who lived a life completely different from hers. With a very different moral code.

'Would you prefer to be alone? I—'

'No,' Rashid stopped her. 'I'm glad of your company.' He, too, indicated the richly coloured cushions. 'Please join me.'

Polly didn't believe him, but she sank down as gracefully as she could manage and carefully tucked her feet beneath her. Soles pointing away from him, as instructed in Minty's manual.

Polly looked up to find Rashid's eyes were glinting down at her. He was *laughing*. Heat washed over her face and with it a sudden, unexpected flash of anger. Polly tilted her chin. 'Am I doing this wrong?'

'No.'

'Then why are you laughing at me?'

The smile in Rashid's eyes intensified. 'You are charming. I wish all visitors to Amrah were as courteous and considerate of our customs.'

'I-I'm trying to follow the rules. There's no point coming here if you aren't...' her voice trailed off as he sat down beside her, close enough that she could feel the warmth of his body '...aren't going to make the effort.'

'I agree. I try to follow them myself.'

'You do?'

'I drink alcohol, but not when I'm in Amrah because it offends so many. Moving between cultures requires dexterity.' Rashid smiled.

His eyes moved over the fine fabric of her *dishdasha*, setting her on fire. He made her feel...out of control. As though she were entirely made up of hormones. 'B-Bahiyaa said I'd be more comfortable in something of hers.'

'And are you?'

'Yes.'

If it weren't for the way he was looking at her. At Shelton she prided herself on being able to handle any situation, but here...she couldn't. But it wasn't being in Amrah that made the difference. It was the garden. The night. *Rashid*. Mostly Rashid.

His clever face concealed so much more than it showed, but when his eyes danced they seduced her. They melted her from the inside out. And every now and then she fancied they hovered on her lips as though he might be thinking what it would be like to kiss her.

Her breath seemed to dry in her throat at the thought of what it would be like to have him kiss her. In her entire twenty-seven years she'd never felt her body wouldn't respond to the instructions of her brain before. She wasn't sure she liked him, but he was the most compelling man she'd ever met.

'You look very beautiful.'

Polly's eyes flew up to meet his. It would be so easy to believe he meant that. Seduced by the moment into doing goodness knew what.

If she wasn't sensible. If she didn't remember Rashid was known in the West as Amrah's playboy sheikh for a reason. Presumably women often dissolved in a pool of oestrogen at his feet. It would be much better for her self-esteem if she didn't become another conquest.

'I am glad you have recovered,' he said softly.

'So am I.' Polly's hands pleated the end of her *lihaf*, watching the silver threads glint in the candlelight.

'The heat can be punishing.'

Polly moistened her upper lip with the tip of her tongue. 'I—I bet the guys are dreading going with me into the desert. They must think I'm a complete liability now.'

'I doubt that.'

Polly dragged her eyes away from his. She'd had six years of making 'small talk'. She could do this. If she just kept breathing in and out he need never know she felt as though a million tiny ants had been let loose inside her. 'Are they joining us here?'

'Baz and John intended to swim here at the palace before having an early night. Graham, Pete and Steve have gone into Samaah. I suspect in search of alcohol in one of the international hotels. Do you wish you could have gone with your friends?'

Polly gave a sudden nervous laugh. 'If I said "yes" that would be a little rude, wouldn't it? And the guys aren't "friends". I met them for the first time at the airport.'

'Colleagues,' he amended.

'Even that sounds a bit grand. I keep pinching myself to prove I'm really here and not dreaming.' Polly turned her head at the sound of people approaching. Men. All dressed in simple white *dishdashas*. She watched wide-eyed as her food was set over a small burner to keep warm. The saffron-coloured rice dish smelt absolutely fantastic.

'This is *maqbous*,' Rashid said as one of the men spooned a portion into a shallow bowl. 'It's a popular Amrahi dish, although not confined to this region. You'll find the same in Oman and Saudi Arabia. Balkrash, too.'

Instead of handing it to her, the man placed it down on the low table in front of her and it was Rashid who passed it across. Then he spoke to the men in Arabic and they silently moved away, leaving behind tall glasses of layered fruit juice and a jug of iced water.

'I hope you will enjoy this more than *gahwa*.'

Polly looked back up into his teasing blue eyes. When he looked at her like that it was really very difficult to remember all the reasons why she shouldn't let herself relax into the moment. She'd had years and years of being responsible. It would be wonderful to act without thinking. To succumb to the playboy prince of Amrah, perhaps?

Crazy.

She carefully combined some of the white meat with the rice for a perfect first mouthful, glad she had something to do.

'It's spicy,' she said, surprised. 'And it's lovely. Are you not eating anything?'

'No.'

Polly felt a sudden wave of renewed embarrassment as she realised all this food was for her. 'You know, I could have waited until tomorrow. There was no need for Bahiyaa to—'

'It is our pleasure.'

It was really too late to protest too much. The food was there, she was hungry and it *was* delicious. She'd been too excited during her flight to eat much, not particularly inspired by what had been served either. 'Thank you.'

Rashid poured her a glass of iced water. He set that on the low table in front of her and, once she'd finished eating, she exchanged her empty bowl for the water. Ice, *ice* cold.

'I think I'm in heaven.'

'I always think that when I come home to Amrah.'

He smiled and Polly felt her own falter. 'Then why spend so much time away?'

He shrugged with typical Arab insouciance. 'I have business which takes me abroad. Hobbies.'

Oh, yes, she knew plenty about those. She'd seen the

smiling pictures of Sheikh Rashid Al Baha with assorted society beauties. It might help control her awareness of him if she remembered that.

'Like your stepbrother I am passionate about horses, but that is more of a mission than a hobby.'

Nothing like Anthony, then. The Beaufort Stud was a means to an end. Not a passion, certainly not a mission. Even Shelton wasn't. He saw the castle as a financial drain.

Polly took another spicy mouthful, determined not to dwell on how precarious Shelton's future was. She couldn't alter Anthony's personality, couldn't inspire him with her love for the castle, any more than his father had been able to. 'In what way a mission?'

'I want to see Arabia acknowledged as the home of racing.' Rashid placed his glass down on the table and looked at her. 'Every thoroughbred can trace its lineage back to one of three sires.'

'Yes, I know. The Darley Arabian, the Godolphin Barb and...the Byerly Turk,' she produced triumphantly, ridiculously glad her marshmallow brain had come up with something sensible.

Rashid sat back against the cushions. 'Trace their heritage back a little further and you discover all three have their roots in Arabia. Racing belongs here. What I have begun here is a fraction of what the Maktoum family have achieved for Dubai, but it will come.'

'Gambling is forbidden here, isn't it?' Polly said, after a moment.

'As it is in Dubai.'

Polly nodded. 'So that must mean your interest is tourism. Particularly since you said your oil reserves are running out. So, why,' she continued, slightly intimidated by the sudden narrowing of his eyes, 'why aren't you more enthusiastic about this documentary?'

'What makes you think I'm not?'

'Are you?'

His sensual mouth twisted into something approaching a smile. 'I have given my permission.'

Which was no answer at all. And he was watching her again as though he expected her to be trouble. She didn't understand why. 'Surely you want people to catch a glimpse of Amrah and be inspired to come here?'

He said nothing. Hard, flinty eyes looked at her, a muscle flexing in his cheek, then he leant forward to pick up his glass again and took a sip. 'Let us say I find it difficult to trust,' he said, at last.

'We really don't intend any kind of political comment. This documentary is to be entirely about Elizabeth Lewis.' Polly looked about the garden, foolishly hurt. There was no reason on earth why he should trust her. He didn't know her. It wasn't personal... 'Was this really here in the time of my great-great-grandmother?'

'It was created for her.'

'It was?'

'It's why there are so many roses. Tradition has it that Elizabeth missed the roses of her English home and so my great-great-grandfather conceived and planted this garden for her. You know they lived here for a time?'

Polly shook her head.

'After their adventure in the Atiq Desert in eighteen eighty-nine they stayed here for a handful of months.' Rashid settled back against the cushions once more, the fierce glitter in his eyes gone. 'You knew they became lovers within days of meeting?'

Polly nodded. The knowledge that their ancestors had been lovers made her feel shy. 'Dr Wriggley said they settled in Al-Jalini.'

'*Elizabeth* was settled there. When it became clear she

wasn't going to return home. It's a beautiful sea port and she lived there until she died in nineteen oh-four.'

'Alone?'

'No.' Rashid picked up one of the fruit juices and handed it across to Polly. 'Al-Jalini is the perfect place to live out a romantic idyll. I think King Mahmoud spent every moment he could with her, much to the anger of his wives. Theirs was an enduring love story.'

'But selfish.' She'd thought a lot about this. 'He was already married and so was she. And Elizabeth was a mother. I've read some letters which say her son was told she'd died and we know her husband drank himself to a premature death. The scandal was too much for him, I suppose.'

'The son being your great-grandfather?'

Polly nodded. Those letters had made her cry. 'It's a strange feeling to be connected to someone as…colourful as her,' Polly said, searching for the right word, 'but when you start to think about the hurt she caused I can't like her particularly.'

Rashid picked up the second fruit juice and sipped, his eyes not leaving her face.

'I do like her courage and zest for living,' Polly said, stumbling on. 'I'd like to have that.' She'd really like to have that, but real life had intervened. She had responsibilities, people she cared for and who cared about her. *As Elizabeth Lewis had had.* 'I know I'd have stayed in England and tended my rose garden there. Not very exciting of me, is it?'

'It depends on the motivation behind the decision.'

'I couldn't have left my child.'

'Mothers do.'

His mother *had*, if what she'd read about him was true. If only there were a nice deep hole in which she could hide herself. For someone who prided herself on her social skills, she was doing appallingly.

She struggled on, 'And, maybe it wasn't as straightforward as it seems. These things often aren't.' She stopped her fingers pleating her *lihaf*.

'What became of the son?'

Polly forced a smile and said brightly, 'Oh, he married and had five children spread over two wives. The youngest son being my grandfather, who became a not particularly distinguished soldier with something of a drink problem. So perhaps *his* grandfather's early demise wasn't entirely due to Elizabeth. It would be nice to think that. My mother remembers her father as being very...handsome but ineffectual.'

'You didn't know him?'

'Oh, no, he died in his forties and his widow became a housekeeper and, family gossip has it, a little bit more to a Major Bradley.' Polly picked up her fruit juice and traced a finger across the condensation on the glass. 'Now, I do remember him. Not that I knew anything about the "little bit more". As far as I was aware she really did just look after his house. They never married.'

'And your mother?'

'Became a shorthand typist and eventually married my father. Who was a chef at Shelton.'

Rashid hadn't moved. His eyes were still on her face, his expression one of polite interest. She'd probably bored him rigid.

'What's in this?' Polly asked, holding out her fruit juice. 'I don't think I've tasted anything like it.'

Rashid moved one long finger up the glass. 'Avocado, orange, pomegranate and mango.'

She took another sip. 'I can taste the orange, but I'd never have guessed avocado. It's lovely.'

'I am glad you like it. Have you lived at Shelton Castle all your life?'

'On and off,' she said evasively. Rashid was being polite and she didn't want that. She wished, for perhaps the millionth time in her adult life, she were more like Minty. It would have been nice to have felt confidently sexy and flirted a little bit with a man who most certainly knew how the game was played.

But she was seriously out of practice. Like the clothes, the easiest way to maintain the peace at Shelton was to keep a low profile. Her life would have been immeasurably worse if Anthony had thought she intended to snare a society husband for herself. Far better to blend into the background.

'Go on,' Rashid prompted, his entire attention focused on her.

'Initially we had a house on the estate. Then he died and we moved out into the village. For a while.'

'But not for long?'

'No.' Polly made a great show of sipping her fruit juice as the silence stretched out between them.

'Please. If it is not intrusive I would like to know about your life.'

He really did sound as if he meant it. Goodness, but he was good. How incredibly easy it would be to allow herself to believe he really wanted to know all about her. *And how foolish.* She ought to have slipped some of those glossy articles in her handbag so she could remind herself how Rashid had become quite so adept at making a woman feel special.

Only she hadn't thought she'd meet him again. Certainly hadn't thought she'd be staying in his home. And couldn't have imagined he would turn any part of his attention on her.

'My mum continued to work at the castle and eventually she became the housekeeper. So we moved back. We had a suite of rooms in the staff quarters...until Mum married Richard,' she said, truncating years into the fewest number of sentences possible.

'Were you pleased?'

'Yes, of course.' She took another sip of her drink, adding when he said nothing, 'I suppose I was shocked, but they were very happy together.'

'And was that why you decided to come back to Shelton Castle after you finished university?'

How the heck did he know that? Surely Minty hadn't thought it necessary to provide him with a full CV...

He must have seen something of her surprise in her face because he smiled. A slight deepening of the tiny lines fanning out from his sexy eyes, which had her stomach perform a complete somersault. 'You have a first from Warwick University in English and Political Science.' Rashid adjusted his powerful body against the cushions, but only so he could see her face more clearly. 'That information was in the paperwork sent to me.'

Ah. If he knew about her interest in politics, maybe that went some way to explaining his concern at her involvement. He needn't have worried. Since leaving university the only politics she'd had time for were the internal ones going on at Shelton.

'My mother found it...difficult to adjust to being the Duchess of Missenden.'

'Difficult?'

'Difficult is probably not the right word,' she concurred. The truth was her mother had found it completely impossible. Anthony had been incandescently angry. Benedict and Simon very little better. 'Dukes don't generally marry their housekeepers. Not in England, anyway. So I came for moral support with Richard's blessing. I meant to spend just a year there but…' Polly shrugged '…time passed and I stayed. And then there was the accident and I…stayed again.'

Nothing like the art of British understatement. Six years of emotional turmoil neatly contained in a handful of sentences.

'Until now.'

'Until now,' she echoed with a smile. 'I think this is the first thing I've ever done entirely for myself. I hope I don't make a mess of it.'

'Why should you?'

'Well…' Polly pretended to hesitate '…there's having to speak directly at a camera as though it were a friend, coping with the heat…'

Rashid laughed and her chest grew tight, as though she'd swallowed too much air. 'How about you? I—I seem to have given you my life story from four years onwards.'

'I was under the impression you had researched me fairly thoroughly,' he said lazily, his voice little more than a rumble.

Her eyes flew up to meet his teasing ones and she felt as pinned as a butterfly in a collector's box. There was no getting away from sexy blue eyes that ripped through every preconception she'd ever had about herself.

'What do you wish to know about me?'

Where to start? It was difficult not to be fascinated by a man who was so completely different from anyone she'd ever met before. He was simply more. More arrogant. More sexy. More inscrutable. More charismatic. *More.*

And yet he had roots in her own country. Those compelling blue eyes reminded her of it. 'Do you really not feel remotely English? Not on any level?'

Rashid leant forward and tore off a piece of *rukhal*

bread and offered it to her. Polly took it and he tore off a second piece for himself. 'I think I made a choice.'

'Between being Arab and English?' She broke off the tiniest piece of her bread and put it in her mouth, watching the frown that formed on his forehead.

'You will have read something of my parents' divorce?'

It was scarcely a question but Polly nodded. She'd certainly done that. It was practically the first thing anyone wrote about him.

'I was eight at the time and very angry when my mother left. I wanted nothing to do with her. I identified completely with my father. My one aim and purpose was to be like him. And that meant embracing everything that was important to him. I wanted to expunge everything English from my life because he hated it.'

'So how did being given an English education fit into that?' she couldn't resist asking.

Rashid smiled. 'I went to the same boarding school and university as my father. Followed that up with a Sandhurst military training, as had my brother Hanif before me. And during the holidays I absorbed everything Amrahi. Poetry. Art. Music.'

'To please your father?'

'Initially. Even horse racing was his passion before it was mine. My father,' Rashid said, reaching for the water jug and refilling Polly's glass, 'insisted we were connected with our Bedouin heritage and the Bedouin have a long tradition as master horsemen.'

So, naturally, Rashid had wanted to excel. Polly accepted her glass back. 'I've only been to the races once in my life. The summer after Mum married Richard. To be honest it seemed more about gambling than sport. I suppose you *could* argue gambling is a sport.'

'Not in Amrah.'

No, not in Amrah. Polly took another piece of *rukhal* bread. 'So, if there's no revenue from gambling, how is the Samaah Golden Cup funded?'

'Private investment.'

'Yours?'

His dark eyebrows rose, the blue eyes beneath them glinting in amusement.

Polly bit her lip and shook her head slightly. 'That must be millions of dollars of "private investment".'

'Twenty-eight million.'

'That's crazy!'

'We have to look to the future. Tourism and international finance is vital to our economy.'

'And do you get a good return on twenty-eight million dollars?' she asked politely.

'I think so. I make sure that I do.'

Six words, but they sent a shiver down her spine. It reminded her of how he'd been at Shelton. That feeling that he would break whatever needed to be broken.

Rashid leant forward and tilted her chin up so he could look directly into her eyes. 'I have a habit of winning.'

'So I've read.'

Then his hand lightly stroked the side of her cheek, burning a trail across her skin. His eyes lingered on her lips. If he kissed her now she wouldn't be able to stop him—even though she knew this was all a game to him.

Humiliatingly, he must know she'd fall into his bed like a ripe greengage from a tree. Almost. There was still the finest steel of self-preservation holding her back.

Rashid's blue eyes glittered down at her, his thumb moving to stroke across her sensitive lips. Slowly. Very slowly, he moved to kiss her.

Her hands came up to hold him off, but one touch of

his lips had them snaking round his neck, pulling him closer. Beneath her fingers she felt the soft curling hair that touched the nape of his neck. Her mouth softened and she heard the guttural sound of satisfaction deep in his throat.

Winning. This was all about winning.

'No.' She pulled back, her breath coming in short sharp bursts.

Rashid's hands still cradled her face, his eyes locked with hers. 'Polly.' His deep voice breathed her name, sending renewed shivers coursing through her body.

'This isn't right. Please.'

His smiled twisted. Then he sat back, watching her face. 'I will escort you back to your room.'

'Th-thank you.' Polly felt by her side for her *lihaf*, which had fallen off unheeded. She balled it up in her hand as sudden cold whipped through her. He must think she was a complete idiot. Any other woman would have just closed their eyes and thanked their lucky stars.

Other women did.

'Come.'

She looked up to find Rashid was already standing. He held out a hand. Polly allowed him to help her to her feet. A faint breeze caught at the light fabric of her *dishdasha*, brushing it against the denim of his jeans.

Polly drew in a ragged breath. She just wasn't made that way. But she was under no illusions. If Rashid truly intended to 'win' she'd be powerless to stop him.

CHAPTER FIVE

RASHID stood looking out across the courtyard, the fountain anything but soothing. There'd been some semblance of normality as he'd escorted Polly back to her room. Years of experience had meant that he was perfectly able to talk about her proposed documentary, the arrangements that had been made to take them into the Atiq Desert, all the while pretending his body wasn't on fire for her.

He screwed up the piece of paper in his hand and aimed it towards the waste bin by the desk. It brushed the edge and fell neatly inside. Rashid looked away, back out towards the central fountain and jagged a hand through his hair.

He'd kissed her. It didn't matter he'd intended it as a kind of test. Somewhere between the thought and the action his motivation had changed. And he'd felt her tremble. Her lips had been warm and pliant against his. Her fingers had been in his hair pulling him closer, urging him on until the moment she'd stopped. Stopped *him*. The control had been all hers.

Rashid swore softly. Inviting them, *her*, to stay in his home had seemed such an inspired idea. He pulled an agitated hand across his face. It felt less inspired now.

'Rashid?'

He spun round to face his sister. She quietly shut the door and walked to stand next to him.

'Are you angry with me?' she asked in Arabic, her voice low.

'Do not bring her to me again. I will make my decisions in my own time and in my own way.'

Bahiyaa turned so she could look at his profile. 'I do not believe Polly is involved in anything criminal.'

'And you know that how?'

'I know my own sex, Rashid. I genuinely believe she is here solely to make this documentary. And,' she continued after a moment of silence, 'she is charmingly excited to be here. I don't think she has been used to have her wishes considered. Rashid, are you listening to me?'

He was listening, to every word. In his heart of hearts he didn't believe Polly was complicit in any crime either. Perhaps it was his sense of self-preservation that had made him cling to that idea longer than was reasonable?

Even so…it was still possible. The timing of their visit was damnable and the stakes were high. If anything appeared in the British press that Hanif's enemies could use against him, Rashid would never be able to live with himself.

Rashid straightened his spine, the expression on his face set as he looked down at his sister. 'Golden Mile *is* sitting in our stables unable to sire anything—'

'I understand that.'

'*Knowingly* sold as a stud horse by Polly's stepbrother.'

'But—'

He pulled an agitated hand through his hair once more. 'The ramifications of that will be far-reaching. There will be people, apparently *good* people, who have been persuaded to take pay-outs. People we know, Bahiyaa.'

'But not Polly. I do not believe it.'

He'd thought…it would be easy to *know*. By changing her plans, having her stay in his home with the opportunity to talk to her…

He hadn't expected desire to cloud his thinking.

He'd been prepared for everything but Polly with her wide eyes and soft curves. She seemed to be a woman of contradictions. At Shelton she had appeared so confident. The way she held herself, the way she moved, talked to people, managed difficult egos with quiet skill had suggested inner confidence. Here in Amrah she was eager to please, *anxious*…

Anxious because she suspected she was out of her depth and knew it?

Rashid left Bahiyaa at the French doors and sat down at his desk, picking up his fountain pen and twisting it between thumb and forefinger.

'What are you going to do?'

Without turning his head he knew Bahiyaa had moved to stand behind him. 'Here Polly can be closely supervised. While filming she can be equally monitored.'

'About Golden Mile?'

'Wait.'

She came round to stand in front of his desk. 'For what?'

'For the evidence to be compiled. Once I am clear as to who was involved and to what extent, I will act.' He looked up. It was a statement of fact. He *would* act. In his own time, in his own way.

He intended to see the Beaufort Stud was put out of business. Anthony Lovell, Duke of Missenden, with it. He would send aftershocks through the entire racing fraternity. And if Polly was part of that…

'Don't let your pride hurt the innocent,' Bahiyaa said

softly, moving towards the door. 'Be very certain where your anger is coming from.'

Rashid watched as his sister left and, for a few moments after the door shut, stayed looking at the closed door. Bahiyaa's meaning was clear. She knew how betrayal affected him. Betrayal touched a nerve that had been left exposed during his childhood.

In among the fiasco that was Golden Mile there was betrayal in plenty. People close to him. People he employed and trusted. Under those circumstances how certain was he the cool, clear logic he prided himself on remained the guiding principle of his actions?

But did it matter? If Polly was as innocent of all involvement as Bahiyaa believed her to be it wouldn't matter her visit here was closely supervised. She would get her documentary. He…would get peace of mind.

He pulled a hand across his face.

Only…

Only he'd *kissed* her. And he could still taste her sweetness in his mouth, feel the pressure of her lips on his. A kiss was nothing. He'd kissed many women, enjoyed their company and taken them to bed.

But…

It had been a long time since he'd connected to… He'd been going to say 'a woman', but the truth was it had been a very long time since he'd allowed himself to connect to anyone. And he knew why that was.

Rashid tapped his pen on the table, waiting. His eyes flicked to his wristwatch. Hanif had yet to return his call—and the wait was hard. While his father still lived there was hope of forgiveness, a chance to heal the hurts. Bahiyaa coped so much better than he did. Perhaps because she had long since ceased to seek her father's approval.

At last the phone rang. 'Rashid.'

'No news to report.' His brother's voice sounded weary. 'He is sleeping a great deal. Talking less.'

'Has he asked for…the family to be gathered?'

He'd chosen his words carefully, but Hanif understood the question. 'I'm sorry, Rashid. There has been no change. Not towards you or Bahiyaa, and I have tried.'

Rashid didn't doubt that. His brother would have done everything possible. He sat back in his chair and stared up at the ceiling.

'He really only wants Raiyah, who would prefer not to be here. Samira makes a duty visit twice a day primarily to stake her claim over Raiyah.'

Rashid smiled wryly at the thought of his brother standing between their father's two wives.

'And I've yet to persuade our grandfather he needs to leave Dholar. It's been one nightmare of a day…'

'Anyone know why we're here?' Pete asked, his shirt damp in places from having dragged it on after an interrupted swim.

John shook his head. 'Something's happened. Please God it's not that Crown Prince Khalid has died. If Amrah goes into mourning, then starts to squabble over the old King's successor, we'll be stuffed.'

Polly sipped mint tea, too sweet for her taste, as Pete came to sit beside her. 'You okay?'

She nodded. There was no time for more. Echoing footsteps and the sound of voices heralded the arrival of Rashid. She'd had a long sleepless night to prepare for this moment. Most of the morning. She was ready. Or thought she was.

'Your Highness—' John began, getting to his feet.

Rashid brushed him aside. 'Please sit.'

Polly knew the moment he saw her. It was a fleeting glance but she knew he'd remembered it all. Their conversation in the garden. Their kiss. It was there as a sudden flare in his eyes and she knew hers responded.

What would have happened if she hadn't pulled back? Would they be lovers now? Would she know what he looked like naked? Know how his skin felt beneath her fingers?

If only she'd been braver. That was the regret. She might never have the chance again to know what a man like Rashid Al Baha would be like as a lover.

The sensible part of her brain saw no problem with that. He was obviously a highly sexual man and, for him, it would have meant nothing. It was different for her. Her heart and soul went with her body. If she became his lover she would carry him with her the rest of her life.

'I have had to make some changes to your itinerary.'

John made a guttural sound as though he were about to speak. Rashid's blue eyes turned on him and the other man sat back to listen.

'We will be starting in Al-Jalini—' Rashid nodded to an aide who passed out neatly typed sheets '—as opposed to the Atiq Desert.'

'Are we allowed to ask why?' Steve asked in his Texan drawl.

A muscle in Rashid's cheek flexed. It wouldn't take much, Polly knew, for him to answer, 'Because I wish it.' Whatever his reasons were, he didn't like being questioned on them.

'We went to some pains to keep the details of your visit private. Unfortunately it would seem our security measures have been breached and we must make adjustments. Your safety while in Amrah is my responsibility.'

'We'll need to run these changes by the London office,' John said after a cursory glance down at his paper.

'It has been done. But, of course, you will wish to confirm.'

Polly looked from John to Rashid and back again. There seemed to be more passing between the two men than the words they spoke.

'"We?" Are you proposing to accompany us, Your Highness?'

'Certainly as far as Al-Jalini.' His tone was uncompromising. Certainly left no room for debate. 'By then there will be clearer intelligence as to whether I need to be concerned.'

John nodded. 'Thank you.'

'If you have any questions about these amendments, please speak to Karim Al Rahhbi,' he said, indicating the aide who had passed round the papers.

Polly made a show of looking at the new itinerary, but the point that interested her most was that Rashid had decided to accompany them. There'd never been even the faintest suggestion of that. Slightly scarier was the way her stomach seemed to have leapt into her chest cavity at the thought of time with him, whatever the cause.

It must have been something quite significant that prompted a man like Rashid to alter his own plans. No one had asked about that. She saw the surreptitious glances that passed between the men and judged they already had a pretty good idea what was going on.

Only no one had thought to include her and it was beginning to get a long way up her nose. Even at Shelton she wasn't considered a bit of fluff. True, she was new to this business, but she had come with a brain and if something was happening that concerned her safety she really wanted to know what it was.

'I don't have any questions about the amendments,' she said, her voice stopping Rashid from leaving, 'other than

I'd like to know why it matters if people know where we are going. Are we in any danger?'

'No.' Rashid's eyes met hers. 'If you were in any danger I would not allow you to stay.'

They were in a room full of people but he managed to make that sound so unbelievably intimate. He meant 'you' as in the entire team, but what she heard was 'you' as in 'her'. There was something so primeval in the desire to be nurtured.

She'd not reached the career heights she'd once hoped for herself, but she considered herself a woman of the twenty-first century. Perfectly able to take care of herself. Nevertheless it was intoxicating to feel protected.

'Then why does it matter if people are aware of our itinerary?'

'Polly—'

'It is all right.' Rashid cut across Baz's instinctive exclamation.

Polly met his blue eyes once more and waited while Rashid reached his decision. If the men of the team had been told something she hadn't, she wasn't going to let him leave without telling her.

'Come with me.'

She wasn't in the mood for peremptory instructions but she did want answers. For a start she'd be really interested to know why she was kept separate from the rest of her team. Not that they seemed remotely bothered about it. But was that because she was a woman?

While she was prepared to be adaptable and accepting of a culture different from her own, she was *stuffed* if she was going to be sidelined by a Western film crew and a man who was half English whether he liked it or not.

Without looking at her so called 'colleagues', she stood up and followed him.

'You are cross,' he observed as soon as they were out of hearing.

'Irritated. They might not have expected you to change our itinerary but the whole "your safety is my priority" wasn't a surprise to them, was it?'

Rashid smiled.

'So why have I been left out of the loop?'

'Because you fainted and missed that conversation.'

That hadn't been the answer she'd expected. She'd been geared up for a fiery discussion on the role of women. Now, with nothing to fight against, she felt deflated.

He held open the door to what turned out to be his office. The only concessions to their being in Amrah were the marble floors and the carved screens folded back from the windows. That aside it was a seriously high-tech room meant for business. And it was enormous. On the far wall was a large plasma-screen television and in front of that a Western-style sofa, upholstered in dark brown leather, with a tub chair either side of that.

Polly watched silently as he walked over to his desk and pulled a remote control from the top drawer.

'You remember I told you when we spoke in England that yours would be the second documentary made about my country?'

Polly nodded.

He placed a DVD into the machine and stood back. 'This is it. I would like you to see it before we talk.'

'Have the boys seen this?'

'They have.'

She sat on the sofa, her eyes fixed on the plasma screen. Rashid placed the remote control on the edge of his desk and walked round to sit in his chair.

He'd told her the content was offensive, but the initial

shots of Amrah were just beautiful. The camera panned across a landscape studded with volcanic remains, then across an endless vista of giant sand dunes. A strange, uncluttered landscape and hauntingly beautiful.

A voice-over quoted Wilfred Thesiger and Polly glanced over at Rashid. There was nothing wrong with any of that. He answered the question in her eyes. 'Watch on,' he said.

Polly settled back and by the end of the short programme she understood exactly what Rashid's objections were. The Amrah they'd presented to the West was one of dogma and extremes. It spoke of a society where women were suppressed and their human rights violated.

It was so unfair. Everything she'd read in preparation for her visit had described a country that was striving to meld all that was wonderful about the East with the best of the West.

She'd admit to being a little confused by some of the customs she'd encountered, the fact that she and Bahiyaa seemed to occupy an entirely different part of the palace from the men was a strange one, but to portray Amrah as they'd done was irresponsible and, as Rashid had said, offensive.

She remained silent as he walked over and removed the DVD from the machine and put it away in its case. He looked across at her. 'I can't deny there are factions in our society who are accurately portrayed here. When my great-grandfather first opened Amrah up to the West there was fierce opposition. My grandfather has continued to encourage Western investment and it is well known my father would have carried on in the same vein. There are people who are deeply suspicious of that.'

He switched off the TV.

'I'm so sorry.' She was angry for him. For his country.

And humiliated by the crassness of hers. No wonder Rashid had been so cautious about allowing a Western film crew into his country. What King Abdul-Aalee had done for Amrah had been amazing and should have been celebrated. 'I'd never take part in a programme like that.'

Rashid smiled. He moved to the chair that was at right angles to the sofa she was sitting on.

'I think it's incredible how much has been done in such a short time. The new schools, hospitals, the emphasis on building a solid infrastructure...'

His smile broadened and Polly felt her insides curl up at the edges. She didn't want to feel like this. She preferred the anger. Felt safer with that. 'Minty would never make a programme like that,' she managed, her voice breathy.

'I am sure she would not.' Rashid brought his fingers together and let them rest against his mouth while he watched her.

He'd watched her yesterday, Polly thought, in just the same way. It was as though he was trying to see inside her, trying to understand more than she said with words. Almost as though she were a specimen under a microscope and then, sometimes, the way he looked at her changed. She became a woman and his pupils dilated.

That was when she felt most afraid. She was hopelessly out of her depth with a man like Rashid Al Baha. It felt a lot like she remembered feeling when she'd been swimming in the sea off Cornwall as a child. There were undercurrents she couldn't see tugging at her, taking her in a direction she knew she shouldn't be going.

The trouble was she wanted to go there. Rashid was excitement. Danger.

When he spoke his voice was low and controlled. 'You have come to Amrah at a crossroads for us politically. My father is dying and the country knows it. The only person who is clinging to a belief that he might be spared is my grandfather.'

Polly heard the edge in his voice that told her how much what he was saying *mattered* to him and irrationally she found it mattered to her. She wished she'd not forced this conversation on him. She ought to have followed the others' lead, been glad of the opportunity to be here at all.

'He is steadfastly refusing to name any successor other than my father.' His mouth twisted. 'While I admire his love and loyalty, it does mean the country is left uncertain of its future direction.'

Rashid paused.

'Who will he choose?' Polly ventured after a moment.

'If his objective is to see his work continue he'll choose my elder brother, Hanif. He's long been considered my father's heir.'

Polly moistened her top lip with the tip of her tongue. 'I still don't understand why it matters if people know where we're going.'

'It might not matter. But Hanif stands for conservative liberalism in a country where there are active extremists.' Rashid's eyes held hers, fiercely blue. 'I have always been aware your visit here might be seen as an opportunity to undermine what Hanif is trying to achieve.'

'In what way?'

'His political opponents could use your visit as propaganda. It would be easy to suggest Hanif is nothing more than a puppet of Western governments.'

'I see.'

'More probably they could seek to embarrass us by compromising your safety.'

News programmes she'd seen over the years of Western

journalists being kidnapped suddenly flashed in her mind. She wasn't brave. She didn't feel any great compulsion to 'get a story out there'. At this moment, given the choice, she'd fly straight back home.

'This morning I received the information that your planned itinerary might have been leaked so I have decided on changes. It is a precaution merely.'

'And you're coming with us?' Polly said, casting an uneasy glance in his direction. If it were a 'precaution merely' why would Rashid Al Baha put aside everything else that claimed his time?

'I am responsible for your safety and I will see no harm comes to you. You have my personal guarantee.'

It was the strangest thing, but Polly didn't doubt it. Looking at Rashid, you simply couldn't doubt he'd deliver exactly what he promised. She'd never had anyone in her life make her feel safe.

Not even in childhood. When her father had died she'd been so scared. Within weeks they'd had to move out of their home on the Shelton estate and buy a small terrace house in Shelton itself. Her room had been painted in gloss red and smelt damp and she'd hated it. For months and months she'd cried herself to sleep, but she'd never told her mother.

Not once. Her father had asked her to look after her and she'd done that. Her role had always been to be 'strong'. Long before the accident that put her mother in the wheelchair. She was still doing it.

But with Rashid Polly felt she could give over control. She looked at his blue eyes and her initial fear receded. He would keep them safe. *Her* safe.

'Are you happy to continue?'

'Of course,' she answered quickly. 'Will we still leave tomorrow?'

'Unless I hear anything which gives me cause for concern.'

'And if you do?'

'I will send you home.'

He stood up and Polly felt compelled to do the same. Their interview was over and he no doubt had much to do. 'How do I get back to rejoin the others?'

'Do you wish to?'

Heat rippled through her. It would certainly be the safest option but, no, she didn't want to. He was an irresistible temptation. The feeling of being on the edge, of not quite knowing what he was thinking and feeling about her was addictive.

'You haven't had a chance to see Elizabeth's garden in daylight. It would be a shame not to. I could show you now.'

Why was he doing his? Her eyes flicked to his lips. What did he want from her?

'If you have the time, I'd like that.'

No one had ever kissed her as Rashid had last night. Not with that expertise and control. It had been a few seconds of pure sensation before sanity had kicked in. But he was like a drug. He'd awoken her to possibilities, things she really hadn't allowed herself to think. And now he was choosing to spend time with her again.

'I will ask for refreshments to be brought to the summer house.'

'There's a summer house?'

'This garden was designed to soothe Elizabeth's longing for home, remember. An English garden must have its summer house. Besides which it provides some welcome shade.' He reached for the phone on his desk and spoke quickly and in Arabic.

This was probably the craziest decision of her entire

life. Polly knew it, but it didn't seem to make any difference.

'That is settled.'

His smile sent shivers coursing through her. A feeling of anticipation. She kept pace as Rashid led her through a maze of corridors. Even if she'd felt at liberty to wander around the palace freely, which she didn't, she wouldn't have had the faintest idea which way to head.

They walked through a Moorish archway and into a formal seating area with low couches. The room was filled with a heady scent that seemed to envelop her. 'What is that smell?'

'*Bokhur.*'

'*Bokhur,*' Polly repeated the unfamiliar word.

Rashid smiled. 'It's incense. Although to say that doesn't communicate its importance to Amrahi households.' He stopped, allowing her to breathe in the complex aroma. 'Every village will have their own *bokhur* maker who will create incense which is unique to that area. The ingredients might be any combination of frankincense, rosewater, sandalwood, ambergris…'

She wrinkled her nose.

'Each recipe is a closely guarded secret, handed down from one generation to the next. And once it is made it is scattered over hot charcoals,' he said, pointing at a silver incense-burner.

It certainly beat the rather bland pot-pourri she placed around the castle, but she wasn't sure she liked it. It was unfamiliar, exotic and slightly cloying as it seemed to seep into the light fabric of her borrowed clothes.

'Do you like it?'

'Perhaps. I'm not sure. It's so different.' But then everything here was so different. *She* was different.

Rashid laughed. 'It is the scent of home.'

She looked at him curiously but, of course, he was right. And for her the 'scent of home' would be newly cut grass, old books and beeswax polish. Nothing as exotic as *bokhur*.

As she went through the doors that led into the garden and into the full heat of the sun she was glad of the co-ordinating *lihaf* Bahiyaa had placed across one shoulder. Deftly, as she'd been shown, Polly placed it over her head.

She looked up and caught Rashid watching her. *Again.* 'It's hot,' she said foolishly.

'And you are fair. You are wise to cover up in the sun.'

Rashid started down one of the paths and, coming into the rose garden from a different direction, Polly immediately saw Elizabeth's summer house. It was open on all sides, more of a pavilion, and smothered in rambling roses.

Elizabeth's summer house. Built for her by a man who had loved her.

'It's beautiful,' she said softly.

Rashid looked down at her. 'I think so.' He watched as she lifted a hand to shade her eyes from the sun, then turned to look back at the palace.

He truly wanted Polly to like this garden, he realised. He loved her wide-eyed enthusiasm. The feeling he was sharing something with her she would treasure.

From the moment his father had given him this palace as his home the rose garden had been a strange attraction. He'd spent years trying to distance himself from his English heritage, but he'd always been drawn to this garden with its strange melding of East and West.

He felt at home here. Peaceful. And that was the purpose of a garden. A place where you could feel at one with yourself and with your God.

'It's not a very English garden, though,' Polly said, looking out across the orange trees, then up at him. 'Don't exactly run to those back home.'

Bahiyaa must have persuaded her to line her eyes in kohl. A dark smoky line around sparkling eyes that were as blue as his own. She looked as much a hybrid as this garden. In traditional Amrahi clothes, hands covered in an intricate henna pattern, she was the embodiment of a fantasy.

It was no part of his plan now to want to kiss her. He'd brought her here to talk. Only it was hard to remember that when his body responded to her with sharp immediacy. He didn't want to talk. He knew what she felt like, tasted like. He knew how her curves fitted against him, how soft her skin was, the warmth of her breath against his mouth, and he craved that.

He hadn't wanted to like her, didn't want to respond to her, but she drew him in anyway. Like a fly on a cobweb, he was more securely caught the more he struggled against it.

But at what cost? Amrah's future rested on the next few days and he'd been indiscreet in what he'd told her earlier. The knowledge that negative publicity would harm Hanif was power if she chose to use it.

He needed to be sure of her reasons for being here. It wasn't enough to believe her innocent. He had to *know*. His feelings for Polly were complicated, but he needed to focus on why he'd arranged for her to stay at his home.

'Fresh oranges still warm from the sun is about as far from a frost-bitten February day as you can get. Even if we manage to restore the orangery we'll never be able to recreate anything like this at Shelton.'

'But it's not a traditional Amrahi garden either,' Rashid countered, watching the sunlight catch at the silver embroidery that edged her *lihaf*, 'although it has elements you'd expect to find in one. The fountain, the long rills of water… Even the simplest Arab garden finds space for water.'

'It's beautiful,' Polly said, looking up at him.

She was happy now. *With him.* If he kissed her now would she stop him as she had yesterday or would she surrender to the inevitable? Because in any other place, at any other time, it would have been inevitable.

'English gardens have fountains, too. At Shelton we have a spectacular one which you can see from the Summer Sitting Room.'

The mention of her stepbrother's ancestral home was as effective as a cold shower. Did Polly know the extent to which Anthony Lovell had borrowed against his inheritance? Quite possibly selling Golden Mile to Rashid had been the last act of a very desperate man.

And desperate men could be very persuasive. And maybe her love for the house was enough of a temptation. Without any interference on his part he couldn't see the duke holding on to his country seat for long.

They walked down the vine-shaded path towards the summer house. 'You always speak of Shelton Castle with such affection.'

Polly looked up at him, a warm smile lighting her eyes. 'I love it. I always have. My mother says it's because I've polished most of it. Which is true. I had my first job at the castle at fourteen.'

Rashid said nothing, hoping his silence would encourage her to speak.

'There's such a sense of history about the place. Every nook and cranny could tell you a story. And we have our own resident ghost.'

'You believe that?'

'I've never seen her but there are plenty who will swear to it. We call her the Mad Duchess, but actually she was Lady Margaret Chenies who was married, pretty much against her will, to the very first Duke of Missenden back at the time of the English Civil War.' Her blue eyes danced with mischief.

'Was she mad?'

'Highly strung, I think, and lived a miserable life.'

'As all ghosts should.'

'Certainly.'

Rashid watched, fascinated at the hint of a dimple. 'Lady Margaret was absolutely devoted to her only son who was killed at the Siege of Gloucester in sixteen forty-three and she threw herself out of the window in her grief.'

'Ah.'

'But there are those who say she was pushed by her philandering husband. She now walks the Long Gallery, which actually wasn't built in sixteen forty-three, calling his name.'

Rashid smiled. It was impossible not to. Her enthusiasm for her subject was infectious—as it had been in the documentary on Shelton. She was a natural in front of the camera and it was really not surprising her friend had decided to utilise her talent.

He felt himself weaken a little more. He wanted to believe her, but if he believed her that would lead to a whole new list of problems.

How possible was it to have an affair with a woman whose life you were destroying? When he took Shelton away from her stepbrother what would she do? Would she hate him?

'Do you intend to do more television work after this?'

Polly shook her head. 'I shouldn't think so. I suppose

if it came my way I wouldn't turn it down, but I don't have any great specialism to bring to anything.'

'What do you plan on doing?'

'I'll return to Shelton.'

'Straight away?'

'Well, Easter is the start of the tourist season and there'll be lots to do to get the house ready in time.'

Again that sparkling enthusiasm, but he fancied he saw something else. Something she wasn't saying. Something that clouded her enjoyment of the castle and her role in it.

They stepped up into the summer house and Polly sat down on the intricate seat facing out towards the small ornamental lake. 'How come everything's so green here?'

Rashid sat facing her. 'There is a complex irrigation system in place, all stemming from a natural spring.'

'Created for Elizabeth?'

He nodded, watching the expressions pass over her beautiful face.

'King Mahmoud must have loved her very much,' she said wistfully. 'It was a shame they had to hurt so many people to be together. It spoils the story for me.'

She kept surprising him. That was not a sentiment he'd have expected to hear expressed by an Englishwoman. In his experience they wanted money and power and would achieve that even if the money and power were found in another woman's husband.

Rashid turned to watch the arrival of the servant bringing fruit juices. Two large jugs. One of lime juice and the other of pomegranate.

He looked back at Polly to see she'd taken off her *lihaf* and shaken her blond hair free. It was all too easy to imagine it spread out on a pillow next to him. Far too easy to want it there.

'Do you have a preference between lime and pomegranate?'

'Isn't lime juice sharp?'

'Try it.' He spoke to the servant in clipped Arabic, who then poured two glass of the lime juice, his head respectfully bowed throughout. It did him enormous credit because the temptation to look at her must have been acute.

If Polly were his he'd want to shield her from every eye but his.

Rashid picked up one of the glasses and sipped. It was dangerous to even think that way. Even if Polly were not related by marriage to the Duke of Missenden she could never play a part in his life. She was as unsuitable a choice as his mother had been for his father.

Destined for disaster. Two cultures that couldn't do anything but clash. It *was* time he decided on a wife, but he wouldn't search for her in the West.

He watched, silently, as Polly took her first sip of lime juice. But all thoughts of finding himself a wife would have to wait. What mattered now was determining if this woman presented a problem to Hanif's succession.

'This is lovely. Really refreshing and clean.' She looked up and smiled. 'My favourite so far.'

It seemed to him her smile filled the garden. 'I'm glad.'

And then there was silence. A faint breeze caught at her shimmering blond hair, a hennaed hand reaching out to brush one wayward strand off her pale cheek.

'I can't imagine ever wanting to leave somewhere so beautiful—especially if it had been created for me.'

There wasn't a movement Polly made that didn't feel erotic. Rashid felt as though his skin had suddenly become two sizes too small for his body.

'Why did she leave here?'

He forced his eyes to scan the sweet-smelling flowers that scrambled through the trees. Anywhere but look at her and her wide-eyed sensual beauty. 'She didn't have the choice. Their love affair was a scandal here, too.'

'Because King Mahmoud was married?'

'He had only two wives when he met Elizabeth and could easily have afforded a third,' Rashid said with a shake of his head. 'The problem was that she was not free to make a commitment to him.'

'But if she hadn't been married that would have been fine?'

He nodded.

Polly pursed her lips. 'There's something wrong with that. Why would any woman agree to marry a man who already had two wives?'

He'd had this conversation many, many times during his years at Cambridge University. Beyond anything else it was the thing that touched a nerve in Western women and he'd come to enjoy the debate.

'Perhaps a woman who trusts her father,' he said, sitting back, watching her face.

It wasn't what he wanted for himself. He wanted a woman who would entrance him all his days, an equal, one who would protect and care for his children with her life, a woman who would love him and only him.

'In my culture a man's wife is chosen by his family, taking into account his status, family background and intellectual capacity.'

'How romantic!'

'The husband and wife bring a shared sense of values and an understanding of duty. Romantic love often comes later.'

'And if it doesn't,' Polly said, her eyes watching him from over the rim of her fruit juice, 'he just gets himself another wife!'

She knew he was enjoying himself at her expense and the teasing glint in her eyes was irresistible. Rashid smiled. 'It is not quite as simple as you make it sound. While a man is permitted up to four wives, I know none of my generation who would choose to do so. Each wife must be treated equally…in all things.

'Had King Mahmoud married Elizabeth he would have needed to create two more gardens as beautiful as this one for his other wives. A man with more than one wife must share his time, his body and his possessions equally. Expensive and physically exhausting, I'm sure you'll agree.'

Rashid sat back and watched the blush that spread across Polly's cheekbones. He couldn't remember the last time he'd seen a woman blush. No Amrahi woman was left alone with him long enough for that to be a possibility and he'd thought Englishwomen had forgotten how to.

'And all rather silly if he can have a mistress anyway.'

'Ah, but that is human frailty at work, not a guiding principle.'

Polly laughed, seemingly because she couldn't help it. Warmth spiralled out in a coil from the pit of his stomach.

'So, will you marry the woman your family chooses?'

There was the difficult question, the one he'd prefer not to answer. He saw the advantages played out all around him, but the honest answer was 'no'. How could he? To marry a woman of your family's choosing required confidence in their ability to choose wisely and with your happiness in mind.

His father and grandfather were remarkable men, men who had achieved great things in the time allotted to them on earth, but he did not trust their judgement.

'When the time comes,' Rashid said firmly, 'I will choose my own wife.'

CHAPTER SIX

'AND Bahiyaa?' Polly asked. 'Will she get to choose her own husband?'

'Bahiyaa is already married. But, the answer to your question is that my sister's marriage was arranged by our father and approved of by my grandfather.'

Polly frowned. There'd not been a whisper of that. Not in all the conversations she'd had with his sister. And Rashid's manner had changed, his jaw was set and his cheekbones flushed.

'Have I met him?'

Rashid shook his head. 'Bahiyaa's marriage was particularly unsuccessful. Eventually she made the decision to leave her husband and seek sanctuary with her own family.'

'But she's not divorced?'

'Her husband doesn't wish it,' he stated bluntly. And then, as though he realised she would need more explanation that that, 'In Amrah a divorce is not an automatic right. Bahiyaa must convince a court she has sufficient grounds. Omeir is an intelligent and articulate man who has been very convincing. And our mistake was not realising soon enough her husband would refuse to let her go.

She has no way now of substantiating her version of events.'

Shock held Polly silent, for a moment. 'And that's it? There's nothing she can do?'

'For the time being.'

It was unfair to push him any further, but she really wanted to know. Not merely from idle curiosity, although she had to admit there was something of that, too, but because she cared about Bahiyaa. Sometimes, when his sister hadn't known she was being watched she'd looked so sad.

The kind of sad that went beyond emotion. Much as her mother had been in the first few months after her father had died. And, being a natural 'fixer', she'd wondered what she could do to help. She'd not imagined anything like this, though.

'Even with a family as influential as yours? Surely if your grandfather intervened on her—'

'Even so.'

Polly let her finger slowly trace the rim of her glass. 'How long has Bahiyaa lived apart from her husband?'

'Four years.'

'*Four?*'

Rashid held up his hand as though to silence her. 'I know. There is huge injustice in what is happening to Bahiyaa. I feel it deeply.' He took another sip of his fruit juice and appeared to be lost in thought.

He sighed. 'When a man takes a wife,' Rashid said quietly, 'our religion teaches us it is a uniting of souls for all of eternity. It is the husband's duty to love and care for his wife throughout her life.'

Put like that it was beautiful. The Christian marriage ceremony was the same. 'To love and to cherish in sickness and health.' So often people didn't manage to live up to those vows, but it was a great starting point.

'And it wasn't like that for Bahiyaa?'

'No.' Rashid's voice took on the steely quality she'd often heard in it. 'Omeir is an influential man from a good family. He's gifted in many areas, but he is also cruel and violent.'

'Violent?'

'To give my father his due I sincerely believe he had no idea when he brokered that marriage.'

Polly sat in stunned silence. Bahiyaa was so lovely. Intelligent, warm and stunningly beautiful. What more could a man want in a wife?

'Of course, Bahiyaa did her best. She is a strong woman and she wanted her marriage to be a success. Its failure has caused her to experience a shame I do not believe she should feel. She was also, rightly as it turned out, not sure of our father's support.'

'Why ever not?' The question shot from Polly's mouth without any thought.

'It is a question of honour. Our family's honour.'

'That doesn't make any sense. *He* was divorced.'

'It is different for a man.'

'It shouldn't be!'

'And my mother is English.' Rashid allowed himself a tight smile, the skin across his cheekbones pulled tight. 'She did not consider herself bound by the precepts of a religion not her own. And I will own she had the full support of her own family.'

But she'd left her son behind. Polly couldn't imagine the pain of that. Whatever had compelled Rashid's mother to do that? He'd spoken of having chosen to be Arab. Perhaps he'd been put in the impossible position of having to choose between parents?

It was a little like treading on eggshells, but she had to ask. 'Did she have to leave Amrah without you?'

'Certainly. She didn't have the legal right to take me without my father's permission and he would never have given it. Perhaps if I'd been a daughter... But even then, I don't think so. By the time she left it would have been as much about punishment as legal right.'

A lump filled her throat. More than a century before Elizabeth Lewis had chosen to leave her child, too, and there'd been such heartache in the wake of that decision. Rashid might give the impression of being invincible, but it was the ultimate rejection.

Polly moistened her lips. 'What made her leave?'

'It is no secret.' Rashid refilled his glass with lime juice and silently offered to refill hers.

She nodded. 'Please.'

'Put simply, my father wished to take a second wife.' He allowed himself a very small smile. 'You will not be surprised to learn my mother objected.'

'Polygamy is not an English concept. He must have known that.'

Rashid placed the jug back down on the tray. 'Indeed. But my father's desire to have a junior wife was predominantly motivated by political necessity and, no doubt, emotional blackmail. My grandfather wished it.'

She sat in silence but, honestly, she couldn't comprehend of any situation that would justify what Rashid's father had done to a woman he'd presumably married for love. *And to his son.*

He'd robbed his young son of his mother. She didn't know what to say. Probably because there was nothing that could be said. The hurts were there, scar tissue covering wounds that had imperfectly healed.

'It was political. In the early years of my grandfather's

reign he favoured his much younger brother, Prince Faisal, as his successor. That was a sensible choice.

'But time passed, and by the grace of God my grandfather lived a long and fruitful life. Eventually it became logical to choose an heir from among his own nine sons.' Rashid picked up his glass, swirling the fruit juice around as though it were whisky.

Polly waited while he sipped. The whole concept of senior and junior wives was alien to her. Having nine sons was unusual. Needing to name one as a successor more unusual still.

But it was his pain that held her silent. He related facts as though they were no more than that, but his features were set like granite.

'My father is the eldest. At the time he was in his mid thirties, a highly educated man, disciplined, popular with the Amrahi people, and already the father of two sons. You would think an obvious choice, but my grandfather was, *is*,' Rashid amended, 'adamant that Amrah's sovereign be entirely of Arab blood.'

It was like being given a key to his soul. So much about Rashid was falling into place. Polly felt such anger. She didn't think she'd ever experienced anything quite as intense. At eight years old this strong, beautiful man had been made to feel he would never be good enough by the people whose business it was to love and care for him.

Rashid stared out across the lake for a few moments. 'Princess Yasmeen, my father's first wife, and the woman my grandfather had selected as a suitable bride, had died young. I assume my father was sincerely attached to her because he refused to contemplate a second marriage.'

'Until he met your mother.' Polly knew what was coming next. She understood. Hanif was a suitable heir. He, Rashid, was not.

'I can't imagine my grandfather was happy about it but my father married her anyway. If he'd thought my grandfather would soften his views, he was wrong.'

Polly blinked hard against the tears prickling behind her eyes.

'Remember Amrah was a young country, newly emerging from a century of isolation. My grandfather was spearheading rapid modernisation and surrounded by voices counselling caution in his choice of successor.'

Rashid's voice grew more distant. 'If anything happened to Hanif they feared my father might be tempted to name me as the future king and gave him an ultimatum. He needed to take a second bride.'

'Could he have refused?'

'He could.' Rashid brought his eyes back to hers. 'He was a grown man. But my grandfather knew he wouldn't. One of my father's strengths is his love and commitment to Amrah. Although my grandfather rightly receives much of the credit for the skilful blend of tradition and modernity here, I think history will recognise my father's contribution.'

For the first time Rashid's voice held a trace of an emotion other than hurt. *Pride.* Crown Prince Khalid might be many things, but he was clearly a father Rashid had looked up to. Loved. Still loved?

She studied him. It was inconceivable that any father wouldn't have delighted in a son like Rashid.

Or grandfather.

King Abdullah had wilfully ripped a young family apart. And Rashid's father had let him.

'There is a history of rebellion in the Muzna region and it was suggested that ties could be strengthened if my father married Sheikh Sulaiman's eldest daughter, Samira.'

There was a hideous logic, but what of Samira? It was hateful for her. 'Did she agree?'

'She was seventeen at the time, offered the chance to become a princess...'

And she'd thought life at Shelton was complicated.

'Within weeks of that marriage my mother returned to England.'

Leaving Rashid behind to be brought up by the woman who'd replaced her. 'That's incredibly sad.'

'As you say,' he conceded.

It was more than sad. It was heartbreaking. For them both. 'Did you see her? Growing up?'

'No.'

Her heart felt so unbearably heavy.

'As a child I only knew she'd chosen to leave. I never questioned my father's judgement.'

'And do you see her now?' she asked, her voice husky.

'Occasionally. She is my mother. I respect her as my mother but I have chosen to embrace the life she rejected.' His voice was, once again, devoid of all emotion. 'There is no fairy-tale ending. She is a woman I barely know.'

Polly stared out across the ornamental lake towards the orange trees, looking but not seeing. 'Did she marry again?'

'Yes.'

'And had more children?' Polly pushed.

'I have two half-sisters. Miranda and Portia.'

Two English sisters. Half-sisters he scarcely knew.

'And Princess Samira and your father have had children together, haven't they?'

'Three sons and five daughters. More recently my father decided to take a junior wife and Princess Raiyah gave birth to twin sons a little over two years ago.'

'So, what's that?' Polly frowned, mentally counting

through Rashid's family. 'Seven sons. Your grandfather must be delighted his plan worked so well,' she said acerbically.

King Abdullah seemed like a Machiavellian puppeteer, pulling the strings of those around him. And Rashid's father a victim of his own ambition. She couldn't like that any more than she liked Elizabeth Lewis's selfishness.

Other people mattered. They *did*. For the first time in six years she was suddenly hugely grateful she understood that. There was nothing more important than the people you loved. The years she'd spent at Shelton seemed years very well spent.

'Except my grandfather is likely to outlive my father. He will need to name a new heir and Samira's eldest son is still young.'

So all that upheaval and heartache might have been for nothing. Crown Prince Khalid was not going to live long enough to be King and his sons might not inherit either. One would have thought, having lived through that, he'd have been more receptive to his daughter's situation.

'What made Bahiyaa take the decision to finally leave her husband?'

The muscle in Rashid's cheek worked painfully. 'Omeir had never left a mark on Bahiyaa where it could be seen, but on that night he threw her against a wall and she broke her wrist putting her hands up to break her fall. When she came to me she had a black eye, bruising to her face and marks around her neck.'

Deep loathing washed over Polly in unstoppable waves. She'd only known Bahiyaa for such a short time but imagining her in that situation brought such revulsion. Thank God she'd had the courage to leave at last. Even in England, where divorce held no stigma, she knew women so often found it hard.

'Three weeks later she lost the baby she'd been carrying.'

Oh, dear God, no! Polly reached out instinctively, her hand lightly touching his. 'She was lucky to have somewhere to come.'

His fingers closed around hers, dark against the paleness of her skin. 'She lives under my protection. She's safe, but she has lost so much. The possibility of children. Companionship.'

Love, Polly added silently. If ever there was a woman capable of loving it was Bahiyaa. 'Couldn't...?' She stared down at their joined hands. 'Couldn't your father do something to help her?'

'He refuses even to see her.'

'Even now?' Polly couldn't keep the shock from her voice. Crown Prince Khalid was dying. Surely *now*, when he realised how short a time he had left, he'd want to see his daughter. Make things safe for her.

'He is adamant Bahiyaa should return to her husband.'

'And be beaten?'

'I have to believe he doesn't think that will happen.'

Her hand moved against his. Of course, he had to believe his father was acting out of ignorance. How could you have any respect left for a man who would allow his daughter to live in fear, particularly when she'd had the courage to ask for help?

It must be doubly painful if that man was someone you'd spent your entire life revering.

'How long is your father expected to live?'

Rashid shrugged. 'Hours. Days. Weeks. His cancer is advanced but he is a strong man. It will take the time it takes.'

And he was going to die without telling his daughter how much he loved her.

She'd been so lucky. Her father had left nothing unsaid. She'd never been in doubt he'd gone away from them only because he'd had to. And that had carried her. Always.

'She seems so calm.'

'She is accepting. I think she's reached the point where she is content not to live in fear. I find the separation from our father more difficult.'

Polly looked up. She hadn't understood that by taking Bahiyaa in Rashid had broken contact with his father, too. That conversation back in Minty's office about why Rashid wasn't doing the 'bedside vigil thing' suddenly seemed glib.

He wasn't there because he wasn't allowed to be there.

Never had Rashid seemed quite so human. Or so desirable. He'd made a conscious decision to do the right thing at enormous personal cost. He was all that was standing between his sister and an unthinkable future.

A strong, sexy, wonderful man. A man you could trust. A man worth loving. Polly's gaze drifted to Rashid's mouth and the lips that had kissed her. She studied the curve of them, the fullness of his bottom lip as compared to the top one. The cleft in his chin.

'Polly.'

From somewhere deep inside her a tear welled up and rolled slowly down her cheek. She wasn't sure why exactly. Whether she was crying for the boy Rashid had been, the man he was now or for Bahiyaa, she couldn't tell. She only knew she felt an overwhelming sense of sadness flow through her.

Rashid moved. He sat beside her and his left hand moved to brush her hair off her face, his thumb coming back to wipe away the moisture on her cheek. His face so close to hers. She could feel his fingers skim her neck. But it was his eyes that caused heat to lick along her limbs.

She wanted him with a passion she really didn't understand. It was a compulsion. A *need*. Something that transcended morality and sense. It wasn't even really about sex. It was about belonging. About recognising that this was the man she'd been waiting for.

'You're so beautiful.'

Incredibly, with the truth of that burning in his blue eyes, she felt beautiful. His hand brushed her cheek, setting the long gold earrings Bahiyaa had given her swinging. She felt them touch her neck.

It seemed such a long time before he lowered his mouth to hers. Every millisecond she was urging him on, willing him to kiss her with all the passion she knew he was capable of.

Rashid's hands cradled her face and his mouth was hard against hers. His kiss was everything it had been yesterday and more. There was desperation in it, a certain knowledge that this passion was beyond wisdom. They lived lives so very far apart. There could be no future. Nothing more than this moment.

But this moment was all she wanted. Heat coursed through her veins and settled in the pit of her stomach. She was beyond excitement.

I want him. The words pounded in her head with each beat of her heart. *I want him to love me.*

His tongue moved against her mouth. The lightest touch on her lips and she heard her own gasp for breath. She wanted to taste him. Feel him invade her body. Her lips parted and her heart thudded against her breasts.

Rashid's hand moved round to the small of her back urging her closer, his left hand tilting her face to allow him maximum access.

There was nothing she wouldn't do for him. *Nothing.* Here, *now*, in Elizabeth's garden, she'd be his lover if that was what he wanted. She only wanted his lips to go on kissing her. Kissing her until she was certain there was no life outside this moment.

Her whole body was humming with a pleasure, a hot ache low in her abdomen. She needed more. Wanted more.

The sound of smashing glass barely pierced her consciousness, but Rashid pulled back, his breathing uneven.

She moaned.

'Your glass,' he said roughly.

No. Inside she was screaming, but her pride kicked in. She ignored the lime juice spread out over the summerhouse floor and bent down to collect slivers of glass in the palm of her hand.

Rashid touched her hair. 'Leave it.'

She placed what she'd gathered already in one neat pile and looked up, knowing that he'd remembered all the reasons why kissing her wasn't a good idea.

'You are too beautiful to resist.'

No one had ever said that to her. It warmed her even as she knew what he was really saying. 'Too beautiful' meant that kiss shouldn't have happened.

The girl she'd been back in England would have agreed. It *was* foolish. She was no more suitable a bride for Rashid Al Baha than his mother had been for his father. She could only be a temporary distraction and if she continued down this path she'd be hurt.

Desperately hurt. For whatever reason Rashid had let her glimpse behind the mask. She knew what motivated him, what had shaped him. She saw more than perhaps even he'd intended.

And she ached to have his arms around her once more. The future didn't seem so very important any more. It would take care of itself and if all she could have were memories she'd settle for those.

Rashid brushed his thumb against her swollen lips and then, with his eyes holding hers, he placed her *lihaf* over her head. 'The heat of the sun is fierce now. I ought to take you back inside.'

Away from him. *Away from temptation.*

'Thank you for telling me about your father. And about Bahiyaa.' Polly tugged at the side of her bottom lip with her teeth in an effort not to cry. 'She is fortunate to have a brother like you.'

It took immense courage to turn away, but she did it. Head high, she stepped down out of the summer house and into the midday sun. Heat seemed to rise up from the marble paving in waves, her legs brushing against the sweet-smelling herbs that spilled out across the warm stone.

'Polly.'

She forced her feet to slow. If her smile was a little too bright it was unlikely Rashid would notice. She turned and waited for him to catch up. 'Which way now? Will the guys still be in the *Majlis*?'

'Quite possibly. Is that where you wish to go?'

No, it wasn't. The thought of having to make small talk with people she scarcely knew didn't appeal in the slightest. What she wanted was solitude and the chance to mull over what Rashid had told her. A chance, too, to understand what was happening to her. 'I think I might like to read for a while.'

Rashid nodded. 'Then I shall take you to find Bahiyaa. She will show you the way to your room.'

It had always been a matter of 'when' not 'if' Bahiyaa would track him down. Not because he imagined Polly would have referred to his sister's unhappy marriage or that Bahiyaa would mind if she had, but because she had become their guest's champion.

Perhaps it was because she was wrongly judged herself she felt a need to protect Polly from what she saw as an unjust accusation? Perhaps it was nothing more than friendship? While Omeir and their father remained intransigent, her life was necessarily secluded and she must often be lonely.

'Polly...'

Rashid saved the work on his computer and gave his sister his full attention.

'Have you reached any conclusions?'

He supposed he must have.

Inadvertently. Nothing about this morning had gone to plan. The questions he had about her stepbrother and her life at Shelton had remained unasked, but it seemed he'd reached a decision all the same.

Rashid rubbed a hand around the back of his neck. He hadn't intended to kiss Polly for a second time any more than he'd intended to bare his soul. But her beautiful moist eyes, her hand in his, and he'd been unable to resist her.

The sweetness of her kiss seemed to reach deep inside him and grab hold of his heart. He'd felt her vulnerability to him and it had enflamed him. What troubled him was the sense of intimacy he felt.

That was new.

He didn't do intimacy. Rashid picked up his fountain pen and twisted it between thumb and forefinger. He liked to play fair. His relationships had always been about sex, need, passion, wanting...

They were not based on conversation. No woman he'd ever slept with had imagined she would occupy a permanent place in his life. If he felt they were getting too close he stepped back.

But Polly had crossed some kind of line. And he didn't

want that. His family's privacy was sacrosanct and yet, for some reason, he'd felt able to talk to her. And, having done so, he trusted her not to use that information to hurt the people he loved.

That had to be his decision. He trusted her. When he looked into her blue eyes he saw honesty—which meant she was going to be hurt.

Because of him.

Rashid glanced across at his sister, who was looking at him with a slight knowing smile.

'She knows nothing, Rashid.'

He pushed his chair back from his desk. 'Perhaps.'

'I have had so many conversations about her life at Shelton Castle. I do not think she cares for her stepbrother at all.'

'He is a thoroughly unpleasant man.'

'She says "weak".'

'That would be right.' Weak, greedy and dishonest. But he was her family, if only by marriage. 'If she dislikes him so much, has she told you why she stays?'

'Because of her mother's accident.'

Bahiyaa twisted the gold bangles on her wrist. 'And have you thought to ask her what her stepbrothers felt about their father's remarriage? What they said?' She moved closer. 'Have you asked her what she fears will be Shelton's future?'

Rashid moved his pen from one hand to the other and back again, twisting it all the time between long, lean fingers.

She smiled. 'I am wondering, Rashid, what you have been talking about for so long. You seem to have discovered very little.'

Her dark, kohl-lined eyes smiled understandingly across the distance between them.

'Surely it would be simplest to ask her about Golden Mile?'

'It need not concern her.'

'Of course it will concern her! Shelton Castle is her home and a place she loves. She has poured her life into it and what you propose to do will rip it from her. You cannot destroy the Duke of Missenden without hurting Polly. And,' Bahiyaa continued with unaccustomed force, 'you are working towards that end while offering her friendship. I do not think she will be able to forgive you that, Rashid. And I'm not sure you will forgive yourself.'

'My honour demands justice.'

'You have the power to temper your justice with mercy if you so choose. Rashid, I *know* you.' Her hennaed hand reached out and touched his arm. 'You will never be content with a girl who has lived her entire life in Amrah. You say that is what you—'

Rashid moved abruptly and set his pen down on the desk. Bahiyaa was hitting too close to home, touching a nerve that was newly exposed. 'When I marry I will choose a girl from my own culture. I will look for the mother of my children.'

'You should choose the woman you love,' Bahiyaa corrected softly. 'And if you love wisely she will be a woman who can help you accept that two cultures have shaped you, Rashid. And your children will be blessed because they have parents who will nurture them in a loving relationship.'

He saw her blink hard. 'You, Hanif and I did not have that. What we experienced was not good.'

What she had experienced in her own marriage had been infinitely worse, Rashid added silently.

CHAPTER SEVEN

RASHID was ready to leave for Al-Jalini long before the appointed early start. Long before the plaintive wail of the muezzin drifted out across Samaah, calling the faithful to prayer.

He'd slept fitfully. Bahiyaa's words had burned deep inside him—as she had intended they should. It was as though she'd held up a mirror to his life and forced him to take a good hard look at it. And having taken a look he wasn't so sure he liked what he saw.

He was still that boy trying to fit in, trying to find acceptance, trying to be better, stronger, make things *right*. Rashid swore softly.

Because he'd known his father was watching for signs of his mother, he'd subjugated everything he could about himself that would remind him of her. And he'd tried to make his father proud of him. He'd rode faster than Hanif, on horses that his brother wouldn't have ventured near. He'd learnt swathes of Amrahi history. Even his love of the desert had been born out of his burning need for acceptance.

But whatever he'd done had never been enough. It was time to accept that and understand why. He had his mother's eyes and, when his father looked at him, he saw her. The woman who had publicly shamed him. There'd been no way back from that.

And in the way of a child he'd come to loathe what he had been told was loathsome. Bahiyaa was right. He needed to come to terms with the fact two cultures had shaped the man he'd become and find a way of balancing them within himself.

Bahiyaa had spoken, too, of his taking a wife. It was time. He yearned for family. To create what he had never really had.

Over the years he and Hanif had spent many hours teasing each other over their father's choice of prospective brides. A second cousin. The daughter of an influential sheikh on whose land there was oil. They'd resisted. Always.

But, when the time came, Hanif would do his duty. His brother knew, and had always known, there was no reason to suppose their grandfather would not place the same stipulations on him as he had on his own son. It was his destiny to marry dynastically and Hanif had accepted it.

His brother would respect the woman his family chose and he would probably be happy. He would derive solace from his children and would pour his energies into the environmental issues that so concerned him. And should his grandfather decide to make him his successor, he would devote the last breath of his body to Amrah and its people.

Rashid's own future path was less well delineated. His choices wider. But he feared Bahiyaa was right. He would not be satisfied by a relationship based on duty and friendship.

He had told Polly he would choose his own bride and he stood by that. He, and only he, would determine what would best suit him in a wife. And what would suit him was a woman who understood he was an Arab at heart.

However he'd come to it, Amrah was the place his soul felt at peace. It was foolishness to suppose a woman brought up with the freedoms of the West would live happily here and that must guide his choice.

It could not, *would* not, be a woman like Polly.

He turned his head at Karim's tap on the door. His aide held the papers he'd been waiting for.

'Everything you asked for is here, Prince Rashid.'

Rashid nodded. 'Leave the file on my desk.' He turned back to fill his lungs with the early morning air, looking out across the courtyard garden.

His feelings about Polly were complicated. Bahiyaa, despite it all, was a romantic, but even she had counselled he 'love wisely'.

'Wisely' could not mean loving a woman who was related by marriage to a man he would ruin. And he *would* have justice. Bahiyaa didn't understand that not to would lay him open to ridicule throughout the racing world. His actions would be moderate but decisive. Not revenge. Justice.

He would also act to minimise the consequences to both Polly and her mother. That was the act of an honourable man.

With no real appetite for the job at hand, Rashid sat himself at his desk and worked his way through the latest developments in their investigation. Written confirmation of what he'd already been told verbally. His agent admitted accepting payment from the Duke of Missenden.

The betrayal of a man he'd considered a close friend had wounded him deeply, but his way was clear. With immense regret he would instruct Karim to make the necessary phone calls. Quietly he would let it be known Farid had forged documentation. He would never be in a position where he could accept a bribe again.

And it saddened Rashid.

As did the details of how Shelton was run, where the day-to-day finance of the castle came from, how many staff were employed on the estate...

What was clear was that Karim's request for the money paid for Golden Mile to be returned could only happen if the Duke of Missenden sold Shelton Castle. And only if he was given a very generous deadline to meet his obligation.

Everything Polly had worked for would be lost. It would be little consolation to her to know it was the consequence of her stepbrother's actions when it was his hand that wielded the justice.

Rashid shut the file and placed a stick-it note on the top, writing *'Action. Proceed as arranged'* in his usual bold hand.

He had no choice, but it was the strangest feeling. He'd finally got the evidence he'd been waiting for, he'd given the instruction to proceed and yet he felt no sense of peace about it. No satisfaction.

And the reason for that was Polly.

Not only had they not turned up anything that incriminated her, they had referred to her as Shelton's 'salvation'. Without her input it seemed her stepbrother would have lost the castle eighteen months ago.

She was the chatelaine of the castle. It was her strength of character that took a skeleton staff and made it possible to host evenings like the one he'd first seen her at.

Sulaiman, one of his most trusted staff members, came in with a low bow. 'Your guests are ready to leave, Your Highness.'

He stood immediately. Surely, Polly would agree he had a right to seek redress for a multimillion-pound fraud perpetrated against him?

But Bahiyaa had hit home. He *had* lied to Polly by omission. And he *was* going to take away something she'd devoted years of her life to. By the time she returned to England her life would have been altered in a way she could never have expected.

Rashid stepped out into the bright sunshine and immediately saw Polly standing a little away from the rest of her team, her hand shading her eyes, looking up at the vast doors to the palace. Just as she'd stood looking out across the rose garden.

She seemed to sense him because she turned and smiled. Involuntarily he walked towards her.

'Karim says we are not permitted to take photographs of the palace. Are you sure about that?'

'Quite sure.'

'Really?'

'It is my home and, therefore, private.'

'Shelton Castle is my home and we allow people to take photographs all the time.'

Guilt washed through him. He needed to tell her everything, but he wanted to do so in a way that would soften the blow.

He liked her. He admired her strength.

And for all he'd told himself he would keep his distance from her he still wanted to kiss her. If he'd been able to he would have held her close and shielded her from life's blows with his own body.

She looked very different from the woman in the rose garden. Her face was clear of make-up, her blond hair secured in a single braid and her clothes were Western. Very much more the woman he'd first met at Shelton.

He wanted to kiss beneath her ear lobe and down the length of her neck to where her clavicle met her collarbone. Run his tongue along her bottom lip, coaxing, teasing...

Beyond foolish. Rashid moved away, walking towards the waiting cars.

Baz looked up from the maps he'd laid out across the bonnet. 'Will we be taking the main coast road?'

He was deliberately slow to answer, and grateful when Steve sauntered over to ask, 'How long a drive? It looks like it'll take the best part of the day.'

Another lie by omission. At least this one was to ensure their safety.

'Your Highness,' Karim interrupted, 'there is a telephone call I think you should take.'

A chill spread through him like ink through water. Rashid forced himself to swallow, finding his voice. 'I apologise. I will be the shortest possible time.' Abruptly he turned on his heel and walked back inside.

Karim kept pace. 'It is His Highness Prince Hanif, Your Highness.'

He nodded, his emotions held taut. Rashid reached across his desk and picked up the receiver. 'What news?'

His brother equally wasted no time. 'I've just spoken to the consultant oncologist and we're talking days. His kidneys have failed.'

It was news he'd been expecting, but it didn't make hearing it any easier. *Days.* Rashid looked up to see Bahiyaa standing in the doorway. 'Is he still able to hold a conversation?' he asked, his eyes watching for his sister's reaction to his question.

'Sporadically. He is taking large doses of morphine and is sleeping most of the time.'

'Has he—?' Rashid began.

'No.'

No. He still refused to see Bahiyaa.

'And I think we have passed the point we might have expected it.'

Rashid shook his head at his sister and she nodded. She had no tears left to cry and that ripped him apart. All that was left was acceptance.

'Rashid, do you want to be here at the end? I'm sure he could be persuaded to see you. Or at the very least you could be sent for as soon as he slips into unconsciousness…'

His hand gripped the receiver until his knuckles showed white. What was the point of that? He could watch his father take his last breath—but only as long as his father wasn't aware he was there to see it.

'No.'

At the other end of the phone there was silence.

'I will make sure nothing goes awry during filming. The next few days will be crucial for you. We will continue as we discussed.'

'Rashid—'

'We agreed.'

There was another lengthy pause. 'Bahiyaa shouldn't be alone. Should—'

'She is here.' Rashid motioned for his sister to come closer and passed her the receiver.

He turned his back to give her privacy, but he couldn't help but hear her side of the conversation. It was punctuated by long pauses in which he could only imagine what Hanif was saying.

'Perhaps it is better like this.' Another pause and then Bahiyaa said, 'Will you ring me as soon as you have… news?'

Quiet and dignified and completely in control of her emotions. Rashid heard the click as Bahiyaa ended the call and he came back to hold her in his arms.

She still didn't cry but stood so stiffly and he couldn't think of a single thing that might comfort her. Her father was dying, so angry with her he refused to see her. 'Do you want me to stay?' he asked softly.

'No.' Bahiyaa pulled back. 'Nothing has changed. I want Hanif to be Amrah's next king. Nothing must go wrong now. When he is King he will be able to give me my freedom.'

That was true. They had talked about it often. Bahiyaa clung to that with tenacity. It was her one hope.

'Omeir will never be able to touch me again. I can endure far more than being here alone knowing that.' She smiled. 'But I am sorry you have suffered because of me. You should be with our father.'

Rashid leant forward and kissed her cheek. 'I am sorry you are suffering because of his blindness. He is wrong and makes his own choice.'

'Where is he?' Baz asked, looking at his watch for the fifteenth time. 'This is ridiculous.'

'He's a prince, we are but mortals,' John quipped, pulling out a cigarette and patting his pocket for matches. 'Light, anyone?'

Polly said nothing. She watched the door, waiting for Rashid to reappear. To be called back like that couldn't be good. It had to be news about his father.

And she cared.

Polly shivered. What *was* happening inside?

Bizarrely, because the circumstances were so dissimilar, it brought back memories of her father's death. Details she hadn't thought of in years came flooding back. She remembered standing in Mrs Portman's red-carpeted hall listening while the other woman spoke about 'getting the little thing in her coat ready' and 'popping her in the taxi'.

Before then she'd thought her father would get better. That had been the longest drive of her life. Eight years old and she'd never been in a taxi on her own before. Her mother had met her at the hospital doors and had held her close.

Polly bit her lip so hard she drew blood. Rashid was no child of eight. Whatever was happening now he would be able to rationalise, but she ached for him. There was unfinished business between him and his father and that would haunt him for the rest of his life.

'Here he is! Now we can get going. 'Bout *bloody* time,' John said under his breath.

Polly spun round to look at Rashid, searching his handsome face for some sign of what had happened. There was nothing to see. His eyes were emotionless.

'I am sorry to have delayed you,' Rashid said by way of a greeting. 'Shall we leave?'

He barely spared her a glance. She shouldn't have expected he would, but it hurt that he didn't look to her. She felt so close to him. Connected.

Because she loved him.

The thought slid into her brain but it brought no surprise. *Of course*, she loved him. He'd let her see the man behind the prince. Nothing she'd read about him had prepared her for that.

She was in love with the man who shielded his sister. The man who loved his brother without rivalry. The man who had sat in the cool of the evening and listened to her. He was exciting. Compelling. A man she could trust with her life.

Except he didn't want that. She tempted him, but she was not what he wanted. He'd been conditioned to want an Arabian wife and she could never be that, however much she loved him.

Polly allowed herself to be steered into one of the waiting cars and, unlike last time, Rashid travelled alone.

She sat back in the soft leather seat, free to notice the way the convoy moved off in perfect unison and the way the outriders took their place at regulated intervals.

She knew what it was like to live among the British aristocracy, but this was a mode of travel she'd no experience of outside of Amrah. Despite the beauty of Rashid's palatial home she'd allowed herself to forget he was royalty.

She was in love with an Amrahi prince. A man of influence and power. No amount of physical chemistry was going to make anything other than a temporary relationship between them possible. It wasn't simply a matter of cultural divide. It was status, expectation, money, connections.

In backing away from their kiss Rashid had been kind. He'd not allowed her to hope.

'Where are we?' Pete asked, cupping his hand to peer out of the tinted window. 'Looks like we're heading for a private airport.' He whistled. 'There are helicopters waiting. Nice.'

All three cars came to a stop in perfect alignment. The motorcycle outriders dismounted and guards with guns took their positions.

'I suppose the great man didn't fancy driving.'

Or didn't think it was safe enough. That had to be a possibility, too. Rashid had personally guaranteed their safety. His father was dead or dying and he was here, keeping his word.

Polly hung back, watching as Rashid disappeared from sight and then waiting until she was directed which helicopter to go to. It was a couple of minutes, no more, before she was climbing in with the blades already spinning above. She settled herself in one of the seats, taking care to fasten the seat belt tightly across her lap, before looking up to see Rashid was at the controls.

It was a visual confirmation of the chasm between them. He lived a life of private planes, helicopters, race horses.

A prince.

She watched as he confidently ran through his pre-flight checks. Then, with a controlled lurch, the helicopter lifted up off the ground. Polly stared, glassy eyed, out of the window as Samaah became an aerial view, the modern motorways cutting a great swathe across it.

This was everything she had dreamed of seeing, the adventure she wanted, but she felt hollow inside. Around Samaah the countryside was vast and empty. For a time. Then the arid stony ground gave way to salt flats and, within minutes, she had her first glimpse of the Arabian Sea. Turquoise blue and edged with Amrah's famous white sands.

A town spread out in the shape of a pear drop and was dominated by three craggy forts, presumably built to protect from marauding forces from the sea. Al-Jalini. And as dramatically beautiful as anything she could have imagined.

Polly held her breath while Rashid swung the helicopter out over the sea and back towards town, coming to land on a designated helipad in the gardens of what looked like a fanciful sultan's palace. It was all arches, marble pillars and a stunning domed atrium.

Baz swore softly beside her. 'Like something out of *Ali Baba and the Forty Thieves*, isn't it?'

She nodded. It was exactly like that. A place for tourists who preferred their experience of Arabia to be sanitised. Polly released her seat belt and reached inside her bag for her sunglasses.

'Let's go.'

She nodded again and followed Baz and John as they stepped down from the helicopter into unexpectedly lush gardens. By the time she turned another pilot was at the controls and Rashid had come to stand beside her, tension radiating from him.

'What is this place?'

'The Al-Ruwi Palace Hotel,' Rashid answered her question crisply, his eyes focused on the helicopters hovering like gnats above. 'I'm sorry if the change of plan has unsettled you but it is safer to fly.'

Polly so desperately wanted to ask about his father. She wanted to reach out and smooth the crease between his eyebrows, kiss away the tiredness in his eyes. There was no opportunity, even had she dared. Baz joined them, smiling broadly. 'Fantastic view coming in. Just wished we'd had a chance to get some shots of that.'

'If you wish I can arrange it,' Rashid said, turning his attention to the second helicopter.

'Bikini-babes everywhere,' John whispered in her ear, reaching into his pocket for his packet of cigarettes. 'Bit different from Samaah.' He stepped away before lighting up and Baz wandered over to join him.

Polly took a sharp intake of breath. She couldn't wait any longer. She had to know. 'Was the news bad?'

A tell-tale muscle pulsed in his cheek. 'Expected.' Rashid met her gaze briefly. 'Hanif will ring when it is over.'

'Shouldn't you be there? With the rest of your family at least?' Rashid shouldn't be here babysitting a Western film crew he'd never really wanted to come.

'I have not been asked for.'

'And Bahiyaa?' She asked the question even though she knew the answer.

'Is content to remain in Samaah.'

'Couldn't she have come here with us?'

Rashid's face broke into a half-smile, the bleak look vanishing. 'To the desert? Bahiyaa would rather shave her head.'

Polly choked on a sudden laugh. It was strange how crying and laughter were so close. Flip sides of the same coin. 'She does hate it, doesn't she? She told me riding camels was a male preserve and that they were welcome to it.'

A frisson of awareness crackled between them.

'S-so, is that true?'

'Among the Bedouin people of the Atiq Desert, yes. Their womenfolk walk behind.'

'Sexist!'

His eyes smiled down at her. 'You have yet to sit on a camel. We will talk after.'

It was their only chance to talk before they were joined by her colleagues.

'I have taken the liberty of arranging rooms here at the Al-Ruwi Palace Hotel. Its security is tight and they're used to accommodating Western visitors. There are good sports facilities, a bar...'

'Did someone say bar?' John asked, looking about him for an ashtray only to have a uniformed hotel employee hurry over.

Polly soon wandered away. Down two broad steps to her right there were fifty or so chefs dotted along the edge of a sweeping circular courtyard and cooking on giant open grills.

'Who knew the Garden of Eden was in Amrah?' Pete said, coming alongside her. 'Something, isn't it?'

Polly looked at him curiously. This wasn't Eden. It was like some fabricated film set. Fun, but not real. Not at all like the beauty of the whitewashed and sand-coloured buildings they'd flown over.

'Rashid wants us to get our room keys and then we can explore what's available here.'

'Sorry. Yes, of course.'

The path meandered through improbable planting and passed four tennis courts. No one paid the slightest bit of attention to them until they walked into the exuberantly decorated reception hall. Then the Amrahi nationals noticed Rashid. Curious eyes turned on them from all directions and those nearest executed deep bows.

And Polly felt sad for him. Sad, not sorry. He wasn't a man you could feel pity for. But, sad, yes. Surrounded by people but essentially very alone. She hung back, noticing the care he took of other people. The skill with which he stopped them becoming over-familiar.

If she could she would have brushed them all aside and given him the peace and solitude he must want. Her own colleagues seemed oblivious to anything other than their own reasons for being in Amrah. It didn't even seem to have occurred to them that Rashid was greatly inconvenienced by their being there.

They didn't seem anything other than thrilled at the prospect of good sports facilities and a bar. Within minutes of noticing the sign they'd made plans for the rest of the morning, planning to meet as soon as they'd seen their luggage safely installed in their rooms.

'You don't like it here, do you?' Rashid said, making her jump.

Polly pushed her sunglasses back up on her head. 'It's…it's…er…' She glanced round at the flame colours of the opulent furnishings, the gilt decoration and mock-sultan palace touches. 'Do you?'

'It wasn't designed to impress for me.'

No, this was strictly for tourists. She glanced up at him.

'I suppose I've seen the real thing. It's not designed for someone like me either.'

Rashid's eyes warmed. 'Ah, but it has a licence to serve alcohol.'

'Naturally important,' Polly whispered back. 'Alcohol is always a primary consideration when you've chosen to holiday in a "dry" country.'

He laughed quietly, holding out a swipe card. 'You'll need this to get into your room.'

'Thank you.'

'And the lifts are this way,' Rashid said, pointing towards the left. 'I will show you the way to your room.'

Her smile wavered as she struggled not to let him see how aware she was of the fact they were alone. Her stomach felt as though it were a mass of frothy bubbles and the thoughts running through her head were a confusing muddle of contradictions.

She wanted to tell him his kiss was the most erotic thing she'd ever experienced—and, of course, she wanted him to know it hadn't bothered her at all. That she understood why he wouldn't want a relationship with her—and to scream at him that he was missing something wonderful.

Because it *would* be wonderful between them. The air was so completely charged when they were together. That couldn't just be one-sided. She didn't believe it. Breathing in, she caught the scent of his skin mingled with a manly fragrance and a shiver whipped through her as his arm brushed against hers.

She had never reacted to a man like this before. *She had never been in love before.*

A glass lift wafted them up to the fifth floor. Polly cleared her throat as the doors parted on a whisper. 'Are you on this floor, too?'

'Two floors above.'

More thoughts crowded into her head. She wanted him to know she understood completely that he'd want to be alone—but that he didn't have to be unless he wanted to. Sometimes, in the darkest times, you needed someone to sit with you, even though they were powerless to truly help.

Polly stepped out onto marble flooring. 'I think I'm that way,' she said, catching sight of the number 7.

'Yes.'

If he needed a friend she could be that. When she reached her room she stopped, checking the number on the door against the one on her swipe card. 'This is it.'

Did she ask him in now for a drink? Or did she offer to meet him for lunch? It *felt* different now they were in the hotel, as though Western rules applied. Not that that helped her much. It mattered too much to feel easy.

'Do you know how these things work?' she asked after her third try at opening her door.

His fingers brushed her hand as he took the swipe card and she swallowed hard.

'Like this,' he said, moving the card in front of a box, which flashed red. 'Now you can turn the handle.'

The door immediately swung open, a tantalising glimpse offered of the room beyond.

'I hope you will find the accommodation to your satisfaction.'

Polly closed her eyes and willed the words to leave her mouth. 'Would you rather be by yourself or would you prefer company?'

'Polly—'

'You must be thinking about your father. About Bahiyaa…'

She heard him exhale and steeled herself to turn round.

'It's going to be a long day if you spend it all by yourself.' She wished she had the right to walk into his arms and simply hold him. Hold him tight and make him feel loved, cared for and accepted. But she didn't. She could only talk. Take his mind off what he couldn't change.

Rashid's indecision was obvious. His firm jaw was clenched hard, his hands balled into fists by his side. Polly turned away and left him to follow or not.

She threw her handbag down on the king-size bed and fought an incongruous desire to laugh as she caught the full glory of the opulent crimson drapes tied back with oversized gold tassels. 'And you really ought to see this,' she said with the quickest of glances over her shoulder.

Rashid came in, the lines about his eyes deepening as he saw what she was pointing at.

'I thought the flame-coloured tea lights downstairs were tacky. But that's wonderful.' She moved over to investigate the room's tea and coffee facilities. 'Oh, and look, I can even do my own version of *gahwa*!'

He smiled but it was clearly an effort.

'I can be quiet, too,' she said gently.

He shook his head as though to deny he thought she needed to moderate her behaviour for him. 'Perhaps I ought to go? I am not very good company.'

'Sit out on the balcony for a while.'

He hesitated.

She peeked inside the mini-bar. 'I can offer you pineapple juice, orange juice, grape juice...with ice!' Polly said, holding up a small bag of ice cubes. 'Now, that's good.'

Again a smile that didn't quite reach his eyes. 'Pineapple with ice would be lovely.'

'This isn't going to compete with the fresh fruit juices you've given me,' she said, taking out two glass bottles.

'This looks exactly like the bottles we have at home.' Polly placed a handful of ice cubes in the bottom of two hi-ball glasses and poured the pineapple juice on top.

When she looked back Rashid had opened the French windows. He didn't turn to smile as she came out to join him. In fact, he didn't look at her at all. His eyes were fixed on a distant point and he looked indescribably weary.

Polly drew a quick shallow breath and then set the drinks down on the table. He'd chosen to stay with her rather than be alone.

'Is there a set time when your brother will call with news?'

Slowly his eyes refocused on her. 'He will ring each evening and, of course, earlier if there is anything to tell me.' Rashid's fingers circled on the rim of his glass.

'And will he ring Bahiyaa or will you?'

'I think we will both call.' He paused, and then said, 'This is...kind of you.'

'This' being the drink, the sitting alongside him, the being company. It felt as if someone had reached inside her and were squeezing her heart so that it cried blood.

'I'm sorry you have to be here,' she said huskily. 'Babysitting us must be the last thing you want to be doing.'

'It is needful.'

If they stayed with the revised itinerary he'd given to them he'd have at least five days in this hotel. Two in the Atiq Desert.

His father was dying. And he shouldn't be here.

Polly let the silence stretch between them. He would talk if he wanted to and she wasn't about to force a conversation on him. What she really wanted to do was tell him everything would be all right. But, of course, it wasn't going to be. His father *was* going to die without Rashid having the comfort of a proper goodbye.

And she couldn't hold him. She shouldn't even reach out to hold his hand. The last time she'd done that it had snapped whatever semblance of control they'd had.

Rashid took a deep breath, seeming to make a conscious effort to rouse himself.

She smiled. 'I suppose the sooner we get this thing shot, the sooner you can go home. I'm not sure the guys are going to want to leave here and go home, though. Pete thinks he's stumbled into Eden and—'

Rashid leant across the table and captured her hand. His fingers interlaced with hers. Dark against the comparative paleness of her skin.

In such a short time she would be back at Shelton. Life would go on exactly as it had done for years. She would read about him, see photographs, but his life wouldn't touch hers again.

He might never hold her hand again. She had to remember this.

CHAPTER EIGHT

RASHID wasn't used to feeling so uncertain. He'd so much he needed to tell her—and the truth was he was reluctant to begin. Polly's beautiful blue eyes were shining with unshed tears. Tears he knew were there for him. Because she cared. He could count on the fingers of one hand the people who really cared about him.

And he was about to shatter her faith in him. If he was truly honest he was going to have to tell her about the suspicions he'd harboured about her. The decisions he'd taken because of that.

He was going to have to tell her that her home would be sold piecemeal. That he knew Shelton's famous Rembrandt was a copy, the original sold two years before. That it was quite possible the remaining Lovell family portraits, amassed over centuries, would be split up and sold to different collectors across the world.

That the detailed conservation programme she'd spent hours, weeks, months putting together would never be brought to fruition. That the young trees she'd had planted might never become the orchard she'd envisioned. That six years of her life had been devoted to something he'd decided to bring to an end.

Was it weak to want to delay the moment? His fingers moved against the palm of her hand. He was going to hurt her and Bahiyaa had known him better than he'd known himself. It was going to crucify him to do it.

'Wh-why are there *so* many copper coffee-pots here?' she asked, a break in her voice.

He loved it that she was nervous around him. Loved seeing the pulse beating at the base of her neck. All his adult life he'd been pursued by women. In the West it was almost entirely physical. Women who wanted the cachet of being known to be his lover. In Amrah, women wanted the status and security he could give them. Polly wanted neither, but her body betrayed her attraction to him and it excited him.

'The *dalla* is a symbol of Arabic hospitality,' he said, releasing her hand. 'The willingness to share what you have with others has its roots in survival.'

'Yes, but why *so* many? Even if this were a stage set you'd expect a few less. I love the idea of *gahwa*, though.' Polly took her sunglasses off her head, then slipped off the band she'd tied her hair back with. Rashid watched, distracted as she ran her fingers through the plait, loosening her hair into a curtain of waves that brushed her shoulders.

'Bahiyaa explained it. It's polite to drink two cups, so your host can feel bountiful, but not three, because that might expose him to want.'

He smiled.

'After you've drunk the second cup you shake it to show you've finished. Next time, if I manage to make it through the experience without fainting, I'll be ready.'

His eyes rested on her lightly sun-kissed face, her earnest expression, as she tried to keep talking so he would have something other than his father's illness to think about.

She was a woman who understood grief. She knew you needed to come in and out of it. In her company he found he could relax. He was interested in what she said and thought. He liked the way her eyes sparkled, the way they changed from blue to almost grey when she passed from happy to sad.

And he loved the way Polly wanted to explore a culture not her own. Her beautiful hands still showed the carefully drawn hennaed pattern his sister had applied, and would for days.

Her eyes followed his gaze. 'Bahiyaa painted it,' she said, self-consciously. Her forefinger traced the outline on her left hand. 'It took hours to dry. I don't think I've ever spent so long doing nothing in my entire life.' She looked up and smiled. 'I've enjoyed Bahiyaa's company so much. I will miss her.'

'And she you.'

'I wish I'd had a sister. Or brother. I think it would have been fun not to be quite so alone.' Then, 'Is…?' Polly stopped, biting the side of her lip.

'Go on.'

The tip of her tongue came out to moisten the very centre of her top lip. 'Is…?' She stopped again, then changed tack. 'Do you feel like an only child?'

Beautiful blue eyes looked across at him expecting an answer to a question no one had ever thought to ask him before. It took him to an area he'd suppressed because it had been easier to see his mother as 'bad' and to see himself only as his father's son.

But, of course, there were so many shades of grey— and the truth was his mother had been kind to her two stepchildren. Had loved them. The sibling bond he shared with Hanif and Bahiyaa had been forged then.

So, no, he didn't feel like an only child. Even though

his grandfather saw a distinction between Hanif and himself, they never had. They were brothers. Bahiyaa was their sister.

'Hanif was four when Princess Yasmeen died. Bahiyaa a baby. Neither of them have strong memories of their own mother.'

And they'd adopted his. They'd been a happy family. A unit. It was his father who had taken a mallet to it. It seemed so obvious now, but it came as a revelation.

'My mother was the only maternal figure they'd known.'

'So losing her was as difficult for them as you.'

No, that wasn't true. As painful and traumatic as his mother's leaving Amrah had been for them all, it was only he who had felt he had to rip out part of himself.

'Do they see her now?'

'Hanif has done.'

'And Bahiyaa?'

Rashid shook his head. 'She has never travelled outside of Amrah.'

'Never?' Polly's eyebrows shot up, her expressive face showing more than just amazement.

'She was married to Omeir at seventeen.'

Even as he said it the full force of what that had meant for Bahiyaa hit him. *Seventeen.* She'd endured a life sentence. Was still enduring it. It was perhaps just as well his father still refused to see him. Anger rolled over him. All the more potent because it had no outlet.

'Rashid.'

He looked up to see Polly watching him, her eyes concerned. Fearful.

'I could hate him,' he said, forcing the words out. There was no one else on earth he could say that to and know they'd hear it for what it was. 'I *do* hate him.'

'Don't.'

She reached out and took hold of his hand, as he had done hers. With infinite care she turned it over and smoothed her hand across his palm.

'My grandma believed the whole of your life was mapped out on the palm of your hand. Everything. Who you married. How many children. Whether you'd be sick. Prosperous.'

The light feather-soft touch of her fingers across his skin made it hard to concentrate, but his anger was evaporating like water in summer. She soothed him.

'She believed there was nothing we could do about any of it. But I've never believed there's a life mapped out for us. It has to be all about choices.'

Still those fingers moved over his hand.

'Some will be good and others not so good. You just have to hope you make enough good ones enough of the time to live a good life. Hating your father would be a bad choice.'

'What he's done is—'

'Wrong,' she finished for him. 'Your father is flawed. He made poor choices at some crucial points of his life. And those choices damaged other people. Hurt you. But he is dying, Rashid. You can be angry about some of the things he's done without forgetting the good things.'

And there *were* good things. It was that that ripped him in two. He wanted things to be black and white. Clearly right or wrong. A person good or bad. It was hard to admire his father so much, want his approval, and yet hate what he refused to put right for Bahiyaa. Then to realise he'd denied him a relationship with his mother and broken promises he must have made to her.

'Your time with him is running out. Can't you see your father before he dies?'

'Perhaps.'

But perhaps not. What had made his father such a good leader of men was his ability to make a decision and stick to it.

Polly's blue eyes were clear and strong. Without a doubt she would risk the rejection. He might, too, if it weren't for Bahiyaa.

'I will go if he asks for me. I cannot go without Bahiyaa.' Hanif aside, he had never spoken about this to anyone. Not even Bahiyaa, though he was sure she suspected.

'Four years ago,' he began, his voice scraping across razor blades, 'when Bahiyaa first came to me I went to see my father.'

It was painful to talk about, but with Polly it was possible. She radiated warmth. Acceptance.

'I told him. I told him about Bahiyaa.'

He had told him everything. He'd described her injuries in graphic detail: the bruises on her face and body, the broken bones and the mental scarring caused by years of living in fear. *Ten years.* He'd told him how Bahiyaa had suffered silently and struggled to cope.

'My father said that Bahiyaa had brought dishonour to our family and that he considered her dead to him. That as long as I chose to shelter her I was not welcome in his home.'

She frowned. 'You haven't seen him since Bahiyaa came to live with you four years ago?'

He nodded.

Polly sat back in her chair and looked at him. 'You are a remarkable man,' she said slowly.

Of all the things he'd expected her to say that hadn't been it. He couldn't have anticipated his reaction to her words either. It was like ice breaking deep inside him.

'I told you Bahiyaa was lucky to have you for a brother, but I hadn't realised quite how lucky. She must have been terrified.'

'She still is. And will be as long as Omeir continues to insist he wants her to come home.'

'Why does he want her to?' Polly reached forward to pick up her glass and drained the last of her pineapple juice.

Who knew? Any man who treated a woman as Omeir had treated Bahiyaa was someone beyond his comprehension. 'He says he loves her, but it's a warped kind of love. It may be pressure from his family. I don't know.'

'She can't go back.'

'No.' Bahiyaa would return to that life over his dead body.

'I should really mind my own business, particularly when it comes to things I don't know anything about. I hadn't realised what taking Bahiyaa in had meant for you. I just can't resist trying to sort everything and everyone out and sometimes they're just not fixable.'

She pulled her hair off her neck and, taking the band from her wrist, twisted it up into a loose ponytail. 'It's so hot. Do you want another drink?'

Rashid shook his head.

'I will.' She got up and went inside for a moment or two, returning with a second pineapple juice with twice the amount of ice. 'I'm sorry you can't see your father before he dies,' she said, sitting down again, 'but I think you're right. Bahiyaa needs you more. What does Prince Hanif say about it?'

'Very little. I've persuaded Hanif it's better if he doesn't. Bahiyaa is safe with me and that's really all that's important. There is nothing to be gained by both of us making the same sacrifice.'

'Difficult for him, though.'

'Yes.'

'I wish life wasn't so complicated,' she said on a sigh.

Rashid watched the shadow pass over her face, and wondered what she was thinking about, fearing he knew.

'It's *so* hot,' she said again, holding the iced glass against her cheek. 'How do people cope in summer?'

'By shutting the doors and giving thanks you live in an age of air-conditioning.' His head nodded towards the French doors propped open. 'It's an option now. You'd be cooler inside.'

She gave a soft laugh. 'That would feel like cheating. There was no air-conditioning when my great-great-grandmother lived here. I wonder how long it took her to adjust to the temperatures. You kind of imagine she'd have taken the whole thing in her stride, don't you?'

A shrill beep caught his attention. 'Is that your phone?'

Polly jumped up. 'Yes, I think it must be. I'm so rubbish with these things. Half the time I've not got it switched on and the other half I forget where I've put it.'

Rashid let his eyes wander out over the manicured gardens of the Al-Ruwi Palace Hotel while he waited for her to return. He still needed to tell her about her stepbrother. There was a situation that wasn't fixable.

'Well, that was Graham,' Polly said, returning. 'Just checking I didn't wish to join them for lunch. I'm really not that hungry when it's hot like this.'

'In Amrah we tend to opt for a simple rice dish midday,' he agreed, absent-mindedly. The trouble with delaying telling Polly the truth was that it felt dishonest, in a way it hadn't when he'd thought she might have been involved.

'Polly?'

She looked up.

'*Why* have you stayed at Shelton Castle? I know you love the house and that you grew up on the estate, but haven't you ever imagined something different for yourself?'

She looked up into his face, her eyes meeting and holding his.

That had to be the key to finding a way of ensuring Polly didn't suffer unduly. She had told him this was the first thing she'd ever done 'entirely for herself' and it was clear she was relishing everything about her Arabian adventure. She seemed to crave excitement. Yet she'd stayed with what she'd known from childhood. There had to be more to that decision than he knew—and if he knew why he would be in a far better position to offer her an alternative.

'What would you do if you had a completely free choice of what to do with your life?' he prompted.

'They're two very different questions.'

'And?'

'Why have I stayed?' she repeated slowly.

He nodded.

She hesitated, her eyes holding real sadness. 'I told you I initially came back because my mother was struggling to adjust to life as the Duchess of Missenden, didn't I?'

'Yes.'

'That…was true, but it was all a bit more complicated than that.' Her fingers splayed out on the table between them.

Rashid waited, by no means sure she would tell him anything.

She looked up. 'It concerns Anthony, so I need you to promise you won't tell anyone.'

She was lovely. The Duke of Missenden deserved no such loyalty and yet he had it.

'If any of this ended up in the British tabloids it would be horrendous.'

'I would never betray your confidence.'

'No. Sorry. It's just I never talk about the family.'

The family' as opposed to '*my* family'. It was a distinction he was beginning to understand. Nick had been right in his assessment of Polly's role at Shelton.

'But it's hardly fair to ask you questions about yours and then refuse to tell you anything about mine. So...' She took a deep breath. 'In order to minimise death duties Richard had already passed ownership of the castle to Anthony by the time he married my mother.

'That's not unusual,' she said in response to his raised eyebrow. 'It really is the only way to make it possible for the great houses to be passed intact from one generation to the next. Crazy, isn't it? You'd think they could work out a better system but, anyway, that's what Richard did. It usually works well.'

But... Rashid waited for the 'but'.

Polly twisted one of her small stud earrings. 'Unfortunately for Shelton, Anthony is a gambler.'

She knew. Relief surged through him.

'Richard said he didn't know, but I think he must have. On some level, anyway. Everyone on the estate knew. But I think we thought Anthony wouldn't touch Shelton.'

'And he did?'

Polly nodded. 'Oh, yes, it's an addiction. As soon as Richard transferred ownership he borrowed huge sums against the house. Sold a number of small things he thought no one would notice.' She tried to smile, but it faltered almost immediately. 'My mother did, of course.'

Her blue eyes looked almost grey. Polly was miles away, thinking about a time that clearly gave her pain. Rashid could all too easily picture how difficult it must have been for the new Duchess to challenge her husband's heir on missing treasures.

'And there was nothing your stepfather could do?'

'He'd transferred ownership. Shelton was Anthony's. But, at the time, Richard and my mother were still living at the castle—' She broke off, drawing in a painful breath. 'Do you want to know all this? Really?'

'I want to know why you have stayed at Shelton.' If it hadn't been so important for him to know Rashid didn't think he could have forced her to continue.

She shrugged. 'Oh, well, this *is* the "why". I'd come home for the summer after I finished at uni. I had some vague plan about doing a PhD but, to be honest, I'd had enough studying for a bit and Richard asked me to help.'

Her face changed, softened, as kinder memories ran through her head.

'He was the loveliest man. Real old school. He believed he was the custodian of Shelton for future generations and his one aim had been to hand the castle on to his heir intact.'

'Only for the heir to start dismantling it.'

'Right. It began with some of the minor paintings Richard had put into storage. Pieces of china. A few clocks. They all went to pay the interest on the loans.'

'And your stepfather knew this?'

'By the time I came home he did. Anthony was quite scared, I think. Everything had snowballed so quickly and he agreed to let his father take on the day-to-day running of the castle again.'

The day-to-day running, which, having read that final report, he now knew was Polly's responsibility.

'We divided the jobs between us. My mother continued as housekeeper. Richard concentrated on the financial side of things. And I tried to drum up new money-making enterprises to make a start on repairing the roof.'

'Successfully?'

'To an extent. Shelton is a money pit. But it was interesting work and it seemed worth doing.' She looked to him as though she were searching for his approval. 'It was only meant to be a very temporary thing.'

Polly brushed a hand across her face. 'Richard was sure Anthony would seek help...'

And, of course, that hadn't happened.

'But, gambling is an addiction and the problem had been there a long time. Richard and my mother moved out of the castle into a house on the estate and that helped maintain the peace. Anthony and Georgina took up residence in the main house.'

'And you?'

'Moved back down to the staff quarters. Much nicer.' She took a breath before continuing, 'But then there was the accident.'

Rashid saw the pulse beat in her neck and her hands move convulsively against her glass. He asked gently, 'Is that how your mother came to be in a wheelchair?'

She swallowed hard, her voice husky. 'Three years ago in May they were coming back from a party. Richard was driving and he had a stroke. Their car hit a ditch and they somersaulted. My mother broke her back but Richard never knew. He had a second stroke within twenty-four hours and died.'

She brushed a hand across her eyes. '*Damn*, I'm sorry. I hate thinking of it.'

'So you stayed.'

'Of course. While I was waiting for her to come home I installed ramps in the ground floor of the house, lowered work surfaces, fitted a bathroom in part of the garage and made a bedroom out of the other part.'

Rashid didn't really need to hear the rest of her story. He could piece it together himself.

'The upstairs I turned into a flat for me and I moved out of the staff quarters. And I tried to take over the things my mother and stepfather had been doing.'

'Why?' He knew few women who'd put their life so comprehensibly on hold. Certainly not for the years Polly had. No wonder she craved adventure. Her life was boxed in by a combination of circumstance and misplaced loyalty.

'Minty says that. She says Shelton is Anthony's responsibility and that I need to move away.' Polly tried to smile. 'And I do. I know I do. Even my mother says I do. But it's hard to let Shelton go. Mentally I accept I need to, but I can't quite do it. It feels like I'm admitting failure.'

'It's not your failure.'

'But I know I'd be letting Richard down. I know he'd have wanted me to carry on as long as Anthony lets me. And, if I left, where would I go? My mother needs care. I have a strange CV.' She took another sip of her drink. 'I've got no references. Unless Anthony can be persuaded to write me one. And, even then, who'd believe it? He's my stepbrother. I'm not sure anyone would take that seriously.'

Rashid frowned slightly. 'Does Anthony *want* you to stay?'

'Hell, no. He'd like to sell the castle. Only he can't quite bring himself to do it while I'm there. It's as though I remind him of his father and make him feel guilty.'

As well he might. Rashid sat back in his chair. Richard had been a man not unlike his friend. From the moment he'd become the Duke of Aylesbury, Nick had spent every thinking, breathing moment planning the future of his crumbling pile of ducal stones. Absolutely determined to secure it for the son he hoped he'd have one day.

'And the Beaufort Stud?' he asked, drumming his fingers on the table. It was beginning to sound as though the only person he'd hurt by dismantling Shelton was Polly.

'It's owned by the Lovell family, and has been for three generations, but it's really Georgina's baby now. She's Anthony's wife, the present Duchess of Missenden.'

'Do you like her?'

'I don't know her. She considers me "staff".'

It was an unholy mess. 'Perhaps,' he suggested carefully, 'it would be better if your stepbrother sold the castle. Then its care could be entrusted to someone who would cherish it.'

'That won't happen.' Polly looked at him. 'Anthony will make much more money if he sells it off in bits and pieces. And I suspect the castle will be divided up into upmarket apartments, sold off on some kind of long lease. That would probably be enough to salvage his pride.'

Of course, she was right.

Most disturbing from his perspective was that, instead of taking from Anthony Lovell something he valued, he was allowing a weak man to abdicate responsibility for wasting his inheritance.

It needed thinking about.

'And my second question?'

Polly looked at him, bemused for a moment, then her eyes seemed to smile. He had no idea how they did that. They seemed to light up from within.

'What would I like to do?' She leant forward and thought for a moment or two, her elbows resting on the table. 'I don't know. I like being here. I like this.'

This. He liked this, too.

Being with her. Talking to her. Even though it wasn't comfortable listening.

'In the end I'll have to go home, though. My mother will always need care.'

'Do you own the house you live in?'

'My mother does.'

That was better than it could have been. At least Anthony couldn't sell it from under them.

'So you see I don't have very much time for dreams. I mustn't waste a moment.' Polly glanced down at her wristwatch. 'There are still over four hours before I need to meet the others.'

'Do you wish to rest?'

'No.' She looked slightly hesitant. 'I was wondering whether we might go and see something of Al-Jalini? Or do you need some time alone? I can easily explore the hotel complex.'

That was the last thing he wanted. Alone he'd have too much time to think. Rashid shook his head. 'It will be a pleasure to show you something of my country.'

An opportunity to salve his own conscience, too. He was as guilty as anyone of not considering Polly's wishes. He might have more justification than most, but he'd arbitrarily taken decisions that would affect her profoundly. 'Where do you wish to go?'

'I don't mind. Somewhere that isn't on the itinerary, perhaps?' she suggested, her eyes sparkling.

Adventure. She craved adventure. And the real Arabia.

'I will arrange that,' he said, standing up. 'There is somewhere I should like to show you.' He smiled. 'Somewhere I think you will like.'

CHAPTER NINE

POLLY let Rashid go. She shouldn't have asked to leave the hotel. Her smile became rueful as she gathered up the glasses and carried them through to her bedroom. She'd a pretty good understanding now of what forces were at work in Amrah. The timing of their visit was difficult. And she ought to be co-operating with the plans Rashid had already put in place, not making things more complicated.

But maybe it would be good for him, too. The cold, shut-down look he'd worn earlier had vanished while they'd been talking.

Polly walked over to the dressing table, her own brush and comb laid out. Her make-up bag to one side. She turned her head to look at her suitcase resting on a stand.

Everything must have been unpacked. She didn't even bother to check. It didn't seem to matter if some faceless someone thought she ought to buy better quality underwear. She had other things to think about. Problems that would all be waiting for her when she got home.

She sat on the edge of the king-size bed and searched her handbag for the small folded piece of paper on which she'd written the international dialling code for the UK and the number of the Al-Ruwi Palace Hotel. Phoning home felt difficult. Her mum refused to talk about what was happening at the castle, saying she preferred to hear all about her daughter's travels, but Polly knew her too well. She could hear the weariness in her voice, the false brightness.

Today was no exception. Her mother was pleased to hear from her. Keen to tell her that Mrs Ripley, who came each morning and evening to help her get in and out of bed, was wonderful. That she'd been out to dinner with friends, and insisted they could talk about the quotes that had arrived from three local plumbers when Polly got home.

Polly ended the call absolutely certain all was not well. Anthony had become more acerbic of late and it was usually her mother he took his frustrations out on. Without her there to deflect the snide comments Polly imagined she'd be having an unpleasant time of it.

And it made her feel more trapped than ever. How could she ever leave? It wasn't in her nature to walk away from people who needed her, but coming to Amrah had made her realise she did want more.

The soft tap on her door startled her, but it brought her head up. She was not going to spoil the now. Time with Rashid was precious, because whatever the future did hold for her it certainly did not hold Amrah's playboy sheikh.

Fixing a smile, she opened the door, but it couldn't have been very convincing because Rashid immediately asked, 'Are you feeling well?'

Polly brushed a hand over her eyes. 'I'm fine. I've just rung home.'

'Are there problems?'

'My mother assures me everything is "wonderful", but I don't believe her.'

'Polly,' Rashid said, stepping close. The lines around his mouth were more defined than she had ever seen them. 'Polly, if there is anything you are worried about, at Shelton, please talk to me.'

She laughed, the sound breaking on a hiccup. She believed Rashid was a man who could move mountains, but the problems at Shelton Castle were beyond his fixing. 'I think you've got enough going on in your life without me pouring out the nonsense in mine.'

Polly turned away to search the drawers for the blue *lihaf* Bahiyaa had insisted she pack.

'Polly—'

She found the scarf and pulled it out. 'I ought to take this. It's so hot out there.'

Rashid nodded, his expression unutterably weary. *His beautiful, strong face.* Polly felt a sharp pull on her emotions, an intense compulsion to smooth the worry lines from his forehead, to reach out and cradle his face between her hands and kiss away everything that was bothering him.

He must be under so much pressure from all sides. It put her troubles into perspective. The future of a kingdom was surely more important than that of a house, however beautiful.

'Are you sure you want to do this?' she said.

'Of course.'

'Really?'

'I would like to spend time with you.'

If she hadn't fallen for him before, she'd have fallen then. Rashid held out his hand and Polly put her own in it, trying to ignore the sense of nervous anticipation.

'Where are we going?'

'You will see.'

The curl of excitement in her abdomen spread. 'Are we walking?'

Rashid smiled down at her, his eyes softening. 'You will see.'

He wasn't going to tell her, but it didn't matter where she was going. She was collecting memories, storing them up against a future that was going to be without him. Rashid led the way back to the glass lifts and, before the doors opened, released her hand, resting his in the small of her back, guiding her in.

She was a twenty-first-century woman, used to holding her own doors open, but that tiny gesture made her feel protected and cared for. Polly glanced surreptitiously up at the darkly handsome man beside her, his skin tawny gold and his chin firm. Tall, broad-shouldered and powerful. She was no size zero but he managed to make her feel delicate. And the expression in his eyes when he looked at her made her feel desirable.

It had been a long, *long* time since she'd felt that.

Rashid didn't touch her again, but she could feel the energy pulse between them. Intense, scary and completely wonderful. She wanted him with a passion that surprised her. One that made a mockery of her morality.

She'd never been promiscuous. Far too much of a people watcher to ever want to be. She'd never understood women who slept with men who clearly viewed their relationships as recreation.

Men like Rashid. He might not be prepared to accept an arranged marriage, but when the time came she was sure he wouldn't choose any of the women he'd been linked to in the British press.

But she was tempted. More than tempted. Would it be wrong? Loving him, would she survive the inevitable parting?

The lift doors slid open and Polly held back as a man stepped forward and bowed. 'All is ready, Your Highness.'

Rashid spoke in Arabic. Then turned back to her. 'The helicopter is waiting for us.'

'We're going by helicopter?'

'Yes, of course.'

Of course. In his world it was just another form of transport. He was an Amrahi prince. He lived in a palace. And for today, right now, he was hers. She wasn't going to think outside this moment.

Where were they going?

'I've only got a few hours before I've got to meet the boys in the foyer.'

'You will not be late.'

'Rashid—?'

He laughed softly. 'Patience.'

For a while she said nothing more, content to be with him. She watched as he went through the pre-flight checks, loving the strength of his hands on the controls.

'Just us?' she asked in surprise as the last of his staff prepared to leave them.

Rashid looked at her. 'We will be safe enough where we are going. Are you scared?'

Not about going without security, no. Of how she reacted to him, yes. She didn't quite recognise the woman she was when she was near him. It *was* frightening, but exciting, too.

'There is no need.'

'I suppose not,' she managed. 'We're not going to be where anyone expects us to be. That has to be safer than following a planned itinerary.'

He smiled and Polly settled back in her seat. This was a golden day. A day that would live on in her head always as being pure magic.

And she still had absolutely no idea where he was taking her. She managed a few minutes, but then she couldn't resist asking again.

'You are a hard woman to surprise,' Rashid said as he took the helicopter along the line of the coast.

Polly turned her head away from him to hide her smile. 'I'm not really used to it.'

Below her the harmonious blend of Al-Jalini's sandstone buildings gave way to a bizarre collection of… houses. Were they houses? She peered closer. 'What are the buildings with the brightly coloured plastic roofs? There.'

Rashid barely needed to glance below him. 'Homes. Traditionally they'd have been thatched, but people improvise with what they have.'

Plastic?

'The walls are made with interlocking sticks. Farther inland it tends be flattened-out oil drums. Over the border into Oman there are *barasti*, which are homes built from palm leaves. It's what's easily available and will provide shelter at little or no cost.'

She hadn't seen that in Amrah before. Samaah was a vibrant and affluent city, Rashid's palace pure fantasy. This was grinding poverty.

'Change takes time,' Rashid said, his eyes on her profile. 'And people are resistant to change. My father insisted affordable housing was built on the outskirts of Al-Jalini, and there are jobs here, but many have preferred to remain in their own communities.' Rashid took the helicopter sharply inland.

'How much farther?'

She caught the edge of his smile. He didn't answer, concentrating on bringing the helicopter down on a flat plain near a dusty hillside.

'Here?' Polly sat up straight in her seat, looking out of the window in disbelief.

He laughed.

'There's nothing here.'

'Look closer.'

She did, and looked out at a collection of puny trees clinging to an arid dusty hillside. A desolate, bleak place.

'As far back as five thousand BC this area was an important centre for frankincense.'

'What happened? Is this climate change?'

Rashid laughed again, jumping down from the helicopter and walking round to help her. He reached up and Polly put her hand in his. She looked down at him and her smile faded as the air crackled between them.

'Jump.' The rich timbre of his voice seemed to reverberate in her chest. His eyes, and the sensuality in them, sent heat to every extremity of her body.

Being with him felt like that. Like jumping. Not sure how safe the landing would be, but knowing the experience would be worth it. If she dared.

'Come.'

Polly lowered herself down, steadied by Rashid's grip on her hand until her feet touched the ground and she became aware of his left hand resting low on her waist. He was so close. She could feel the strong, hard planes of his torso. Even feel the beat of his heart.

Neither moved. A handful of centimetres apart and the moment stretched on. And on. Polly waited, her eyes caught by the fierce intensity of his.

She dragged air into lungs that had seemed to forget they had a function as his hand moved to cradle her cheek, his palm warm against her face. His eyes impossibly tender. He moved so slowly. There was time, plenty of time to pull back if she'd wished to, but she didn't.

She stood there waiting to breathe.

This kiss was different. Different from before. This time she knew she loved him and that changed things.

Polly closed her eyes, savouring his breath on her lips before the first fleeting touch of his mouth.

So teasing. Warmly sensual.

His touch was almost reverent.

Polly felt the fear recede. She wanted this. For however long, whatever he could give her.

She wanted him to remember this moment.

Remember her.

Her lips parted and Rashid's hold on her head became firmer, his kiss more insistent.

Warm. Soft. Sexy. She felt as though she were melting from the inside out, and that had nothing to do with the strong Amrahi sun.

His tongue traced the line of her bottom lip and her hands clung to him as passion engulfed her. A tsunami-type wave that swept away everything before it. And, finally, she understood what had prompted Elizabeth to leave her family.

This. It was this.

The desire for this and its discovery. There was nothing clean and sanitised about this emotion. It was raw. Dangerous. Compelling.

Her fingers closed on the material of his *dishdasha*, the air warm and sultry around her and her senses full of the scent of his skin, of spice and musk.

Slowly, his eyes watching for her reaction, he pulled back. His right hand moved to pull the band from her hair, the silky softness falling about her face as Rashid reached for her again. His mouth compelling and sensual.

She loved him.

Loved him.

His tongue slipped into her mouth and she felt her tremble the length of her body, a fierce dragging sensation of need low in her stomach. His hands, either side of her face, held her prisoner.

'Polly.' Rashid's voice was hoarse, almost desperate. His arms held her close, his forehead resting on hers, waiting for the world to steady.

He eased back, one thumb tracing the line his tongue had taken over her sensitised bottom lip. 'You enflame me.'

And you me.

'I do not wish… I have no right to seduce you.'

Polly reached out and traced the deep indenture by the side of his mouth. 'I kissed you back,' she whispered.

'Polly, I…' The words seemed wrenched from him, his hold on her convulsive. 'Not now. This cannot happen.'

He was right, of course. He couldn't make love to her on a dry and dusty hillside, but the feeling of rejection was intense. She'd all but offered herself to him. And she'd never done anything like that before in her entire life.

This cannot happen.

She wanted to ask why. More than anything she wanted to change his mind. But Rashid had already stepped back.

'This afternoon was supposed to be for you. I wished…' He rubbed an impatient hand across his face. 'I want you to have memories to take away with you. Good memories.'

So did she. She wanted those memories filled with him.

'Polly, I—'

'Don't!' She didn't want to hear any explanations of anything. She was doing well to be still standing. If it had been possible she'd have taken herself away to a dark place and curled herself in the smallest possible ball. 'I understand.'

'Polly.'

'No, really. It's fine.' She neatly sidestepped him and

stood looking out at the desolate place he'd brought her to. 'Where does frankincense come from now?'

'Here.' Rashid moved closer. 'The fabled golden city Queen of Sheba saw has long gone, but the trees are still here.'

Polly blinked hard, fiercely determined to pretend she was just fine.

'All that has really changed is its commercial value. Frankincense is no longer as valuable as gold. Once upon a time men made their fortunes trading it against spices from India and caravans took it across the entire continent.'

He started towards the stony and uneven ground. Polly followed, still bemused as to how this bleak landscape could ever have been a golden city. Rashid stooped and picked up a sharp stone, which he then jabbed against the flaky tree bark.

Polly watched as an oozing blob of sap bubbled up out of the slash in the tree. 'That's frankincense?'

'And it's still harvested today and sold around the world.' He pulled a bit and rubbed it between his finger and thumb. It gathered together into a glutinous ball which he flicked away.

'I'd no idea it came from trees.'

'As a child I thought it was magical.' He seemed to be lost in thought, as though a bittersweet memory was crowding in around him.

His father was dying.

Immediately Polly felt guilty. There must be so much going on in his mind. Huge pressures crushing in on him. Nothing mattered so much in the face of that. She reached out and caught his hand. 'Thank you. For showing me this.'

Rashid looked down to where their fingers were

joined. His thumb moved against her palm. 'There is somewhere else.'

'Wh—?' she began, but he shook his head.

'You will see. Come, there is plenty of time yet.'

It would have been possible to negotiate the uneven ground alone, but she liked the feel of his hand in hers. 'Can you land these things anywhere?' she asked as they approached the helicopter.

Rashid lifted their joined hands and pressed a kiss against the inside of her wrist. 'That depends on the skill of the pilot.'

'Can *you* land them anywhere?'

His blue eyes took on a sinful glint. 'You had better hope so.'

Polly's stomach performed a complete somersault. She climbed up into the helicopter and settled herself into the seat. Was it really possible to fall in love so completely and so quickly? Or was this like a desert mirage, nothing more than a distant reflection?

She glanced over at his strong profile. She only knew she'd give up everything to be with him. If he asked her to. This place, this country... She could love it.

Within moments they were airborne, the frankincense trees dotted below her. 'Has anyone tried to find the city?'

'Archaeologists. Adventurers.' Rashid turned his head to look at her and smiled. 'Your great-great-grandmother. No one has yet found incontrovertible proof one way or the other. Amrah is a country which holds its secrets closely.'

A mystical land. Polly stared out of the window as the stony land gave way to scrubby sand and, in the distance, wide-open desert. She turned back to Rashid. 'The Atiq Desert?'

He nodded and excitement whipped through her body.

'Not where you plan to film, but my home. The place I return to.'

The Atiq Desert stretched out endlessly. Not as she'd imagined it. It was a landscape studded with volcanic remains. Jet-black against the pale gold of the sand.

'It's amazing.' Then, 'There are people.'

'Bedouin. "Conquerors come and go, but it is only the Bedouin who stay,"' Rashid quoted softly.

'Camels! Rashid…'

Rashid wished he could watch her face, but he needed to concentrate on landing safely. Her excitement was contagious. Whether or not the reality of Bedouin life would live up to her romantic dreams he couldn't say, but he wanted her to experience it.

In many ways, if it didn't it would help when the time came to watch her leave. And she would leave. She'd return to a life he was dismantling. Khalid would already have acted on his instructions. He'd wondered, today back at the hotel, whether her mother had said something and that was why she'd been crying.

She had been crying. And he'd ached for her. For what he was about to do to a place she loved so much. If she knew would she still quiver in his arms? Bahiyaa's words echoed in his head: 'I do not think she will be able to forgive you that, Rashid.'

'Have they come to meet us?' Polly asked, turning back from the stationary cameleers and their bad-tempered charges.

Rashid landed the helicopter with minimum sand disturbance. 'You wished to ride a camel.' He smiled at her inarticulate squeal beside him.

'You arranged this. How? But, how did you do this in such a short time?'

'I am a prince,' he teased, 'and we princes of the

desert have a centuries-old method of communicating with our own.'

Polly wasn't fooled for a minute. Her eyes sparkled. 'You used a mobile.'

'Even the Bedouin have cell phones these days,' he agreed.

She was addictive, Rashid thought, loving the low chuckle she gave. If he could he would do more than this for her. Any dream she had he would strive to give her.

Anything that did not touch on his honour.

Anything but Shelton's reprieve.

'This is incredible! And Elizabeth came here?'

'With King Mahmoud. Without a doubt. This is his tribe. His people.'

'Am I dressed all right?' Polly asked suddenly, reaching down for her *lihaf*.

'You are beautiful. And you are with me. These men are my friends, my kin.'

Her beautiful eyes looked up at him.

'And,' he said with a smile, 'they will think you are dressed very unwisely.'

Polly smiled and twisted the scarf around her head, the blue of the *lihaf* bringing out the deep sapphire colour of her eyes. She was more than beautiful. And he felt a fierce spurt of pride at the thought these men would think she was his.

His.

A possessive word. A word that sounded good to him.

Kareem, the man who had first sat him on a camel, came forward to greet them, bowing low.

Rashid moved close to Polly, saying quietly, 'They do not speak any English.'

There was no time for any more before the *chanteur* offered his welcome. '*Ahlan beekum. As-salaam alaykum.*'

'*Wa alaykum as-salaam,*' Polly replied formally. She shot a mischievous look in his direction. 'How was that?'

Her pronunciation needed a little work but it was impressive. As she was a foreigner, an *ajnabi*, not one of the men present would have expected that. He hadn't. But Polly was a continual surprise to him.

Rashid went through the important process of enquiring after everyone's health, one eye on Polly as she took in the camel asserting his male dominance by blowing out his throat lining.

Her blue eyes looked to him for reassurance and he smiled. 'Ready?'

'For what?'

'Your camel ride?'

Polly looked hesitantly at the wizened little man coming towards her, gesturing back at a large one-humped camel. That had been her fantasy, but faced with the reality she was less sure. It was really only the glinting amusement in Rashid's eyes that spurred her on.

She pointed at the camel, hoping her body language would convey what needed to be said.

Kareem nodded, stopping by a white camel. 'Ashid.'

'*Ashid?*' Polly queried, looking back at Rashid.

'The name of your camel,' he said, strolling over with a smile.

Polly was pleased Ashid hadn't been the one blowing out its neck like bubblegum. She turned, disconcerted, when Kareem started to make a noise that she could best describe as being like a cappuccino machine.

'He's asking it to sit.'

After a moment's hesitation Ashid obliged, sinking down on its knees. Perilously perched on top of the single hump was a roll of fabric.

This couldn't be any harder than mounting a horse,

Polly told herself firmly. She allowed Rashid to help her sit astride. 'Tuck your feet up behind,' he instructed, 'and grip with your knees.'

He'd barely finished speaking before Kareem gave an instruction that had Ashid lurching upwards. Polly let out a shriek and looked down to see Rashid's laughing eyes watching her. She clutched at the makeshift saddle, glad another one of the cameleers had Ashid firmly on a lead.

She was too busy trying to get her feet up behind her to watch Rashid climb on his own 'ship of the desert'. The heat was sizzling hot, scorching through the light scarf. Polly looked curiously at the turbanlike headgear the Bedouin wore, but Rashid was too far away to ask anything about it and within moments she was concentrating on adjusting to the camel's movement.

Once she'd got used to the bouncing it was reasonably comfortable. The heat was something else. Minty's insistence they try to film everything during the cooler months made absolute sense. Polly kept her eyes firmly on the tree they seemed to be making for.

It had the appeal of lights flickering in a cottage window on a stormy night back home. It spoke of safety and rest. But she loved every minute of her camel ride. She turned round to smile at Rashid, so happy she wanted to laugh.

Her desert prince looked as though he'd been born to ride a camel. Which, in a way, he had. The animal's uneasy gait didn't produce the same lurching it did for her. He was able to talk to the men walking beside him, laughing as one of them struck up a tuneless chanting. From the other men's reactions she assumed the lyrics were probably quite rude.

'So was Bahiyaa right? Do you think riding camels should be reserved for men?' Rashid asked as she inelegantly climbed off Ashid.

'I think the jury is still out.' Her legs felt a little as if they'd turned to jelly. Rashid seemed aware of that because he reached out to steady her, his hand coming to rest on the small of her back.

'You did well.'

She laughed. 'Surprised?'

'Not as much as I thought I'd be,' he answered. 'Now we get lunch and a rest before we head back to Al-Jalini.'

Polly walked gratefully under the shade of the shrubby tree. 'Is this an acacia tree?'

He nodded, pulling the rolled fabric off Ashid and bringing it over for her to sit on.

'How does it survive out here?'

Rashid came to sit beside her. 'It has root systems which spread out a hundred feet or more. As you get nearer the wadi there are considerably more than here.'

She watched as the cameleers tied the front legs of the camels together, turning to Rashid with an impulsive, 'Does that hurt them?'

'No. Annoys them, perhaps,' he said. 'There is a saying among the Bedouin that you should never trust a camel. You can't take any chances. To lose your camel out here would be like being shipwrecked.'

Polly had thought she'd read fairly extensively, but there was so much she wanted to know. Everything about the Atiq Desert fascinated her. The men had already lit some kind of a brazier. Kareem was involved in a complicated process of pouring liquid from one pot to another from a flamboyant height.

'Wh—?' she began.

Rashid settled back into the shade of the tree, more at peace than Polly had ever seen him. He'd described this as his home, and it seemed it was. His palace home was sumptuous, but it came with much responsibility.

Here there was just space. Quiet, all bar the sound of camels complaining and munching on the thorny branches of the acacia tree. It felt so much like sitting in the centre of history. The birth place of three world religions. The petty squabbles of Shelton, her concern over its long-term future, suddenly seemed so very unimportant.

She turned her head to find Rashid was watching her, his blue eyes unfathomable. 'This is the most amazing place I've ever seen.'

He smiled.

'What is he doing?' she asked with a look at Kareem. 'Making tea.'

She looked back as the cameleer poured the liquid into several glasses already laid out on a tray.

'Water is precious here and is treated like vintage wine.'

Polly knew Rashid's eyes didn't leave her face as she first sipped the frothy tea. Over the rim of his own glass, Rashid's eyes were wickedly teasing.

'*Shukran,*' she murmured as Kareem returned her glass a second time. The flavour was slightly different. Sweeter. Perhaps a result of tea and sugar continuing to blend.

In twenty-seven years Polly didn't think she'd ever experienced such peace. It was partly Rashid, partly the incredible privilege of being here in a magical place he loved. Real happiness bubbled inside her.

The tallest man, the one who'd guided Ashid, stretched out some dough rather as you would a pizza. It was all fairly surreal. As meals went it was one of the simplest she'd ever eaten. She'd no idea what the men around her were saying, but she loved the laughter and their easy camaraderie.

'It's time we were leaving,' Rashid said, breaking in on her thoughts.

Polly experienced a wave of disappointment and then her innate sense of responsibility kicked in. 'I wish... I hope I can come back here one day.' She smiled up at him, fighting an inexplicable desire to cry. 'Thank you.'

Rashid caught her chin, tilting her face so that he could look deep into her eyes. 'Pollyanna Anderson, you are a remarkable woman,' he said, almost echoing her words to him.

It wasn't a declaration of love, not in any conventional sense, but it felt like it.

CHAPTER TEN

THE flight back to the Al-Ruwi Palace Hotel seemed to take no time at all. Al-Jalini, beautiful though it was, didn't have the charm of the desert and the hotel gardens were an unnatural splash of green.

Polly felt as if she'd left a little piece of her heart behind. She looked down at her watch. 'I should have time for a shower before I meet the boys,' she said with false brightness. 'Then we're off to the souk. According to Dr Wriggley it's one of the oldest in Amrah.'

Rashid nodded. 'You'll walk under the same tall arch Elizabeth did.'

'Will you be there?'

Polly saw the muscle pulse in his cheek and knew his answer before he gave it. 'There is no need. You will have security with you.'

She could feel him slipping away from her. 'What will you do?'

'Work.' His monosyllabic reply set her at a distance. She knew, logically, that he would have to. He'd taken hours off today to help the film crew, ensuring their safety, and then spending time with her this afternoon. But...

It felt more than that. As though the weight of the world had come back to rest on his shoulders.

'When will you speak to Prince Hanif again?'

'This evening.' Rashid brought the helicopter down on the hotel's helipad. Within seconds her door was opened and hotel staff were helping her down.

Polly flicked the scarf from her head and shook out her hair as Graham ambled over. 'Where have you been?'

She felt a ridiculous reluctance to tell him. It was as though the sound man was trying to force his way into something intensely precious. Private. 'We've flown over the Atiq Desert,' she evaded, turning back to watch Rashid step down from the helicopter.

He came over. 'I will leave you.'

There was nothing Polly could say. Not with Graham overhearing every word. And that was probably just as well, because what was there to say? She wanted to reach out and touch him. Hold him. Take the pain of whatever he was experiencing away, make it hers.

Rashid held himself stiffly, completely inaccessible. The man she'd kissed so passionately had vanished.

'Graham.' He nodded at the other man. 'I will see you both later this evening, perhaps?'

By the time Steve had decided they'd filmed enough for the day Polly was exhausted. She'd walked up and down one section of the souk more times than she could remember, each time exclaiming at the same stalls of silver-ware. She'd loved the canopied roof of palm fronds, the feeling of walking in the footsteps of her great-great-grandmother, but her mind had been elsewhere.

It was with Rashid, wondering whether he'd any news about his father. Whether he'd spoken to Bahiyaa.

'Drink?' John asked as they walked into the foyer. 'Or shall we get something to eat first?'

'What about the prince? Might be a good idea to ring up? See if he wants to join us?' Baz looked over at the reception area and then back at them. 'What d'you reckon?'

'Do it,' John said. 'We'll wait in the bar. Come find us.'

Polly let herself be guided towards the largest of the hotel's bars, edged with small seating booths. She missed the quiet of the desert. She wanted to be with Rashid. There was a slight possibility he might decide to join them, but she doubted it.

She sat cradling her chilled pineapple juice, one eye on the entrance watching for Baz to return. The tall Yorkshireman walked over shaking his head. 'Nope. Didn't actually get to speak to Sheikh Rashid. Spoke to his aide. The one from Samaah. He flew in an hour or so ago,' he said, pulling a face. 'I think the Crown Prince might be a goner.'

Polly put her pineapple juice down on the table. 'Did he say that?'

'No. Didn't say anything at all which is why I think there's been some bad news. Wasn't supposed to be here, was he?'

Pete pushed a beer across in Baz's direction. 'What'll that mean to us?'

'We'll be out of here, won't we? No way Minty is going to keep us here if it looks like the country is going to be unstable for a bit.'

There were a few disgruntled murmurs.

Baz added, 'She didn't like the changes to the itinerary. Think she'd have had us home then if she hadn't wanted not to offend Sheikh Rashid. I reckon we'll be out.'

Polly quietly slipped away, leaving her juice scarcely

touched on the table. Baz was almost certainly right in thinking Karim Al Rahhbi's arrival at the hotel couldn't be a good sign. She wasn't quite sure what she actually intended to do now. She simply knew she couldn't sit there making small talk when Rashid might need her.

She'd no particular reason for thinking it, but she suspected he'd told her things about his family he'd not discussed with anyone else. Other people might know that when Prince Khalid died Rashid would lose the father he loved and any hope of reconciliation with him, but she knew how he truly felt about that. He hadn't had a chance to say 'goodbye'. Nothing that would make the loss of his father easier to bear.

Polly hesitated at the main reception desk and then turned towards the glass lifts. Vaguely she remembered the guys talking about Rashid being booked into the penthouse suite. That seemed likely and it was quite possible they wouldn't give that information out at the desk even if she asked them. Better to go and see.

It wasn't until the lift doors opened on the seventh floor she wondered what she was going to actually *do*. She'd been acting on pure instinct, but now she realised it might be a little more complicated than to burst into his suite and demand to see him.

She was such an idiot. Karim Al Rahhbi would be there. Security staff. He wouldn't be alone.

But he still might need her.

Polly wrenched her bag open and pulled out the piece of paper on which she'd written the numbers she'd needed when she called her mother. It was the best idea she had. Better anyway than being turned away at the door.

She rang the hotel's number and waited while the receptionist answered. 'Hello, I'm Ms Pollyanna Anderson from Room 7 on the fifth floor. Can you put me through to His Highness, Prince Rashid bin Khalid bin Abdullah Al Baha's suite please?' She even managed to sound confident.

Even so, she was slightly surprised when the line crackled and a voice spoke. 'Miss Anderson, this is Karim Al Rahhbi. The prince is resting—'

'Yes, I know.' She cut across him. 'Ask him if he wants to speak to me.'

There was a significant pause while Karim decided to do just that. 'I will do so,' he said in his perfectly correct English. 'One moment, Miss Anderson.'

The line crackled again and it seemed to Polly it stayed that way for the longest time. More than enough time to realise what a huge assumption she'd made. The last thing she wanted to do was to make things more difficult for Rashid—and she didn't want to embarrass herself either.

The truth was *she* had a need to be here because she loved him. She couldn't bear knowing he was hurting and not be with him. That didn't mean he felt the same way.

And then came the realisation Rashid's aide might have flown to Al-Jalini on entirely different business. Rashid might have declined joining them because he preferred other company. He might…

'Polly?'

The pressure in her heart on hearing his voice was painful. 'Is there news? We thought—'

'My father has died.'

'Oh, Rashid. I'm so…*so* sorry.'

It was the end, then. Of so many things.

Polly stood clutching her mobile phone, so many thoughts passing through her mind. She thought of Bahiyaa. Of Rashid. Of what it would mean to Amrah.

And she thought of Minty and knew she'd be flying back to the UK first thing in the morning.

It was possible they'd return to Amrah to finish making their programme, but that would only be if there was political stability. There would be no need for her to see Rashid after today. Their lives would separate, just as she had always known they would.

She might see him again at a distance. At Shelton, perhaps, surrounded by beautiful women vying for his attention. As they'd been that first time. Or perhaps she'd never be any closer to him than seeing a picture in a magazine.

'Where are you?'

It was tempting to lie. 'I'm outside.'

'Outside?'

'Your suite,' she clarified. 'Seventh floor. Just by the lifts.' Nothing quite like committing emotional suicide, Polly thought. If he hadn't realised she'd fallen in love with him he'd surely know it now. Her heart was beating so hard it actually hurt.

And then she saw him, standing at the far end of the corridor, phone to his ear.

'Polly.'

'Hello.' She pulled the phone from her ear and ended the call. 'I wanted to know what had happened. Was it peaceful? The end?'

Rashid held his phone loosely in his left hand. 'I believe so. I scarcely know, I…'

He brushed his free hand across his eyes. 'Come in.'

She paused only long enough to stow her phone away in her bag, then walked slowly up the length of the corridor. What she wanted to do was run at him, wrap her arms around him and hold him so tight.

Reality wasn't quite like that, though. There was this enormous fear of being rejected, of having not quite understood what had been going on between them. And then there was Rashid's expression. The skin on his face appeared so pale it was almost translucent and his eyes were bleak. Unseeing.

He drew her in, past the bodyguards standing at the doorway. Karim stood up and moved to greet her. '*As-salaam alaykum.*'

'*Wa alaykum as-salaam,*' she murmured.

The one thing she didn't feel was 'peace'. Karim looked past her.

'Please leave us for a few minutes,' Rashid said. 'I will send for you the moment Miss Anderson leaves.'

What was left of hope shrivelled. She would be leaving. Soon. And Rashid had things he needed to be doing. Things that didn't involve her.

The door clicked shut. So quiet and yet it sounded loud to Polly. 'Have I broken some rule by coming here?' she asked, meeting his eyes properly for the first time.

Rashid shook his head. 'Karim is aware I have something to tell you. It must be done before you leave.'

'Am I leaving?'

Something flared in his eyes. For a moment Polly was glad to see an expression of something and then fear kicked in. She was leaving. He had said so.

'Within the next couple of hours,' Rashid concurred. 'Karim has already made all the necessary arrangements.'

Polly found herself a chair and sat down. That probably broke some Amrahi etiquette, but she wasn't so sure her legs were going to hold out much longer if she kept on standing. Everything was going wrong. It was happening and she was powerless to stop it.

'I have spoken to your friend, Miss Woodville-Brown, and she sees no reason to delay your departure.'

'Is there danger?' Polly asked in a small voice.

'There is a significant risk of terrorist incident.'

'I—'

'The choice isn't yours to make,' Rashid cut across her.

'No.'

'My grandfather is in shock and has yet to name his successor. He has three days.' Rashid paced across to the window and drew back the curtains.

From where she was sitting Polly could see the garden illuminations, Rashid's reflection in the window.

'We have a grieving and very elderly King. Men opposed to Hanif becoming King will need to act quickly. And they will.'

Rashid's voice was like flint. 'All embassies will council caution during this interim period, remove what personnel isn't considered essential. God willing, it will be of short duration.'

'I'm so sorry.' She could think of nothing else to say. 'What will you do?'

'As soon as I know you are safe I will return to Samaah.'

'To Bahiyaa?'

'I need to be seen in the city. By being there I can instil confidence, minimise the consequences of the next few days.'

Dangerous things. He might even be killed. 'Ra—'

'Polly,' he interrupted her, 'there is something I need to tell you. Something you will discover as soon as you return home.'

His words seemed torn from him. Polly lost all desire to speak at all. There seemed a recklessness about Rashid now. A steely determination to do what had to be done and she had the strangest presentiment that what needed to be done was going to hurt.

'When I came to Shelton…'

Polly nodded because he paused.

'I did so because I wished to see your brother. Step-brother,' he corrected.

'A-about Golden Mile?'

'You knew?'

Polly flinched at the barklike tone of his question. 'I thought. Henry, Anthony's butler, said you were Golden Mile's secret purchaser. And I knew you were angry.'

'Do you know why?'

She shook her head. Weariness seemed to be seeping into her bones. It was over. All over. What she wanted was a quiet lie-down. Somewhere private where she could lick her wounds.

Instead she was going to have a long flight home. She would have to present a calm face to the world. Hide the heartbreak that was tearing her apart.

'Anthony isn't a man to do business with though. It seemed to make sense.'

'You are right.'

Polly looked up and caught the edge of Rashid's anger. It was gone in a moment, but she'd seen it all the same. Anthony had created a powerful enemy.

He seemed to brace himself to say what came next. His jaw was set firm, his eyes holding hers with a fierce determination. 'When I gave permission for this documentary to be made, I did so against my better judgement.'

'I know. You showed me the docu—'

'No, Polly. Yes, the documentary was a factor, but…' He turned away from her as though he thought it might be easier to speak if he couldn't see her face. 'I thought you might be involved.'

'In what?' Her voice was a husky whisper, her mind racing.

'Golden Mile is unable to sire anything.' He waited,

allowing her time to process what that meant. 'There were all the usual safeguards in place. All the usual checks: bloods, X-rays, airways, movement and sperm.'

She'd thought leaving Amrah, leaving Rashid, would have been painful enough; she hadn't anticipated anything like the agony she was now suffering. 'What did you think I was here to do?' she managed.

But she didn't need his answer. All those conversations. The times when he'd taken her to one side to talk to her. The interest he'd shown in her life. In Shelton. All were given a new perspective now.

'I thought you may have come to discredit Amrah. Discredit me. To find something that would hold me silent. Perhaps. I wasn't sure.'

The fact he'd not been sure didn't feel like much of a concession. Pain ripped through her. She'd been such a fool. A gullible, *stupid* fool.

'Why would I do that?'

'Because you love Shelton.' Rashid straightened his shoulders. 'And I'm going to take it.'

Shelton. This part was harder to understand. 'But surely...if Anthony has done something criminal...' *Surely he'd go to prison?* There had to be systems in place to protect against that kind of thing.

'I have offered him the option of repaying what he has stolen from me as I'd prefer it wasn't generally known my own agent, my own men, took bribes to cheat me.'

'He has no money. The more valuable paintings were sold months ago to private collectors. We only have copies. There's nothing—'

'He has Shelton.'

And then she understood.

It was like a dam bursting. For so long she'd lived in expectation that she wouldn't be able to keep the castle safe. She'd imagined this moment. The moment when she heard that everything Richard had strived for had been lost. But she had never imagined the words coming from the man she loved.

Tears welled up and fell down her cheeks unheeded. She scarcely knew they were there. All she felt was pain. Intense, cruel pain.

Rashid had never felt anything for her. He'd made her believe he cared, that he genuinely *liked* her. He'd made her feel special. He'd kissed her as though he wanted her with a passion that matched her own.

All lies.

'Polly, if there were another way I—'

'You'd let Anthony keep the castle?' She didn't believe that for one moment. Rashid was an implacable enemy and this touched his honour. She understood that.

'No. I can't do that.' He pulled a hand across the back of his neck. 'But I don't want this to hurt you or your mother. I will see the dowager duchess is—'

Polly stopped him. She didn't want Rashid feeling sorry for them, for her. If the only thing she could take away from Amrah was the tattered remains of her pride, so be it. 'I think you've got enough to be thinking about at the moment. I will see we're all right.'

'Polly!'

She stood up. 'It was all a lie, wasn't it?' she asked huskily. 'You. Me. Today.' Her voice broke on that last word. Their fabulous time in the desert. The sense of home.

'No, I—'

'Don't! Please don't.' She didn't want to hear the lies. No more. She didn't want him saying how much he'd enjoyed her company or any other spurious platitudes. The fact was he didn't love her. Nothing else really mattered but that.

She made an ineffectual swipe at her face. 'If I'm flying back to England tonight I'd better gather my things together.'

'Pol—'

'No!' Polly stood up, holding him off with her hand. 'No more. You will do what you need to do. I will take care of what I have to.'

Somehow, and she wasn't sure how, she managed to find her way out of the room. Karim looked up as she walked past but she kept on going, her back straight.

'Miss Anderson, allow me,' Karim said, coming to stand beside her and pushing the button that called the lift.

'Thank you.'

'I have already arranged for a helicopter to take you and your colleagues to the airport.'

'*Shukran.*' *Thank you.* Perhaps the last time she'd ever use those words because she couldn't ever imagine coming back to Amrah. Minty would find a replacement when the time came.

'*Afwan.* I will escort you myself. Shall we say within the hour?'

Polly nodded just as the lift doors closed.

'Polly, you need to sit down. Pace yourself.' The dowager duchess sat with a box of cutlery on her lap. 'The auction isn't for a couple of months yet.'

'I want this done.' *Done and finished.*

'Darling, Richard would have understood. None of this is of your making.'

Polly brushed a grubby hand across the side of her cheek. She knew that. It wasn't that that was eating away at her. The eight weeks since she'd left Amrah had passed so slowly and they'd been filled with difficult decisions.

The paintings they'd had copied quietly disappeared.

The 'Rembrandt' she took home, and had it propped up against her bedroom wall. Staff had been given their notice and had already begun to leave. Sotheby's auctioneers were coming next week to begin their valuations and it wanted only Anthony's word before the castle was officially on the market. Though he obviously had no intention of being in the country when he gave it.

Polly climbed the steps and held up two copper jelly moulds. 'I suppose these might be worth something.' She heard footsteps. 'Henry, have you—?'

'His Highness Prince Rashid bin Khalid bin Abdullah Al Baha, Your Grace.'

Polly looked round, almost falling from the steps she was standing on. She stood looking foolishly at Rashid, so handsome in a soft caramel linen suit.

Her mother turned her wheelchair around. 'I have heard a great deal about you. Since I'm sure you are aware my stepson left the castle weeks ago, I imagine you've come here to speak to my daughter. Henry,' she said, lifting up the cutlery box, 'put that on the table and then take me for a cup of tea in the housekeeper's room.'

Polly managed an inarticulate sound.

Her mother merely smiled and looked up at Rashid and Shelton's elderly butler. 'I am ready for a break. Polly is exhausting.'

'Have you come here to see Anthony? I'm afraid he isn't here. He—'

'No, I've come here to see you.'

She stepped down and placed the copper moulds down on the central kitchen table, then wiped her dusty hands down the sides of her jeans. 'We were going to open these old kitchens to the public some time next year. I'm not sure how much all this will realise, but something—'

'Polly—'

'Anthony had already gone by the time I got home.' She pulled the plastic clip from her hair and let it fall down around her shoulders. If she had to see Rashid again she wished she'd been dressed for it. Some sharp business suit. Make-up on. 'I'm doing what I can to raise your money but it takes time. I've spoken to Karim about it and he—'

'Yes, I know.' Rashid stepped forward and took hold of her hands. 'Polly, I have something to say—'

She gave a half-hiccup, half-cry and pulled her hands away. 'I don't like listening to the things you have to say.' Then, 'I'm sorry.' Polly turned back to face him. 'I do know none of this is your fault. It's Anthony's. I know. I—'

'But you are facing the consequences.'

'I'm mopping up the mess.' She took a shaky breath and attempted to change the subject. 'Prince Hanif was named as your grandfather's successor. You must be pleased.'

'Yes.'

Rashid's eyes didn't leave her face and Polly felt a compulsion to keep talking. 'And everyone seems to have accepted that. In fact, Minty was saying—'

'Polly, I have brought something to show you.' Rashid handed over an envelope.

She looked up at him. 'Wh—?'

'Please read it.'

A muscle pulsed in Rashid's cheek. He was nervous. Uncertain of her reaction. *And it mattered to him.* Polly looked down at the stiff envelope and carefully drew out the official-looking document inside.

He'd bought Shelton. But more than that. Much more.

Tears burnt the back of Polly's throat. So much so she found it difficult to get the words out. 'You've given it away? I don't—'

'I'm setting up a charitable trust to ensure Shelton's long-term future. I can stop this if you think it's wrong,' he said quickly. 'It will take time to finalise but this way Anthony and all future Dukes of Missenden will retain the right to live in an apartment at the castle. I know it's not the same...'

It was better than the same. Shelton would be safe. Its management would be in the hands of people who cared about it and who had the skills to protect it. But...it made no sense.

Rashid intended to allow Anthony the use of an apartment within his ancestral home without cost. The future Dukes of Missenden, too. For as long as the line continued unbroken. He was pouring a staggering amount of money into the trust fund to begin the most pressing conservation work.

Why? She knew how much Beaufort Stud Farm would realise and it wasn't enough to compensate him for this.

'Why would you do this for Anthony?'

'I want to do this for you,' he said quietly.

'But the money you spent on Golden Mile. You'll never—'

'The money was never important.' Rashid's hands found their way to his jacket pockets. 'What mattered was that Anthony should not be allowed to profit.'

'He does from this. He can still live at the castle. He—'

'And his son can, and his son's son. Isn't that what's important to you? What was important to your late stepfather?'

Polly nodded, tears threatening to choke her.

'And I found that what really mattered to me, beyond everything else, was you.'

Polly brought a hand up to cover her mouth, hoping that would somehow stop her from crying.

'I hurt you, and I'm sorry.' She shook her head but he continued anyway. 'I hurt you when all I want to do is make you happy. Keep you safe. Fill your life with adventure. Polly, I love you.'

It was like a dam bursting. Emotion flooded through her. It didn't matter she was standing in a dusty, unused Victorian kitchen. That she was in old jeans and an even older baggy shirt.

Rashid stepped forward and his thumbs smoothed away the tears on her cheeks, before he bent to kiss each eyelid.

'You need an Arab wife.'

'I need you,' he countered, his voice firm. 'I choose you. I want you to be the mother of my children. The woman who lives her life by my side. My equal. My heart.'

It was hard to think clearly when his hands were stroking her face, his eyes caressing her. 'My mother—'

'May well want to spend time in England, but I've put in ramps, lowered work surfaces…' He smiled. 'I choose you.'

Me. He wants me. Loves me.

'And once Hanif is secure we can even live in England if that's what you want. Polly, I have discovered my life is empty without you in it. I ache for you.'

As she ached for him.

'I can't settle to anything. I can't concentrate.'

Polly reached up and smoothed out the deep frown lines on his forehead. 'I do love you.'

His arms closed about her, fiercely possessive. Incredibly he hadn't been sure of her answer. She laughed up at him, letting all the love she felt for him show in her eyes. 'And I can love you in Amrah. But what I can't do is share you.'

Rashid placed a kiss beneath her ear and then another by her eye. 'Or I you. I will love you, and only you, until the day I die.'

His beautiful, sexy blue eyes held hers for a long, long moment until he was absolutely certain she believed him. And then he kissed her.

Really kissed her.

Marrying the
Scarred Sheikh

BARBARA McMAHON

Barbara McMahon was born and raised in the southern United States, but settled in California after spending a year flying around the world for an international airline. After settling down to raise a family and work for a computer firm, she began writing when her children started school. Now, feeling fortunate in being able to realise the long-held dream of quitting her 'day job' and writing full-time, she and her husband have moved to the Sierra Nevada Mountains of California, where she finds her desire to write is stronger than ever. With the beauty of the mountains visible from her windows and the pace of life slower than that of the hectic San Francisco Bay Area where they previously resided, she finds more time than ever to think up stories and characters and share them with others through writing. Barbara loves to hear from readers. You can reach her at PO Box 977, Pioneer, CA 95666-0977, USA. Readers can also contact Barbara at her website, www.barbaramcmahon.com.

To Kelly-Anne, Jeff, Justin, Dylan and Bridgette:
Family is always best. Love from me.

CHAPTER ONE

ELLA PONTI walked along the shore. The night was dark. The only illumination came from the stars overhead. No moon tonight. The wavelets gurgled as they spent themselves on the sand. Alexander had loved walking in the dark and she felt a closer tie than any other time.

He'd been dead for over a year. The crushing pain of his death had eased, as others had told her it would. Only a lingering ache where her heart was reminded her constantly that she would never see him again.

Sighing, she looked to the sky. The stars sparkled and shimmered through the heat of the night. Turning slowly, she looked at the black expanse that was the Persian Gulf. Nothing was visible. Some nights she saw ships sailing silently through the night, their lights gliding slowly across the horizon. Nothing there tonight. Turning toward home, she began walking, splashing lightly through the warm water at land's edge.

What a contrast this land was, she mused as she enjoyed the silence. Here at the seashore it was as beautiful as any Mediterranean resort; lush plants grew in abundance. She loved the leafy palms, the broad-leaf ferns and the flowers were nothing short of breathtaking. Each house around the estate she lived on seemed to flourish with a horticulturist's delight.

She enjoyed sitting out in the afternoons in the shady nooks of the garden, smelling the blend of fragrances that perfumed the air. While only a short distance from the capital city of Alkaahdar, it felt like worlds away from the soaring skyscrapers of the modern city.

She would go to bed when she reached her place. It was already after midnight. She liked to work late, as she had tonight, then wind down by a walk on the deserted beach—alone with only the sand, sky and sea.

With few homes along this stretch of beach, only those who knew the place well knew where to turn away from the water to follow winding paths through lush foliage that led home. Ella knew exactly where to turn even in the dark.

From a distance, as she walked along, she saw a silhouette of another person. A man, standing at the edge of the water. He was almost in front of where her path opened to the beach. In all the months she'd lived here, she'd never seen another soul after dark.

Slowing her pace, she tried to figure out who he might be. Another person who had trouble sleeping through the night? A stranger exploring the beach? Or someone intent on nefarious activities?

Ella almost laughed at her imagination. The homes along this stretch of beach belonged to the fabulously wealthy of Quishari. There were guards and patrols and all sorts of deterrents to crime. Which was why she always felt safe enough to walk alone after dark. Had that changed? She had only nodding acquaintances with her neighbors. Ella kept to herself. Still, one of the servants at the main house would have told her if there were danger.

She could cut diagonally from where she was to where the path left the beach, avoid the stranger entirely. But her curiosity rose. She continued along splashing in the water. The flowing skirt she wore that hit her midcalf was already wet along the hem. The light material moved with the slight breeze, shifting and swaying as she walked.

"Is it safe for a woman to walk alone at night?" the man asked when she was close enough to hear his voice.

"Unless you mean me harm, it is," she replied. Resolutely, she continued walking toward him.

"I mean no harm to you or anyone. Just curious. Live around here?" he asked.

As she walked closer, she estimated his height to be several inches over six feet. Taller than Alexander had been. The darkness made it impossible to see any features; even his eyes were hidden as he tilted his head down to look at her. No glimmer of light reflected from them. The traditional white robes he wore were highlighted by the starlight, but beyond that, he was a man of shadow.

"I live nearby," she replied. "But you do not. I don't know you."

"No. I'm here on a visit. I think." He looked back out to sea. "Quite a contrast from where I've been for the last few weeks."

She turned to look at the sea, keeping a safe twelve feet or so of space between them.

"Rough waters?"

"Desert. I wanted to see the sea as soon as I got here. I've been traveling for almost twenty-four hours straight, am dead tired, but wanted to feel the cool breeze. I considered going for a swim."

"Not the safest thing to do alone, especially after dark. If you got into trouble, who would see or hear?" Though Ella had gone swimming alone after dark. That had been back shortly after Alexander's death when she hadn't thought she cared if something happened or not. Now she knew life was so precious she would not wish harm on herself or anyone.

"You're here," he said whimsically.

"So I am. And if you run into trouble, do you think I could rescue you?"

"Or at least go for help." With that, he shed the robe, kicked off the shoes he wore.

Startled, Ella watched. Was he stripping down to nothing to go for a swim?

It was too dark to know, but in a moment, he plunged into the cool waters of the Gulf and began swimming. She had trouble following him with her eyes; only the sounds of his powerful arms cleaving the water could be heard.

"So I'm the designated life guard," she murmured, sitting down on the sand. It was still warm from the afternoon sun. Sugar-white and fine, at night it nurtured by its warmth, soft to touch. She picked up a fistful letting it run between her fingers. Idly she watched where she knew him to be. She hoped he would enjoy his swim and not need any help from anyone. She hadn't a clue who he was. For tonight, it was enough he had not had to swim alone. Tomorrow, maybe she'd meet him or maybe not.

Ella lost track of time, staring out to sea. So he came from the desert. She had ventured into the vast expanse that made up more of Quishari than any other topography. Its beauty was haunting. A harsh land, unforgiving in many instances, but also hiding delights, like small flowers that bloomed for such a short time after a rare rainstorm. Or the undulating ground a mixture of dirt and sand that reminded her of water. The colors were muted, until lit by the spectacular sunsets that favored the land. Once she'd seen an oasis, lost and lonely in the vast expanse of the desert. But her fervent imagination found it magical. Water in the midst of such arid harshness.

She wished she could capture that in her own work. Show the world there was more to the desert than endless acres of nothing. She began considering plans for such a collection. Maybe she'd try it after finishing her current project. Tomorrow was the day she tried the new technique. She had the shape in mind of the bowl she wanted to make. Now she had to see if she could pull it off. Colors would be tricky, but she wanted them to swirl in glass, ethereal, hinting and tantalizing.

She felt relaxed as the moment ticked by. It was pleasant in the warmth of the night, with the soft sound of the sea at her feet and the splashing in the distance. Would the man ever get tired?

Finally she heard him approach. Then he seemed to rise up out of the water when he stood in the gradual slope. She rose and stepped back as he went directly to where his robes lay and scooped them up.

"You still here?" he asked.

"As designated life guard. Enjoy your swim?"

"Yes, life giving after the heat of the desert." He dried himself with the robes, then shrugged into them.

She turned. "Good night."

"Thanks for keeping watch."

"I don't know that I would have been any help had you gotten into trouble," she said, turning and half walking backward to continue along the shore.

"Shall I walk you home? It would be easy enough for me to do." He stood where he was, not threatening.

"No." She did draw the line there. She knew nothing about the man. It was one thing to run into a stranger on the beach, something else again to let him know where she lived—alone.

"I might be here tomorrow," he said.

"I might be, as well," she replied, then quickly walked away. She went farther down the beach and then cut into a neighbor's yard. She didn't want to telegraph her location. Hopefully he couldn't see enough in the darkness to know which path she'd taken. She walked softly on the edge of the neighbor's estate and soon reached the edge of the property she rented. Seconds later she was home.

* * *

Khalid watched until he could no longer see her. He had no idea who the woman was or why she was out after midnight on a deserted beach. He was dripping. Taking a last look at the sea, or the dark void where it was, with only a glimmer of reflected starlight here and there, he turned and went back to the house his grandmother had left him last summer. Her death had hit him hard. She'd been such a source of strength. She'd listened to his problems, always supportive of his solutions. And she had chided him often enough to get out into society. He drew the line there. Still he cherished her wisdom and her sense of fun. He would always miss her.

He thought about the woman on the beach. He could only guess she wasn't all that old from the sound of her voice. But aside from estimating her height to be about five feet two inches or so, he didn't know a thing about her. The darkness had hidden more than it revealed. Was she old or young? Slender, he thought, but the dress she wore moved in the breeze, not revealing many details.

Which was probably a good thing. He had no business being interested in anyone. He knew the scars that ran down his side were hideous. More than one person had displayed shock and repulsion when seeing them. Like his fiancée. Damara had not been able to cope at all and had fled the first day the bandages had been removed and she'd seen him in the hospital after the fire.

His brother, Rashid, had told him more than once he was better off without her if she couldn't stick after a tragedy. But it didn't help the hole he'd felt had been shot through his heart when the woman he'd planned to marry had taken off like he was a horrible monster.

He'd seen similar reactions ever since. He knew he was better off working with men in environments too harsh for women to venture into. Those same men accepted him on his merits, not his looks.

He had his life just as he wanted it now. Except—he had to decide what to do with the house his grandmother left him. It had been a year. He had put off any decisions until the fresh ache of her dying had subsided. But a house should not sit empty.

He walked swiftly across the sand to the start of the wide path that led straight to the house. It was a home suited for families. Close to the beach, it was large with beautiful landscaping, a guesthouse and plenty of privacy. The lawns should have children running around as he and his brother had done. As his father and uncles had done.

The flowers should be plucked and displayed in the home. And the house itself should ring with love and laughter as it had when he and Rashid had been boys visiting their father's parents.

But the house had been empty and silent for a year. And would remain that way unless he sold it. It would be hard to part with the house so cherished by him and his family. Especially with the memories of his beloved grandmother filling every room. But he had no need for it. His flat in Alkaahdar suited him. There when he needed it, waiting while he was away.

As he brushed against an overgrown shrub, his senses were assaulted by the scents of the garden. Star jasmine dominated the night. Other, more subtle fragrances sweetened the still air. So different from the dry, acrid air of the desert. Instantly he was transported back to when he and Rashid had run and played. His father had been alive then, and of course his grandmother. Who knew the odd quirks of fate, or that he'd end up forever on the outside looking in at happy couples and laughing families. That elusive happiness of families denied him.

Not that he had major regrets. He had done what he thought right. He had saved lives. A scar was a small price to pay.

He entered the house through the door he'd left open from the veranda. Bed sounded really good. He'd been traveling far too long. Once he awoke, he could see what needed to be done to get the house ready for sale.

* * *

Ella woke late the next morning. She'd had a hard time falling asleep after meeting the stranger on the beach. She lay in bed wondering who he was and why he'd been traveling so long. Most people stopped when they were tired. No matter, she would probably never see him again. Though, she thought as she rose, just maybe she'd take another walk after midnight tonight. He said he'd be there. Her interest was definitely sparked.

But that was later. Today, she wanted to try to make the new glass piece that had been taking shape in her mind for days.

After a quick breakfast at the nook in the kitchen, Ella went to her studio. As always when entering, she remembered the wonderful woman who had sponsored her chance at developing her skill as a glassblower and who had offered to help her sell her pieces when they were ready. She missed her. She pursued her passion two-fold now—for herself and for her benefactor.

In only moments, she was totally absorbed in the challenge of blending colors and shapes in the bowl she was creating.

It was only when her back screamed in pain that Ella arched it and glanced at the clock. It was late afternoon— she'd been working for seven hours straight. Examining the piece she'd produced, she nodded in satisfaction. It wasn't brilliant by any means, but it had captured the ethereal feel she wanted. For a first attempt at this technique, it passed. A couple more stages to complete before the glass bowl was ready for a gallery or for sale. A good day's work.

She rubbed her back and wished there was some way she could pace herself. But once caught up in the creative process, it was hard to stop. Especially with glass. Once it was at the molten stage, she had to work swiftly to form the pieces before it cooled. Now it needed to go into the annealer that would slowly cool it so no cracks formed. This was often the tricky part. Especially when she had used different glass and different color mediums that cooled at different rates.

It would end up as it ended up. She tried to keep to that philosophy so she didn't angst over every piece.

Once the bowl was in the oven, she went back to her kitchen, prepared a light meal and carried it to the small terrace on the shady side of the house. The air was cooling down, but it was still almost uncomfortably warm. She nibbled her fruit as she gazed at the flowers that grew so profusely. Where else in the world would she be so comfortable while working on her art? This house was truly a refuge for her. The one place she felt safe and comfortable and almost happy. She'd made it a home for one.

Thinking about the flat she'd given up after Alexander's death, she knew she had traded their happy home for her own. It had taken her a while to realize it, but now she felt a part of the estate. She knew every flower in the garden, every hidden nook that offered shade in the day. And she could walk the paths at night without a light. It was as if the cottage and estate had welcomed her with comforting arms and drawn her in.

So not like the home of her childhood, that was for sure. She shied away from thinking about the last months there. She would focus on the present—or even the future, but not the past.

Taking a deep breath, she held it for a moment, listening. Was that a car? She wasn't expecting any friends. No one else knew where she was. Who would be coming to the empty estate? The gardener's day was later in the week. For a moment she didn't move. The car sounded as if it were going away. Soon the sound faded completely. Only then did Ella relax.

After she ate, she rose and walked around the cottage. Nothing seemed disturbed. How odd that the car sounded so near. Had the sound been amplified from the road, or had it been in the drive for some reason?

The late-afternoon sun was hot. She debated taking a quick swim, but reconsidered. She wanted to walk along the beach tonight to see if the stranger returned. For the first time in over a year, she was curious about something—someone. Not many people shared her love of the night. Did he? Or had last night been only an aberration because of his long trip? Where in the desert had he been? She'd like to visit an oasis or drive a few hours into the desert, lose sight of any signs of man and just relish the solitude and stark beauty that would surround her.

She needed a car for that. Sighing softly, she considered renting a vehicle for such an expedition. Maybe one day in the fall.

Ella could scarcely wait until midnight. Very unusual, her impatience to see if the man was there again. For a year she'd felt like she was wrapped in plastic, seeing, but not really connected with the rest of the world. Yet a chance encounter in the dark had ignited her curiosity. She knew nothing about him, except he liked the sea and wasn't afraid to swim after dark. Was he old or young? Did he live nearby or was he sneaking through the estates to gain access to the private beach?

Would he be there tonight?

Promptly at the stroke of twelve, Ella left her home to walk quickly through the path to the beach. Quickly scanning from left to right, she felt a bump of disappointment. He was not there. Sighing softly for her foolishness, she walked to the water's edge and turned to retrace last night's steps.

"I wondered if you would appear," the familiar voice said behind her. She turned and saw him walking swiftly toward her. His longer legs cut the distance in a short time. No robes tonight, just dark trousers and a white shirt.

"I often walk at midnight," she said, not wishing him to suspect she'd come tonight especially to see if he were here.

"As do I, but mainly due to the heat of the day."

"And because you don't sleep?" she asked.

He fell into step with her.

"That can be a problem," he said. "For you, too?"

"Sometimes." Now that he was here, she felt awkward and shy. Her heart beat a bit faster and she wondered at the exhilaration that swept through her. "Did you catch up on your sleep after your trip?"

"Got a few hours in."

"Holidays are meant for sleeping in late and lazing around," she said, trying to figure out exactly how to ask questions that wouldn't sound as if she were prying.

"If I were on holiday, which I'm not, I still require little sleep."

"Oh, from what you said…" She closed her mouth.

"I did come off a job at an oil field west of here. But I'm here on business. Personal business, I guess you'd say."

"Oh." What kind of business? How long would it take? Would she see him again after tonight? Not that she could see him exactly. But it was nice to share the walk with someone, if only for one night.

"I have some thinking to do and a decision to make," he added a moment later.

"Mmm." She splashed through the water. There was a slight breeze tonight from the sea which made the air seem cooler than normal. It felt refreshing after the heat of her workshop.

"You speak Arabic, but you're not from here, are you?" he asked.

She looked up and shook her head. Not that he could likely see the gesture. "I've studied for years, I can understand it well. Do I not speak it well?"

"Yes, but there is still a slight accent. Where are you from?"

"Italy. But not for a while. I live here now."

"With family?"

She hesitated. Once again safety concerns reared up. "Do you think I need a chaperone?" she asked, shying away from his question.

"I have no idea. How old are you?"

"Old enough." She stopped and turned, looking up at him, wishing she could see him clearly. "I am a widow. I am long past the stage of needing someone to watch out for me."

"You don't sound old enough to be a widow."

"Sometimes I feel a hundred years old." No one should lose her husband when only twenty-eight. But, as she had been told before, life was not always fair.

"I'm sorry for your loss," he said softly.

She began walking again, not wanting to remember. She tried to concentrate on each foot stepping on the wet sand. Listen to the sea to her right which kissed the shore with wavelets. Feel the energy radiating from the man beside her. So now he'd think she was an older woman, widowed and alone. How old was he? She had no idea, but he sounded like a dynamic man in his prime.

"Thank you." She never knew how to respond to the comment. He hadn't known her husband. He hadn't loved him as she had. No one would ever feel the loss as she did. Still, it was nice he made the comment. Had he ever lost a loved one?

They walked in silence for a few moments. Then she asked, "So what did you do at the oil field?"

"I consult on the pumps and rigs. My company has a retainer with Bashiri Oil among others to assist when new fields are discovered. And to put out fires when they erupt."

"You put out oil fires?" She was astonished. She had seen the pictures of oil wells burning. Flames shot a hundred feet or more in the air. The intense heat melted and twisted metal even yards from the fire. She found it hard to work with the heat in her own studio with appropriate protective gear. How could anyone extinguish an oil well fire? "Is there any job more dangerous on earth?"

He laughed softly. "I imagine there are. It's tricky sometimes, but someone has to do it."

"And how did you get interested in putting out conflagrations? Wasn't being a regular fireman enough?"

"I'm fascinated by the entire process of oil extraction. From discovering reserves, to drilling and capping. And part of the entire scenario is the possibility of fire. Most are accidents. Some are deliberately set. But the important thing is to get them extinguished as quickly as possible. That's why we do consultation work with new sites and review existing sites for safety measures. Anything to keep a well from catching fire is a good thing. It's an interest I've always had. And since I could choose my profession, I chose this one."

"I just can't imagine. Isn't it hot? Actually it must be exceedingly hot. Is there a word beyond hot?"

He laughed again. She liked the sound of it. She smiled in reaction, not at all miffed that he was laughing at her questions.

"Oh, it's hot. Even with the special suits we wear."

He explained briefly how they dealt with fire.

Ella listened, fascinated in a horrified way. "You could get killed doing that," she exclaimed at one point.

"Haven't yet," he said.

She detected the subtle difference in his voice. He was no longer laughing. Had someone been injured or killed fighting one of those fires? Probably. The entire process sounded extremely dangerous.

"They don't erupt often," he said.

"I hope there is never another oil fire in the world," she said fervently. "No wonder you wanted to go swimming last night. I'd want to live *in* the sea if I ever survived one of those."

"That is an appeal. But I'd get restless staying here all the time. Something always draws me back to the oil fields. A need to keep the rigs safe. And a sense of need to return burning wells to productivity. Duty, passion. I'm not totally sure myself."

"So it's the kind of thing you'd do even if you didn't need to work?"

He laughed again. "Exactly."

She stopped. "This is as far as I usually go," she said.

"Ben al Saliqi lives here, or he used to," Khalid said, turning slowly to see the house from the beach. Only the peaks of the roof were visible above the trees that lined the estate, a soft glow from the lamps in the windows illuminating the garden.

"How do you know that?" she asked. There was hardly any identifying features in the dark.

He turned back to her. "I spent many summers here. At my grandmother's house," he said. "I know every family on the beach—except yours."

"Ohmygod, you're one of the al Harum men, aren't you? I'm your tenant, Ella Ponti."

CHAPTER TWO

"MY TENANT?" Khalid said.

"I rent the guesthouse on your grandmother's estate. She was my patron—or something. I miss her so much. I'm so sorry she died."

"She rented out the guesthouse? I had no idea."

"I have a lease. You can check it. She insisted on drawing one up. Said it would be better for us both to get the business part out of the way and enjoy each other's company. She was wonderful. I'm so sorry she died when she did. I miss her."

"I miss her, as well. I didn't know about this," Khalid said.

"Well, I don't know why you don't. Haven't you been running the estate? I mean, the gardener comes every week, the maids at the house keep it clean and ready."

"This is the first I've visited since her death. The servants know how to do their job. They don't need an overseer on site."

"It's the first visit in a long while. You didn't visit her the last few months she lived here. She talked about her grandsons. Which are you, Rashid or Khalid?"

"Khalid."

"Ah, the restless one."

"Restless?"

"She said you hadn't found your place yet. You were seeking, traveling to the interior, along the coast, everywhere, looking for your place."

"Indeed. And Rashid?"

"He's the consumed one—trying to improve the business beyond what his father and uncles did. She worried about you both. Afraid—" Ella stopped suddenly. She was not going to tell him all his grandmother had said. It was not her business if neither man ever married and had children. Or her place to tell him of the longing the older woman had had to hold a new generation. Which never happened and now never would.

"Afraid of what?" he asked.

"Nothing. I have to go back now." She began walking quickly toward home. How was she to know the mysterious stranger on the beach was her new landlord? She almost laughed. He might hold the lease, but he was nothing like a landlord. He hadn't even visited the estate in more than a year. She knew, because she'd never seen him there and she'd live here for over a year and had heard from his grandmother how much she wished to see him beyond fleeting visits in the capital city.

He easily caught up with her. Reaching out to take her arm, he stopped her and swung her around.

"Tell me."

"Good grief, it's not that big a deal. She was afraid neither of her grandsons would marry and have children. She was convinced both of you were too caught up in your own lives to look around for someone to marry. She wanted to hold a great-grandchild. Now she never can."

"She told you this? A stranger."

Ella nodded. "Yes. We became friends and had a lot of time to visit and talk. She came to the guest cottage often, interested in what I was doing." And had been a rock to lean against when Ella was grieving the most. Her gentle wisdom had helped so much in those first few months. Her love had helped in healing. And the rental cottage had been a welcomed refuge. One guarded by the old money and security of the al Harum family. Ella had found a true home in the cottage and was forever grateful to Alia al Harum for providing the perfect spot for her.

Sheikh Khalid al Harum came from that same old money. She hadn't known exactly what he did but it certainly wasn't for money. No wonder his grandmother had complained. It was a lucky thing he was still alive.

"And what were you doing?" he asked, still holding her arm.

"Working. You could call her a patron of the arts."

"You're a painter?"

"No, glassblower. Could you let me go?"

Ella felt his hold ease. His hand dropped to his side. She stepped back and then headed for home. So much for the excitement of meeting the stranger. She could have just waited until she heard him at the main house and gone over to introduce herself.

Now she wanted to get home and close the door. This was the grandson who was always roaming. Was he thinking of using the house when in the capital city?

"Oh." She stopped and turned. Khalid bumped into her. She hadn't known he was right behind her. His hands caught her so she didn't fall.

"Are you planning to sell the estate?" she asked.

"It's something I'm considering."

"Your grandmother wanted you to have it. She'd be so hurt if you just sold it away."

"I'm not selling it away. It's too big for one man. And I'm not in Alkaahdar often. When I am, I have a flat that suits me."

"Think of the future. You could marry and have a huge family someday. You'll need a big house like that one. And the location is perfect—right on the Gulf."

"I'm not planning to ever marry. Obviously my grandmother didn't tell you all about me or you'd know the thought of marriage is ludicrous. So why would I want a big house to rattle around in?"

Ella tried to remember all her sponsor had said about her grandsons. Not betraying any confidences, not going into detail about their lives, she still had given Ella a good feel for the men's personalities. And a strong sense that neither man was likely to make her a great-grandmother. The longing she'd experienced for the days passed when they'd been children and had loved to come to her home had touched Ella's heart. Alia had hoped to recapture those happy times with their children.

"Don't make hasty decisions," she said. Alia had died thinking this beloved grandson would live in her home. Ella hated the thought he could casually discard it when it had meant so much to the older woman.

"My grandmother died last July. It's now the end of May. I don't consider that a hasty move."

Ella didn't know what tack to use. If he wanted to sell, the house was his to do so with as he wanted. But she felt sad for the woman who had died thinking Khalid would find happiness in the house she'd loved.

"Come, I'll walk you back. You didn't use the path last night that leads to the house or guesthouse," he said.

"I didn't know who you were. I didn't want to indicate where I lived," she said, walking back. The night seemed darker and colder. She wanted to be home. So much for looking forward to the evening walk. Now she wished she'd stayed in the cottage and gone to bed.

"Wise. You don't know who might be out on the beach so late at night."

"I've been taking care of myself for a long time. I know this beach well." She was withdrawing. There was something liberating about walking with a stranger, talking, sharing. But something else again once actually knowing the person. She'd be dealing with him in the near future. She didn't know this man. And until she did, she was not giving out any personal information.

A blip of panic settled in. If he sold the estate, where would she go? She had made a home here. Thought she'd be living in the cottage for years to come. She had to review the lease. Did it address the possibility of the estate being sold? She knew Madame al Harum had never considered that likelihood.

As soon as she reached the path, she walked even faster. "Good night," she said. She wasn't even sure what to call him. Sheikh al Harum sounded right, or did she use his first name, as well, to differentiate him from his brother who also was a sheikh? She was not used to dealing with such lofty families.

When she reached her house, she flipped on the lights and headed for the desk. Her expenses were minimum: food, electricity and her nominal rent. It wasn't as if the al Harum family needed her money. But she had needed to pay her way. She was not a charity case. It wasn't a question of money; it was a question of belonging. Of carrying out her dreams. Madame al Harum had understood. Ella doubted the sheikh would.

She read the Arabic script, finding it harder to understand than newspapers. She could converse well, read newspapers comfortably. But this was proving more difficult than she expected. Why hadn't she asked for a copy translated into Italian?

Throwing it down in disgust, she paced the room for a long time. If she had to leave, where would she go? She studied the cream-colored walls, the soft draperies that made the room so welcoming. Just beyond the dark windows was a view of the gardens. She loved every inch of the cottage and grounds. Where else would she find a home?

The next morning Ella was finishing her breakfast when one of the maids from the main house knocked on the door. It was Jalilah, one who had also served Alia al Harum for so many years.

"His Excellency would like to see you," she said. "I'm to escort you to the main house."

So now he summoned her—probably to discuss her leaving. "Wait until I change." She'd donned worn jeans and an oversize shirt to work around the studio. Not the sort of apparel one wore to meet with a sheikh. Especially if doing battle to keep her home.

Quickly she donned a dress that flattered her dark looks. It was a bit big; she'd lost weight over the last few months. Still, the rose color brought a tinge of pink to her cheeks.

Her dark eyes looked sad—as they had ever since losing Alexander. She would never again be the laughing girl who had grown up thinking everything good about people. Now she knew heartache and betrayal. She was wiser, but at a price.

Running a brush through her hair, she turned to face the future. Was there a clause in the lease that would nullify her claim if the estate was sold? As they walked across the gardens, she tried to remember every detail about the terms Madame al Harum had discussed.

She entered the house and immediately remembered her one-time hostess. Nothing had changed since the last time she'd visited. It was cool and pleasant. The same pictures hung on the walls. Her first vase from her new studio still held a place of honor on the small table in the foyer, holding a cascading array of blossoms. She'd been so happy it had been loved.

The maid went straight to the study. Ella paused at the doorway for a moment, her eyes widening in shock as she got a good look at Sheikh Khalid al Harum. He looked up at her, catching the startled horror in her expression. His own features hardened slightly and she felt embarrassed she'd reacted as she had. No one had told her he'd been horribly burned. The distorted and puckered skin on his right cheek, down his neck and obviously beneath his shirt, disfigured what were other-wise the features of a gorgeous man. She'd been right about his age—he looked to be in his prime, maybe early thirties. And he was tall as she noted when he rose to face her.

"You wanted to see me?" she said, stepping inside. She held his gaze, determined not to comment on the burn, or show how sympathetic she felt at the pain he must have en-dured. She'd had enough burns herself in working with mol-ten glass to know the pain. Never as big a patch as he had. What was a fabulously wealthy man like he had to be risking his life to fight oil fires?

Her heart beat faster. Despite the burn scar, he was the best-looking guy she'd ever seen. Even including Alexander. She frowned. She was not comparing the two. There was no need. The sheikh was merely her new landlord. The flurry of attrac-tion was a fluke. He could mean nothing to her.

"Please." He gestured to a chair opposite the desk. "You're considerably younger than I thought. Are you really a widow?"

She nodded as she slipped onto the edge of the chair. "My husband died April a year ago. What did you wish to see me about?"

He sat and picked up a copy of the lease. "This. The lease for the guesthouse you signed with my grandmother."

She nodded. It was what she expected. He held her future in his hands. Why didn't she have a good feeling about this?

"How did you coerce her to making this?" he asked, frown-ing at the papers.

Ella blinked. "I did not coerce her into doing anything. How dare you suggest such a thing!" She leaned forward, de-bating whether to leave or not at his disparaging remark. "She offered me a place to live and work and then came up with the lease herself so I wouldn't have to worry about living ar-rangements until I got a following."

"A following?"

"I told you, I blow glass. I need to make enough pieces to sell to earn her livelihood. Until that time, she was—I guess you'd say like a patroness—a sponsor if you would. I rented the studio to make my glass pieces and she helped out by making the rent so low. Did you read the clause where she gets a percentage of my sales when I start making money?"

"And if you never sell anything? Seems you got a very cushy deal here. But my grandmother's gone now. This is my estate and if I chose to sell it, I'm within my rights. I don't know how you got her to sign such a lopsided lease but I'm not her. You need to leave. Vacate the guest quarters so I can renovate if necessary to sell."

Ella stared at him. "Where does it say I have to leave before the end of the five years?" she asked, stalling for time, trying to think about what she could do. Panic flared again. It has seemed too good to be true that she'd have a place to live and work while building an inventory. But as the months had gone on, she'd become complaisant with her home. She couldn't possibly find another place right away—and she didn't have the money to build another studio. And not enough glass pieces ready to sell to raise the money. She was an unknown. The plans she and his grandmother had discussed had been for the future—not the present.

"I do not want you as a tenant. What amount do you want to leave?"

She didn't get his meaning at first, then anger flared. "Nothing. I wish to stay." She felt the full force of his gaze when he stared at her. She would not be intimidated. This was her *home*. He might see it as merely property, but it was more to her. Raising her chin slightly, she continued. "You'll see on the last page once I begin to sell, she gets ten percent of all sales. Or she would have. I guess you do, now." She didn't like the idea of having a long-term connection with this man. He obviously couldn't care less about her or her future.

Madame al Harum had loved her work, had encouraged her so much. She appreciated what Ella did and would have reveled in her success—if it came.

Sheikh Khalid al Harum saw her as an impediment to selling the estate.

Tough.

"I can make it very worth your while," he said softly.

She kept her gaze locked with his. "No."

"You don't know how much," he said.

"Doesn't matter. I have the lease, I have the house for another four years. That will be enough time to make it or not. If not, I'll find something else to do." And she'd keep her precious home until the last moment.

"Or find a rich husband to support you. The estate is luxurious. You would hate to leave it. But if I give you enough money, you'll be able to support yourself in similar luxury for a time."

She rose and leaned on the desk, her eyes narrowed as she stared into his.

"I'm not leaving. The lease gives me a right to stay. Deal with it."

She turned and left, ignoring her shaky knees, her pounding heart. She didn't want his money. She wanted to stay exactly where she was. Remain until those looking for her gave up. Until she could build her own future the way she wanted. Until she could prove her art was worth something and that people would pay to own pieces.

Khalid listened to the sound of her hurried footsteps, then the closing of the front door. She refused to leave. He glanced at the lease again. As far as he could tell, it was iron tight. But he'd have the company attorneys review. There had to be a way. He did not want to sit on the house for another four years and he suspected no one would buy the place with a tenant in residence. What had his grandmother been thinking?

He leaned back in his chair and looked at the chair his unwanted tenant had used. Ella Ponti, widow. She looked like she was in her midtwenties. How had her husband died? She was far too young to be a widow, living alone. Yet the sadness that had shone in her eyes until the fire of anger replaced it, showed him she truly mourned her loss. And he felt a twinge of regret to be bringing a change to her life.

Yet he couldn't reconcile her being in the cottage. Had his grandmother been taken in? Was Ella nothing more than a gold digger looking for an easy way in life? Latch on to an old woman and talk her into practically giving her the cottage.

He was on the fence about selling. He remembered his grandmother in every room. All the visits they'd shared over the years. Glancing around the study, he hated to let it go. But he would never live in such a big house. Which left selling the estate as the best option.

He should have visited his grandmother more often. He missed her. They'd had dinners together in Alkaahdar when he was in town. Sometimes he escorted her to receptions or parties. But long weekends at the estate doing nothing were in the past. And in retrospect she'd asked after him and what was going on in his life more than he'd asked after hers. Regrets were hard to live with.

Though if she'd seen Ella's reactions, maybe she would have stopped chiding him that he made too much of the scar. Ella's initial reaction had been an echo of his one-time fiancée's own look of horror. He knew it disgusted women. That was one reason he spent most of his time on the oil fields or in the desert. He saw the scar himself every morning when he shaved. He knew what it looked like.

Shaking himself out of the momentary reverie, he picked up the phone to call the headquarters of Bashiri Oil. The sooner he found a way to get rid of his unwanted tenant, the better.

* * *

Ella stormed home. She did not want to be bought out. Why had Khalid al Harum come to the estate at this time? He'd never visited in all the months she'd live here, why now? She had her life just as she wanted it and he was going to mess it up.

And how dare he offer her money to move? She was not going anywhere. She needed this tranquil setting. She'd gradually gotten over the fierce intensity of her grief. She owed it to Alia al Harum. The older woman had such faith in her talent and her ability to be able to command top money for her creations. She had strongly encouraged Ella to prove it to herself. And she would for the memory of the woman who had helped her so much.

And no restless grandson was going to drive her away.

She shrugged off the dress and tossed it on the bed. So much for dressing up for him. He only wanted her gone. She pulled on her jeans and oversize shirt. Tying her hair back as she walked, she went to the studio. The glass bowl she'd created yesterday still had hours of graduated cooling to complete before she could take it from the oven. She was impatient to know if it would be as beautiful as she imagined. And flawless with no cracks from irregular cooling, or mixing different types and textures of glass that cooled at different rates. Fingers crossed. Patience was definitely needed for glasswork.

In the meantime, she picked up her sketchbook and went to sit by the window. She could do an entire series in the same technique if the bowl came out perfect. She stared at the blank page. She was not seeing other glass artwork, but the face of Khalid al Harum. What a contrast—gorgeous man, hideous scar. His grandmother had never mentioned that. She'd talked of her grandchildren's lives, her worry they'd never find happiness and other memories of their childhood.

When had the fire happened? He could have been killed. She didn't know him, nor did she care to now that he'd tried to bribe her to leave. But still, how tragic to have been burned so severely. She looked at the couple of small scars on her arms and fingers from long-ago childhood scrapes. Fire was dangerous and damaging to delicate human skin. Every burn, no matter how small, hurt like crazy. She shivered trying to imagine a huge expanse of her body burned.

Had it happened recently? It didn't have that red look that came with recent healing. But with all the money the al Harums had, surely he could have had plastic surgery to mitigate the worst of the damage.

Impatient with her thoughts, she rose and paced the studio. She needed to be focused on the next idea, the next piece of art. She had to build a collection that would be worthy of an exhibit and then of exorbitant prices. Had Madame al Harum spoken to the gallery owners as she had said she would do when the time was right? Probably not. Why speak of something that was years away from happening.

"Great. It's bad enough he'll try to get me off the property. I truly have no place to go and no chance of getting a showing if I don't have someone to vouch for me," she said aloud. She could scream.

But it would do no good.

"Deal with it," she said to herself. She'd take the advice she'd given him and make sure she made every moment count. He might try to evict her, but until she was carried kicking and screaming from the studio, she'd work on her collection.

The day proved interminable. Every time she'd start thinking about Khalid al Harum, she'd force her mind to focus on designing pieces using the swirling of blues and reds. It would work for a few moments, then gradually something would drift in that had her thinking about him again.

She didn't like it one bit.

After dinner, she debated taking a walk on the beach. That usually cleared her mind. But after the last two nights, the last thing she wanted was to run into *him* again.

She sat on her terrace for a while, trying to relax. The more she tried to ignore his image, the more it seemed to dance in front of her. She was not going to be intimidated by him. Jumping to her feet, she headed down the path to the beach. She'd been walking along the shore for months. Just because he showed up was no reason to change her routine.

When she stepped on the sand, she looked both ways. No sign of anyone. Slowly she walked to the water, then turned south. If he did come out, chances he would head north as she had the last two nights. She'd be safe from his company.

It didn't take long for the walk to begin to soothe. She let go of cares and worries and tried to make herself one with the night.

"I took a guess," a voice came from her right.

Khalid rose from the sand and walked the few yards to where she was. "I thought you might go a different way to-night and I was right." The smug satisfaction in his tone made her want to hit him.

"Then I'll turn and go north," she said, stopping and fac-ing him. She'd tried an earlier time and a different direction. Had he come out to the beach a while ago to wait for her? She ignored the fluttery feeling in her stomach. So he came out. It probably was only to harangue her again about leaving.

"I am not stopping you from going in either direction," he said. He stood next to her, almost too close. She stepped back as a wavelet washed over her feet. The cool water broke the spell.

"You are of course welcomed to walk wherever you wish," she said. She began to walk again along the edge of the water.

Khalid walked beside her.

The silence stretched out moment by moment. Ella had lost all sense of serenity. Her nerves were on full alert. She was extremely conscious of the man beside her. Her skin almost tingled. She could see him from the corner of her eye—tall, silhouetted against the dark sky. She didn't need this sense of awareness. This feeling of wanting to know more. The desire to defend herself to him and make him change his mind and want her to stay in the guesthouse until the lease expired.

She kept silent with effort, wondering if she could outlast him. It grew harder and harder to keep silent as they went along.

"I called an attorney," he said at last.

She didn't reply, waiting for the bad news. Was there an escape clause?

"You'll be happy to know the lease is airtight. You have the right to stay as long as you wish. The interesting part is, you have the right to terminate before the end but my grandmother—and now me—didn't have the same right."

She'd forgotten. Madame al Harum had insisted Ella might wish to leave before five years and didn't want her to feel compelled to remain. At the time Ella had not been able to imagine ever leaving. She still didn't want to think about it. Would four more years be enough time?

"So if you wished to leave, I'd still make it lucrative for you."

"I don't live here for the money," she said.

"Why do you live here? You're not from here. No family. No husband. What holds you to the guesthouse, to Alkaahdar?"

"A safe place to live," she said. "A beautiful setting in a beautiful country. I also have friends here. Quishari is my home."

"Safe? Is there danger elsewhere?" he countered, focusing in on that comment.

She stopped to look at him. She wanted to get this through to him once and for all. "Look, I came here at a very hard time in my life—just after my husband died. Your grandmother did more for me than anyone, including making sure I had a place to live, to work, sheltered from problems and a chance to grieve. I will forever be in her debt. One I can now never repay. It hit me hard when she died. I grieve for her, as well. Now I'm coming to a place of peace and don't wish to have my life disrupted because you want to get rid of a home she loved and left to you in hopes you'd use it. Do not involve me in your life. I have no interest in taking a gazillion dollars to leave. I have no interest in disrupting my life to suit yours. I want to be left alone to continue as I have been doing these last months. Is that clear enough for you?"

"Life changes. Nothing is as it was last year. My grandmother is dead. Yes, she left me the estate in hopes I would settle there. You saw me this morning. You know why I'll never marry. Why should I hold on to a house for sentimental reasons, visiting it once or twice a year when some other family could enjoy living in it daily? Do you think it is easy for me to sell? I have so many memories of my family visiting. I know I'll face pressure from others in the family to hold on to it. But it's more of a crime to let it sit vacant year after year. What good does that do?"

"Why will you never marry? Did the fire damage other parts of you?" she asked, startled by his comment.

"What?"

She'd surprised him with that question.

Oh, this was just great. Why had she opened her mouth? Now she had to clarify herself. "I mean, can you not father children or something?"

He burst out laughing.

Ella frowned. It had not been a funny question.

"So you're all right in that department, I guess," she said, narrowing her eyes. "So what's the problem?"

He leaned over, his face close enough to hers she felt the warmth of his breath. She could barely see his eyes in the dark. "As I said, you saw me this morning. What woman would get close enough for me to use those other parts?" he asked very softly.

She stared into his eyes, as dark as her own, hard to see in the dim light of the stars. "Are you stupid or do you think I am? You're gorgeous except for a slight disfiguration on one side. You sound articulate. I expect you are well educated and have pots of money. Why wouldn't someone fall for you? Your grandmother thought you should be married. Surely she'd have known if there was a major impediment."

"I do not wish to be married for my money. I have a temper that could scare anyone and, I assure you, looks count a lot when people are looking for mates. And my grandmother saw only her own happy marriage that she wished replicated for her grandsons."

"So again I say what's the problem?"

"Maybe you are stupid. This scar," he said, reaching for her hand and trailing her fingers down his cheek, pressing against the puckered skin.

He let her hand go and she left it against the side of his face. The skin was warm, though distorted. Lightly, she brushed her thumb against it, drifted to his lips which had escaped the flame. Her heart pounded, but she was mesmerized. His warmth seemed to touch her heart. She felt heartbreak for his reasoning. He was consigning himself to a long, lonely life. She knew what that was like. Since Alexander's death, hadn't she resigned herself to the same?

But the circumstances were different. She had loved and lost. Khalid needed to feel someone's love, to know he was special. And to keep the dream his grandmother had so wanted for him.

Khalid was shocked. Her touch was soft, gentle, sweet. Her thumb traced a trail of fire and ice against his skin. No one had touched him since the doctors had removed the last of the bandages. When he released her, he expected her to snatch her hand away. It was still there. The touch was both unexpected and erotic. He could feel himself respond as he hadn't in years.

"Enough." He knocked her hand away and took a step back. "Tell me what it would take to get you to leave the guest house."

"Four years," she replied, and turned to resume her walk.

He watched as she walked away along the sea's edge. She was serious. At least at this moment. She didn't want money. She wanted time.

Why was she here? Was there anything in his grandmother's things that explained why she'd befriended Ella Ponti and made that one-sided deal with her? He hadn't gone through all her papers, but that would be his next step first thing in the morning.

He remained standing, watching. She didn't care if he walked beside her or not. If this was her regular routine, she'd been coming for nightly walks for a year. She didn't need his company.

Why had he come out tonight? He usually kept to himself. He couldn't remember the last time he'd sought out a woman's company. Probably because it would have been an exercise in futility. Ella had seen him in broad daylight. Tonight it had been like the last two: wrapped in darkness he could almost forget the burn scar. She had treated him the same all three nights.

Except for her touch tonight.

Shaking his head, he almost smiled. She shocked him in more ways than one. Was the reaction just that of a man too long without a woman? It had to be. She had done nothing to encourage him. In fact, he couldn't remember another woman standing up to him as she had, both tonight and earlier this morning. Deal with it, she'd said, dismissing his demand she leave as if it were of no account.

Which legally it proved to be. Maybe he'd stop pushing and learn a bit more about his unwanted tenant before pursuing other avenues. She intrigued him. Why was she really here? Maybe it was time to find out more about Ella Ponti, young widow living so far from her native land.

CHAPTER THREE

MAYBE she had finally gotten through to him, she thought as she walked alone. He had not followed her. Good. Well, maybe there was a touch of disappointment, but not enough to wish he was with her.

She clenched her hand into a fist. His skin had been warm, she'd felt the strong line of his jaw, the chiseled outline of his lips. Not that she wanted to think about his lips—that led to thoughts of kisses and she had no intention of ever kissing anyone else. It almost felt like a betrayal of her love for Alexander. It wasn't. Her mind knew that, it would take her heart a bit longer to figure that out. She still mourned her lost love.

"Alexander," she whispered. It took a second for her to recall his dear face. She panicked. She couldn't forget him. She loved him still. He'd been the heart beating in her. But his image wavered and faded to be replaced by the face of Khalid al Harum.

"No!" she said firmly. She would dismiss the man from her thoughts and concentrate on something else, anything else.

Wildly, she looked around. Out to sea she spotted a ship, gliding along soundlessly in the distance. Was it a cruise ship? Were couples and families enjoying the calm waters of the Gulf? Would they be stopping in one of the countries lining the coast? Maybe buy pearls from the shops or enjoy the traditional Arab cuisine. Maybe couples would be dancing. For a moment she regretted she'd never dance again. She was young to have loved and lost. But that was the way life was sometimes.

She had her art.

Stopping at last, she gazed at the ship for a long moment, then glanced back up the beach. Khalid al Harum stood where she'd left him. Was he brooding? Or just awaiting her return. She studied his silhouette and then began walking toward him. She had to return home. It was late and she'd had enough turmoil to last awhile.

When she drew even she stopped. "Now what?"

"Now we wait four years," he replied.

That surprised her. Was he really going to stop pressuring her? Somehow she had not thought he'd give up that easily. Yet, maybe he was pragmatic. The lease was valid. She had the law on her side—even against a sheikh. Dare she let her guard down and believe him?

"Since we'll be neighbors for the time, might as well make the best of things," he said.

That had her on instant alert. He didn't strike her as someone who settled for making the best of any situation unless it suited his needs and demands.

"And how do we do that?"

"Be neighborly, of course." He walked beside her. "Surely you visited with my grandmother from time to time."

"Almost every day," she said. "She was delightful. And very encouraging about my work. Did you know you have one of my early pieces in your house?"

"What and where?"

"The shallow vase in the foyer. It's a starburst bowl. Your grandmother liked it and I gave it to her. I was thrilled when she displayed it in such a prominent place."

"Maybe I'll come by one day and see your work."

Ella wasn't sure she wanted him in her studio or her house. But she probably had to concede that much. If he truly stopped pushing her to leave, she could accept a visit or two.

"Let me know when," she said.

Khalid caught up on some e-mail the next morning and then called his brother. Rashid was the head of Bashiri Oil. Khalid was technically equal owner in the company, along with an uncle and some cousins, but Rashid ran the business. Which suited Khalid perfectly. He much preferred the oil fields to the offices in the high-rise building downtown.

"What's up?" Rashid asked when he heard his brother's voice. "Are you still in Hari?"

"No, I'm at Grandmother's estate. Did you know she rented out the guesthouse last year?"

"No. Who to?"

"An artist. Now I'm wondering why the secrecy. I didn't know, either." Another reason to find out more about Ella Ponti.

"Good grief, did he convince her to sponsor him or something? What hard-luck story did he spin?"

"Not a he, a she. And I'm not sure about the story, which is the reason for the call. Can you have someone there run a background check? Apparently Ella has an airtight lease to the premises and has no intention of leaving before the lease expires—in four more years."

"A five-year lease? Have someone here look at it."

"Already done. It's solid. And she's one determined woman. I offered her as big a bribe as I could and she still says no."

"So, look for dirt to get her out that way." Rashid suggested.

"No, I think I'll go along with it for a while. I just want to know more about her. I respect Grandmother's judgment. She obviously liked the woman. But she also knew her and I don't."

There was a silent moment before his brother spoke again. "Is she pretty?"

"What does that have to do with a background check? She's a widow."

"Oh. Sure, I'll have one of the men call you later and you can give him what you have to start with. Bethanne and I are dining with Mother tonight…care to join us?"

"I'll take a rain check. I'm going through Grandmother's things. I still can't believe she's gone. It's as if she stepped out for a little while. Only, she's never coming back."

"Planning to move there?"

"I was thinking of selling the place, until I found I have an unbudgeable tenant."

"Then good for the widow. None of us wants you to sell."

"It's not your place. You got the villa south of the city."

"Where I think Bethanne and I will live. You love the sea. Why not keep it?"

"It's a big house. You don't need it—you have your own villa by the sea. Why let it sit idle for decades?"

"Get married and fill it up," his brother suggested.

"Give Mother my love and have someone call me soon," he said, sidestepping the suggestion. Rashid should know as well as he did that would never happen. But his brother had recently become engaged and now had changed his tune about staying single. He was not going to get a convert with Khalid.

Ella's words last night echoed. He shook his head. Easy to say the words in the dark. Harder to say when face-to-face with the scars.

He hung up the phone and looked again at the vase sitting on his desk. He'd taken it last night from the foyer to the study. It was lovely. Almost a perfect oval, it flared at the edges. From the center radiating outward was a yellow design that did look like a sunburst. Toward the edges the yellow thinned to gossamer threads. How had she done it? It was sturdy and solid yet looked fragile and enchanted. He knew his grandmother had loved it.

Seeing the vase gave validity to Ella's assertion she was an artist. Was she truly producing other works of art like this? Maybe his grandmother had seen the potential and arranged to keep her protégée close by while she created. She'd been friendly and helpful to others, but was an astute woman. She must have seen real talent to encourage Ella so much. So why not tell the rest of the family?

Khalid rose and headed next door. It was time he saw the artist in her studio, and assessed exactly what she was doing.

He walked to the guest cottage in only seconds. Though it was close, because of the lush garden between it and the main house there was a feeling of distance. He saw a new addition, obviously the studio. How much had his grandmother done for this tenant?

He stepped to the door, which stood wide-open. He could feel the heat roiling out from the space. He looked in. Ella was concentrating on her project and didn't notice him. For a long moment Khalid watched her. She wore a large leather apron and what looked like leather gloves that reached up to her elbows. She had dark glasses on and straddled a long wooden bench. At one end a metal sheet was affixed upon which she turned molten glass at the end of a long tube. As he watched, the glass began to take shape as she turned it against the metal. A few feet beyond was a furnace, the door open, pouring out heat.

Her dark hair was pulled back into a ponytail. He studied her. Even attired as she was, she looked feminine and pretty. How had she become interested in this almost lost art? It took a lot of stamina to work in such an adverse environment. It had to be close to thirty-seven degrees in the room. Yet she looked as cool as if she were sitting in the salon of his grandmother's house.

Slowly ,she rotated the tube. She blew again and the shape elongated. He was afraid to break her concentration lest it cause her to damage the glass globule.

She looked up and frowned, then turned back to her work.

"What do you want?" she asked, before blowing gently into the tube again.

"To see where you worked." He stepped inside. "It's hot in here."

"Duh, I'm working with fire."

He looked at the glowing molten glass. She pushed it into the furnace. No wonder it was so hot; everything inside the furnace glowed orange.

She pulled out the molten glass and worked on it some more. Khalid began to see the shape, a tall vase perhaps. The color was hard to determine as it was translucent and still glowed with heat.

He walked closer, his scar tissue reacting to the heat. He crossed to the other side, so his undamaged cheek faced the heat. How did she stand it so close for hours on end?

"Do you mind if I watch?"

"Not much I can do about it, is there?" she asked with asperity.

Khalid hid a smile. She was not giving an inch. Novel in his experience. Before he'd been burned, women had fawned over him. He and Rashid. He'd bet Ella wouldn't have, no matter what.

"Did my grandmother build this for you?"

"Mmm," she mumbled, her lips still around the tube.

"State of the art?"

"Mmm."

He looked around. Other equipment lined one wall, one looked like an oven. There were jars of crushed glass in various colors. On one table were several finished pieces. He walked over and looked at them. Picking up a vase, he noted the curving shape, almost hourglasslike. The color was pastel—when held up so the white wall served as a background, it looked pale green. When on the table, it grew darker in color contrasting with the wood.

He wondered how much all this cost and would his grandmother ever have made any money as a return on her investment. She must have thought highly of Ella to have expended so much on an aspiring artist.

He looked at the other pieces. He wasn't a connoisseur of art, but they were quite beautiful. It was obvious his grandmother had recognized her talent and had encouraged it.

When he glanced back at Ella, she was using a metal spatula to shape the piece even further. He watched as she flattened the bottom and then began molding the top to break away from the tube. Setting the piece on the flat bottom, she ran the spatula over the top, gradually curving down the edge. He watched her study it from a couple of angles, then slide it onto a paddle and carefully carry it to the oven. She opened the top doors and slid it in, closing the doors quickly and setting a dial.

Turning, she looked at him, taking off her dark glasses.

"So?" she said. Her skin glowed with a sheen of perspiration.

"Interesting. These are lovely," he said, gesturing to the collection behind him. Trying to take his eyes off her. She looked even more beautiful with that color in her cheeks.

"I hope so. That's the intent. Build an inventory and hit the deck running. Do you know any art dealers?" she asked hopefully.

Khalid shook his head. His family donated to the arts, but at the corporate level. He had no personal acquaintance with art dealers.

She sighed and untied her apron, sliding it off and onto the bench. "Me, neither. That was another thing your grandmother was going to do—introduce me to several gallery owners in Europe. Guess I'll have to forge ahead on my own."

"Too bad you can't ride in on the al Harum name," he murmured.

Her eyes flared at that. Was he deliberately baiting her to

ee her reaction? He liked the fire in her eyes. It beat the hint of sadness he saw otherwise.

"I was not planning to ride in on anyone's name. I expect my work to stand on its own merits. Your grandmother was merely going to introduce me."

"Still, an introduction from her would have assured owners ook a long look before saying yea or nay, and think long and hard about turning down a protégée of Alia al Harum. She spent a lot of money in some galleries on her visits to France and Italy."

"I don't plan on showing in Italy," she said hastily.

Khalid's suspicions shot up. She was from Italy—why not show in her home country? He'd given what information he had to a person at the oil company to research her background. Now he wanted more than ever to know what brought her to Quishari, and how she'd met his grandmother.

"Do you think you can sell enough to earn a living?" he asked.

"Your grandmother thought so. I believe her, so yes, I do. don't expect to become hugely wealthy, but I have simple needs, and love doing this creative work, so should be content f I ever start selling."

"Have you sent items out for consideration?"

"No. I wanted to wait until I had inventory. If the pieces sell quickly, I want more in the pipeline and can only produce a few each month. I have a five-year plan."

He met her eyes. Sincerity shone in them. It seemed odd o have this pretty woman talk about five-year plans. But the onger he gazed at her, the more he wanted to help. Which was otally out of character for him. He broke the contact and gave a final glance around the studio. Heading for the door, he paused before leaving. "I say give it a test run, send out some of your best pieces and see if they'll sell. No sense wasting five years if nothing is worth anything."

* * *

Ella stared out into the garden long after Khalid had left. He made it sound so simple. But it wasn't. What if she didn't sell? What if her pieces were mundane and mediocre? She could live on hope for the next few years—or have reality slap her in the face and crush her. She was still too vulnerable to venture forth to see if her work had merit. Madame al Harum had been so supportive. Now she ran into a critic. She had to toughen up if she wanted to compete in the competitive art world. Could she do it?

She cleaned up, resisting the temptation to peer into the lower part of the annealer to check the progress of the piece she'd done yesterday. She hoped it would be spectacular. Maybe Khalid al Harum was right. She should not waste time creating glass pieces if they would never sell. The slight income from Alexander's insurance would not carry her forever. If she couldn't make a living with glass, she should find another means to earn her livelihood.

Only, she didn't want another means. She loved making glass.

Once she finished cleaning the studio, she grabbed her notebook and went to sit on the terrace. The arbor overhead sheltered it from the hot sun. She enjoyed sitting outside when planning. It was so much more pleasant than the hot studio. She opened the pages and began to study the pictures she'd taken of the different pieces she had already made. She had more than one hundred. Some were quite good, others were attempts at a new technique that hadn't panned out. Dare she select a few pieces to offer for sale?

What if no one bought them?

What if they skyrocketed her to fame?

She did not want to rock the boat. She liked life the way it was. Or the way it had been before Khalid al Harum had arrived.

Idly she wondered what it would take to get rid of him. The only thing she could think of was moving out so he could sell the estate. She wasn't going to do that, so it looked as if she were stuck with him.

He was so different from his grandmother. Distracting, for one thing. She'd known instantly when he appeared in the doorway, but had ignored him as long as she could. Of course he had the right to visit his property, but his grandmother had always arranged times to come see what she was working on. There was something almost primordial about the man. He obviously was healthy and virile. She was so not interested in another relationship, yet her body seemed totally aware of his whenever he was near. It was disconcerting to say the least.

And distracting.

Ella stayed away from the beach that night. She listened to music while cataloging the pieces she thought might do for a first showing. She only had a couple of photos of the first batch of vases and bowls she'd made when she moved here. She needed to take more pictures, maybe showcase them in one of the salons in the main house. It was an idea she and Madame al Harum had discussed.

Good grief, she'd have to ask Khalid and she could imagine exactly what he'd say to her proposal. Or maybe she could sneak in when he wasn't there. Surely there was an oil field somewhere in the world that needed consulting. If he'd take off for a few days, she was sure Jalilah would let her in to photograph the pieces sitting in prominent display in the main salon. It would add a certain cachet to her catalog and maybe garner more interest when she was ready to go.

She went to bed that night full of ideas of how to best display the pieces she would put in her first catalog. The only question was if she dare ask Khalid for permission to use his salon for the photographs.

* * *

By the time morning arrived, Ella regretted her decision to forego her walk. She had slept badly, tossing and turning and picturing various scenarios when asking Khalid for his help. Maybe she should have been a bit more conciliatory when discussing her lease. She planned to stand fast on staying, but she could have handled it better.

Only she disliked subterfuge and manipulation; she refused to practice it in her own life.

After a hasty breakfast, she again dressed up a bit and headed for the villa. Walking through the gardens, she tried to quell her nerves. The worst he could do was refuse. The guesthouse had a small sitting area, not as lavish as the main dwelling. She could use that, but she longed for the more elegant salon as backdrop for her art.

Jalilah opened the door when she knocked.

"I'd like to see Sheikh al Harum," Ella said, hoping she looked far more composed than she felt.

"He has someone visiting. Wait here."

Ella stood in the foyer. Her vase was gone. She peered into the salon; it wasn't there, either. Had something happened to it? Or had Khalid removed it once he'd learned she made it? That made her feel bad.

"Come." The maid beckoned from the door to the study.

When Ella entered, she stopped in surprise. Two men looked at her. Except for their clothing, and the scar on Khalid's cheek, they were identical.

"Twins?" she said.

Khalid frowned. "Did you want something?"

"Introduce us," the other man said, crossing the room and offering his hand.

"My brother," Khalid said.

"Well, that's obvious." Ella extended her hand and smiled. "I'm Ella Ponti."

"I am Rashid al Harum. You're the tenant, I take it."

She nodded. "Unwanted to boot."

"Only because I want to sell," Khalid grumbled. "Rashid is trying to talk me out of it, too."

"Good for you. I told him your grandmother wanted him to have the house. She could have left it to a charity or something if she hadn't hoped he'd live here," she said.

"It's a too big for one man," Khalid said.

"So—"

He raised his hand. "We've been over that. What do you want?"

Rashid glanced at his twin. "Am I in the way?"

Ella shook her head, bemused to see her vase in the center of Khalid's desk.

"Not at all. I came to ask permission to photograph some of my work in the salon. Give it a proper showing—elegant and refined. The guest cottage just doesn't have the same ambiance."

"You want to take pictures of my house?" Khalid asked. "Out of the question."

"Not the house, just some of my special pieces sitting on a table or something which would display them and give an idea of how they would look in another home. The background would be slightly blurred, the focus would be on my work."

"Use the table in your workroom."

"That's elegant."

He frowned. "I don't see—"

"—any problem with it," Rashid finished before his twin could finish. "I was admiring your vase when you arrived. Khalid explained how you made it. I'd like to see more of your work. I bet Bethanne would, as well."

"She'd do anything you say," Khalid grumbled.

"Bethanne?" Ella asked.

"My fiancée. She's making some changes to my villa in preparation of our marriage and moving in there."

"So the consumed one is getting married—wouldn't my grandmother love to know that?" Khalid asked.

"What are you talking about?" Rashid asked, glancing at his twin.

"Nothing, only something your grandmother said to me once. I'm happy for you and your fiancée. You might tell your brother how happy you are so he could go find someone to make a life with and leave me alone," Ella said hastily.

Rashid looked at her and then Khalid.

"Forget it. We've been over this before. I'm not marrying," Khalid growled.

Rashid looked thoughtful as he again looked back and forth between the two others in the room.

"I, uh, have to be leaving. I'll bring Bethanne by tomorrow if that suits you, Ella. She'd love to see the glass objects. Khalid, you have what you asked for. Let me know if you need more." He nodded to both and left, a small smile tugging at his lips.

Ella hated to see him go. He was much easier to be around than his brother.

"So I can use the salon?" she asked. Rashid had indicated yes, but it was still Khalid's place and his decision she needed.

"What if I say no?" he asked, leaning casually against the side of the desk.

"Then I'll pester you until you say yes," she replied daringly. "Maybe it'll help sell some of my work earlier than originally planned and I could move away sooner."

"How much sooner?"

"I don't know, five days?"

A gleam of amusement lit his eyes. "For such an early move, how can I refuse?"

"Thank you. I'll give credit in my brochure so everyone will know you helped."

"No. No credit, no publicity."

She started to protest but wisely agreed. "Okay. I'm cooling a couple of pieces now and once they are ready, I will begin taking pictures. I appreciate this."

"You weren't on the beach last night," he said.

He had been, obviously.

"I, uh, needed to get to sleep early. Big day today."

"Doing what?"

"Coming to ask you about the salon" sounded dumb. What else could she come up with?

He watched her. Ella fidgeted and looked around the room. "Just a big day. Why is my vase in here?"

"I was looking at it. I thought it was mine."

"I guess. I should have said why is the vase I made in here instead of the foyer."

"I wanted to look at it. I like it."

She blinked in surprise. "You do?"

Amusement lurked in his eyes again. "You sound surprised. Isn't it good?"

She nodded. "I just can't imagine you—"

"Having an eye for beauty?"

"I wasn't exactly going to say that."

"You haven't held back on anything else."

"You are very exasperating, do you know that?" she asked.

"Makes a change from other names I've been called."

If he drove the other people he knew as crazy as he did her, she wasn't surprised.

Khalid stood and moved around to sit at the desk.

"So, you'll be on the beach tonight?" he asked casually.

Ella shrugged. "Thanks for letting me use the salon for the photographs."

"One caveat," he said, glancing up.

She sighed. It had been too good to be true. "What?"

"I get to give final approval. I don't want certain prize possessions to be part of your sales catalog. No need to give anyone the idea that more than your glass is available."

"Done." She nodded and turned. At the door she stopped and looked at him over her shoulder. "I do expect to take a walk tonight as it happens."

She wasn't sure, but she suspected the expression on his face was as close to a smile as she'd seen.

CHAPTER FOUR

ELLA and Khalid fell into a tentative friendship. Each night she went for a walk along the beach. Most evenings Khalid was already on the sand, as if waiting for her. They fell into an easy conversation walking in the dark at the water's edge. Sometimes they spoke of what they'd done that day. Other times the walks were primarily silent. Ella noted he was quieter than other men she'd known. Was that his personality or a result of the accident? She gathered the courage to ask about it on the third evening after he said she could use the salon.

"How did you get burned?" she asked as they were turning to head for home. She hadn't wanted to cut the walk short if he got snippy about her question.

"We were capping a fire in Egypt. Just as the dynamite went off, another part of the well exploded. The shrapnel shredded part of my suit, instant burn. Hurt like hell."

"I can imagine. I've had enough burns to imagine how such a big area would be almost unbearable. Were you long in hospital?"

"A few months."

And in pain for much of that time, she was sure. "Did you get full mobility back?"

"Yes. And other parts were unaffected."

She smiled at his reminder of her attempt at being tactful

when he said he wouldn't marry. A burned patch of skin wouldn't be enough to keep her from falling for a man. She suspected Khalid was too sensitive to the scar. There were many woman who would enjoy being with him.

"Good. What I don't get is why you do it?"

"Do what?"

"Put your life at risk. You don't even need to work, do you? Don't you have enough money to live without risking life and limb?"

He was quiet a moment, then said, "I don't have to work for money. I do want to do what I can to make oil production safe. Over the last fifty years or so many men have died because of faulty equipment or fires. Our company has reaped the benefit. But in doing that we have an obligation to make sure the men who have helped in our endeavors have as much safety guarding them as we can provide. If I can provide that, then it's for the good."

"An office job would be safer," she murmured.

"Rashid has that covered. I like being in the field. I like the desert, the challenge of capturing the liquid crude beneath the land, or the sea. I like knowing I'm pitting my skills and experience against the capricious nature of drilling—and coming out on top more than not."

"Still seems ridiculously dangerous. Get someone else to do it."

"It's my calling, you might say."

Ella was silent at that. It still seemed too dangerous for him—witness the burn that had changed his life. But she was not someone to argue against a calling. She felt that with her art.

She turned and he caught her hand, pulling her to a stop. She looked up at him. The moon was a sliver on the horizon, the light still dim, but she could see him silhouetted against the stars.

"What?"

"My mother is hosting a reception on Saturday. I need to make an appearance. I want you to go with me."

Ella shook her head. "I don't do receptions," she said. "Actually I don't go away from the estate much."

"Why?"

"Just don't," she murmured, turning to walk toward home. He still held her hand and fell into step with her.

"Consider it payment for using the salon," he said.

"You already agreed to my using the salon. You can't add conditions now."

"Sure I can—it's my salon. You want to use it, consider this part of the payment. It's just a reception. Some people from the oil company, some from the government, some personal friends. We circulate, make my mother happy by being seen by everyone, then leave. No big deal."

"Get someone else."

He was silent for several steps.

"There is no one else," he said slowly.

"Why not?"

"I've been down that road, all right? I'm not going to set myself up again. Either it's you, or I don't go. My grandmother helped you out—your turn to pay back."

"Jeeze, talk about coercion. You're sure it'll only be people who live here in Quishari?"

"Yes. What would it matter if foreigners came? You're one yourself."

"I am trying to keep a low profile, that's why," she said, hating to reveal anything, but not wanting to find out her hiding place had been found.

"Why?"

"I have reasons."

"Are you hiding?" he asked incredulously.

"Not exactly."

"Exactly what, then?" He pulled her to a stop again. "I wan to hear this."

"I'm in seclusion because of the death of my husband."

"That was over a year ago."

"There's a time limit on grieving? I hadn't heard that."

"There's no time limit, but by now the worst should be be hind you and you should be going out and seeing friends Maybe finding a new man in your life."

"I see my friends," she protested. "And I'm not going dow that road again. You're a funny one to even suggest it."

"When do you see friends?"

"When they come to visit. I'm working now and it's no convenient to have people over. But when I'm not in the mids of something, they come for swimming in the sea and alfresc meals on my terrace. Did you think I was a hermit?"

"I hadn't thought about it. I never see these friends."

"You've lived here for what, almost a week? No one ha come in that time. Stick around if you're so concerned abou my social life."

"Mostly I'm concerned about your going with me to th reception this weekend."

"No."

"Yes. Or no salon photos."

Ella glared at him. It missed the mark. He couldn't see he that well. And she suspected her puny attempts at putting hin in the wrong wouldn't work. He did own the estate. And sh did need permission to use the salon. Rats, he was going t win on this one. She did not want to go. She was content i her cottage, with her work and with the solitude.

Only sometimes did it feel lonely.

Not once since Khalid had arrived.

Dangerous thoughts, those. She was fine.

"All right, we'll go, greet everyone and then leave."

"Thank you."

They resumed the walk, but Ella pulled her hand from his. They were friends, not lovers. No need to hold hands.

But her hand had felt right in his larger one. She missed the physical contact of others. She hadn't been kissed in ages, held with passion in as long. Why did her husband have to die?

"I'll pick you up at seven on Saturday," he said.

"Fine. And first thing tomorrow, I'm coming to take photographs. I don't want to miss my chance in case you come up with other conditions that I can't meet."

He laughed.

Ella looked at him. She'd never even seen him smile and now he was laughing in the darkness! Was that the only time he laughed?

"I expect I need to wear something very elegant," she mumbled, mentally reviewing the gowns she'd worn at university events. There were a couple that might do. She hadn't thought about dressing up in a long time. A glimmer of excitement took hold. She had enjoyed meeting other people at the university, speaking about topics far removed from glass making. Would the reception be as much fun? She felt a frisson of anticipation to be going with Khalid. She always seemed more alive when around him.

"You'll look fine in anything you wear," he said easily.

Just like a man, she thought, still reviewing the gowns she owned.

The next morning Ella carefully took two of her pieces, wrapped securely in a travel case, and went to the main house. Ringing the doorbell, she was greeted by Jalilah.

"I've come to take pictures," she said.

"In the salon, His Excellency has told me. Come." The maid led the way and then bowed slightly before leaving.

Ella put the starburst bowl on one of the polished mahogany tables.

Khalid appeared in the doorway. He leaned against the jamb and watched.

"What do you want?" she asked, feeling her heartbeat increase. Fussing, she tried pictures from different angles. She could hardly focus the lens with him watching her.

"Just wanted to see how the photo shoot went."

"Don't you have work to do?"

"No."

She tried to ignore him, but it was impossible. She lifted the camera and framed the bowl. She snapped the picture just as the doorbell sounded. She looked at Khalid. "Company?" she asked. Maybe someone who would take him away from the salon.

He looked into the foyer and nodded. "Rashid and Bethanne. Good timing. They can help."

"Help what?"

"You get the best pictures. You want to appeal to the largest number of buyers, right?"

"Of course." The sooner she started earning money, the sooner she might move.

"Hello," Rashid said, coming into the room with a tall blond woman. "Ella, this is my fiancée, Bethanne Sanders. Bethanne, this is Ella Ponti. Now, can you two talk?" he asked in Arabic.

"I also speak Italian and French and English," Ella said, crossing the room to greet the pair.

Switching to English, Rashid said, "Good, Ella speaks English."

"I'm so delighted to meet you," Bethanne said, offering her hand.

Ella shook it and smiled. "I'm happy to meet you. My English is not so good, so excuse me if I get things mixed."

"At least we can communicate. And you speak Arabic. I'm learning from a professor at the university. That's not easy."

"And the maid," Rashid said softly.

Bethanne laughed. "Her, too."

"Would that be Professor Hampstead?" Ella asked.

"Yes, do you know him?" Bethanne asked with a pleased smile.

"My husband worked at the university in language studies. I know the professor and his wife quite well. He's an excellent teacher."

"We came to see your work," Rashid said. "I see you've started on the pictures."

"Photographing some pieces for a preliminary catalog. I'd like to see if I can move up my timetable for a showing. Once I have enough pictures, I can make a small catalog and circulate it."

"Why are you taking pictures here?" Bethanne asked, walking over to look at the bowl. "Oh, this is exquisite. You made this? How amazing!" She leaned over and touched the edge lightly but made no move to pick it up.

"I think the ambiance of the other furnishings here will show it off better. I want the background to be blurry, with only the glass piece in clear focus, but to give the feel that it would fit in any elegant salon."

"And Khalid was all for the project, obviously," Rashid said with a glance at his twin.

"Obviously—she's here, isn't she?" Khalid said. "You two can help with the project. Give us an unbiased perspective and select the best pictures."

"I'd like to see the other pieces you've made," Bethanne said.

"I'm happy to show you. Shall we go now?"

"Finish the pictures of these, then when you go to your studio, you can bring some more over," Khalid suggested.

The next couple of hours were spent with everyone giving opinions about the best angle for pictures and which of the different art pieces Ella had created should be included.

Rashid said he'd see if his mother had some recommendations on art galleries who would help.

Ella felt as if things were spinning out of control. She and Alia al Harum had discussed the plans, but they'd been for years down the road. Now so much was happening at once.

Khalid looked over at her at one point and said, "Enough. We will return to the main house and have lunch on the terrace. Bethanne, you haven't told Ella what you do. I think she'll be interested."

Ella threw him a grateful smile. "I'll just tidy up a bit and join you."

Rashid and Bethanne headed out, but Khalid remained behind for a moment.

"They only wanted to help," he said.

"I'm glad they did."

"But you're feeling overwhelmed. You set the pace. This is your work, your future. Don't let anyone roll over you."

"Good advice. Remember that next time you want your way," she said, sitting down on her bench, touched he'd picked up on her mild panic and dealt with it. She hadn't expected such sensitivity from the man.

"You are coming for lunch?"

"Yes. I just need a few minutes to myself."

"I'll come back for you if you don't show up in twenty minutes."

"Did anyone tell you you're a bit bossy?" she asked.

"Twenty minutes," he said, and left.

Ella took less than the twenty minutes. After a quick splash of cool water against her face, she brushed her hair and lay down for ten minutes. Then hurried to the main house. Khalid and the others were on the terrace and she walked straight there without going through the house.

Lunch was delicious and fun. It was a bit of a struggle to

remember to speak English during the meal, but she was confident she held her own in the conversation that ranged from Bethanne's career as a pilot to Rashid's recent trip to Texas to the reception on Saturday night.

"Are you coming?" Rashid asked his brother at one point.

"Yes," Khalid said.

Rashid and Bethanne exchanged surprised looks.

"Great."

"I'm bringing Ella," Khalid continued.

Both guests turned to stare at her. She smiled brightly. Was this such an amazing thing? Surely Khalid had brought other women to receptions before.

"Condition of using the salon for the pictures," she murmured.

"Of course," Rashid said with another quick glance at his fiancée.

"Great. Maybe you could go shopping with me before then," Bethanne said. "I'm not sure I have anything suitable to wear."

Ella hesitated. She hadn't been shopping except for groceries since her husband's funeral. Dare she go? Surely it would be okay for one afternoon. It wasn't as if anyone was hanging around the main streets of the city looking for her.

"I don't know if I would be much help." She felt Khalid's gaze on her and glanced his way.

"Help or not, don't women love to buy beautiful dresses?"

"I don't need one. I have several," Ella said.

"Come help me find several," Bethanne urged.

Rashid watched the interaction and then looked at his brother. He narrowed his eyes when Khalid never looked away from Ella.

"Okay, I'll go tomorrow afternoon," Ella said fast, as if afraid she'd change her mind.

When lunch finished, Ella thanked her host and fled for her cottage. She'd had more activity today than any time since

Alexander had died. And she'd agreed to go shopping—out along the main district of Alkaahdar. Surely after all this time it would be safe. She had a right to her own life. And to live it on her terms.

That night she debated going for a walk. She was getting too used to them. Enjoying them too much. What happened when Khalid moved on? When he went to another oil field to consult on well equipment, or had to go fight a fire. That thought scared her. He was trained; obviously an expert in the field. He knew what to do. It was dangerous, but as he'd explained, except for that one accident, he'd come through unscathed many times.

But that one could have killed him. Didn't he realize that? Or another one similar that might rip the helmet and protection totally off. She shivered thinking about it.

She went for her walk, hoping he'd be there. It was better than imaging awful things that could happen.

He sat on the sand near the garden.

"It's warm," he said when she appeared, letting some sand drift from his hand.

"Sometimes I sit on the beach in the night, relishing the heat held from the day."

"Sand makes glass," he commented.

"Yes. I've heard that lightning strikes on beaches produces glass—irregular in shape and not usually functional. I'd like to see some." She sat beside him. "I like the fact I'll know your brother and Bethanne at the reception."

"And me."

"Yes, and you. We aren't staying long, right."

"I said not long. Why are you nervous? You've been to university receptions—this would be sort of the same, just a different group of people. You'll be bored out of your mind with all the talk about oil."

She smiled at his grumbling. "Is that the normal topic?"

"With a heavy presence of Bashiri executives it usually is. The minister of finance is not in charity with us right now. Rashid closed a deal he didn't like. But I'm sure a few million for pet projects will sweeten his disposition."

Ella didn't want to talk about money or family. She jumped up. "I'm going to walk."

He rose effortlessly beside her and kept pace.

"Tell me more about the oil fields you've been to," she said, looking for a way to keep her thoughts at bay. She liked listening to Khalid talk. Might as well give him something to talk about.

The next afternoon Ella had a good time shopping. Once inside boutiques, she didn't glance outside. While in the car she had seen no one that appeared to be paying the two of them any attention. Bethanne was fun to shop with. She looked beautiful in the elegant cool colors that went so well with her blond hair. Twice, salesclerks offered jewel-tone dresses and Bethanne had suggested Ella try them on. Of course the sizes were wrong. Ella was slight, almost petite, not nearly as tall as the American. She was tempted, but conscious of her limited funds, cheerfully refused. She had dresses that would suit. She wasn't going to spend a week's worth of groceries on a dress she'd wear for about an hour.

Bethanne decided on a lovely blue that mimicked the color of her eyes.

"Done. Let's get some coffee. And candied walnuts. They're my favorites," she said when she received the dress in a box.

Having the chauffeur stow the dress in the limo's trunk, Bethanne asked him to take them to an outside café. When they found a coffee house with outside seating on a side street, she had him wait while she and Ella went for coffee.

"This was fun," Bethanne said. "I hope we can become friends. I will be marrying Rashid in a few months and don't know but a handful of people in Quishari. And most of them don't speak English. So until I master this language, I'm left out of conversations."

"I would like another friend. Tell me about Texas. I've never been to the United States."

"Where have you been that you learned so many different languages? And that's not even your career, like the professor's is."

"I went to school in Switzerland for a few years and in England."

"And the Arabic?"

"That I learned because Alexander was learning it and planned to come to an Arabian country to work."

"Alexander was your husband?" Bethanne asked gently.

Ella nodded. "We knew each other from when we were small. I loved him it seems all my life."

"I'm sorry for your loss," Bethanne said.

"Me, too." Ella didn't want to think about it. Every time she grew sad and angry. It had happened. Nothing could change the past. She had to go on. Today she was with a new friend. And beginning to look forward to the reception on Saturday.

Ella worked through the next two days culling her collection, deciding which pieces to display and which to hold in reserve.

She tried on the dresses she'd worn to university events, dismayed to find she had lost more weight than she'd thought. They all were loose. Finally she decided on a dark blue long gown that shimmered in the light and almost looked black. If she wore her hair loose, and the pearls she received when she was eighteen, she'd do. It wasn't as if it were a real date or anything. But she wanted to look nice for Khalid's sake. If he broke his normal habit of nonattendance, it behooved her to look her best.

* * *

Saturday evening, Ella prepared for the reception with care. She had some trepidation about venturing forth into such a large gathering, but felt safe enough since the guests would most likely all be from Quishari. Her hair was longer than she usually wore. The waves gleamed in the light. She hoped she would pass muster as a guest of a sheikh. Her heart tripped faster when she thought of spending the evening with his family and friends. And some of the leaders of the country. She planned to stay right by Khalid's side and remind him how soon they would leave.

Promptly at seven he knocked on the door of the cottage. She picked up a small purse with her keys and went to greet him.

"You look lovely," he said when she opened the door.

She thought he looked fantastic. A man should always wear a tux, she decided.

"I could say the same. Wow, you clean up good."

"Ready?"

"Yes." She pulled the door shut behind her. To her surprise, Khalid had a small sports car waiting. She had expected a limousine as Rashid used. She liked the smaller car; less intimidating. More intimate.

"If we were going for a spin in the afternoon, I'd put the top down. But not tonight."

"Thank you. I spent hours on my hair."

"Literally?"

She laughed, feeling almost carefree for the first time in months. "No, I just washed and brushed it."

He reached over and took some strands in his fingers. "It feels soft and silky. I wondered if it would."

She caught her breath. His touch was scarcely felt, yet her insides were roiling. She looked out the windshield, trying to calm her nerves. It was Khalid, cranky neighbor, reluctant landlord. She tried to quell the racing of her heart.

When they arrived at the reception, Ella was surprised to

find it held in a large hotel. "I thought your mother would have it at her home," she commented when he helped her from the car. A valet drove the sports car away.

"Too many people, too much fuss. She prefers to have i taken care of here."

"Mmm." Ella looked around. She hadn't been to such a elegant event in years. Suddenly she felt like a teen again proud to be going to the grown-up's affair. Excited. She could do this, had done so many times before. But she preferred smaller gatherings, friends to share good times. Like she and—

No, she was not going there. Tonight was about Khalid She owed him for his reluctant help. So she'd do her best to be the perfect date for a man of his influence and power.

"Khalid, I'm so glad you came. Rashid said you would— but your track record isn't the best." A beautiful woman came up and embraced him. She smiled at him, patted his good cheek then turned to look at Ella.

"Salimeia, may I present Ella Ponti. Salimeia is my cousin," Khalid said, looking somewhat self-conscious.

Ella couldn't imagine he felt that way. She was aware of his self-confidence—almost arrogance when around her. She watched as he gave a quick glance around the gathering.

An older woman, dressed in a very fashionable gown came over, her eyes fixed on Khalid.

"I am so glad you came," she said, reaching out to grab hi hands in hers.

"Mother, may I present Ella Ponti. Ella, my mother Sabria al Harum."

"Madame, my pleasure," Ella said with formal deference

"How do you do?" Khalid's mother looked at him in ques tion, practically ignoring Ella.

"I'm glad he came, too. Mo is here. I'll find him and tell him you're here," his cousin said. She smiled and walked away.

"Ella is my tenant," he clarified.

She looked horrified. "Tenant? You are renting her the house your grandmother left you?"

"No, she has the cottage on the estate and has lived there for a year. Didn't you know about her, either?"

Ella expected the woman to shoo her out the door. She was not the warm, friendly woman her mother-in-law had been.

Sabria al Harum thought for a moment. "The artist Alia was helping?" she guessed.

Ella nodded once. She felt like some charity case the way the woman said it.

"I did not know she had her living on the premises." She said it as if Ella was a kind of infestation.

"I do live there and have an airtight lease that gives me the right to stay for another four years," Ella said with an imp of mischief. She did not like haughty people.

"Nonsense. Khalid, have our attorneys check it out." His mother sounded as if any inconvenience could be handled by someone else.

Ella hid a smile as she looked at Khalid.

"Already done, Mother. Ella's right, she has the right to live here for another four years."

Other guests were arriving. Khalid took Ella's arm and gently moved her around his mother. "We'll talk later," he said. "You have other guests to greet."

"Gee, is she always so welcoming?" Ella said softly, only for his ears.

"No. She is very conscious of the position our family holds in the country. Perhaps because she came to the family as an adult, not raised as we were. Come, I see someone I think you'll enjoy meeting."

She went willingly, growing more conscious of the wave of comments that were softly exchanged as they passed. She caught one woman staring at Khalid, then looking at Ella. Giving in to impulse, she reached out to take his arm. It au-

tomatically bent, so she could have her hand in the crook o
the elbow. He pressed her against his side. She moved closer
head raised.

Khalid introduced her to a friend and his wife. They chatte
for a few moments, Khalid mentioning Ella's art. Both wer
interested.

"My uncle has a gallery in the city. Do send me your cat
alog so I can send it to him," the wife said.

"I would love to. Thank you." Ella replied.

They mingled through the crowd. Once the complete cir
cuit of the ballroom had almost been made, she tugged o
Khalid. He leaned closer to hear her over the noise. "Onc
we've made the circle, we leave, right?"

"If you're ready."

"Ah, Khalid, I heard you came tonight." A florid faced
overweight man stepped in front of them. "Tell your brothe
to stop sending our business outside of the country. There ar
others who could have handled the deal he just consummate
with the Moroccans." He looked at Ella. "Hello, I don't be
lieve we've met."

"Ella, the finance minister, Ibrahim bin Saali. This is Ell
Ponti."

The minister took her hand and held it longer than needed
"A new lovely face to grace our gatherings. Tell me, Mis
Ponti, are you from Quishari?"

She tugged her hand free and stepped closer to Khalid
"I've lived here for years. I love this city."

"As do I. Perhaps we can see some of the beauty of the cit
together sometime," he said suavely.

Ella smiled politely. "Perhaps."

"Excuse us," Khalid said, placing his hand at the small o
her back and gently nudging her.

They walked away.

"That was rude," she said quietly in English.

"He was hitting on you."

"He's too old. He was merely being polite."

"He does not think he's too old and polite is not something we think of when we think of Ibrahim."

She laughed. "I don't plan to take him up on his offer, so you're safe."

Khalid looked at her. "Safe?"

She looked back, and their eyes locked for a moment. She looked away first. "Never mind. It was just a comment."

Khalid nodded, scanning the room. "I think we've done our duty tonight. Shall we leave?"

"Yes."

He escorted her out and signaled the valet for his car. When it arrived, he waited until Ella was in before going to the driver's side. "Home?"

"Where else?" she asked.

"I know a small, out-of-the-way tavern that has good music."

"I love good music," she said.

He drove swiftly through the night. What had possessed him to invite her to stay out longer? She had attended the reception, he got some points with his mother, though she hadn't seemed that excited to meet Ella. They could be home in ten minutes.

Instead he was prolonging the evening. He'd never known anyone as interesting to be around as his passenger. She intrigued him. Not afraid to stand up to his bossiness, she nevertheless defended Ibrahim's boorish behavior. He smiled. Never could stand the man. He had been afraid for a moment Ella might be tempted by Ibrahim's power and position. Not his Ella.

He had to give her credit. No one there had guessed she'd come as part of a bargain. No one made comments about how such a pretty woman was wasting her time with him.

The tavern was crowded, as it always was on Saturday nights. It was one place few people recognized him. He could

be more like anyone else here, unlike the more formal event
his mother hosted. There were several men he knew and
waved to when they called to him. Shepherding Ella to the
back, they found an empty table and sat, knees touching.

Ella looked around and then at Khalid. "I hear talk and
laughter, but no music."

He nodded. "It starts around eleven. We're a bit early. Want
something to eat or drink?"

"A snack would be good. We hardly got a chance to sample
the delicacies your mother had available."

"Want to go back?"

"No. This suits me better."

"Why is that?" he asked. He knew why he preferred the
dim light of the tavern, the easy camaraderie of the patrons.
The periodic escape from responsibilities and position. But
why did she think it was better?

"I don't know anyone."

"That doesn't make sense. Wouldn't it be better to know
friends when going to a place like this?"

She shrugged. "Not at this time."

"Did you have a favorite spot you and your husband
liked to frequent?" he asked. He wanted to know more
about her. Even if he had to hear about the man who must
have been such a paragon she would never find anyone to
replace him.

She nodded. "But I don't go there anymore. It's not the same."

"Where do you and your friends go?" he asked.

"Nowhere." She looked at him.

Her eyes were bright and her face seemed to light up the
dark area they sat in.

"This is the first I've been out since my husband's death.
Friends come to visit me, but I haven't been exactly in a party
mood. But this isn't like a real date or anything, is it? Just paying you back for letting me use the salon for my pictures."

"Exactly. You wouldn't want to go on a real date with me.
know about that from my ex-fiancée."

"What are you talking about?"

"This." He gestured to the scar on the side of his face.

"Don't be dumb, Khalid. That has nothing to do with it. I
.till feel married to Alexander and am faithful."

Khalid nodded and looked away, feeling her words like a
physical blow. Even if they got beyond the scar, she would
never be interested in him. She loved a dead man. He wished
they'd gone straight home. She could be with her memories,
and he could get back to the reality of his life. Only her words
had seemed so wrong.

CHAPTER FIVE

HE LOOKED back at her. "You're not serious? You are no
married—that ended when your husband died. And you are
far too young and pretty to stay single the rest of your life."

She blinked in surprise. "I'm not that young."

"I'd guess twenty-five at the most," he said.

"Add four years. Do you really think I look twenty-five?"
She smiled in obvious pleasure.

Khalid felt as if she'd kicked him in the heart. "At most,
said. Even twenty-nine is too young to remain a widow the
rest of your life. You could be talking another sixty years."

"I'll never find anyone to love like I did Alexander," she
said, looking around the room. For a moment he glimpsed the
sorrow that seemed so much a part of her. He much preferred
when she looked happy.

"My grandmother said that after her husband died. But she
was in her late sixties at the time. They'd had a good marriage
Raised a family, enjoyed grandchildren."

"I had a great marriage," she said.

"You could again."

She looked back. "You're a fine one to talk. Where's you
wife and family?"

"Come on, Ella, who would marry me?"

"No one, with that attitude. How many women have you asked out in the last year?"

"If I don't count you, none."

"So how do you even know, then."

"The woman I was planning to spend my life with told me in no uncertain terms what a hardship that would be. Why would I set myself up for more of the same?"

The waiter came and asked for drink orders. Khalid ordered a bowl of nuts in addition.

"She was an idiot," Ella said, leaning closer after the man left.

"Who?"

"Your ex-fiancée. Did she expect life to be all roses and sunshine?"

"Apparently." He felt bemused at her defense. "Shouldn't it be?"

"It would be nice if it worked that way. I don't think it does. Everyone has problems. Some are on the inside, others outside."

"We know where mine is," he said.

She shocked him again when she got up and switched chairs to sit on his right side. "I've noticed, you know," she said, glaring at him in defiance.

"Noticed what?" He was growing uncomfortable. He tried to shelter others from the ugly slash of burned skin.

"That you always try to have me on your left. Are you afraid I'll go off in shock or something if I catch sight of the scar?"

"No, not you."

"What does that mean?"

"Just, no, not you. You wouldn't do that, even if you wanted to. I'd say your parents raised you very well."

"Leave my parents out of any discussion," she said bitterly.

"Touch a nerve?"

She shrugged. "They and I are not exactly on good terms. They didn't want me to marry Alexander."

"And why was that?"

"None of your business."

The waiter returned with the beverages and plate of nuts. Ella scooped up a few and popped them into her mouth.

"Mmm, good." She took a sip of the cold drink and looked at the small stage.

"I think your musicians are arriving."

So his tenant was at odds with her parents. He hadn't considered she had parents living, or he would have expected her to return home after her husband's death. Now that he knew they were alive, it seemed strange that she was still in Quishari and not at their place. His curiosity rose another notch. He would nudge the researcher at the oil company to complete the background check on his tenant.

Khalid spent more time watching Ella as the evening went on than the musicians. She seemed to be enjoying the music and the tavern. He enjoyed watching her. They stayed until after one before driving home.

"Planning to take a walk on the beach tonight?" he asked.

"Why not?" she asked. "I'm still buoyed up by that last set. Weren't they good?"

"I have enjoyed going there for years. We'll have to go again sometime."

"Mmm, maybe."

He didn't expect her to jump at the chance. But he would have liked a better response.

"Meet you at the beach in ten minutes," she said when she got out of the car.

"No walking straight through?" he asked.

"I don't know about you, but I don't want to get saltwater and sand on this gown. And I'd think it wouldn't be recommended for tuxedos, either."

Khalid changed into comfortable trousers and a loose shirt and arrived at the beach seconds ahead of Ella.

They started north. The moon was fuller tonight and spread

a silvery light over everything. Without much thought, he reached for her hand, lacing their fingers together. She didn't comment, nor pull away. Taking a deep breath, he felt alive as he hadn't in a long while.

"I appreciate your going with me tonight. My mother is always after me to attend those things for the sake of the family," he said.

"She would have been happier without me accompanying you," Ella said.

"She doesn't like anyone who shows an interest in her sons. Unless it's the woman she's picked out. Did you know Rashid almost had an arranged marriage?"

"No, what happened?"

"His supposed fiancée was to be flown in on the plane Bethanne delivered. Only she never left Morocco. When he fell for Bethanne, Mother was furious. I think they are getting along better now, but I wouldn't say Mother opened her arms to Bethanne."

"I bet your grandmother would have loved her."

"She would have loved knowing Rashid was getting married."

For a moment Khalid felt a tinge of envy for his brother. He had found a woman he adored and who seemed to love him equally. They planned a life in Quishari at the other home their grandmother had left and had twice in his hearing mentioned children. He'd be an uncle before the first year was out, he'd bet.

"Bethanne doesn't strike me as someone who cares a lot about what others think of her," Ella said.

"I'm sure Mother will come around once she sees how happy Rashid is. And once she's a grandmother."

Ella fell silent. They walked for several minutes. Khalid wondered what she was thinking. Had she wanted to be a mother? Would her life be vastly different if she had a small child to raise? She should get married again.

She was right—that was easy enough for him to say. They were a pair, neither wanting marriage for different reasons. Maybe one day another man would come along for her to marry. Once she was out, showing off her creations, she'd run into men from all over the world.

Khalid refused to examine why he didn't like that idea.

"Ready to head back?" she asked.

He nodded, but felt curiously reluctant to end the evening. He liked being with Ella.

The return walk was also in silence, but not without awareness. Khalid could breathe the sweet scent she wore, enjoy the softness of her hands, scarred here and there by burns from her work. She wore a skirt again. He didn't think he'd seen her in pants except when working at her studio. It made her seem all the more feminine. He didn't want the evening to end. Tomorrow would bring back the barriers and status of tenant and landlord. He had no more reasons to seek her out or take her out again. But he wanted to.

"I can get home from here," she said when they reached the path.

"I'll walk that short distance." He was not ready to say good-night.

When they reached the cottage, she tugged her hand free. "Good night. I enjoyed the tavern. And am glad I got to meet your mother even if she wasn't as glad to meet me."

He reached for her, holding her by her shoulders and drawing her closer. "I'm glad you went with me."

"We're even now, right?" Her voice sounded breathless. He could see her dimly in the light from the moon, her eyes wide, her mouth parted slightly.

With a soft groan, he leaned over and kissed her. He felt her start of surprise. He expected her to draw away in a huff. Instead, after a moment, she leaned against him and returned his kiss. Their mouths opened and tongues danced. Her arms hugged him closer and his embraced her. For a long moment they kissed, learning, tasting, touching, feeling.

She was sweet, soft, enticing. He could have stood all night on the doorstep, kissing Ella.

But she pushed away a moment later.

"Good night, Khalid," she said, darting into the house and shutting the door.

"Good night," he said to the wooden door.

This was not going to be their last date, no matter what Ella thought.

Ella leaned against the door, breathing hard. She closed her eyes. She'd kissed Sheikh Khalid al Harum! Oh, and what a kiss. Unlike anything she'd ever had before.

"No!" she said, pushing away and walking back to the kitchen. She wanted water, and a clear head. She loved Alexander. He was barely gone a year and she was caught up in the sensuousness of another man. How loyal was that? How could she have responded so strongly. Good grief, he'd probably think she was some sex-starved widow out to snare the first man who came along.

How could she have kissed him?

She took a long drink of water, her mind warring with her body. The kiss had been fantastic. Every cell in her tingled with awareness and yearning. She wanted more.

"No!" she said again. She had her life just as she wanted it. She did not need to become the slightest bit involved with a man who wanted her to leave so he could sell a family home.

On the other hand, maybe she should do just that. Put an end to time with Khalid by moving away.

She went to her bedroom and dressed for bed, thoughts jumbled as she brushed her teeth. She had a good place here, safe and perfect for making new pieces of art. She wasn't going anywhere. She just had to wait a little while; he'd get tired of being here and be off on some other oil field consultation and she'd be left alone. She just had to hold out until then. No more night walks. No more kisses.

Though as she fell asleep, she brushed her lips with her fingertips, remembering their first kiss.

The next morning Ella went to her studio, ready to work. She had to focus on her plans for the future and forget a kiss that threatened to turn her world upside down.

Easier said than done. Her dreams last night had been positively erotic. Her first thought this morning was that kiss. And now she was growing warm merely thinking about Khalid and his talented mouth. Why had he showed up? Why not go consult at some oil field and leave her in peace.

Try as she might, as the morning wore on, she couldn't get last night off her mind. Finally putting a small dish into the annealer to cool down, she decided to go see Khalid and make sure he knew she was not interested in getting involved.

She cleaned up, had a light lunch and then went to broach him at his home.

When she rang the bell, Jalilah opened the door, looking flustered. "Come in, things are hectic. His Excellency is leaving in a few minutes."

"Leaving?" This was perfect. He was leaving even earlier than she planned. He'd probably been as horrified by their kiss as she had been. He'd leave and if he ever came back, they'd have gotten over whatever awareness shimmered between them and they could resume the tenant-landlord relationship.

"A fire. He and his team are gathering at the airport in an hour."

Fear shot through Ella. He was going to another fire. For a moment she remembered Alexander, bloodied and burned from the car crash. He'd been coming after her. He hadn't deserved to die so young. She didn't like that memory any more than the one that flashed into her mind of Khalid burned beyond recognition. Nothing as unforgiving as flames.

She walked swiftly to the study, where Khalid was speaking on the phone. Entering, she crossed to the desk.

"See you then," he said, his eyes on her. "Got to go now."

"You can't go put out a fire," she said.

He rose and came around the desk. Lightly brushing the back of his fingers against her cheek, he asked, "Why not. It's what I do."

"It's too dangerous. Don't you have others who can handle that?"

"Others work with me on these projects. It's another one at a well Bashiri Oil has down on the southern coast. It blew a few months ago and it's burning again. Something's wrong with the pump or operators. Once this is capped, I plan to find out why it keeps igniting."

"It's dangerous."

"A bit. Are you all right? You have circles beneath your eyes."

She brushed his hand away. "I'm fine. It's you I'm worried about. What if something goes wrong? You don't have to do this. Send someone else."

"Something has gone wrong—a well is on fire. My team and I will put it out and do our best to make sure it doesn't happen again. I have to do this. It's what I do."

"It's too dangerous."

"I like the danger. Besides, what does it matter who does it as long as it gets put out? If not me, another man would be in danger. Maybe one who has a wife and children waiting at home."

She couldn't reach him. He would go off and probably get injured again. Or worse.

"Don't go," she said, reaching out to clutch his arms. She could feel his strength beneath the material, feel the determination.

"I have to—it's what I do."

"Find another job, something safer."

"Not today," he said, and leaned over to brush his lips against hers. "Come on, you can walk me out."

She stepped back, fear rising even more. What if something happened to him? She'd planned to tell him to stay away, but not like this.

When they reached the foyer, she noticed the duffel bags and heavy boots. He lifted them easily and nodded to Jalilah to open the door. A moment later they were stowed into the back of the small sports car. Ella followed him like a puppy, wishing she had the words to stop him. The seconds flew by. She could not slow time, much less stop it. But if she could, she would. Until she could talk him out of this plan. What if something happened to him?

"See you in a few days," he said easily.

"I hope so," she replied. But what if she didn't? What if she never saw him again? The feelings that thought triggered staggered her. She didn't want to care. That way lay heartache when tragedy struck.

She rounded the car and stood by him as he opened the driver's door. "Come back safely," she said, reaching up to kiss him. All thoughts of putting distance between them vanished. She couldn't let him go off without showing just a hint of what she felt. She would not think of all that could go wrong, but concentrate on all that could go right.

He let go the car door and kissed her back, cupping her face gently in his hands. His lips were warm but in only a moment she felt cold when he pulled away.

"I'll be back when the job's done," he said, climbing into the car. "Stay out of trouble," he said, and pulled away.

She watched for a moment, then with an ominous sense of foreboding, returned to her cottage. She felt as if she was in a daze. Fear warred with common sense. He knew what he was doing. Granted it was dangerous. But he'd done it before. And he did not have a death wish. He would take all necessary precautions.

Changing into work clothes, she went to the studio. She could always lose herself in art.

But not, it appeared, today. She tried to blow a traditional bowl, but the glass wasn't cooperating. Or her technique was off. Or it was just a bad day. Or she couldn't concentrate for thinking of Khalid. Glancing at her watch, she wondered where he was. She should have asked questions, found out where the fire was. How long he thought he'd be gone.

After two hours of trying to get one small project done, she gave up. Her thoughts were too consumed with Khalid. If he'd left the airport an hour ago, he could already be in harm's way. She paced her small studio, wondering how she could find out information about the fire. She did not have a television. She tried a radio, but the only programs she found were music.

Finally she went to the main house. When the maid answered the door, Ella asked to use the phone. She had done so a couple of times when Madame al Harum had lived here, so Jalilah was used to the request. Ella hoped Khalid had not given instructions to the contrary.

Jalilah showed her into the study and left. Ella stayed in the doorway for a moment. Everything inside instantly reminded her of Khalid. How odd. She'd visited Madame al Harum in this room many more times than she had her grandson. But he'd stamped his impression on the room in her mind forever.

She went to the phone. Who could she call but his brother. She hunted around for the phone number of Bashiri Oil and when she found it on a letterhead, she tried the number. It took her almost ten minutes to get to Rashid's assistant.

"I'm calling for Sheikh Rashid al Harum," she said for about the twentieth time.

"Who is calling?"

"Ella Ponti. I'm his brother's tenant in the house his grandmother once owned," she repeated.

"One moment, please."

On hold again, Ella held on to her composure. What would she do if Rashid wasn't there? Or wouldn't take her call? She had no idea how to reach Bethanne, who might be an ally.

"Al Harum." Rashid's voice came across the line sounding like Khalid's. She closed her eyes for a second, wishing it were Khalid.

"It's Ella Ponti. Khalid left this morning to put out a fire. Do you know anything about that?"

"I do. It's on one of the wells in the southern part of the country. Why?"

"I, uh…" She didn't know how to answer that. "I wanted to make sure he's all right," she said, wondering if Rashid would think her daft to be asking after his brother with such a short acquaintance.

"So far. The team arrived a short time ago. They assess the situation then plan their attack. It could be a day or two before they actually cap it."

Two days he could be in danger and she wouldn't know? This was so not the answer she wanted.

"Um, could you have someone keep me updated?" she asked tentatively. She didn't know if Sheikh al Harum would be bothered, but she had to ask. Surely there was some clerk there who could call her once something happened.

"I worry about him, too," Rashid said gently. "I'll let you know the minute I hear anything."

"Thank you. I'm using his phone. I don't have one. Jalilah can get me." She hung up, a bit reassured. She didn't want to question her need to make sure he was safe. She'd feel the same about anyone she knew who had such a dangerous job.

Ella sat in the desk chair for several moments. She studied the room, wondering what Khalid thought about when he sat here. She suspected he missed his grandmother more than he might have expected. The older woman had spoken so lovingly about her grandsons. Their family sounded close.

Except perhaps their mother. Or was her hesitancy welcoming women into the fold mere self-protection. It would be too bad to have someone pretend affection if they were only after money. How would she become convinced? Nothing had convinced her parents Alexander had not been after their money. They hadn't seemed to care that their only daughter was very happy in her marriage. The constant attempts to end the union had only alienated them. Ella hoped Madame al Harum never resorted to such tactics, but accepted Rashid's choice and wished him happiness.

She stood up and went back to her place. She didn't want to think about her parents, or Alexander, or anything in the past. She didn't want to worry about a man she hardly knew. And she didn't want to worry about the future. For today she'd try to just make it through without turmoil and complications, fear and dread.

Shortly after lunch there was a knock at the door. When Ella opened it, she was surprised to see Bethanne.

"Hi, I thought you might wish for some company," she said.

"Come in. I'm glad for company. I couldn't work today."

"I wouldn't be able to, either, if Rashid was doing something foolishly dangerous."

When they were on the terrace with ice-cold beverages, Ella smiled at her new friend. "What you said earlier, about Rashid being in a dangerous position—ever happen?"

"Not that I know about. And I would be sick with worry if he went off to put out an oil well fire."

"You and he are close, as it should be since you will be marrying him. Khalid is my landlord."

Bethanne laughed. "Right. And Madame al Harum and I are best friends."

Ella wrinkled her nose slightly. "I don't think she thinks in terms of friends."

"Well, not with the women who might marry her sons."

"I heard she helped arrange a marriage, but it didn't take place."

"Good thing for me. Rashid was going along with it for business reasons. Honestly, who wants to get married for business reasons? I'm glad he caught on."

"And the other woman?"

"She ran off with a lover and I have no idea what happened after that. But she obviously had more sense than my future husband. Much as I adore him, I do wonder what he was thinking considering an arranged marriage. I can't imagine all that passion— Oops, never mind."

Ella looked away, hiding a smile. She remembered passion with Alexander when their marriage was new. The image of Khalid kissing her sprang to mind. Her heart raced. She experienced even more passion that night. She did not want to think about it, but couldn't erase the image, nor the yearning for another kiss. Would that pass before he returned?

She had not helped her stance by kissing him goodbye. She should have wished him well and kept her distance.

"If they don't get the well capped today, they'll try tomorrow," Bethanne said, sipping her drink. "And if that doesn't work, Rashid wants to go there. If we do, want to fly with us? I took the crew down. They spent the entire flight going over schematics of the oil rig. It's in the water, you know. You'd think with the entire Persian Gulf at their feet it would be easy enough to put out a fire."

Ella laughed, but inside she stayed worried.

Bethanne was wonderful company and the two them spent the afternoon with laughter. Ella was glad she'd come to visit.

Except for a very few friends from the university, she didn't have many people she saw often. She had wanted it that way when Alexander first died. Now she could see the advantage of going out more with her friends. It took her mind off other things. Like if Khalid was safe or not.

The next morning she took an early walk along the beach. She never tired of the changing sea, some days incredibly blue other days steely-gray. She loved the solitude and beauty. During the day other people used the beach and she waved to a family she knew by sight. Watching the children as they played in the water gave her a pang. She and Alexander never had children. They thought they had years to start a family. They had wanted to spend time together as a couple before embarking on the next stage of family life.

His death cut everything short. She wished she'd had a baby with him. Would a child have brought her more comfort? Or more pain as every day she saw her husband in its face? She'd never know.

When she returned to the cottage, she saw a black car parked in front of the main house. Staying partially hidden behind the shrubs, she watched for a moment. It was not Khalid's sleek sports car. Was Madame al Harum visiting? Surely she knew her son was gone. Unless—had something happened. She could scarcely breathe. If Khalid had been injured, would Rashid send someone to tell her?

A moment later a man came from the house and got into the car, swiftly driving away.

Ella caught her breath at the recognition. She pulled back and waited until the car was gone before moving. In only seconds she was home, the door firmly locked behind her. How had they found her? She paced the living room. Obviously the maid had not given out where she lived or he would have camped on her doorstep. But it was only a matter of time now before he returned. Maybe he wanted to speak to the sheikh. Good grief, Khalid didn't know not to give out the information. His grandmother had been a staunch ally, but Khalid was looking for a way to get her to leave early. Had he any clue? Could she convince him not to divulge her whereabouts if her brother came calling again?

He had no reason to keep her home a secret. In fact, she could see it as his benefit to give out the information and stand aside while he tried to get her to return home.

Pacing did little but burn up energy, which seemed to pour through her as she fretted about this turn of events. She had grown comfortable here. She liked living here, liked her life as she'd made it since Alexander's death. She was not going home, no matter what. But she did not want the pressure Antonio would assert. Should she leave before Khalid returned? If he didn't know where she was, he couldn't give the location away.

But she didn't want to leave. Not until she knew if he was all right. What if the fire damaged more than equipment? Men could die trying to put out an oil fire. She so did not need any of this. She'd worked hard the last year to get her life under control.

Drawing a deep breath, she went to her desk and pulled out a sheet of paper. She'd make a list of her choices, calmly, rationally. She'd see what she could do to escape this situation—

Escape. That's what she wanted. Could Bethanne help? She could fly her to a secret location and never tell anyone.

Only, would she? And how much would it cost to hire the plane? Maybe she should have sold some of her work to give herself more capital. She had enough for her needs if she was careful. But a huge chunk spent on a plane trip could wreak the financial stability she had. Did she have the luxury of time? She could find a bus to take her somewhere in the interior. But not her equipment. Not her studio.

She couldn't leave that behind. It was her only way to make the glass art that she hoped was her future.

Jumping up, she began to walk around, gazing out the window, touching a piece of glass here and there that she'd made. What was she going to do?

There was a knock on the door. Ella froze. Had he found her already? Slowly she crossed the room and peeked out of the small glass in the door. It was Jalilah.

Ella opened the door.

"Hello," the maid said. "I came to tell you someone was at the house earlier, asking after you. He said the sheikh had sent inquiries to Italy. I remember Madame's comments when you first came here to live. She wanted you to have all the privacy you wanted. I told the man the sheikh was away from home and did not know when he would return."

"Thank you!" Ella breathed a sigh of relief. She had a respite. No fear of discovery today.

But—Khalid had sent inquiries to Italy? Why?

Jalilah bowed slightly and left.

Had Khalid sought to find other ways to get her to leave? Anger rose. How dare he put out inquiries? Who did he think he was? And more importantly, who did he think she was? He couldn't take her word?

After a hasty lunch Ella could barely eat, she went to the studio, trying to assess how much it would take to move her ovens, bench and all the accoutrements she had for glassblowing. More than a quick plane ride west.

Maybe she could leave for a short while, let her brother grow tired of looking for her again and when he left, she'd return. Only, what if Khalid then told him when she returned. She'd never be safe.

She heard a car and went to the window, peering out at the glimpse of the driveway she had. It was Khalid's car. He was home.

Without thinking, she stormed over to the main house. The door was shut, so she knocked, her anger at his actions growing with every breath.

Jalilah opened the door, but before she could say a word of greeting, Ella stepped inside.

"Where is he?" she demanded.

"In the study," the maid said, looking startled.

Ella almost ran to the study door. Khalid was standing behind the desk, leafing through messages. He hadn't shaved in a couple of days, the dark beard made him look almost like a pirate—especially when viewed with the slash of scar tissue. His clothes were dirty and she could smell the smoke from where she stood. None of it mattered.

"What have you done to my life?" she asked.

CHAPTER SIX

HE LOOKED up. "Hello, Ella."

"I mean it. What gives you the right to meddle in things that don't concern you? You have ruined everything!"

"What are you talking about?" he asked.

"You sent inquiries to Italy, right?"

He lifted a note. "Garibaldi?"

"If you wanted to know something, why not ask me? I told you all you needed to know. I told you more than I've told anyone else."

"Who is Antonio Garibaldi?" he asked, studying the note a moment, then looking at her. His eyes narrowed as he took in her anger.

"He's my brother. And the reason my husband is dead. I do not wish to have anything to do with him. How could you have contacted them? How could you have led them right to me? I've tried so hard to stay below the radar and with one careless inquiry you lead them right to me. I can't believe this!"

"Wait a second. I don't know what you're talking about. Your family didn't know you were living here?"

"If I had wanted them to know, I would have told them."

"How did your brother cause your husband's death? Didn't you say it was a car crash? Was your brother in the other car?"

"No. He practically kidnapped me. He lured me to the

airport with the intent of getting me on the private jet he'd hired. Only someone told Alexander. He was coming to get me before Antonio could take me out of the country. He crashed on the way to the airport. The police, thankfully, stepped in and stopped our departure." She looked away, remembering. "So I could identify Alexander's body."

She burst into tears.

Khalid looked at her dumbfounded. In only a second he was around the desk and holding her as she sobbed against his chest.

"He had a class. He should have been safely inside, teaching, instead he was trying to come to my rescue," she said between sobs. She clutched a fistful of his shirt, her face pressed against the material, her tears soaking the cotton. She scarcely noticed the smoke. "He would still be alive today if Antonio hadn't forced me. *Alexander.*" She cried harder.

Khalid held her close, her pain went straight to his heart. He'd felt the anguish of losing a woman he thought he would build his life with. But his anger soon overcame any heartache. This woman was still devastated by the loss of her husband. What would it be like to mean so much to someone? He thought about his brother and the woman he was going to marry. Bethanne loved him; there was no doubt to anyone who saw them together. She'd be as devastated if something happened to Rashid.

Khalid knew that kind of attachment, that kind of love, was rare and special. Her husband had been dead for more than a year. Ella should have moved on. But the strength of her sobs told him she still mourned with an intensity that was amazing. The emotions told of a strong bond, a love that was deeply felt.

He had never known that kind of love. And never would.

Finally she began to subside. He didn't know what to do but hold her. He'd caused this outburst by his demand to know more. Had the man at Bashiri Oil been clumsy in his research?

Or was the family on alert for information about their daughter? Was her brother's involvement the cause of the estrangement, or did it go deeper? Khalid wanted answers to all the questions swirling around in his mind.

But now, his first priority was to make things right with Ella.

Slowly he felt her hands ease on the clutching of his shirt. A moment later she pushed against his chest. He let her go, catching her face in his palms and brushing away the lingering tears with his thumbs. Her skin was warm and flushed. He registered the softness and the vulnerability she had with her sorrowful eyes, red and puffy.

"I did not know making an inquiry would cause all this," he said. "You are safe here. I will not let anyone kidnap you. Tell me what happened."

She pushed away and stepped back. "I'm not telling you anything. You tell my brother when he contacts you again that you have no idea where I'm living. Make him go away. Make sure he never finds me."

"You think he'll come again?" Khalid asked.

"Of course. He's tenacious."

"Why should he come for you?"

"My family wants me home. I want to stay here. If you can't guarantee I can stay, I'll have to disappear and won't tell you where I go."

Two weeks ago Khalid would have jumped at the offer. He wanted his tenant gone so he could put the estate up for sale. But two weeks changed a lot. He wasn't as anxious to sell as he had once been. He liked living near the sea. He liked the after dark walks along the shore. He did not want his tenant to leave and not give a forwarding address.

More importantly, he wanted to know the full story of what was going on. How could she be so afraid of her family?

"How old are you?" he asked, stepping back to give her more space.

"Twenty-nine. You know that. What does that have to do with anything?"

"As far as I understand the laws in most countries, that makes you an adult, capable of making your own decisions on where to live."

"You'd think so," she said bitterly, brushing the last of the tears from her face. She walked to the window and peered out but Khalid didn't think she saw the colorful blossoms.

She rubbed her chest, as if pressing against pain. "Alexander and I were childhood sweethearts. My parents thought we'd outgrow that foolishness. Their words. They had a marriage in mind for me that would probably rival what your mother had for Rashid. Combining two old Italian families, and merging two fortunes that would only grow even larger over the years."

Khalid frowned. He made a mental note to get in touch with the man at the company who had been doing the research for him. What had he discovered?

"So you and Alexander married against parental wishes. It happens."

"When they discovered where we were living, Antonio came and said I had to return home. There would be an annulment and the arranged marriage would go forth. I laughed at him, but he was stronger than I was and soon I was in a car heading for the airport. The rest you know. I managed to dodge him at the police station and then hid until I thought he'd left Quishari. Mutual friends contacted your grandmother who offered me a place to live. I'm forever grateful to her. I miss her a lot. She really liked my work, and I think she liked me. But more importantly—she gave me a safe haven. I'll never forget that."

"I'm sure she did," Khalid said, stunned to learn this. Had his actions threatened the haven Ella clung to? He would have to take steps to remedy the situation.

Ella turned and looked at him.

"If my actions caused this, I will fix it," he said.

"If? Of course they did. No one has ever come here before. Why did you have to ask about me. I told you about me."

"I wanted to know more. My grandmother never mentioned you. My family doesn't know about you. What you told me was limited."

"You're my landlord—you know all you need to know about me. I pay my rent on time and I have a lease. I don't trash the place. End of story."

"I want more."

"Well, we don't always get what we want in life," she snapped.

Khalid stared at her, seeing an unhappy, sad woman. One to whom he'd brought more pain and suffering. It didn't come easy, but he had to apologize. "I'm sorry."

She shrugged. "Sorry doesn't change anything."

"It lets you know I didn't deliberately cause you this grief. I said I'd fix it and I shall."

"How? Erase my brother's memory? Put up guards so no one can get on the estate? Wouldn't that also mean no one goes off, either? I had things going just fine until you showed up."

"Sit down and we'll get to the bottom of this." He went around the desk and called Bashiri Oil. In less than a minute he was speaking to the researcher in the office who had been asked to find out more about Ella Ponti. He listened for a solid five minutes, his expression impassive as the man recited what he'd discovered, ending with...

"One of her brothers was in the office yesterday, trying his best to get more information. We know better than to give that kind of information. He accosted people in the halls and in the parking area. Finally we had security remove him from the premises. But I'd watch out—he's looking for his sister and seems most determined."

"I, also, can be determined," Khalid said softly.

"True, Excellency. And I'd put my money on you."

Khalid ended the call.

"It appears the inquiries I had made did cause your brothe to return to Quishari. He is staying at the Imperial Hotel. H has made a pest of himself at the company headquarters, ques tioning everyone trying to locate you. Why is it so importan that you marry the man your parents picked out? Surely tha was years ago. You said you'd been married for four years and Alexander has been dead for one. What is so compelling?"

"To further the dynasty, of course. And ensure the mone doesn't go outside the family or the family business—wine. have a trust, that I can't access for another couple of years. Bu my father was convinced Alexander wanted only my money He was wrong. Alexander loved me. We lived modestly on hi income from the university. We were so happy."

Tears filled her eyes again, and Khalid quickly sought a wa to divert them. He was not at all capable of dealing with woman's tears. He wished he'd never thought to find out mor about the woman his grandmother had rented the cottage to.

"I'll go see your brother and make sure he leaves you alone." She blinked away the tears, hope shining from her eyes. "You will?"

Khalid nodded, loath to involve himself in her family dy namics, but he felt responsible for causing the problem. "I' shower, change and go to the hotel myself."

Ella thought about it for a moment, then nodded once "Fine, then. You take care of it." She turned and went to th door, pausing a moment and looking back at him. "I'm glad you got home safely. The fire out?"

"Yes."

"Did you find out what caused it?"

"I believe so. We have taken steps to make sure there won' be another one at that rig."

"Good." She left.

Khalid rubbed the back of his neck. He had better get changed and to the hotel before her brother annoyed even more people. Or came back and found Ella.

Ella kept her house locked up all day. She knew her brother. He would not likely be sidetracked from his goal just on Khalid's say-so. Not that she would buck the power of the sheikh. He could probably buy and sell her brother without batting an eye. And it was his country. His family was most prominent. Antonio would find no allies in Quishari. Served him right. She couldn't forget the last time she'd seen him. If he had never come last year, Alexander would be alive today.

As the afternoon waned, Ella wondered if Khalid had truly gone to see her brother. She had not seen him return. What if he'd changed his mind? Upon further consideration, he had to know this would be the perfect way to rid himself of the tenant he didn't want. The more Ella thought about it, the more certain she was that was what happened. It could not take Khalid hours to go tell Antonio to go home.

Restless, she set off for her walk when it was barely dark. She doubted she'd sleep tonight. In fact, she might best be served by packing essentials and contacting Bethanne to ask for a ride someplace. At this point, Ella would take anyplace away from Alkaahdar.

She walked farther than normal, still keyed up. When she came to a more populated area, she sat near the water. There were others still on the beach. A small party had a fire near the water, and were sitting around it, laughing and talking. She watched from the distance. How long had it been since she felt so carefree and happy?

When that party began breaking up, Ella realized how late it was—and she still had a very long walk home. She rose and walked along the water, the moon a bright disk in the sky. She was resigned to having to leave. There didn't seem to be any choice unless she wanted her family to take over her life. And that she vowed would never happen. She was not some pawn for her father's use. She liked being on her own. Loved living in Quishari. She'd have to find a way.

She slowed when she drew closer to the estate. Would Khalid be on the beach? She wasn't up to dealing with him tonight. She'd made a fool of herself crying in his study. She didn't want to deal with any more emotion. She was content with her decisions and her walk. A good night's sleep was all she wanted now. Tomorrow she'd begin packing and slip away before Antonio found her. She'd contact her friend Marissa to come after she was gone to pack up her glass art. Once she was settled somewhere, she'd see about resuming the glassblowing.

Khalid saw Ella slip through the garden on her way to the cottage. He had tried her place earlier, but she was already gone. Now she was back. It was late, however. He needed to tell her how the meeting with her brother had gone, but maybe it would be best handled in the morning.

He sat in the dark on the veranda, watching her go to her home. A moment later the lights came on in one room, then another. Before a half hour passed, the cottage was dark again. He hoped she had a good night's sleep, to better face tomorrow. He knew she would not be pleased with what he had to tell her.

The next day it rained. The dreary day seemed perfect to Ella as she packed her clothes in one large suitcase. She put her cosmetics in a smaller suitcase and stripped the bed, dumping the sheets into the washer behind the kitchen. She'd leave the place as immaculate as it had been when she moved in. The only part she couldn't do much with would be her studio. She hoped Khalid would permit her friend to come to clea∢

away her things. If not, so be it. It wouldn't be the first time she'd started over. She was better equipped now than she had been a year ago.

The knock on the door put her on instant alert. She would not open to Antonio no matter what. Slowly she approached the door, looking through the glass, relieved to see it was Khalid.

Opening the door a crack, she stood, blocking the view into the living room. "Yes?" she said.

"I need to talk with you," he said. Today he wore a white shirt opened at the throat. His dark pants were obviously part of a suit. Was he going somewhere for business later?

"About?"

"Your brother, what do you think?"

"You saw him?"

"I did. Are you going to let me in or are we going to talk like this?"

She hesitated. "Is it going to take long? Either you got rid of him or you didn't."

He pushed against the door and she gave in, stepping back to allow him to enter.

She shut the door behind him and crossed to the small sofa, sitting on the edge. He took a chair near the sofa.

Wiping suddenly damp palms against her skirt, she waited with what patience she could muster.

"I saw your brother at the hotel. He is very anxious to talk with you. Seems there's a problem with your family that you only can help with."

"Sure, marry the man they picked out."

Khalid nodded. "Apparently there have been some financial setbacks and your family needs an influx of cash that the wedding settlement would bring."

She frowned. "What setbacks? The wine business is doing well. We've owned the land for generations, so there's no danger from that aspect. I don't understand."

Khalid shrugged. "Apparently your younger brother has a gambling habit. He's squandered money gambling, incurring steep debts which your father paid for. That didn't stop him. Unless they get another influx of cash, and soon, they will have to sell some of the land. It's mortgaged. They've been stringing creditors along, but it's all coming due soon and they are desperate."

"Giacomo has a gambling problem?" It was the first she'd heard about it. She frowned. For a moment she pictured her charming brother when she had last seen him. He had still been at university, wild and carefree and charming every girl in sight. They'd had fun as children. What had gone wrong?

"While I'm sorry to hear that, I don't see myself as sacrificial lamb to his problem. Let my father get him to marry some wealthy woman and get the cash that way." She could see her patriarchal father assuming she would be the sacrifice to restore the family fortunes.

"Both your brothers are already married."

Ella was startled at the news. She realized cutting herself off from the family when she married Alexander had meant she wasn't kept up-to-date on their activities. When had her brothers married? Recently? Obviously during the years she and Alexander had lived in Quishari.

"Apparently Antonio feels it is your duty to the family to help in this dire circumstance," Khalid said dryly.

"He's echoing my father. I have no desire to help them out. And I certainly am not going to be forced into marrying some man for his money to bail Giacomo out of a tight place." Antonio had always looked out for her and Giacomo. Looks as if he was still looking out for their younger brother. What about her?

Khalid nodded. "I knew you would feel that way."

"Does he know I live here?" she asked.

Khalid shook his head. "He could end up coming here to see me again and discover you around. But I did not tell him where you lived."

"I'm leaving."

He looked surprised at that.

"Going where?"

"I don't know yet. But I'm not telling anyone. That way they can't find me again."

"Would it be so bad to be in touch with your family? I can't imagine being cut off from Rashid."

"That's different. Your mother isn't trying to marry you off to the woman she wants. Just listen to what Antonio said—I'm to come home and marry some man for his fortune. You don't want to be married for money, why would you support that?"

"You know I wouldn't. Would it hurt to listen to what he has to say?"

"I'm not going back to Italy."

He shook his head. "I'm not suggesting that. Parents can't arrange marriages for their offsprings."

"Your mother tried with Rashid."

"And it came to nought. I don't see her doing anything now but eventually accepting Bethanne will be his wife."

"She tried it, that's the point. She may try with you."

"I doubt it. She doesn't like the scars any more than another woman would."

"Honestly, I can't believe you harp on that. So you have a scar. Try plastic surgery if you don't like it. In truth, it makes you look more interesting than some rich playboy sheikh who rides by on his looks."

"Playboy sheikh?" he said.

Ella leaned forward. "This is about my problem, not yours."

"Of course." The amusement in his eyes told her he was not taking this as seriously as she was. Why should he? He had power, prestige, money. She had nothing—not even a family to support her.

"So did Antonio leave?" she asked.

"Not yet. He wants to see you. Hear from you that everything is fine."

"And try to kidnap me again to take me home."

"No. I, uh, made it clear he could not do that."

"How?"

Khalid looked uncomfortable. "Actually by the time the meeting was drawing to an end, I was a bit exasperated with your brother."

Ella laughed shortly. "I can imagine. He's like a bulldog when he's after something. So what did you tell him?"

"That you and I were engaged."

Ella stared at him for a long moment, certain she had misheard him. "Excuse me?" she said finally, not believing what echoed in her mind.

"It seemed like a good idea at the time."

"You told my brother we were engaged? You don't even like me. We are not engaged. Not even friends, from what I can tell. Why in the world would you say such a thing?"

"To get him to back down."

"I don't believe this. You're a sheikh in this kingdom. You could order people to escort him to the country borders and kick him out. You could get his visa denied, declare him persona non grata. You could have—"

"Well, I didn't do any of that."

She blinked. "So Antonio thinks we're engaged."

Khalid nodded.

"And that's it? He's going home now?"

"After he's met you and is satisfied you are happy with this arrangement."

For a moment Ella felt a wave of affection for her brother. She didn't always agree with him, but for him to make sure she was happy sounded like the brother she remembered with love. However—

"No."

"No what?"

"I'm not taking that chance. I don't want to see Antonio. I don't want him to know where I live." She looked at him with incredulity. "You don't think they expect you to give the family money if I were really going to marry you, do you? He's probably just as happy with you as candidate as whomever they had picked out in Italy."

"I mentioned that I have a few thousand qateries put away for the future."

"Utterly stupid," she said, jumping to her feet. "I cannot believe you said that. You go back and tell him you were joking or something."

Khalid rose, as well, and came over to her. "Ella, think for a moment. This gets you off the hook. We'll meet him for dinner or something. Show we are devoted to each other. And that you have no intention of returning to Italy. Then he'll be satisfied and take off in the morning. You'll be safely ensconced here and that's an end to it. Once your family finds another way to deal with the debt, you can write and say the engagement ended."

She considered the plan. It sounded dishonest. But it also sounded like it might work. If she could convince Antonio she was committed to Khalid. Glancing out the window, she wondered if she could look as if she loved the man to distraction when her heart was buried with Alexander.

Yet, he knew her. He could believe she'd fallen in love. He'd often teased her for being a romantic. And her family would welcome Khalid like they never had Alexander. This time they had no reason to suspect he was interested in her money. Next to him, she was almost a pauper.

"Do you think it'll work?" she asked, grasping the idea with faint hope.

"What could go wrong?" he asked. "You'll convince your brother you're deliriously happy. He'll go home and you'll go back to making glass art."

"What do you get out of this?" she asked cynically.

"No more tears?" he said.

She flushed. "Sorry about that."

"No, I didn't mean to make light of it. Just make sure you don't have another meltdown. I'll be gone again soon so you'll have the place to yourself again, like before."

"So you're not planning to sell?"

"Maybe not for a while. I find I'm enjoying living by the water."

"Okay. We'll try your plan. But if he doesn't leave, or tries anything, I'm taking off."

Khalid arranged dinner at a restaurant near the hotel. He picked Ella up at seven and in less than twenty minutes they arrived at the restaurant. She saw her brother waiting for them once they entered.

"Ella," he said in Italian, coming to kiss both cheeks.

"Antonio," she replied. It had been almost a year since she'd seen him. He looked the same. She smiled and hugged him tightly. No matter what—he was still her older brother.

He shook hands with Khalid. Soon all three were seated in a table near the window that looked over a garden.

"We've been worried about you," Antonio said.

"I'm fine."

"More than fine. Engaged to be married again." He gave her a hard look.

She looked at him. "And?"

"It will come as a surprise to our parents."

"As learning about Giacomo's gambling problem surprised me."

Antonio flicked a glance at Khalid and shrugged. "A way

will be found to get the money. Family needs to support each other, don't you think?"

When the waiter came for the order, conversation was suspended for a moment. "Khalid doesn't speak Italian. He speaks English or French, so you choose," Ella said in English.

"English is not so good for me. But for, um, good feelings between us, I speak it," Antonio said.

"Ella tells me your family has been in the winemaking business for generations," Khalid said. "You are a part of that operation?"

Antonio nodded. "I sell wine. Giacomo helps father with the vineyard and the make. My father wants Ella to come home. She goes a long time."

"Maybe in a while. She cannot come now," Khalid said flatly.

Antonio looked surprised that anyone would tell him no. Ella hid a smile and took a moment to glance around the restaurant. The tables were given plenty of space to insure a quiet atmosphere and offer a degree of privacy for the customers. Her eye caught a glimpse of the minister of finance just as he spotted her.

"Uh-oh," she said softly in Arabic. "The minister is here."

Antonio frowned. "If we speak English, all speak," he said.

"Sorry, I forgot," she replied, looking at Khalid for guidance.

A moment later the minister was at their table.

"Ah, the lovely Madame Ponti," he said with a smile, reaching out to capture her hand and kiss the back. "Rashid, I didn't expect to see you with Madame Ponti," he said with a quick glance at Khalid.

Khalid stood, towering over the older man, exposing the scar when he faced him. "Minister," he said.

"Ah, my mistake. Khalid. No need to get up. I'm on my way out and saw you dining." He smiled affably at Antonio. "Another guest?"

"Ella's brother." Good manners dictated an introduction

which Khalid made swiftly. Explaining Antonio was Italian and didn't speak Arabic.

"English?" he asked.

Antonio nodded.

"Welcome to Quishari," the minister said with a heavy accent.

"Happy to be here. We are celebrating good news—Ella's engagement."

CHAPTER SEVEN

ELLA was struck dumb. She wished she could stuff a sock in her brother's mouth. Her horrified gaze must have shown, as Khalid reached out and touched her shoulder.

"Congratulate us, Minister. You are the first outside the family to know," he said easily.

His grip tightened and she tried to smile. What a disaster this was turning out to be. Khalid must be furious. That's what they got for trying to put something over on Antonio.

"My felicitations. I have to say I am not surprised after seeing you at your mother's event the other evening."

Khalid nodded, releasing his hold on Ella's shoulder as if convinced she would not jump up and flee—which she strongly felt like.

"Don't let me keep you from dinner," the minister said as the waiter approached with their meals on a tray.

When he left, Ella gave a sigh of relief. Maybe Khalid could catch him later and explain. She needed to concentrate on getting her brother on the next plane to Italy.

"Mother and father will want to meet your fiancé," Antonio said as they began to eat. "You two should visit soon. I can wait here a few days and return with you."

"Unfortunately I am unable to get away for a while and Ella must work on her art," Khalid said.

"Art?" Her brother looked puzzled.

"You have not seen the beautiful glass pieces she makes?" Khalid asked in surprise.

"Oh, those." Antonio gave a shrug. "I've seen bowls and such. Nice enough."

Ella knew better than to take offense at her brother's casual dismissal of her work. He had thought it an odd hobby when she'd been younger. But she'd come a long way since those early attempts. Not that she needed to show him. If Khalid was successful in getting him to leave, she'd be grateful. If not, then maybe Plan B would work better—get Bethanne to fly her somewhere far away and tell no one.

The meal seemed interminable. Ella wanted to scream at her brother to leave her alone. She couldn't forget his part in Alexander's death. If he had not tried to take her home last year, Alexander would still be alive.

Everything was different. When they finished eating, Khalid escorted them to the curb where the limo was waiting. Ushering them both inside, he gave instructions for Antonio's hotel and settled back.

"We will drop you at your hotel and in the morning I will arrange for the limousine to pick you up to take you to the airport. Ella will contact your parents when it is convenient to visit."

Never underestimate the power of money, status and arrogant male, she thought as she watched her brother struggle with something that would assert his own position. But one look from the dark eyes of the sheikh had Antonio subsiding quietly.

"As you wish. My father will be delighted to learn his daughter is engaged to one of the leading families in Quishari. I hope you both can visit soon."

The ride home from the hotel was in silence. Ella didn't know whether to be grateful to Khalid or annoyed at his outlandish handling of the situation. If the minister hadn't learned of the bogus engagement, they could have muddled through without any bother.

"What if the minister says something?" she asked.

"Who's he going to tell? We are not that important in his scheme of things. You worry about things too much," he said, studying the scenery as they were driven home.

"At least I didn't go off half-cocked and say we were engaged. Too bad he speaks English. The language barrier could have prevented it. I doubt he speaks Italian."

Khalid looked at her. "Your brother will return home, tell your parents you are safe and go on with his life. Once things settle down, you can tell them things didn't work out."

She laughed nervously. "I doubt things will settle down. They will push for marriage."

"Tell them I am not ready."

"Oh, Khalid, if they really need money for Giacomo, then my guess is the next step is get me safely married to you and hit me up for some money. If you were poor as Alexander was, they would never be satisfied with a marriage between us."

"You're an adult. Just tell them no."

"Antonio tried to force me from the country last time. Just say no doesn't work with my family."

"He won't try you in the future, not as long as you live in Quishari."

"Then I may never leave," she said, still worried about the entire scenario.

Khalid had the limousine stop by Ella's cottage and dismissed the man. He escorted her to her door.

"Thanks for dinner, and for standing up for me," she said, opening it.

"That's what fiancés are for," he said, brushing back her hair and kissing her lightly on the lips.

He turned and walked to the villa, wishing he had stayed for a longer good-night kiss. He had hidden it from Ella, but he was worried the minister could stir up trouble that would be hard to suppress.

When he entered the study a few moment later, the answering machine was flashing. He pressed the button.

"What's this I hear about your engagement? You couldn't tell me before the minister?" Rashid's voice came across loud and clear—with a hint of amusement. "Or did he get it wrong? Call me."

Khalid sighed and sank onto the chair. Dialing his brother, he wondered if he could finesse this somehow. It was hard sometimes to have a twin who knew him so well.

"Hello."

"Rashid, it's Khalid."

"Ah, the newly engaged man. I didn't have a clue."

"It's not what you think?"

"So what is it?"

Khalid explained and heard Rashid's laughter. "Sounds almost like Bethanne and me. We pretended she was my intended to close the deal I was working on when the woman I expected didn't show up. Watch it, brother—fake engagements have a way of turning real."

"Not this time. In fact, I wasn't going to tell anyone beyond Ella's brother. Once he was back Italy, she'd be left alone."

"Now you have the minister calling me and undoubtedly Mother to congratulate us on your engagement. And I know from experience, Mother isn't going to be happy."

"She should be glad anyone would even consider marrying me with this face."

"Not if it isn't someone she picked out—which I'm coming to believe means someone she can boss around. Bethanne isn't exactly docile. So what's the plan?"

"I haven't a clue. It would have gone smoothly if the minister hadn't come over. Her brother would have left and things would have returned to normal."

"Whatever that is these days." Rashid was quiet for a moment, then said, "Any chance…"

"What, that she'd want to marry me? Get real. First off, I'm not planning to marry. Your kids will carry on the line. And second, she's still hung up on her dead husband. And I see no signs of that abating. She was crying over him today."

"Fine, you've played the role of hero, rescuing her from her brother. Would that make her feel she owes you? Maybe vacate the cottage so you can sell the place sooner?"

"I wouldn't use that to get her gone."

Rashid was silent.

"Anyway, things will work out."

"Call me if you need me," Rashid said.

When he hung up, Khalid contemplated finding a job ten thousand miles away and staying as long as he could. Who would think inheriting a beautiful estate could end up making him so confused.

The phone rang again.

When he answered, he sighed hearing his mother's greeting.

"I just had an interesting call," she began.

"I know." For a split second he considered telling her the truth. But that fled when he thought of her calling to set the minister straight. He would not like having been lied to.

"Is it true? Honestly, if I had thought you were planning to marry, which you have stated many time you are not, I know several nice women who would have suited much better than a widow of dubious background."

"I know her background."

"I don't. Where is she from? Are you certain she wants to marry you to build a life together, or is she in it to keep the cottage? Once her career takes off, will she leave for greener fields?"

"Who knows what the future holds," he said.

"Your father used to say that all the time. Honestly, men.

I suppose I have to have another party to introduce her formally to everyone like I did with Bethanne."

"Hold off on that, Mother."

"Why?"

His mother was sharp; anything out of a normal progression would raise doubts. And he didn't want Ella talked about, or word to reach her family that the engagement wasn't going strong.

"You just had a party…we can wait a few weeks." Maybe by then something would occur to him that would get him out of the situation. He'd thought it the perfect answer to getting rid of Ella's brother. The first time in recent months he did anything spontaneous and it grew more complicated by the moment. Give him a raging oil fire any day.

"Nonsense. I'll call your aunt. She'll be thrilled to hear you are getting married and want to help. We had given up on you, you know."

Hold that thought, he wanted to say. But for the time being, he'd go along with her idea. He wondered if Ella would. Or if she'd put an end to it the minute her brother took off in the morning. She hadn't welcomed the idea when he first told her.

He went to change into casual clothes and headed for the beach. He didn't know if she'd join him on a walk tonight. He could gauge her reaction by her manner if she did show up.

When he reached the beach, there was no sign of her. He'd wait a bit. It wasn't that late.

Sitting on the still warm sand, he watched the moonlight dance on the water. The soft night breeze caressed. The silence was peaceful, tranquil. Why did men make things so complicated. A quiet night surrounded by nature—that's what he needed. That's what he liked about the desert. The solitude and stillness.

He heard her walking through the garden. Satisfaction filled him. She was coming again. Despite their differences, he felt closer to her in the dark than he did anyone except Rashid. Theirs was an odd friendship; one that probably wouldn't last through the years, but perfect for now.

"I wondered if you'd want to go walk," she said, walking over and sitting beside him. "You were right, you know. I overreacted, but this was a perfect scheme to get rid of Antonio. You know, of course, that had this been real, the minute we married, he'd be hitting you up for money."

"It crossed my mind," Khalid said. Antonio didn't know him well—nor ever would. But giving money away to people who wasted it was not something he did. Though he could understand family solidarity. Wonder if there were a different way to handle the situation.

He rose and reached out his hand to help her up. With one accord, they left their shoes and began walking to the water. Once on hard-packed sand, they turned north.

Khalid liked the end of the evening this way. Ella was comfortable to be around. With the darkness to cloak the scar, he had no hesitation in having her with him. She didn't have to see the horrible deformity and he didn't have to endure the looks of horror so often seen in people when they were around him. Not that he'd caught even a glimpse of that with Ella after that first day. She seemed to see right through the scar to the man beneath.

"At least we don't have to worry about that. I'm still working on a catalog and will see if I can get a showing earlier than originally planned. Once I have a way to earn a living, I'll be out of your way."

"There is one complication," he said.

"What?"

"My mother thinks we are engaged and is planning a party to announce it to the world."

"What? You've got to be kidding? How did your mother find out?" She stopped walking and stared at him.

"She called me tonight. The minister wasted no time. He
has it in for Rashid and I expect is trying to gain an ally with
mother in getting insider info or something."

Ella shook her head. "I can imagine how delighted she is
to think we're engaged. Did you set her straight?"

"No."

"Why not?"

He refused to examine the reason. He felt protective toward
Ella. He didn't want anything to mar her happiness—especially
her family. It seemed she'd had enough grief to last a lifetime.

"Seemed better not to."

"Well, tell her in the morning."

"Or, let her think that for a while. What does it hurt?"

Ella thought about it for a moment. "Maybe no one," she
said reluctantly.

"If people think you are engaged to me, it'll give you a bit
of a step up when going to galleries."

"I wouldn't pretend for that reason."

"But you would to keep your family out of your life."

"I didn't know my younger brother had a gambling problem. He was the cutest little boy. So charming."

He took her hand and tugged her along and resumed walking. "I know. Family pressure can be unrelenting, however. If
they think you are already out of reach, they have to look elsewhere for financial help. Personally I'd kick the man out and
tell him to make a go of it on his own."

"You talk a hard line, but I bet you would try to work
something out if it were Rashid," she said.

Khalid knew that to be true.

"I'm not sure it's fair to you," she continued.

"Why not? I'm the one who started the entire convoluted
mess."

"I know, which I think is totally off the wall. But no one who
knew us would believe we could fall in love and plan to marry."

"Because of the scar," he bit out.

She whacked him on his arm with her free hand. "Will you stop! That has nothing to do with anything. I'm still grieving for my husband. I don't want to ever go through something like that again. It's safer to go through life alone, making friends, having a great career, but not putting my heart on the line again. It hurts too much when it's shattered."

"Safer but lonely, isn't it?"

Ella glanced at him. Was he lonely? On the surface he had it all: good looks, money, family behind him. The downside would be the job he did. Yet because of the scarring on his face, he pulled away from social events, hadn't had a friend come to visit since he'd been in the main house. And to hear him talk, he was shunned by others.

She'd seen some looks at the reception, fascinated horror. Her regret was he had to deal with rude, obnoxious people who didn't seem to have the manners necessary to deal with real life.

"Come on," she said, pulling her hand free. "I'll race you to that piece of driftwood." With that, Ella took off at a run for the large log that had washed up on shore during the last storm. She knew she couldn't beat Khalid; he'd win by a long margin. But maybe it would get them out of gloomy thoughts. She felt she'd been on a roller coaster all day. It was time to regain her equilibrium and have some fun.

She'd taken him by surprise, she could tell as he hesitated a moment before starting to run. She had enough of a head start she thought for a few seconds she might win. Then Khalid raced past her, making it look easy and effortless.

Ella was gasping for breath when she reached the log. He was a bit winded, which helped her own self-respect.

"Do you often race at night?" he asked.

"No one can see me and I can race the wind. It's better than racing you, for I can convince myself I win."

He laughed and picked her up by her waist and twirled them

both around. "I win tonight," he said, and lowered her gently to the ground, drawing her closer until they were touching from chest to knees. He leaned over and kissed her sweetly.

Ella closed her eyes, blocking out the brilliant blanket of stars in the sky. Hearing only her own racing heartbeat and the soft sighing of the spent waves. Soon even they were lost to sound as the blood roared through her veins, heating every inch of her. She gave herself up to the wonderful feelings that coursed through her. His mouth was magic. His lips like nectar. His strong body made her feel safe and secure, and wildly desirable.

Time lost all meaning. For endless minutes, Ella was wrapped in sensation. She could have halted time and lived forever in this one moment. It was exquisite.

Then reality intruded. Slowly the kiss eased and soon Khalid had put several inches between them. She stepped forward not wanting to end the contact. His hands rested on her shoulders and gently pushed her away.

"We need to get back before things get out of hand," he said.

She cringed and turned, glad for the darkness to hide her embarrassment. How could she so wantonly throw herself at him when he made it perfectly clear he was not interested in her that way. His gesture with the fake engagement was merely a means to offer some protection to her. If her brother had never shown up, never threatened her, Khalid would never in a million years have pretended that they were involved.

And that was fine by her.

She increased her pace.

"Are we racing back?" he asked, easily keeping pace.

"No." She slowed, but longed to break into another run and beat him home, shut the door and pull the shades. She was an adult. She could handle this—it was only for the length of time to get to her cottage. Then she'd do her best from now on to stay away from Khalid al Harum!

* * *

That vow lasted until the next day. Ella spent the early hours working on a small bowl that would be the first of a set, each slightly larger than the previous. She concentrated and was pleased to note she could ignore everything else and focus on the work at hand.

It was past time for lunch when she stopped to get something to eat. In the midst of a project, she became caught up in the process. But once it was safely in the annealer, thoughts of last night surfaced.

Jalilah knocked on the door before Ella had a chance to fix something to eat.

"His Excellency would like to see you," she said.

"I'm getting ready to eat," Ella said. "Tell him I'll be over later."

Jalilah looked shocked. "I think he wants you now," she said.

"Well, he can't always have what he wants," Ella said. "Thanks for delivering his message. Tell him what I said. Maybe around three." She closed the door.

Who did he think he was, expecting her to drop everything just because he summoned her? He had delusions if he thought she'd drop everything to run to him.

In fact, she might not go at all.

Except her curiosity was roused. What did he want?

She prepared a light lunch and ate on her small veranda. The hot sun was blocked by the grape-covered arbor. The breeze was hot, blowing from the land and not the sea. She wouldn't stay outside long.

Sipping the last of her iced tea, Ella heard the banging on the front door. Sighing, she rose. It didn't take a psychic to know who was there. Dumping her dishes in the sink on her way to the front of the cottage, she wondered if she dare ignore him.

Opening the door, she glared at him instead. "What do you want?"

"To talk to you," he said easily, stepping inside.

She moved to allow him. It was that or be run over. He wa quite a bit larger than she was.

Closing the door, she turned and put her hands on her hip "About what?"

"My mother is hosting another party. This time to formall announce our engagement. We need to go."

"Are you crazy? This has gone on long enough. Tell he the truth."

"Not yet. You need to make sure your family turns else where for relief from your brother's gambling. It's only on evening. You'll meet people, smile and look as if you like me

"I'm not sure I do," she said, narrowing her eyes. "This ge more complicated by the moment."

"We need to invite some of your friends to make it seem real

She crossed her arms over her chest. This was unexpecte "I'm not involving my friends. Besides, no one would believ it. They all know how much I loved Alexander. And do yo really think they'd believe you'd fall for me?"

"So pretend."

"We don't have to pretend anymore. Antonio's gone an it was for his benefit, right?"

He was silent for a moment.

"Right?" she repeated.

"He did not leave as we thought."

"Why not?" She frowned. What was her brother doing? H wasn't waiting for the wedding, for heaven's sake, was he'

"Now how would I know what your brother thinks…I ju met him. But the limo showed up at the hotel in time to get hi to the airport for the first flight to Rome and he said he'd change his plans and would be remaining in Quishari a bit longer."

"Great." She walked across the room and turned, walke back, trying to think of how to get out of the mess the men her life had caused.

"I'll go away," she said.

"After the announcement," he replied.

She looked at him. He was calm. There was a hint of amusement in his eyes. Which made her all the more annoyed. "This is not a joke."

"No, but it's almost turning into a farce. I thought telling him would shut him up. Do you think I want the world to think I got engaged again and then a second fiancée breaks the engagement?"

She had not thought about that at all.

"Then you break it," she said.

"That'll look good."

"Well, one of us has to end it, so you decide. In the meantime, I do not want to go to your mother's. I do not want the entire city to think we are engaged. I do not—"

He raised a hand to stop her.

"Then you come up with something."

"I wouldn't have to if you hadn't told my brother."

"You could have told him the truth at dinner last night."

She bit her lip. She did not want to return to Italy. She would not be pressured day and night by parents trying to talk her into a marriage with some wealthy Italian to shore up her brother's losses. The days when daughters were sacrificed for the good of the family were long past. If only her father would accept that.

"Okay, so we pretend until Antonio leaves. Can we hurry him on his way?" she asked, already envisioning her mother's tearful pleas; Giacomo's little boy lost entreaties; Antonio begging her to think of the family reputation. She loved her family, but she wasn't responsible for them all.

"He's your brother. I could never hurry Rashid. The more I'd push, the more he'd resist."

She nodded. "Okay, so brothers are universal. Somehow we have to get him to leave me alone."

"So we'll convince him tonight that it's an arrangemen
meant to be and maybe he'll leave."

"Or hit you up for a loan."

Khalid frowned. "Do you really think that's the reason fo
the delay?"

"I don't know." Maybe her brother just wanted to make
sure she was happy. Yet he'd been right there when her parents had railed against her for marrying Alexander and neve
said a word in her behalf. She had no intention of letting any
of her family dictate her life.

"What time do we go to your mother's?"

"I'll pick you up at seven."

"How dressy?"

"About like last time. Do you need a new dress?"

She looked at him oddly. "I have enough clothes, thank you
What—do you expect everyone to hit you up for money?"

"No. But women always seem to need new clothes. I ca
help out if you need it."

"I do not." She studied him for a moment. Thinking abou
her own family, she knew there were some shirttail relative;
who had asked her father for handouts. He'd refused and
when she was a child, she wondered why he didn't share
Once she was older, she realized some people always have
their hands out.

For a moment she wished she had brought some of her
clothes from home. She and her mother had shopped at the
most fashionable couturiers in Rome. She'd left them behind
when joining her husband in Quishari. The dresses for receptions were more conservative. She wished at least one woul
make Khalid proud to be escorting her.

Then she remembered the red dress she'd bought from a
shop near campus. Her friend Samantha had urged her to buy
it. She'd never worn it. It was too daring for a professor's wife
But for tonight, it might just be the thing. Sophisticated and

elegant, it was far more cosmopolitan than anything else she now owned. She smiled almost daringly at Khalid. If he insisted they continue, she'd show him more than he bargained for.

He studied her for a moment, a hint of wariness creeping into his expression.

"Until tonight," he said.

She nodded, opening the door wide and watching him as he started to leave.

"I don't think I trust your expression," he said.

She feigned a look of total innocence. "I'm sure I have no idea what you're talking about, darling."

He tapped her chin with his forefinger. "Behave."

She laughed and shooed him out the door. Tonight might prove fun. She was not out to impress anyone, nor kowtow to them. Madame al Harum would be horrified. The minister might wish he'd kept his mouth shut. And her brother would learn not to mess with his sister's life anymore.

Ella was ready before the appointed time. She'd tapped Jalilah's expertise in doing up her hair. She remembered the maid had a talent for that which her former employer had used. The dress was daring in comparison to the gowns Ella had worn to the university functions. The thin crimson straps showed brilliantly against her skin, the fitted bodice hugged every curve down to where the skirt flared slightly below the knees. The satiny material gleamed in the light, shifting highlights as she walked. She had her one set of pearls she again wore. The dress really cried out for diamonds or rubies, but Ella had neither. The high heel shoes gave her several inches in height, which would add to her confidence. She was ready to face the world on her terms.

Khalid arrived at seven. He stared at her for a moment, which had Ella feeling almost giddy with delight. She knew she'd surprised him.

"You look beautiful," he said softly.

She felt a glow begin deep inside. She felt beautiful. The dress was a dream, but the color in her cheeks came from being near Khalid. She knew she would do him proud at the reception, and give others something to think about. All too soon this pretend engagement would end, but until midnight struck, she'd enjoy herself to the fullest. And make sure he did, as well. He deserved lots for helping her out without question.

"Thank you. So do you," she said with a flirtatious smile.

He gave a harsh laugh. "Don't carry the pretense too far," he said. "This is a dumb idea."

"It was yours," she reminded him.

He laughed again, in amusement this time. "Don't remind me. I say we ditch the reception and go off on our own. You look too beautiful to be stuck in a room full of my mother's friends."

"You're not thinking. What would your mother say. She went to all the trouble to celebrate what she thinks is a happy occasion. You can't disappoint her."

"You got it right first time—it's hard to think around you the way you look right now."

Ella smiled, delighted he was so obviously taken with how she looked. The dress was really something and she didn't ever remember feeling so sexy or feminine. The hot look in Khalid's eyes spiked her own temperature. Maybe his idea of not going out had merit.

"Let's go wow them all. And when we've put in our appearance, we'll dash back here and take a walk on the beach. Much more fun that the ordeal ahead." Filled with confidence from his reaction, she could hold her own with his mother and anyone else who showed up.

CHAPTER EIGHT

WHEN they arrived at his mother's apartment building, Ella was impressed. It looked like a palace. They were admitted by the uniformed doorman and quickly whisked to the top floor by a private elevator.

"The family home, no hotel," she murmured.

"Only a few intimate friends, like maybe a hundred. You never gave me a list of your friends, so I had one of my assistants contact the university and find out who your friends were. Told them it was a surprise."

Ella gave a loud sigh. "You just can't leave things alone, can you? Did you drive everyone insane while growing up?"

"Hey, I had Rashid to help me then."

"But not now?"

"He knows, but he is the only one besides you and me. Unless he told Bethanne. I forget there is a new intimate confidant with my brother. That'll be interesting—learning how to deal with that aspect."

Entering the large flat that overlooked Alkaahdar, Ella was struck by the large salon, ceilings at least twelve feet high. A wall of windows opened to a large terrace. The room held dozens of people yet did not appear crowded. Classical artwork hung on the walls. The chandelier sparkled with a thousand facets. The furniture looked more Western than Arabian, chosen for elegance and style.

"Khalid, you should have been here before the first guests," his mother chided, coming to greet them. She looked at Ella, her eyes widening slightly. "You look different tonight," she said taking in the lovely dress and the sophisticated hairstyle.

Ella inclined her head slightly. "I've been told I clean up good," she said cheekily.

Sabria al Harum didn't know how to respond.

Khalid gave his mother a kiss on her cheek. "We're here, that's the important thing. I can't believe you managed such a crowd on less than a day's notice.

"Everyone here wishes you well, son," she said, eyeing Ella as if she wasn't sure how to react to her.

Ella slipped her arm through Khalid's and leaned closer. "We are honored you did this for us on such short notice, aren't we, darling?" she said, smiling up at him.

"Indeed we are, *darling*," he said back, his eyes promising retribution.

"Mingle, let people congratulation you," Sabria said. She gave Ella an uncertain look.

Rashid crossed the room with Bethanne. He grinned at Khalid and Ella. "Congratulations, Brother," he said, then leaned in and gave Ella a kiss on the cheek. "Keep him in check," he said.

"I couldn't believe it when Rashid told me," Bethanne said, glancing around. She hugged Ella, and said in English. "I think it's fabulous."

Ella giggled a little. "Outlandish, I thought," she replied, one arm still looped with Khalid's.

Antonio came over, bowing stiffly.

"I thought you went home," Ella said when he stopped beside them.

"There were one or two things to deal with before I left. I

spoke to our parents. They wish you both happiness in your marriage," he said. "If I had left, I would have missed this."

"And wouldn't that have been too bad," she murmured in Arabic.

"Come," Khalid said, "let me introduce you to some friends."

As they stepped away from the entry, they were surrounded by people who were mostly strangers to Ella. However one or two familiar faces had her smiling in delight to see again, though inside she felt guilty to be deceiving everyone.

Conscious she needed to convince her brother nothing would deter her from marrying Khalid, she stayed within touching distance all evening, reaching out sometimes to touch his arm as if to ground herself. Once when she did, he clasped her hand, lacing their fingers together and holding it all the while he carried on a conversation with a friend.

The finance minister saw Khalid with Ella and broke away from the small group he was talking with and came over to them.

"Your mother must be so pleased, both her sons are taking the next step to insure the family continues."

"There's more to marriage than having children," Khalid said dryly.

"Ah, but nothing like small ones around to keep you young."

"Do you have children?" Ella asked.

"Not yet."

"Yet you and your wife have been married for many years," Khalid said.

For a moment the minister looked uncomfortable, then he changed the subject. "So are you and your brother marrying at the same time? Or as Rashid is the elder, will you defer to him?"

"Our plans are not yet firm," Khalid responded. "Excuse us, please, I see some friends of Ella's have arrived." Khalid moved them toward the door where two couples were standing, looking around in bewilderment.

"How do you know they are my friends?" she asked recognizing her friends.

"They look out of place. They obviously don't know anyone else here."

Greetings were soon exchanged. Though Ella's university friends were startled by the scar on Khalid's face, they quickly hid it and greeted him as warmly as they did her.

"I had no idea," Jannine said. "Though we haven't seen much of you this last year. I guess a lot has happened that I don't know about."

"It has been a hectic and busy year," Ella said vaguely. If this had been a true engagement, she would have shared the news with her friends immediately. She knew they'd wish only happiness for her.

"So, how are you doing with your glassmaking?" Joseph asked. He looked at Khalid. "You've seen her work, of course."

"Yes. Exquisite. She's planning a showing before too much longer. I predict a spectacular future for our artist."

"Do tell us all," Monique said.

Ella was pleased her friends had come on such short notice and silently vowed to keep in touch better. They'd been part of her life for several years and were each interesting people. She talked about the tentative plans for getting into a gallery someplace. They listened attentively, only now and again darting a glance at Khalid.

A moment later, he touched Ella's shoulder.

"Someone I must speak to. I'll leave you with your friends." He left and she watched as he crossed over to an elderly man. Turning back to her friends, she found all eyes on her.

"He's one of the richest men in the country, you know," Jannine said. "How in the world did you land him?"

"Good grief, Jannine, is that how you refer to me? I feel like a large-mouth bass," her husband said.

Everyone laughed.

"Okay, maybe that was not quite what I meant."

"So did you mean how did Ella attract him? She's pretty, young and talented. What's not to like?" Monique said.

"You all are twisting my words and you know it. Tell all, Ella."

She glossed over details mentioning simply that she had been renting a cottage on a family estate and they met that way. The rest they knew. "Tell me what's going on at the university. I've been so out of touch."

Joseph began telling her about professors and students she might remember. She enjoyed catching up on the news, but felt distant, as if that part of her life was over and she was no longer connected as she once had been. It felt a bit lonely.

Glancing around at one point, she saw Khalid and Rashid both talking with the elderly man. They were in profile, left sides showing. Stunning men, she thought. Then Khalid turned and caught her eye. Once again the ruined side of his face showed. She swallowed a pang of regret for the damage and smiled. That was easily overlooked when his dark eyes focused on her. Then she felt as if everything else faded away and left only the two of them in a world of their own.

"She's got it bad," Jannine said, laughing.

"What?" Ella asked, turning back to her friend.

"He's gone five minutes and you're already looking for him. How long until the wedding?"

"I'm not sure. We haven't made plans yet."

Antonio came over at that point. Ella made introductions and the group began talking in English, a common language for them all.

"This is a night of firsts," Jannine said. "I didn't even know Ella had family. She never spoke of you."

Her husband nudged her.

"Oh, sorry. Was that not the thing to say?"

Antonio looked at her. "You never spoke of us? Ella, we are your family."

"Who wouldn't accept my husband," she replied.

As the others looked on, she wished she could march her brother away and find Khalid. She was tired of the pretense, tired of trying to smile all the time when she wanted to rail against Antonio for getting her into this mess.

"But you like al Harum better, scar notwithstanding" Joseph muttered in Arabic.

Ella narrowed her eyes. "Khalid is a wonderful man. He puts out oil fires. Do you know how dangerous that is? He was injured trying to stop a conflagration. There are very few people in the world who can do something like that. And did you ever stop to think how much pain and agony he went through with such severe burns?"

Khalid put his hand on her shoulder. "Defending me?"

"There's no need," she said, glaring at Joseph.

Antonio watched, glancing between Joseph, Ella and Khalid.

"No offence meant, Ella," Joseph said.

"None taken," Khalid said. "Please, help yourselves to refreshments. I want to borrow Ella a moment to introduce her to an old friend."

He took her hand in his and they moved toward the man she'd seen before. Rashid and Bethanne were talking with him.

"He was a friend of my grandparents, Hauk bin Arissi. Unfortunately he is thrilled with our engagement. It is awkward, to say the least. I do not like deceiving people."

"You should have thought of that."

"Or left you to your brother?"

Before Ella could respond, they were beside Hauk bin Arissi. Introductions were made.

"Ah, Khalid, you and your brother have once again surprised me. The antics you used to do. Your grandmother would be so happy today—both her precious grandsons embarking on a lifelong partnership with such beautiful women."

"You are most kind," Ella said.

"Ah, and you my dear, already speak our language."

"I've lived in Alkaahdar for several years. Studied the language before that."

"You speak it well."

"Thank you. My reading is not as proficient."

He waved his hand dismissively. "Have Khalid read to you. The evenings my wife and I enjoyed reading from the classics. I do miss that."

She glanced at Khalid, a question in her eyes.

"We all miss her, Hauk."

"So how did you two meet. I've heard about Bethanne's piloting."

"She lives on Grandmother's estate, the one I inherited."

"So he inherited me," Ella said.

"Are you the artist? The glassmaker? Alia told me about your excellent work. I saw the vase you made for her. It looks like captured sunshine."

Ella smiled. "Thank you for telling me. I miss her so much."

Hauk studied her a moment, then looked at Khalid. "You, also, have found a treasure. See you treat her appropriately."

Khalid bowed slightly. Ella saw the amusement in his eyes. For a moment she wished this was real. That he would treasure her and treat her appropriately. The thought startled her. This was one evening to get through, not let their pretense slip. Soon things would go back to normal.

By the end of the evening, Khalid's temper was held by a thread. His mother was pushing for a wedding date, pushing to learn more, pushing period. The minister watched Ella more than Khalid thought wise. His wife had been unable to attend, and Khalid did not like the way he eyed Ella. Rashid teased him, which normally he'd accept in good stead. But tonight, it rubbed him wrong.

He and Ella spent most of the evening together, except

when she was visiting with her friends. It was growing late when she came over to him and smiled sweetly at the couple he was talking with.

"Will you please excuse us?" she asked, drawing Khalid away.

With the same smile on her face, she leaned closer, to speak only to him.

"My feet hurt, my cheeks hurt, I'm getting very cranky so suggest we leave very soon."

He leaned forward, breathing in the scent of her perfume, something flowery that he had grown familiar with over the last few weeks.

"I was ready to leave about two hours ago."

"I could have gone then. We've been here long enough, right? Your mother can't complain."

"She will, but that's her way. Come, follow me."

He led the way down a corridor and in moments they were in the primary hallway of the building. In seconds they descended in the elevator and were outside.

Ella leaned her head back and drew in a deep breath. It was all he could do to resist leaning over and kissing her. But standing in front of the building with the doorman and valet parking attendants standing mere feet away wasn't conducive for such activities.

Ella was tired. The strain of pretending she was wildly happy with a new engagement, and the anxiety over her brother, was wearing on her. To make matters worse, she almost wished she and Khalid were engaged. He had been most attentive tonight, hovering over her like he couldn't stay away. He even seemed the tiniest bit jealous when he spoke to the finance minister. He was so good in his role he almost had her convinced.

What would it be like to be engaged to him? Fabulous. She knew that without a doubt. He would lavish attention on the woman he chose for wife. She sighed softly, wishing she could imagine herself as his wife. To share their lives, to have his support of her art would be beyond wonderful.

Suddenly she was jealous of the unknown woman who would one day see past his own barriers and find a way into his heart. She would be the one to receive his kisses and caresses. She would be the one to share nights of passion and days of happiness. Ella could see them living on the estate his grandmother had left him—with a half dozen children running around, laughing and shouting with glee.

"Are you all right?" Khalid asked.

Ella hoped he couldn't read minds. "Of course. Just tired."

"So no walk along the beach tonight?"

Did he enjoy their shared time as much as she did? Unlikely. He probably liked walking and didn't mind if she accompanied him. The darkness hid all things. Was that special for him?

"Not tonight." She'd have to decide how to handle this. Everything was complicated. She was drawing closer and closer to Khalid and while he seemed to enjoy her company, she wasn't sure he was seeing her as anything but the woman who leased his cottage. Who was an impediment to his selling the estate.

When they reached home, Ella dashed into the cottage even before Khalid got out of the car. She closed the door and hurried to her bedroom, already unfastening the necklace. She didn't want to be thinking about kisses and caresses and dark nights alone with the man. He tantalized her with things she had thought lost forever.

Her life with Alexander had been all she ever expected. And when he died, she thought a part of her had, as well. But could she find another life, one unexpected but fulfilling nevertheless? Khalid was so different from Alexander it was amazing to her she could think of him in such terms.

Alexander had been kind, gentle, thoughtful. Khalid was exciting, provocative, dynamic and intense. Yet she felt more alive around him than any other time in life. Colors seemed more vivid. Experiences savored longer. Nebulous longing rose, solidifying into a desire to be with him.

She put the pearls on the dresser and peeked out of her curtains. She could only see a small corner of the main villa from this room. Nothing to show Khalid had gone to the study or his bedroom. Or, would he take a walk on the beach tonight without her. That first night he'd not known she was there. Did he often swim alone after dark?

Suddenly she felt daring. Taking off her dress, she slipped on her bathing suit. Just maybe she'd go swimming in the dark. So much the better if he were there, as well.

Pulling on a cover-up, she hurried to the beach. The moon was waning, but still cast enough light over the beach to see a pile of material near the water. Scanning the sea, she thought she saw him swimming several yards offshore. Smiling at the thought of reading his mind, she dropped her own things by his and plunged into the warm water. It felt energizing and buoyant. Swimming toward him, she saw when he first realized she was there.

Treading water, he waited for her to get closer.

"What are you doing here?" he asked.

"I didn't want a walk. But a swim sounded nice," she replied. When she drew closer, she also tread water. "Do you swim every night?"

"Not every night. But many. I like it."

"Always after dark."

"Easier that way."

"How far do the scars go?"

Khalid stared at her for a long moment, then motioned her closer. When she paddled nearer, he reached out and caught one hand, drawing her up to him. Tracing the ruined skin down his right side, he tried to gauge her reaction in the dim light. Most women would be horrified. The scarring went across part of his chest and his upper arm. It no longer pained him, except to look at.

She kicked closer and brushed against him. Instant heat. It had been a long time since he'd slept with a woman. He was already attracted to Ella, but her touch sent him over the edge. He pulled her into his arms and kissed her, kicking gently to keep them both above water. Then he forgot everything except the feel of her in his arms. Her silky skin was warm in the water. Her hair floated on the surface, tangling with one hand as he held her closer. Her kiss spiked desire for more—much more.

The water covering them both brought him back to sanity.

She broke away and laughed, shaking her head. Water flew from her hair, splashing against him.

"Romantic," she said, pushing up against him again, wrapping her arms around his neck. "Unless you drown us." Her lips were close, then she brushed against him, teasing, tantalizing. She trailed light kisses along his lips, across to his left cheek, then to his right one. He pulled away.

"Don't," she said softly, cupping his ruined cheek with her hand. "Khalid, you make me forget everything. Don't pull away and bring reality back. This is a night just for us." Again she kissed him and this time he didn't hold back. He relished the feel of her in his arms, the length of her petite body pressed against his, banishing the loneliness of the last few years. He felt more aware of every aspect of life than ever before. All because she kissed him.

They were both breathing hard when the kiss ended. Khalid wanted to sweep her ashore and make love to her on the sand. He even began swimming that way, but stopped when he realized she was swimming parallel to the shore.

"It's a glorious night for a swim," she called out, swimming away with each stroke.

He'd been fooling himself. He knew what women saw when they looked at him. The night hid the scars, but light would expose them for the awful things they were. He'd take what he could get and ignore the vague yearning for even more.

He swiftly caught up with her.

"I thought you said it was unsafe to swim after dark," he said, keeping pace with her.

"If one is alone, it is. I'm not alone, I have you."

Together they swam along the coast, only turning back when Khalid began to fear she would tire out before reaching their things. Ella seemed as full of energy at the end as when they started. And once their towels and clothes were in sight, she stopped and tread water again. Curious, he stopped, too, and was greeted with a wave of water. A tap on his shoulder as he shook his head to clear the water from his eyes was followed immediately by "You're it!"

Ella dove under the water and for a moment he didn't know which direction she'd gone. When she resurfaced some yards away, he struck out. She laughed and dove beneath the water again. This time she appeared near the shore. Khalid laughed and reversed direction. By the time he reached her, she was already standing and hurrying up the shallow shelf to reach the beach.

Snatching up her towel, she wrung out her hair and then dried herself, all the while moving back, watching him.

"Dangerous games you play, Ella," he said, walking steadily toward her.

"It was fun." She laughed, but kept backing away.

Khalid pursued, gaining ground with every step.

"It was. But you don't play fair. Why leave the water?"

"I'm tired. That was a long swim." She giggled and stepped back. "I'm leaving my cover-up behind," she said.

"Come and get it."

"I'm not that dumb."

"No one said you were dumb," he said, reaching out to catch her.

She laughed but came willingly into his arms. "Khalid, you are the dangerous one," she said just before he kissed her.

The next morning Khalid stood on the veranda on the side of the house nearest Ella's cottage, looking toward the sea. He'd had breakfast early, checked in with the office and debated taking a consulting job that had been offered or sending his second in command. The time away would give him some perspective. Last night replayed itself like an endless film. He should have pushed for more. But his respect for Ella wouldn't allow him to press for more than she wanted. And it appeared as if kisses were the limit of her willingness.

He should take the job.

"The maid said I'd find you here," Rashid said behind him.

Khalid turned. His casual clothes contrasted with the Western suit and tie that Rashid wore.

"And she was right. What's up?" he asked his brother.

"Just came by to see you." Rashid pulled a chair away from the small table and removed his suit jacket, hanging it across the back. Sitting, he looked at his brother, eyebrows raised in silent question.

Khalid came across and pulled out another chair, sitting opposite his twin.

"I heard from an oil company in Egypt. They want us to come vet their new well."

"Are you going?" Rashid asked.

Khalid shrugged. "Don't know."

"You usually jump at foreign assignments."

"I've been to Egypt before."

"More than once. Maybe your new fiancée is keeping you closer to home."

"I don't need that from you. You know the entire thing escalated out of hand. Damn, I was only trying to help out my tenant. I told you."

Rashid smiled at that. "Right. Somehow I guess I forgot."

"Like you ever would. Is that why you're here? To rehash the entire affair?"

"Ah, you've moved on to an affair now."

"No, I have not. I stepped in to try to keep her family from pressuring her. Once her brother leaves, end of story." He rose and paced to the edge of the stone floor, then turned back.

"What would you have done?" he asked.

"The same thing, I'm sure. Actually I came by to see if you were at all interested in her. She seemed devoted to you last night. Maybe this could develop into something good."

The scene in the water and on the sand flashed into mind. Khalid wasn't sharing that with his brother, twin bond or not. "An act." Had it all been an act? He hoped not.

"A suggestion only—" Rashid began.

"What?" Khalid felt his barriers rise.

"Give the relationship a chance. She's a nice woman. Talented, pretty. She loved the country, gave up her family for her first husband. Is loyal."

"Makes her sound like a dog or something."

"I'm trying to get through to you that not everyone is Damara. She was shallow and superficial and at the first setback fled. In retrospect, you got a lucky break. What if you were married and she couldn't stay for the long haul."

"I'm sure she felt she caught the lucky break." He turned back to gaze at the sea, remembering the scene in the hospital—he so doped up because of the searing pain and the one person beside his twin he thought he could count on instead shredding their relationship. As he watched the water sparkle beneath the sun, that image was replaced with a scene from last night: Ella's splashing him and then laughing.

Ella kissing his damaged skin. Ella.

More than anything, he loved her laugh.

Scowling at his thoughts, he turned back to Rashid.

"I'm taking off. The job in Egypt will last a couple of weeks at least."

"Give my suggestion some thought."

"There's nothing like that between us. She needed help. I gave it. She's locked into the cottage legally—nothing I can do to get rid of her before the lease expires. We'll muddle through. Not everyone is like you. Enjoy what you have with Bethanne. Don't try to find a happy ending here."

Rashid rose, slung his jacket over his shoulder and looked at his brother. "Okay. I gave it a shot. Your life is yours. Just don't screw it up any more than you can help."

Khalid laughed. "Thanks for the vote of confidence."

Once Rashid left, he went to the study and called his office. "Make the arrangements…I'll leave this afternoon," he told his assistant.

Ella had expected to hear from Khalid, but he had not sent word for her to come to the main house, nor visited. She kept busy sorting the glass pieces, pleased to study some and find they were better quality than she remembered. Stepping back a bit helped her gain perspective. The piece might not have attained her vision for it, but it was still good.

She had early pieces grouped together. Later ones separated. Definitely an improvement in the later ones. Maybe she should have a seconds sale—knock off the prices of the earlier less-than-perfect pieces. But only after she had started selling.

The pictures she had taken in the house looked great. She'd see about contacting a printer to make them into a booklet.

As much as she tried to concentrate on work, she was on

tenterhooks for Khalid. Last night had been amazing. She'd hated to go home alone.

But this morning—nothing.

Finally she took a light lunch on her veranda. Maybe she should just go over and find out what he was doing. Or if he had gone into his office today. It was a workday after all. She'd gotten used to his being available whenever she wanted. How spoiled was that?

She refused to hang around like some lovelorn idiot. She had her own life. If it coincided with his once in a while, so much the better.

The day seemed to last forever. She cleaned her small cottage. Did a load of laundry, even cooked dinner which was not something she often did. Finally—it was dark. Normally she walked after eleven, but even though it was scarcely past nine, she couldn't wait.

She headed for the beach. No sign of Khalid. She knew she was early. Slowly she walked to the water's edge. She'd wait.

Which wasn't easy to do when every nerve clamored for him. She sat on the warm sand, the water lapping the beach a few feet from her toes. Picking up handfuls of sand, she let it slip between her fingers. Last night had been surreal. One part at the party Khalid's mother had given. The other—the real part—had been swimming in the warm sea. She smiled remembering how much fun she'd had. How much she liked being with Khalid.

Glancing over her shoulder, she wondered what time it was. How long before he came?

CHAPTER NINE

THE next morning Ella headed to her studio, firmly intending to push all thoughts of a certain sheikh from her mind. It did not take a two-by-four hitting her on the side of the head to get it. He had not shown at the beach last night. When she finally gave up and returned home, all lights in the main house were off. Had he gone out?

It didn't matter. He was merely her landlord. Nothing else. She would not let herself believe there was something special between them. If there was any special feelings, they were obviously one-sided—on her side.

Now she was going to focus on her career and leave all men out of the equation until she was firmly on the path to money. Next place she lived, she wanted to own. To be able to come and go when she pleased and not worry about someone trying to evict her because of their own agenda.

Firing up the oven, she chose the glass shards carefully, then melted the different colors, picking them up one at a time on her wand. Slowly the glasses melded and when she began shaping the blob, she was pleased with the greens and blues and turquoise that began to show through. Taking her time, concentrating on the task at hand, Ella fashioned a large flat plate.

It was early afternoon when she was satisfied and put the

art piece in her annealer. Stretching to work out the kinks in knotted muscles, she went to the cottage for lunch. For the first time in hours her mind flipped to Khalid. Where was he? Despite her vow to refrain from thinking about him, now she could think of nothing else.

She wished he'd stroll around the corner of the veranda on which she sat and smile that lopsided smile that crinkled the skin around his eyes and caused her to catch her breath. Saunter over and sit casually in the chair, his dark eyes sending shivers down her spine as she lost herself in them.

She was becoming too involved with the man. He'd made it clear he was not interested in any relationship—short or long-term—and she'd do best to remember that.

Yet when she remembered the fun they'd had playing in the water, the drugging kisses that had her clamoring for more, it was hard to believe. Didn't actions speak louder than words? His actions showed he liked her. She wanted to spend more time with him. It was the first time since Alexander's death she'd had such an interest in anyone. Khalid was special. She felt stirred up every time they were together. When apart, she longed to see him again. Even if he never did more than talk about his work, she relished the moments together.

Frowning, she sat back in her chair and gazed toward the sea. She had a small glimpse of it from this place on her veranda. Normally it soothed. Today, however, she was more worried than before. She could not be falling for the man. She could list a dozen reasons why that would be such a bad idea—starting with she could get her heart broken.

Yet, testing her feelings as she might test a toothache, she had to admit there were a lot of similarities to falling in love. She wanted to be with him. Felt alive in his presence. Knew he was very special. Yet she didn't believe he was perfect. He could be short-tempered at times. And his idea that no one would ever find him attractive because of the scar was dumb.

Sure, it was disfiguring, but he was more than a swatch of skin on the right side of his face and neck.

When he spoke to her, she felt like she was the only person in the world. The flare of attraction wasn't dying down. His kisses spiked her senses like nothing else had. And his protective view was intriguing. Her own family didn't feel that obligation, yet he'd stepped in without being asked to try to thwart her brother's goal.

She leaned back in the chair, trying to relax. She should just go along with things—pretend to be engaged and see what happened. Only it was hard to play that part when half the couple had vanished.

Perhaps vanished was a bit strong, she argued. He had not come to the beach last night nor stopped by today. He had no need to. Except she wanted him to.

She jumped up and cleared her dishes. After rinsing them off, she changed into a cool sundress, brushed her hair and headed for the main house.

Jalilah answered the door to her ring.

"Madame Ponti," she said politely.

"Is His Excellency in?" Ella asked.

"No. He has flown to Egypt."

"Egypt?" Ella hadn't expected that. "When will he be home?"

"I cannot say. He took a large suitcase, so I suspect a few days at least."

Ella thanked the maid and turned to return home. Walking slowly through the garden, she wondered why he hadn't told her. She almost went back to see if he had responded to a fire. That would cause every moment to be precious as he packed and left and he might not think to let his fake fiancée know of his plans. But the maid had said he had a large suitcase and might be gone a while. No sense of urgency in her tone. Had he just left?

Ella debated calling Bethanne to ask if she knew what Khalid was doing, but decided she would not.

Still at the front of the main house, Ella turned when a ca
drove down the driveway. She recognized her brother ever
before he got out of the vehicle.

"Ella," he said.

"Antonio. What are you doing here?"

"I came to speak to Khalid al Harum. I've spoken witl
father and he entrusts me to handle things. Are you visiting
as well?"

"What things?" Did he not know she lived on the estate'
If not, she didn't plan to tell him. She was more interested in
what her father wanted Antonio to handle.

"Marriage settlements," Antonio said after a moment'
hesitation.

"Dowery?" she asked, walking closer to her brother.

He looked uncomfortable. "Not exactly."

"Exactly what? I've moved away from home. I was marriec
several years to another man. I can't imagine why there woulc
be any talk of settlements unless you plan to see if Khalic
would give something to get out of the mess Giacomo caused
Which I absolutely forbid."

"Forbid? You can't do that—it's between me and your future husband."

"If you even speak to him about that, I'll refuse to marry
him," she said recklessly. She would not put Khalid in sucl
a situation. She was embarrassed to even think of her family
asking the man for money. It would be bad enough if they
were madly in love and truly engaged. But this was humiliating. She would not let Antonio do it.

He studied her for a moment. "If you don't marry him, you
can come home and marry someone else."

"I may never marry again," she said, stepping up to her
brother and tapping his chest with her forefinger. "But I sure
will never marry someone I don't love. Giacomo got himsel
into this mess, let him get himself out of it. I am not a pawr

to be used like in feudal days. I can't believe even our father would consider such a thing."

"Your family needs you," Antonio said, capturing her hand and pushing it away. "The sheikh has more money than anyone we know. He wouldn't miss a few thousand euros. Let him help us."

"No! I mean it, if you talk to him about this, I'll vanish and it'll be years before you find me next time."

Her brother stared at her for a long moment. "We need help, Ella," he said softly. "Where else can we go? We cannot make it known in Italy or the business will suffer. If we don't get an infusion of cash soon, it will come out. A company in dire straits loses business which could help it get out of trouble. Then take-overs are bandied about. The business has been in our family for generations, for centuries. Would you see all that gone?"

"No, of course not. Look for other ways. Mother's jewelry—"

"Most already copied in paste and the originals sold."

That surprised Ella. Things were worse than she envisioned.

"Is Giacomo still gambling?" Ella asked, horrified at the lengths her family had already gone. She felt herself softening to them. They had practically excommunicated her when she married Alexander. But they were still her family. The problem seemed larger than she'd realized from what Antonio said.

"No. But the fallout is lasting."

"Go home, Antonio. If I can, I'll send some money." It was too bad her trust fund was not available until she turned thirty. Maybe she could borrow against that. Or she could see about selling some of her artwork. Madame al Harum had thought it had merit. Would others?

He looked at the house.

"Khalid is not home. He had a business trip to Egypt. I don't know when he'll be back."

Antonio nodded. "Very well, then. Come visit, Ella. Your mother misses you."

"One day." It was hard to overlook the obstacles her parents had thrown in her way when she had married Alexander. But she knew her husband never wanted her to be parted from her family. He would not want her holding on to wrongs of the past.

She watched Antonio drive away and began to walk back to the cottage. Alexander would not have wanted her to be a widow all her life, either. He had loved life, loved her and would always want the best for her. Including another husband who could bring her happiness.

Wistfully, she wished Khalid had the same thoughts.

It was amazing the absence of one slightly standoffish man made. As the days went by, Ella gradually resumed her former routine. Working during the day, long walks after dark. Always alone. Only her enjoyment of being alone had been disturbed. She missed Khalid. Which only went to reinforce her belief she had to get on with her life and not grow attached to him.

The bright spot in the week was a visit by Bethanne. She was driving a new car Rashid had just bought for her and wanted to take Ella for a spin.

"It's no fun to have a brand-new convertible and have no one to share it with," she said as the two began driving away from the estate.

"And Rashid doesn't want to go?"

"He has one of his own. I'm sure he's not as enchanted with the convertible as I am. Isn't it great?" She drove to the coast highway and flew along the sea. Ella glanced at the speedometer once and then quickly looked away. Obviously the pilot in Bethanne had no qualms about flying low. Instead of worrying, Ella relaxed and enjoyed the ride. The blue of the

Persian Gulf was on their right. The road was straight and smooth. The wind through her hair made her feel carefree and happy. With sudden insight, she realized she was happy. In this day, in this moment. Worries were gone. Plans and projects on hold. Nothing held her back. She could enjoy this time and not feel sad or guilty.

It had taken a long time, but she knew she was ready to embrace life again. To find all it had to offer and enjoy every speck of the journey—even the heartbreaks and hardships.

"You're quiet," Bethanne said with a smile. "What are you thinking?"

Ella told her and Bethanne nodded. "I know the feeling. But I have an excuse. I'm in love. The colors in the sea seem brighter because Rashid's in my life. The flowers more delicate and lovely, especially when I'm in the garden with him. But I bet coming out of grieving is like falling in love with life again. I'm so sorry for your loss, but time does heal wounds. I was so devastated when I learned my dad was really dead. I grieved both before and after I found out. Then I realized he had loved life. He had done exactly as he had wanted throughout and had no regrets at the end. That's what I want."

"No regrets?"

"No regrets and feeling I lived life to the fullest. Which means even more than I expected before I met Rashid. He's so fabulous."

Ella laughed. "So says a woman in love."

"I know, and I'm so proud of him I could burst, and happy he loves me as much." She flicked Ella a glance. "How is Khalid these days?"

She gazed at the sea. "I wouldn't know. He's on a business trip."

"Still in Egypt?" Bethanne asked.

Ella nodded. "I have no idea when he'll be back."

"I'll ask Rashid if you like."

She hesitated. She didn't want to make demands or have him think she had any expectations. But she did want to know how he was, what he was doing, when she'd get to see him again. Ella almost groaned. She had it bad.

"Please." Khalid need never know she'd asked after him. When he returned, she'd play it cool, not going for walks, no expecting him to spend time with her. But for now—she wanted any information she could get.

Trying to change the subject, Ella asked about how much flying Bethanne was doing these days and the subject of Khalid was dropped.

That evening Ella was summoned to the main house by the maid for a phone call. It was Bethanne.

"Rashid said Khalid is still in Egypt. He called him to see when he was coming home. Turns out he's thinking about visiting some of the oil fields in the interior of Quishari before coming home. Stalling do you think?"

"Why would he?" Ella said, her heart dropping at the news he would be gone even longer.

"I could fly you inland, if you like," Bethanne said.

Ella blinked.

"You know, you could get some great ideas from seeing some of the nomadic people and the colors they use in weaving cloth. And there is an austere beauty of the desert that find enchanting at all times of the day, from cool sunrise to the spectacular sunsets."

"It's tempting."

"I'll ask my darling fiancé if we can go tomorrow. That way, when Khalid shows up, you'll already be there."

Ella wanted to protest, but she closed her mouth before the words would spill out. She longed to be with him again. Here was a chance to see him in the kind of environments he worked. Not in fire suppression, but as a consultant to oi fields. She'd never seen an oil pump and had only the vaguest idea of how everything worked from discovery to gasoline in her car. It would be educational.

She laughed at her foolishness. She was going to see Khalid! "You're on. And tell Rashid thank you very much!"

The next morning Bethanne picked Ella up and drove them to the airport in her new car.

The gleaming jet sat in solitary splendor in a private section of the airport. Service personnel scrambled around, making sure the jet was ready to fly. Ella watched with fascination as Bethanne changed her personality into a competent pilot, double-checking all aspects of the plane before being satisfied. She invited Ella into the cockpit, and talked as she went through the preflight routine. In only moments they were airborne. Ella leaned forward to better see the landscape below them. The crowded developed land near the sea gradually grew less and less populated until they were flying over desert sand. In the distance, toward the west, she saw hills, valleys and mountains. The flight didn't take long, and went even faster fascinated as she was by the sights below.

She knew Bethanne had been half joking when talking about getting new ideas, but Ella already had a bunch of them crowding in her mind. She had brought her sketchbook, but it was in her bag. Her fingers itched to get down the ideas. She would love to capture the feeling of the burning sand, the starkness of the open land. The contrast with the sea and distant mountains.

"Nice, huh?" Bethanne said.

"Beautiful. It's so lush where I'm from in Italy. And I've lived in Alkaahdar since arriving. I had no idea the desert could be beautiful."

"It's not to all. But I love it. Rashid tells me if I wish, he will build us a villa by an oasis surrounded by endless desert.

I'm still too new at everything in Quishari to wish to change a thing. But the thought tantalizes."

"I think I should like that, as well. As long as there was enough water at the oasis."

They circled the town of Quraim Wadi Samil on the edge of an oil field and then Bethanne landed.

Ella watched the pumps on the field with their steady rise and fall as they made their approach. She regretted losing them from view as they landed.

"That's where Khalid will be tomorrow," Bethanne said. "Rashid arranged for someone to pick us up and drive us to the hotel. Once I know Khalid's arrived, I'll return home."

"Stranding me here?" Ella said. She hadn't expected that.

"Hey, he's good for helping a damsel in distress."

Ella laughed, growing nervous. What if he was more annoyed than anxious to help? And she wasn't exactly stranded. She'd be able to take a bus back to the capital city, or even one of the daily commercial planes.

Bethanne arranged for them to go to the hotel that Khalid would use when he arrived. She and Ella checked in and agreed to meet for lunch, then take a short tour of the town.

By dinnertime, they'd both showered, changed and were sitting in the lobby.

Bethanne watched the double doors to the street while Ella sat with her back to them.

"He just walked in," Bethanne said, smiling. She looked at Ella. "Go say hi and ask him to join us for dinner. We'll want to hear all about Egypt."

Ella rose and turned, her heart kicking up a notch when she saw him. He wore a dark suit and white shirt with blue and silver tie. He looked fantastic. She took a breath and crossed the lobby, her eyes never leaving him. She saw when he turned slightly and saw her. For a moment she thought she saw welcome in his eyes. Then he closed down.

"Ella, is everything all right?" he asked, crossing the short distance to meet her.

"Everything is fine. Did you have a good trip to Egypt?"

Khalid's eyes narrowed slightly, then he looked beyond her and saw Bethanne. She raised one hand in a short wave and grinned.

Khalid looked back at Ella. He hadn't expected to see her. One reason he'd decided to stop off at Quraim Wadi Samil was to delay returning home. But she was standing right in front of him, her eyes dark and mysterious, shadowed with a hint of uncertainty. He clenched his fists at his sides to keep from reaching out and pulling her into a hug that he might not ever let go.

"We wondered if you'd like to join us for dinner," she said quickly. "Tell us about your trip."

"You didn't come all this way to have dinner and hear about my trip," he said.

"Actually I'm getting new ideas for more glass pieces. You should see the sketches I've done since I've arrived. I'm hoping to go to the oil fields tomorrow." She stopped abruptly.

"With whom?" he asked, feeling a flare of jealousy that someone would show her around.

"You?" she said.

Khalid relaxed a fraction. His voluntary exile for the last week hadn't done anything to kill his desire for this woman. Now she was right here.

"I don't usually eat dinner in restaurants," he said slowly.

She nodded. "I know, eating alone is awkward in public places. But you'll have me and Bethanne so it'll be fun."

Fun? The stares of the other customers? The whispers that ran rampant as speculation abounded?

"I'm glad to see you again," she was saying. "I've missed you at night when I walk along the beach." Her eyes were shining with more happiness than he'd ever seen before. For another smile, he'd face the horror of others at the restaurant.

He'd make sure he was seated by a wall, with the damaged side of his face away from other diners.

"I need to check in, then it will be my pleasure to escort two such lovely ladies to dinner."

She reached out and touched his arm, pulling her hand back quickly as if unsure of a welcome.

"We'll be waiting." With another smile, she turned and walked back to Bethanne.

Dinner did not prove to be the ordeal Khalid had expected. As if in one agreement, the seating went as he wanted. With fewer people having to see the scar, they were more ignored than he normally experienced. For the first time in years, he enjoyed dining out. The food was excellent. The conversation lively. The more he grew to know Bethanne, the more he understood his brother's love for the woman. Yet his eyes kept turning to Ella. She was feminine and sweet. He detected a difference but couldn't put his finger on it. Was she more confident? Had the sadness diminished around her eyes?

"So Rashid called and doesn't want me to wait until tomorrow to return home. I'm leaving right after dinner," Bethanne said.

Ella looked startled. Khalid watched her as she turned to the other woman. "I thought we'd stay a day so I can see everything here."

Bethanne looked at Khalid. "You can show her around, can't you? She wants to see an oil field. You could explain things. And show her the sunrise. I think the colors in the sky are amazing."

Khalid knew a setup when he saw one. But instead of arguing, he looked at Ella. Another day together suited him. "Fine. We'll watch the sunrise together, I'll take you to the oil fields."

"And see she gets home safely?" Bethanne said.

Amusement warred with irritation. He suspected this was not Ella's plan but one of his soon to be sister-in-law's. Yet why not give in with good grace. He had to admit he'd missed Ella while in Egypt. More than once he'd seen something he'd wanted to share with her. Had almost called her a couple of times.

Dangerous territory, but he was a man who lived with danger. He liked being with her. There was no harm in that. It was only if he let himself dream of a future that could never be that he risked more than he wanted to pay.

Ella couldn't fall asleep after returning to her room. She was too much a night person to go to bed early. Yet Khalid had made no suggestion about spending time with her in the evening. Bethanne had now taken off for Alkaahdar. Ella sat at the window, watching the dark sky display the sparkles of lights from a million stars. There was no beach to walk along. It was too late to wander around town alone. There was nothing to do but think and that she didn't want to do.

She drew out her sketchpad, but instead of sketching various pieces of glass she wanted to try, she drew quick vignettes of Khalid—walking along the beach, swimming in the sea, leaning against his desk.

She also sketched him in traditional Arab robes, like he'd worn the first night she'd met him. She'd love to see him attired like that again. Did he wear the robes in the desert? Slowing in her drawing, she let her imagination drift as she thought about an oasis like Bethanne had talked of. What would it be like to have a small house in the scant shade of the palms surrounding a small pool of clear water? She envisioned a rooftop veranda that would provide a 360-degree view when the heat of the day dissipated. Quiet. Silent except for the wind sweeping across the sand. Sometimes the sand hummed in harmony. Would they feel cocooned together in a world apart?

She filled several pages with sketches, then tossed the

tablet aside. Restlessness was getting her nowhere. She had best go to bed and hope to fall asleep quickly. She'd spend tomorrow with Khalid.

He was waiting for her when she stepped into the lobby the next morning. She greeted him and joined him in the small restaurant attached to the hotel for breakfast. The croissants were hot, the jam her favorite—grape. The coffee was dark and aromatic. She sipped the rich beverage, trying not to stare. Khalid looked fabulous. His dark eyes met hers.

"Ready for the scenic tour?" he asked.

"Ready. I have a hat, sunscreen and a long-sleeved shirt to put on at midday to protect against the sun."

"I have hired a Jeep for our use, and stocked it with a cooler and plenty of cold water. Even lunch."

She smiled in anticipation. "Lovely, a picnic, just the two of us."

"I know a place you'll love," he said.

She would love anyplace he showed her. Looking away before she made a fool of herself, she finished her meal.

In no time they were in the open Jeep, weaving their way through the streets of the old town. The sandstone walls blended with the color of the desert. Bright spots of blues and red punctuated the monotonous walls. Soon the crowded streets fell behind. The homes were farther and farther apart until they were left behind and she and Khalid continued straight for the oil field she could see in the distance.

Fascinated by the acres of oil pumpers slowly rising and falling as they drew the oil from deep in the ground, she ignored what was behind her, trying to see what was ahead.

"Amazing. How did anyone know there was oil here?" she asked. There was nothing in the sparse desert to differentiate it from any other area.

"Geologists can find it anywhere. My father is the one who started this field. For Bashiri Oil, of course."

She looked around. "Was the town this big when the oil was discovered?"

"No. First the drilling and now the activity of the wells boosted the population considerably. It was a small, sleepy oasis way back when oil was first discovered. Inhabited by a few families who had lived here for generations. It was on the trade routes and the migration of nomadic people, so this was a resting place for caravans."

"Now it's another city, though small. With an airport."

Khalid laughed. "With an airport. Did Bethanne really bring you here to get ideas for your glass?"

"That was one reason," she said, staring straight ahead.

She caught a glimpse of him from the corner of her eye when he looked at her. "And another?"

"To see you."

He didn't respond, so Ella looked at him. "Surprised?"

"A bit."

"I think we need to get straight on what we're doing," she said.

He looked at her again, then back to the road. "We're going to see the wells, then have a picnic."

"About this fake engagement. I think Antonio has finally returned home. That should be the end of that matter. Interesting, don't you think, my parents are not against my being engaged to you a stranger, but objected to my marriage to Alexander whom they had known for years."

"Money is important to a lot of people. You are not one of them," he said.

"I think people are much more important. And experiences in life. I'm enjoying today. I have never gone very far into the desert. And I've never been to an oil field." She gave him a shy look, "Nor with a sheikh."

"Hey, I'm a man like any other."

Oh, no, she thought privately. *You are unlike anyone else in the world.* For a moment she wanted to reach over and touch him, grasp his hand and hold on and never let go. Her heart beat faster and colors seemed brighter. She loved him. Closing her eyes for a moment, she wondered when it had happened. How it could have happened. And what she could do to make sure he never knew.

Khalid was the perfect guide when they reached the oil field. He introduced her to the foreman and then gave her an abbreviated tour, explaining how the wells were drilled, capped and put into production. He even told her how something minor could go wrong and cause a fire. She had a healthy respect for the men who worked the fields, their lives in danger if any one of a myriad of things went wrong.

After their visit to the oil field, he drove them straight into the desert. It was just past noon. The sun glared overhead. The air was hot, the breeze from the moving car not doing much to cool. Ella had donned her hat and long-sleeved shirt and was sweltering. She was about to suggest they give up this expedition and return to the air-conditioned comfort of the hotel when she saw the faint suggestion of green in the distance. She stared at the spot gradually seeing the palms as they drove close. A cluster of trees offering a respite to the monotonous brown of the sand.

"The oasis?" she asked, pointing to the spot.

"Yes. A small wadi that holds enough water for a few humans or animals, it can't support a settlement. But there is plenty of water for the trees and shrubs that grow around it. And it provides a nice shady spot in a hot afternoon."

Ella studied the contrast of the golden-brown of the desert with the surprise of green from the trees. It gave her an idea for a new art piece. Could she do a palm, leaning slightly as if wishing to touch the earth? Maybe a small collage with blue glass at the base surrounded by a smoky golden glass with the palm rising.

Khalid stopped in the shade and turned off the engine. For a moment only silence reigned. Ella felt the heat encompass them, then a slight cooling from the shade. She turned and smiled at him.

"It's beautiful here. I know now why Bethanne says she'd like a home in the desert with water nearby. It would be lovely. I could live in such a place."

"Sometimes when things get too much, I come here for a few days." Khalid studied the water, the pond a scant four feet in diameter. The palms were spread out, their roots able to find enough moisture to support them even some distance from the pool.

"Surprisingly the water is cool," he said.

"In this heat?" she asked.

"Come."

He got out of the Jeep and waited for her at the front. When she joined him, he reached over to take her hand, leading her to the water's edge. They sat on the warm sand. Ella trailed her fingers in the water.

"It is cool!" she said in amazement. The water felt silky and refreshing. "How did you find this place?"

"Exploring when I was a kid. Rashid and I spent lots of time exploring while my dad spent time in the town. We learned later it was to visit a woman who had had a child by him."

Ella looked at him in surprise.

He looked back. "We never met her. She died, the daughter. My father's only daughter. He kept her hidden from my mother, understandably. She died in a plane crash that claimed Bethanne's father's life. My father died only days later—we think of a broken heart. Rashid and I haven't mentioned it around Mother."

"Does she know?"

"We don't know. But out of respect we have not brought it up. If she does, it must hurt her and if she doesn't, we don't want to have her learn about it at this late date."

Ella nodded, understanding. She wished her family was as loving and concerned for each other instead of always thinking of money and how to expand the vineyard or protect the family name.

"Your mother is lucky to have you two," she said wistfully. Would she ever have a child? A strong son who would look like his father? Or a beautiful little girl with dark eyes and a sparkle that telegraphed the mischief she might get into?

CHAPTER TEN

THE afternoon was pleasant in the shade. Khalid had brought blankets to spread on the sand. The picnic lunch was delicious. Ella ate with relish. The cool water from the pool completed the meal. Afterward, Khalid made sure the blankets were in the shade and lay down. Closing his eyes, he looked completely relaxed.

Ella watched him for a time, growing drowsy. Finally she lay down and closed her eyes. The quiet and peace of the oasis enveloped her and before long, she slept.

When she awoke, Khalid was nowhere to be seen. The Jeep was parked where he'd left it so she knew he hadn't gone far. She splashed cool water on her face and then rose, folding the blankets and putting them in the back of the Jeep.

"Khalid?" she called.

He appeared a moment later from behind a sand dune. "Just checking things out," he said, walking back to the shady area.

"Sandstorms can wreak havoc in this area. That's what brought down the plane my father's daughter was on. Yet time and again, this oasis reappears. I was trying to figure out why. Ready to return to town?"

Ella nodded, feeling reluctant to end the afternoon. She looked around, imprinting every bit of the scene in her mind. It would forever be special—because of Khalid.

The sooner they were back among others, the sooner she could get her emotions under control. She really wanted to stay. To camp out under the stars. To share feelings and thoughts on the vastness of the desert and the beauty found despite the harshness.

To tell him he was loved.

That she could not do. She hurried to the Jeep and jumped in.

Quraim Wadi Samil seemed to shimmer in the late sunshine as heat waves distorted the air. They drove into the town and straight to the hotel. Ella felt wrung-out with the heat. She would relish the coolness of the hotel. She began to long for the cottage by the sea. At least there seemed to always be a breeze by the Gulf.

"Dinner at seven?" Khalid asked as they entered the lobby.

"That's perfect." It would give her time to shower and change and cool down.

Her room was spacious with little furnishings to clutter the space. She lay down for a few moments, wondering if there could be any future between her and Khalid. His fake engagement had been to help her out, made public by the minister. Since he already had it in for Khalid's family, they dare not end the engagement so soon without negative gossip. Yet the longer it lasted, the more people would expect to see them together, and expect plans for a wedding to be forthcoming.

She wished she was planning a wedding with Khalid. She would so love to spend the rest of her life with him. It would be very different from the life she had before. Khalid had a stronger intensity with life than she was used to. Was it because he flirted with death whenever dealing with oil fires?

The thought of him being injured again had her in a panic. Would he consider not doing that in the future?

As if they had a future.

Ella rose and went to take her shower. She had some serious thinking to do. She could not bear to fall more in love with the man and then have fate snatch him away. Maybe it was time to consider going back to Italy and finding a life she could live there. She'd already lost one man she loved. She could not go through that again.

At least if she left, she could always remember Khalid as he was today. And hope to never hear of his death. As long as he was living in the world, she could find contentment. Couldn't she?

Khalid met Ella at the elevator when she stepped off in the lobby at seven. He had been tempted to go to her room, but had mustered what patience he could to wait for her in a public place. She'd looked perfect that afternoon sleeping in the shade at the oasis. He'd wanted to touch her cheeks, faintly pink. Her hair looked silky and soft. He had touched her hair before and knew its texture.

He was playing a fool's game, tempting fate by spending time with her. What if he became attached? He knew what he could expect from life. He'd made his peace with being alone years ago. His work was interesting and challenging. Especially when fighting fires. He liked the men he worked with. Liked being consulted by Rashid from time to time.

But he couldn't change reality. A scarred and bitter man was not going to appeal to a pretty woman like Ella. He'd help her out because he disliked the way her brother was handling things. And her family sounded totally unlike his. Despite the scarring, his family rallied around when needed.

He moved away from the pillar where he'd been leaning when she stepped out. Her look of expectancy touched him. When she spotted him, she smiled. Khalid felt it like a punch in the gut. It always made him feel whole again. She didn't seem freaked out by the scar. He still remembered the night she had cupped his cheeks, touching the damaged skin without revulsion. He'd never forget it.

"I thought I wouldn't want to eat again after that lavish lunch," she said as she hurried over to meet him. "But now that I've cooled down, I'm famished."

"Then let's hope they have enough food to fill you up."

She laughed. He almost groaned. Her laugher was like water sparkling and gurgling over rocks in the high country. Light and airy and pleasing. He wished he could hear it all his life.

"So tomorrow we return home?" she asked as they walked to the restaurant.

"Yes. We'll summon a plane if you like."

"I'd love to see the country between here and the coast, but not in a hot Jeep like today. It was fine for a short foray into the desert, but for the long drive home, I'd like more comfort."

"Your wish is my command," he said. He did wish he could do anything for her she wanted. An air-conditioned car would be easy. Could he help with selling her artwork? He knew nothing about that. But his mother did. If she'd just warm up to Ella a little, she'd be a tremendous help.

He had a life-size picture of that ever happening. Rashid was head over heels in love with Bethanne, and his mother still chided him for not seeking the woman she had wanted him to marry. He wasn't head over heels in love with Ella. But he liked being with her. Liked hearing her take on things. It gave him a different perspective.

He loved hearing her talk period. Her voice carried a trace of accent. Her Arabic was quite fluent, but softer than most women's. He liked it.

"Khalid!"

He looked at her.

"What?"

"I asked how long it would take to drive back to the coast. Where were you?" She peered up at him.

"Woolgathering. It takes about eight hours. It's a long and boring drive. The road is straight as a stick and there's nothing but sand and scrub bushes as far as the eye can see. We can do it, but I'd rather fly home and spend the afternoon at the beach."

"That does sound nice."

The maître d' appeared and showed them to a secluded table. He presented the menus with a flourish then quietly bowed away.

"No argument? I thought you wanted to drive home," he said.

"Well, you've obviously been across the desert and if it looks all the same, maybe I don't need to experience it for eight hours. You can take me on another trip to the desert if I need more inspiration," she replied, looking at the menu.

"Maybe."

She looked up and grinned. "We are supposed to be engaged, remember?"

"I thought you wanted to talk about that," he said. He had not planned for things to get complicated when he'd told her brother they were engaged. How was he to know it would come out and his mother would make a big production about it?

"So I do. How do we get out of it?"

He stared at her—realizing for the first time he did not want to get out of it. He could understand her haste in ending the agreement. Hadn't his fiancée tossed him over because of the scar? But he wanted Ella to pretend a bit longer.

"We can say we fought on this trip and the deal is off," he said slowly.

She looked at him thoughtfully. "So whose fault was it?"

He met her gaze, almost smiling. "Does it matter?"

"People will ask. And if they don't, they will speculate."

"Have it be mine. It doesn't matter."

"Of course it does," she said passionately. "If you break it off, that's not very nice of you. And if I do, that doesn't reflect well on me."

"So I play the villain. It won't impact my life."

She shook her head slowly. "Not fair. You tried to help me

out. And I appreciate it. Antonio would still be here trying to coerce me back to Italy if you hadn't."

"So if I can't break it off and you can't, we don't." Was that the solution? Keep the engagement going long enough for her to feel more comfortable around him. Would she ever see beyond the exterior to what he thought and felt? Could she ever fall in love with him?

Unlikely. She still loved her dead husband. And he sounded like a paragon. Intellectual. A professor. What did an oil field roustabout have to offer in comparison? Granted he had position in the country, but she hadn't been very impressed being seen with a sheikh. He had money, but she came from money herself and was unimpressed. Not like other women he'd dated years ago. In fact, nothing seemed to impress Ella. That was one thing he loved—*liked*—about her. Money and stature and material items others were impressed by seemed inconsequential to her. She liked people—and it didn't seem to matter what they had or did; if they were of interest to her, she was friendly. If not, she was cordial. And someone who knew her well could easily tell the difference.

"So we stay engaged for a while longer," she mused. "Suits me." Her attention turned back to her menu.

Khalid felt a strange relief at her compliance. At least for a while longer, they continued being engaged.

And didn't engaged couples kiss?

The thought sprang to mind and wouldn't leave. He glanced at her. Her attention on the menu, he had ample time to study her lips, imaging them pressed against his again. Imagine feeling her soft body against his, passion rising between them.

If he didn't stop soon, he'd embarrass himself. He wanted dinner ordered eaten and over. They could walk to the square. The day's heat was abating. It would cool down soon as the desert did at night. They could find a secluded spot and watch the stars appear. And he'd hold her and kiss her and pretend for one night everything was normal.

It almost worked that way. They agreed to stroll through town when dinner finished. And when they found a parapet over-looking a city garden, they leaned against the still-warm stone and tried to make out the plants in the garden. But the light faded quickly. Turning, Ella looked up at the sky. "It's grow-ing darker by the second. Soon a million stars will show."

He nodded and stepped closer, bringing her into his arms. "And you are more beautiful than all of them," he said, and kissed her.

Nothing was normal about that kiss. He felt every inch of his body come alive as he deepened the kiss. She responded like she had been waiting as long as he had. Her mouth was sweet and tender and provocative. Her curves met his mus-cles and tempted him even more. Her tongue danced with his, inflaming desire to a new level. The parapet disappeared. The stars were forgotten. There remained only the two of them, locked in an embrace that he wanted to go on forever.

Forgotten was the hideous scar that so repulsed others. Gone was the fear he would never find a woman to overlook the distortion even for a night. Khalid felt he was soaring. And he loved every moment.

If only it could last forever.

But it was not fair to Ella to kiss her when he'd coerced her into this engagement. Slowly he broke off the kiss, pleased when she followed him as he pulled back—obviously not wanting to end the kiss.

He was breathing hard when they parted. She was, too.

"Wow," she said, then turned. "I think we should go back to the hotel."

He wanted to agree—if she meant they'd go to his room. He wanted to make love to her so badly he ached from head

to toe. Yet nothing she'd said or done gave him any indication that was where her thoughts were heading.

They turned and walked back toward the hotel.

"Did you arrange for Bethanne to pick us up tomorrow?"
she asked as they came into the light spilling into the street
from the hotel.

"She'll be here at nine."

"Good."

When they entered the lobby, Ella quickened her pace.
She punched the elevator button almost savagely. She hadn't
looked at him once since they came into the light.

"Ella, if you're upset—"

"Why would I be upset?" she asked in a brittle tone. "Engaged couples kiss all the time."

The elevator arrived and she stepped in, punching the
number for her floor.

Khalid hesitated, then remained where he was. She did
look up as the doors began to close.

"See you in the morning," he said before she was lost from
view.

Turning, he went back outside. A long walk—like maybe
to Alkaahdar—was required. He hoped he had his head on
straight come morning.

Stupid, stupid, *stupid!* How could she have responded so
freely to Khalid's kiss. No wonder she drove him away. He
didn't even want to escort her to her room. Probably thought
she'd jump him and drag him inside. Ella paced her room,
slapping the wall when she reached it. Turning, she paced to
the other wall, slapped it. What could she do to make things
come right? She knew he had only helped her out. There was
nothing there. How could she have responded so ardently?

Because she loved him and knew he had been lacking in
love for years. She wanted to hold him close, pour out her

feelings, let him know she loved him beyond anything. But to do so would probably have him running for the nearest exit. A kindness to help her out of a jam didn't mean he was falling for her. He had his life, she had hers.

"Stupid!" she almost shouted the word.

Taking a deep breath, she crossed to the bed and sat down hard. Nothing was going right. She was at odds with her family, had lost her husband—whom she was having trouble remembering when every time she tried her mind saw Khalid. She felt a flare of panic. She couldn't forget Alexander. He'd been her childhood sweetheart. They'd had a nice marriage. At one time she thought he was the only man for her.

Only Khalid had a way of making her forget him. Forget the sweet love they'd shared for the hot and passionate feelings that sprang to life anytime she saw Khalid. Or even thought about him.

Daydreams about what life together could be like. And fears for his safety. She had to get away. Pack her things, face her parents and take complete charge of her life. She didn't have to marry anyone. It wasn't her fault her brother had a gambling problem. Time he faced the music and not expect her to martyr herself on his behalf.

And if she made it big in art, great. If not, maybe she could do stained glass work, or something to keep doing what she loved. It wasn't the same as sharing a life with a man she felt passionately about. But it would have to suffice.

If she could make it on her own. Somehow she must find a way to be self-supporting.

Which meant staying in the cottage was her best bet—the lease was solid for another four years. Khalid would get tired of hanging around and move on. Or sell the estate with the cottage occupied. She could make sure she didn't walk along the beach at night. Or venture outside if she knew he was in residence.

She'd faced worse. She could do this.

"But I don't want to," she wailed, and burst into tears.

The next morning Ella felt more composed. She ate a small breakfast in her room. Made sure no traces of last night's tears showed and descended to the lobby promptly at nine. Khalid was nowhere to be seen. She hadn't gotten the time wrong, had she?

One of the porters saw her and came over. "I will take your bag. You should have called down. The taxi is waiting."

So he wasn't even going back with her. That should help. But Ella felt the loss to her toes. Much as she'd talked herself into staying away from him in the future, she still hoped to fly back with him this morning. Saying goodbye silently so he'd never know, but having a few more hours of his company. Now even that was denied her.

The gleaming white jet sat on the runway with a bevy of men working around it. The cab stopped near the plane and a man rushed over to get her bag. She felt like royalty. Tears stung as she tried to smile and walked to the plane. She missed Khalid and it had been less than ten hours since she'd seen him.

Bethanne popped out of the opened doorway. "Hey, let's get a move on. I've got another run later," she said with a wide smile.

It must not be odd that Khalid wasn't with her, Ella thought as she ran lightly up the stairs.

"Where to later?" she asked, hoping Khalid would not be a topic of conversation.

"To take Khalid and his crew to that fire, of course. Didn't he tell you? Since I was already airborne when the call came in, he's staying here and I'm flying back to get the rest of his crew and then we'll head for Kuwait."

Ella felt her heart freeze. "Another fire?" she said. He had not told her. He had not contacted her at all that morning. Which should show her more than anything how nebulous their connection was. It was not her business after all. He saw no reason to inform her.

"A double from what I understand. Want to sit up in the cockpit? We can talk as I fly."

In a surprisingly short time they were airborne. Ella was so curious about the fire she could hardly sit still. Respecting Bethanne's need for concentration, she kept quiet until the pilot leveled out.

"There, all set. We're heading for the capital city now," Bethanne said.

Ella looked at her. "Tell me about the fire. Khalid didn't say a thing to me about it."

"It's in Kuwait and a bad one. Apparently two wells, connected somehow, ignited. Seven men are known dead and a couple of others are missing. They says it's burning millions of gallons of oil. And hot enough to be felt a half a mile away."

"He can't put it out," Ella said, staggered trying to imagine the puny efforts of men to extinguish such a raging inferno.

"You know Khalid, he'll do his best. And my money's on him."

"Someone should stop him," Ella said.

"What?" Bethanne looked at her. "He'll be okay. He always comes through."

"He got burned pretty badly one time," Ella reminded her.

"Freak accident."

"Which could happen again. Good grief, if the heat is felt so far away, what would it be like close enough to cap it? It's probably melting everything around it and there'd be nothing to cap."

"So they put out the flames, let the oil seep and figure out a way to get into production again. That's what Khalid does, and he's really good at it, according to Rashid. Who, by the way, also wishes he wouldn't do this job. But he knows Khalid is driven to do this and won't stand in his way."

Ella nodded, fear rising like a knot in her throat. She swallowed with difficulty, every fiber of her being wanting to see Khalid again.

She gazed out the window, wishing they'd arranged to ride back together in that air-conditioned car she'd wanted. They would have been out of contact, and someone else would be tapped to try to put out the oil fire. He'd be safe.

"When did the call come?" she asked.

"It happened last night. I suspect they called him once they saw what happened. He's the world's best, you know."

"He should retire."

Bethanne reached out and squeezed Ella's hand. "I know, I'd feel that way if it were Rashid. But women can't change men. My mother told me that fact years ago when explaining how she and my father married and then divorced. She had hoped having a family would be enough for him, but it never was. Some men are meant to do more adventurous things than others."

"I'd hardly call putting out raging oil fires adventurous—more like exceedingly dangerous. Why couldn't he have been a professor or accountant or something?"

Bethanne shrugged. "You might ask yourself why you're engaged to the man. You knew what he did. Yet you plan to marry. It's not going to get easier, but support is important."

Ella couldn't tell her why they were engaged. Apparently Rashid had kept Khalid's secret. Ella couldn't tell anyone she considered leaving Quishari because of Khalid. Maybe the decision would be taken from her. There was nothing she could do now but pray for his safety. She wished they'd ended the evening differently. That she had told him how much she cared. That she'd dare risk everything to let him know she loved him. Would she ever get that chance?

The flight seemed endless. She wanted more information. Could she call Khalid when they landed? She knew Bethanne was flying his crew back to Quraim Wadi Samil to pick him up and fly them all to Kuwait. He'd still be at the hotel. For a moment her mind went blank. What was the name of the hotel? She had to call him, tell him to be careful.

"Rashid will meet the plane," Bethanne said after responding to flight control. She began descending. Ella could see the city, the blue of the Gulf beyond. But the beauty was lost, fear held her tightly. "He's not going, is he?" Ella asked.

"No, he's taking you home. I'll be back late tonight. He didn't want you to be alone."

"Maybe I can work to take my mind off things," she said. The truth was she couldn't think about anything except Khalid and the danger he was facing.

"Go with Rashid. He'll have the most current information about Khalid and the crew. Besides, he's swinging by his mother's place to update her. Dealing with Madame al Harum is enough to take anyone's mind off troubles. That woman is a piece of work."

Ella smiled despite her worry. "At least we have that in common. Do you think she'll ever come around to accepting you?"

"My guess is once I have a baby or two."

Ella blinked and gazed out the window. What if she and Khalid married and she had a baby? She remembered thinking about a little dark-eyed little girl, or a couple of rambunctious boys that looked just like Khalid. How would she ever stand it if they wanted to grow up to be oil firefighters.

"Madame al Harum must be beside herself with worry," she said. "I would be if it were my son going to fight that fire."

"I would never let a son of mine grow up to do that," Bethanne said.

"Thought you said a woman can't change a man."

"Well, then I'd start with a little boy."

Ella laughed. Then almost cried when she thought more about the danger Khalid faced. How he'd once been an adorable little boy, running at the beach, playing with his twin. How quickly those years must have flown by.

Rashid was standing beside a limo when the plane taxied up to the hangar. There were a half dozen men near him with duffel bags and crates. As soon as the engines were shut down, men began swarming around the plane, loading everything. It was being refueled even as Ella stepped down the stairs. Bethanne followed, then hugged Rashid tightly.

"I wish you'd let someone else fly the plane," he said.

"I'm going. Don't argue. It's Khalid you should be worried about. I'll pick him up and then take them all to Kuwait. I'll be home late tonight. You take care of Ella. I think she's in shock."

"No, I'm fine. I think I should go home."

"You're coming with me," Rashid said.

She looked at him, almost seeing Khalid. Certainly hearing that autocratic tone of his. They looked so alike, yet so different.

"Any news?" she asked.

"Nothing beyond what we learned earlier. Once we reach home we'll call Khalid. He's been talking with the oil field people so will have the latest intel. This all you have?" he asked as one of the men put her bag in the trunk of the limo

"Yes. It was a short trip." Too short if it was to be the last time she saw Khalid.

Ella went with Rashid to his mother's home. He did not speak on the ride except to try to reassure her that Khalid knew what he was doing and wouldn't take any foolish risks. "Especially now," Rashid said.

Ella nodded, wishing they'd never embarked on this stupid fake engagement. Everyone thought he'd be extra careful but Rashid knew Khalid had no special reason to be extra cautious. She knew he wouldn't be foolhardy, but so many things could go wrong. What if there was another explosion and his suit was torn again. She couldn't bear to think of the pain he'd go through while healing.

Or what if things went really, really wrong?

"My mother can be a bit difficult. We know she loves us. Sometimes I think it's hard for a mother to realize her children are grown and have their own lives."

Ella thought about her parents. "Sometimes they just want to control children forever."

"Or maybe they get used to it and find it hard to let go."

"Your mother doesn't have to like me," she said.

"No, but it would make family life so much more comfortable in the future, don't you think? We do celebrate happy occasions together—holidays, birthdays."

"Bethanne said once she was a grandmother, she'd come around."

Rashid laughed. "That's our hope. But not right away. I want her to myself for a while."

Would Khalid ever want someone to himself for a while? She wished it would be her.

Madame al Harum was distraught when they arrived. She rushed to the door. "Have you heard anything more?"

"No, Mother," Rashid said, giving her a hug. "He's still in Quraim Wadi Samil. Bethanne just took off to get him. It'll be a few hours before they're in Kuwait."

"Call him. I need to talk to him," she ordered.

"You and Ella."

The older woman looked at Ella as if seeing her for the first time. "Oh." She frowned. "Of course."

"We both want Khalid safely back," Ella said.

Madame al Harum nodded. "Come, we will call him."

* * *

Khalid had maps and charts spread around him when the phone rang.

"Al Harum," he said, hoping this was another call from the site, updating the situation.

"Khalid, it's your mother. I wanted to tell you to be careful."

"I always am, Mother." He leaned back in his chair, pressing his thumb and forefinger against his eyes. He'd been studying the layout of the oil field, where the pipes had been drilled and the safety protocols that were in place. He figured he could recite every fact about that field in his sleep.

Glancing at his watch, he noted the plane would be arriving in less than an hour. He had talked to his second in command before he boarded and all the gear they needed was either on the plane or being shipped directly to the fire.

"We will watch over Ella for you," she said.

Khalid's attention snapped back to his mother. Ella. He should have told her this morning before she left, but he'd already been involved in learning all he could from the source. He hadn't wanted to interrupt the phone call to go tell her goodbye.

"She returned safely?" he asked.

"Yes. She's here. Take care of yourself, son."

Before Khalid could say anything, he heard Ella's soft voice.

"Khalid?"

"Yes. You got back all right, I see."

"I didn't know until we were on the plane what was going on. I wished you had told me. You will be careful, won't you?"

"I always am." He was warmed by the concern in her voice.

"From what I've heard, this one is really bad."

He heard a sound from his mother in the background.

"It does seem that way. I'll know more when I get there, but so far, this is probably the most challenging one we've tried."

"I guess I couldn't talk you out of going?" she asked hopefully.

He laughed, picturing her with her pretty brown eyes, hair

blowing in the sea breeze. "No, but I wish I didn't have to leave you. Not that I'd take you to a fire. I enjoyed yesterday." He wished he could pull her into his arms this moment and kiss her again. If he hadn't already been on the phone, nothing would have stopped him from explaining this morning—and taking another kiss for luck.

"Me, too."

He waited, hoping she'd say more. The silence on the line was deafening.

"I better go. I'm expecting another call," he finally said. Nothing was going to be decided on the telephone.

"Okay. Take care of yourself. I'll be here when you get back."

He hung up, wondering where else she'd be but at the cottage. She had a lease for another four years. And at this moment, he was grateful for his grandmother's way of doing things.

The phone rang again and this time it was the field manager in Kuwait. Time to push personal agendas on the back burner. He had a conflagration to extinguish.

CHAPTER ELEVEN

ELLA chafed at the way time dragged by. Rashid stayed for a while, then claimed work needed him and took off. Leaving her with Madame al Harum. Ella knew she'd be better off at home. She could try to take her mind off her worry about Khalid with work. Here she had nothing. She rose from the sofa where she'd sat almost since she'd arrived and walked to the window which overlooked the city. It looked hot outside. She'd rather be at the beach.

"I think I'll go home," she said.

"Stay."

Turning, she looked at Khalid's mother. "There's nothing to do here. At home I have work that might distract me from worry."

Sabria al Harum tried to smile. "Nothing will make you forget. I had years of practice with my husband when he went on oil fields. Always worrying about his safety. And he did not try to put out fires. I now worry about Khalid. Rashid assures me he knows his job. But he cannot know what a fire will do."

"It makes it worse since he was injured once," Ella said, looking back out the window.

"Yet you don't seem to mind his scar."

Ella shrugged. "He is not his scar, any more than he is defined by being tall. It's what's inside that counts."

There was a short silence then Sabria said, "Many people

don't grasp that concept. He was terribly hurt by the defection of his fiancée when he was still in hospital."

"She either freaked or was not strong enough to be his wife. Khalid is very intense. Not everyone could live with that."

"You could."

Ella nodded, tears filling her eyes. She could. She would love to be the one he picked to share his life. She would match him toe-to-toe if he got autocratic. And she would love to spend the nights in his arms.

"He was like that as a little boy," Sabria said softly.

When Ella turned, she was surprised at the look of love on her hostess's face. "Tell me," she invited. She was eager for every scrap of knowledge she could get of Khalid.

"I have some pictures. Come, I'll tell you all about my wild twins and show you what I had to put up with." The words were belied by the tone of affection and longing.

Ella was surprised at the number of photo albums in the sitting area of Sabria al Harum's bedroom. The room was bright and airy, decorated in peach and cream colors, feminine and friendly. She would never have suspected the rather austere woman to have this side to her.

Pulling a fat album from the shelves behind the sofa, Sabria sat and patted the cushion next to her for Ella to sit. Placing the album in Ella's lap a moment later, she opened it. For the next hour, the two women looked at all the pictures—from when two adorable babies came home in lacy robes, to the smiling nannies who helped care for them, to the proud parents and on up to adulthood. There were fewer pictures of the two young men, too busy to spend lots of time with their parents. Then she paused over one last picture.

"This was the one taken just before the fire that scarred my son so badly. He has never had his picture taken since. People can be cruel when faced unexpectedly with abnormalities—

whether scarring or handicaps. He was doubly injured with the loss of his fiancée. He has so much to offer."

Ella nodded. A mother always said that, but in Khalid's case, it was true.

The phone rang. Sabria rose swiftly and crossed to answer the extension in her sitting room.

"Thank you," she said a moment later.

"That was Rashid. The team has taken off from Quraim Wadi Samil. They'll be in Kuwait in a couple of hours. There's nothing to do but wait."

"Then come with me to my studio. I'll show you my work and you can advise me. Madame Alia al Harum thought I had promise. I want to earn a living by my work, but if it is really impossible, maybe I should find out now, rather than later."

"You will not need to work once married to Khalid."

Ella had no quick response. Only she and Khalid knew there would be no marriage.

"Come and see."

Sabria thought about it for a moment then nodded. "I believe I should like to see what you do."

The afternoon passed slowly. Sabria looked at all the work Ella had done, proclaiming with surprise how beautiful it was. "No wonder my mother-in-law thought you had such promise. You have rare talent. I know just where I'd like to see that rosy vase. It would be perfect in my friend's bedroom. Perhaps I shall buy it for her. When will you begin to sell?"

Ella explained the original plan and then her idea to start earlier. Soon she and Sabria were discussing advantages and disadvantages of going public too soon, yet without the public feedback, how would Ella know which ideas were the most marketable.

Ella wasn't sure if it was the situation, or the fact Sabria was finally receptive to seeing her as an individual—no someone out to capture her son's affections—but she felt the tentative beginning of a friendship. Not that Sabria would necessarily wish to continue when the engagement was broken. Ella could see the dilemma—who took the blame? She didn't want to. Yet in fairness, she needed to be the one. Khalid had been helping her. He did not need any more grief in his life.

They called Rashid for news before eating dinner on the veranda. Nothing new. Ella made a quick spaghetti with sauce she'd prepared a while ago and frozen. The camaraderie in the kitchen was another surprise. Ella thought she could really get to like Khalid's mother.

"I'm going now," Sabria said after they'd enjoyed dinner and some more conversation. Ella could listen to stories about the twins all week. Darkness had fallen. It was getting late. Nothing would change tonight. Khalid had told Rashid they needed to plan carefully since the fire was involved with two wells.

When she took a walk on the beach before going to bed, Ella looked to the north. She could see nothing. The fire was too far away. But she could imagine it. She dealt with fire every day—controlled and beneficial. Raging out of control would be so different. She offered another prayer for Khalid's safety. Her decision to leave was best. She could see about selling what she'd already done and arrange shipping to Italy of her annealer and crucible and glass. She'd establish herself somewhere near enough to see her parents, but far enough away to make sure they knew she was not coming back to the family. Not until her brother's situation was cleared up.

In the meantime, she did her best not to focus on Khalid, but everything from the beach to the house next door reminded her of him. She could picture him standing in her doorway. Looking at the art she had created. Holding the yellow vase in his house that his grandmother had loved. She ached with loneliness and yearning. Could she get by without him over the years ahead?

She had to. There was no future for her in Quishari. That part of her life was over.

Tomorrow she'd begin packing and making arrangements to move.

The next two days were difficult. Ella made Rashid promise to call her the moment he learned of anything—good or bad. There was nothing else she could do, so she began packing. She ordered shipping cartons and crates and enlisted the help of Jalilah to help her. Carefully they wrapped the fragile pieces in packing materials, then in boxes, then crates. It was slow work, but had to be done carefully to insure no breakage during transit.

Every time Khalid's cordless phone rang, Ella's heart dropped, then raced. She'd answer only to hear Rashid's calm voice giving her an update. The materials had arrived. The maps had been updated. The plan was coming together. There was never a personal message for her. What did she expect? Khalid had far more important things to worry about.

But each time Rashid hung up, Ella's heart hurt a bit more. One word, one "tell Ella I'm okay," would have sufficed.

On the third day, Ella could see the progress. She had arranged for the shipping agent to pick up what was already packed. He would hold it at the depot until everything was ready and ship all at once. She and Jalilah were talking when Ella heard a car. Glancing out the window, she saw Rashid and Bethanne get out and hurry toward the cottage.

Fear swamped her as she rushed to the door. "What happened?" she called before they could speak.

Bethanne came to her first, hugging her tightly. "He'll be okay," she said.

"What?" Sick with fear, she looked at Rashid.

"Another well exploded. The fire is worse than ever. Khalid was hit by flying debris. One of the crew was killed, but

Khalid's in hospital. He's going to be okay. We're going now. You come with us."

Ella wanted to refuse, but her need to see him was too strong. She had to make sure he was truly okay before leaving.

"I just need my purse and passport," she said. She dashed to the house, Bethanne with her. "Bring a change of clothes and sleepwear. We're planning to stay as long as we need to," she said.

Ella went through the motions, but her thoughts stuck on Khalid. "He's really all right?"

"No, but he will be. So far he's still unconscious. We hope we're there by the time he wakes up," Bethanne said, helping fold clothes and stuffing them in the small travel bag.

Time seemed to stop. Ella felt like she was walking through molasses. She remembered hurrying to Alexander's hospital bed—too late. He had died from the car crash injuries before she was there to see him. She couldn't be too late for Khalid.

She sat on the edge of the bed.

"I can't go," she said.

Bethanne stopped and looked at her. "What?"

"I can't go." She pressed her hands against her chest, wishing she could stop the tearing pain. Khalid. He had to be all right!

"Yes, you can. And will. And greet him with all the love in your heart. He cannot have another fiancée abandon him when he's in the hospital."

Ella looked at Bethanne. "I'm not—" Now was not the time to confess she wasn't really his fiancée. "I'm not abandoning him. But I don't think I can go into a hospital."

"We'll be right with you. Come on. That's all you need. Get your passport and let's go."

Four hours later they entered the hospital. Ella felt physically sick. The few updates Rashid had obtained during the flight had not been encouraging. Entering the new hospital, Ella felt waves of nausea roil over her. "I need a restroom," she said, dashing to the nearest one. Bethanne followed.

After throwing up, Ella leaned limply against the stall wall. "I can't do this again," she said.

"He'll be okay, Ella. He's not Alexander. He'll pull through," Bethanne said, rubbing her back.

"Go on up. I know Rashid needs to see him instantly. I'll clean up and be right behind you." She wanted a few moments to herself. She could do this. She had to. The thought of Khalid lying helpless in bed was almost more than she could stand. But she also wanted to see him. At least one more time. And assure herself he was alive and would recover.

She tried hard to think of this as visiting a sick friend. But as she walked down the corridor, the smells that assailed her reminded her vividly of the frantic dash to see Alexander. Only the times got mixed up. She felt the fear and panic, but it was for Khalid. The door was ajar to the room she'd been directed to. She stood outside, drawing in a deep breath, hoping she wouldn't lose her composure.

Rashid stepped out, smiling when he saw her. "I'm calling Mother. He's awake. And probably wondering where you are." He flipped open his mobile phone and hit a speed-dial number. Walking down the corridor, he began to speak when his mother answered.

Ella turned back to the room, stepping inside. Immediately she saw Khalid, the hospital bed raised so he was sitting. His face was bandaged, both eyes looked blackened. His right shoulder was also bandaged. Bethanne was on the far side, talking a mile a minute in English. Khalid watched her; he hadn't seen Ella yet.

Which was a good thing. It gave her time to get over her shock, give a brief thanks he was awake and seemingly able to recover. Pasting a smile on her face she stepped into the room.

"You scared me to death!" she said.

Khalid swiveled around, groaned at the movement, but looked at her like she was some marvelous creation. Her heart raced. Nothing wrong with his eyes.

"You came," he said.

"You said you'd keep safe." She walked over to the bed. Conscious of Bethanne watching her, she leaned over and kissed him gently on the mouth. His hand came up and kept her head in place as he kissed her back.

"Don't hurt yourself," she said, pulling back a few inches, gazing deep into his eyes.

"I didn't think you'd come," he said, pulling her closer for another brush of lips.

"Why ever not?" Bethanne asked. "If Rashid were injured nothing could keep me away."

"And nothing could keep me away," Ella said. She straightened and took his hand in hers, feeling his grip tighten. Studying him, she shook her head.

"You look horrible," she said.

He laughed, and squeezed her hand. "I feel like a truck ran me over. That was something we didn't expect—another explosion. I think they had the wells linked in a way that didn't show on the maps."

"I heard one of your men died. I'm so sorry."

"Me, too."

She leaned closer. "But I'm glad it wasn't you."

"I'm going to find Rashid. We'll be back." Bethanne waved and headed out of the room.

"When Rashid first came in, I thought you hadn't come," he said.

"Well, some of your fiancées might desert you in hospital, but not all," she said lightly, hating for him to know how much it had taken for her to come. She was so glad she had, but the fear she'd lived with wouldn't easily be forgotten.

He laughed again. Despite his injuries, he seemed the happiest she'd ever seen him.

"Did that blow to the head knock you silly?" she asked.

"Maybe knocked some sense in me. I lay here thinking, after I woke up, what if you didn't come? We haven't known each other that long. What if you didn't care enough to come."

"What if I knocked you up side the head again to stop those rattled brains. Of course I would come. I had to see that you were all right. I couldn't just take Rashid's word for it."

"Why?"

She looked at their linked hands. "I care about you," she said.

"How much?"

She met his gaze. "What do you mean, how much?" she asked.

"I want to know how much you care about me—what's hard about that?"

"Like, more than spinach but less than chocolate?"

His gaze held hers, his demeanor going serious. "Like enough to marry me, stay in Quishari and make a life with me?"

Ella caught her breath. For a moment she forgot to breathe. Did he mean it? Seriously?

"Are you asking me to marry you?" she said. "I mean, for real?"

He nodded. "I am. I hated to say good-night to you in Quraim Wadi Samil. Hated even more leaving for Kuwait without having another kiss. Then I woke up here and realized, life is unexpected. I could die here today, or live for decades. But I knew instantly either way, I wanted you as part of my life. I love you, Ella. I think I have since you touched my cheek on the beach weeks ago. A woman who wasn't horrified by how I look. Who could see me clearer in the dark than anyone in the light. A woman who had been through a lot already, and valued people for who they were, not what they could offer monetarily. Did I also mention who sets my entire body on fire with a single kiss?"

Warmth and love spread through her as she smiled at his words. "You didn't. Maybe we need another check on that." She leaned over and kissed him.

"Are you saying yes?" he prompted a few moments later.

"I am. I love you. I never expected to say those words again after Alexander's death. But you swept into my life, running roughshod over any obstacles I might throw up. I can't pinpoint the moment I fell in love, but I can the moment I realized it. I will love you forever."

"The fire is still going," he said.

"And are you planning to put it out?"

"Might be involved in the planning. But right now I don't feel up to standing to kiss you, so doubt if I'll be leading a foray close to the flames."

"This time," she murmured, remembering what Bethanne had said. She wouldn't want to change a thing about this man.

"This time. But I'm careful. I'm still here, right?"

"Right. Here's hoping there are no more fires in your future."

"Only the one you set with your kisses," he said.

Ella laughed, seeing an entirely different side of the man who had captured her heart. And to think, she almost missed this. She'd have some quick unpacking to do when she got back to the cottage. She couldn't bear for him to think she was leaving. She'd tell him—after a while. After he was convinced of her love as she was already convinced of his.

"I love you, Ella, now and always."

"I love you, Khalid. Now and always."

EPILOGUE

"I'M GETTING car sick riding with my eyes closed," Ella said, still gripping the edge of the door to help with the bouncing. They'd left Quraim Wadi Samil a while ago. In the last ten minutes, Khalid had insisted she close her eyes—he had a surprise for her. It couldn't be the oasis; she'd already seen that. What else was out in this desert?

"Almost there," he said, reaching out to grasp her free hand in his, squeezing it a little.

She felt the car slowing. Then it stopped. The desert wind brought scents of sand, scant vegetation and—was it water?

"Open your eyes," he said.

She did and stared. They were at the oasis. The late afternoon sun cast long shadows against the tall palms, the small pool of water—and the sandstone house that looked as if it had miraculously sprung up from the ground.

"What? Is that a house?"

He left the Jeep and came around to her side, taking her hand to help her out. "It's our house. Ours and Rashid's and Bethanne's. She doesn't know yet. He'll bring her out next week. We have it first."

Ella looked around in astonishment. "You built it here miles and miles from anywhere? How could you get all the materials, how—never mind, money can achieve anything. This is fantastic! I want to see."

He smiled and led her across a flagstone patio to the front door. Lounge chairs rested on the patio, which gave a perfect view of the pool and palms. Opening the door, he swept her into his arms and stepped inside. "Isn't this what newlyweds do?" he asked at her shriek of surprise.

"Yes, in Italy. I didn't know you did it in Quishari." She laughed, traced the new scar on his face and pulled his head down for a kiss. She was so full of love for this husband of hers. And so grateful for his full recovery—with one or two new scars which only made her love him more.

"Why not at our home when we married?" she asked.

"We had the reception there—how could I carry you over the threshold? You were already inside."

"Hmm, good point."

He set her on her feet and turned her around. The small room was furnished with comfortable items. Large windows gave expansive views. Two of her glass pieces were on display. Taking a quick tour, Ella discovered the small kitchen, bath and two large bedrooms.

"This is so lovely," she said, returning to the center of the main room. Khalid had done all he could to make her life wonderful. He'd backed her art exhibit, which turned out wildly successful. She had orders lined up for new pieces.

They'd attended Bethanne and Rashid's wedding in Texas. And then done a quick tour of several larger cities in the United States which Ella had enjoyed with her new husband.

On their way back to Quishari, they'd stopped in Italy so he could meet her parents. Even settled Giacomo's remaining debts, with a stern warning to never gamble again—which only reiterated what her father had decreed. She'd protested, but Khalid had insisted he wanted to have harmonious relations with his new in-laws.

Which she still hoped for with his mother. One day at a time, she reminded herself. At least they'd been married in Quishari, which Madame al Harum liked better than Rashid and Bethanne's wedding.

"The best is outside. Come," Khalid said, drawing her out and around to the side of the house where stairs led to the flat roof.

When they reached the upper level, Ella exclaimed at the loveliness. Pots of flowers dotted the hip-high wall. Several outdoor chairs and sofas provided ample seating. The view was amazing. Slowly she turned around, delight shining in her eyes.

"This is so perfect."

He smiled at her and drew her into his arms. "I wanted something special for us to get away to sometimes, just the two of us. To enjoy the quiet of the desert and the beauty of this oasis."

She smiled, then frowned a little.

"You don't like it?"

"I love it. It's just…" She bit her lower lip and glanced around, then back at Khalid. "It won't be just the two of us."

"Rashid and I plan to keep the other informed when we want to use the house. We won't be here when they are. Or I can just tell him forget it, we want it all ourselves."

"Don't you dare. It's not that. We're having a baby," she blurted out. "Darn, that was not the way I wanted to tell you," she said.

Staring at his stunned face, she almost laughed. "Well, we've been married for four months and not exactly celibate. What do you think?"

"I'm stunned. And thrilled." With a whoop, he lifted her up and spun her around. "How are you feeling? When is it due? Do we know if it's a boy or girl? How long have you known?"

She laughed, feeling light and free and giddy with happiness. She thought he'd be happy; this confirmed it.

"You know Bethanne and Rashid are expecting. She gave me a full rundown on the symptoms she was feeling, from morning sickness to constantly being tired. Only, I don't have any of those. I feel fine. But there are signs and I had it confirmed yesterday. I was going to tell you last night, but then you had that meeting, and then we flew to Quraim Wadi Samil and here we are. Really, this turns out to be the best place to tell you. I loved our picnic here months ago. I'm so thrilled with this new house. We'll have only happy memories here. Do you know we're probably going to have our baby within weeks of Rashid and Bethanne's?"

"So our child will grow up with theirs," he said with quiet satisfaction.

She nodded, already picturing two small children playing on the beach by their home. Or coming here with parents to explore the desert.

"Do you think we'll have twins?" she asked.

"Who cares—one at a time or multiples, we'll love them all."

"All?"

"Don't you want a dozen?" he teased.

She laughed. "No, I do not. A couple, maybe three or four, but not twelve."

"Whatever makes you happy. You have made me happy beyond belief. I love you, Ella." He drew her into his arms and kissed her gently. "You changed everything beyond what I ever expected."

She smiled at him, not seeing the scars, only the love shining from his eyes. "You are all I'll ever want," she said, reaching up to kiss him again on the rooftop of a house made for happy memories.

Hot reads!

These 3-in-1s will certainly get you feeling hot under the collar with their desert locations, billionaire tycoons and playboy princes.

**Now available at
www.millsandboon.co.uk/offers**

24 new stories from the leading lights of romantic fiction!

Featuring bestsellers Adele Parks, Katie Fforde, Carole Matthews and many more, *Truly, Madly, Deeply* **takes you on an exciting romantic adventure where love really is all you need.**

Now available at:

www.millsandboon.co.uk

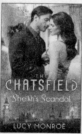

Discover more romance at

www.millsandboon.co.uk

- ❤ WIN great prizes in our exclusive competitions
- ❤ BUY new titles before they hit the shops
- ❤ BROWSE new books and REVIEW your favourites
- ❤ SAVE on new books with the Mills & Boon® Bookclub™
- ❤ DISCOVER new authors

PLUS, to chat about your favourite reads, get the latest news and find special offers:

- Find us on facebook.com/millsandboon
- Follow us on twitter.com/millsandboonuk
- ❤ Sign up to our newsletter at millsandboon.co.uk